Silent Storm

Ida Lambert

SSDIA™ Inc.
St. Louis • Missouri

International Standard Book Number: 978-0-9891652-04-4

Printed in the United States of America

Published by SSDIA™ Inc.

Revised Edition June 2014

Lambert, Ida

Silent Storm: / Ida Lambert

ISBN: 978-0-9891652-04-4

In memory of my mother, brother, and all those whose lives have been touched by the ravages of cancer, and/or other devastating diseases.

This is based upon a true story. Some of the settings are real, nevertheless, with the exception of public officials in their official capacity and public figures, none of the characters in Silent Storm exist outside of the author's imagination.

1

Dr. Burton hovered over the microscope on his desk, squinting at the slides smeared with the blood of his patients. It was only a few minutes before his 8:30 appointment. Although the doctor's patient load was heavy today, Porter Lance's friend, Dave, would be squeezed in.

After loosening the collar around his neck, Dr. Burton ejected photographs of blood from the slide holder. He was expecting several patients from out of state, some as far away as Wisconsin--quite a distance from Aberdeen, a little town at the southern tip of Idaho. They came in search of a different kind of diagnosis, a new insight into their illnesses; for many, Dr. Burton was the last hope.

Soon Dr. Burton's assistant appeared in his doorway. With a warm smile, she greeted the doctor. "John is here. Would you like him to come in?"

"Yes, Anna, bring him in."

A frail, trembling man stood outside the doctor's office, his bent frame supported by a cane. His skin resembled a dried peach. The eyes, red from pain, were sunken. His clavicle protruded underneath his open collar.

Anna wrapped her arm around John's waist, lending support until at last he was seated in the chair just left of Dr. Burton. Fear gleamed in his eyes.

"Hello John. I'm Dr. Burton. How are you feeling?"

"Not so good, I'm afraid."

"What seems to be the problem?"

"I'm so weak and tired. I'm in constant pain. I have trouble urinating. When I think I'm through I have to go again, even at night."

"Okay, let's see what's going on. I'll need your left little finger. It'll sting a bit, but you can... I think you can handle it."

Dr. Burton squeezed John's finger; a quick poke with the lancet forced a drop of blood which settled into a small bubble on his finger tip. The doctor held it steady for some thirty seconds before smearing five drops of blood in descending sizes onto a glass slide. The last was the size of a ballpoint pen tip.

The doctor put the slide into a holder after which an assortment of donut-shaped red blood cells appeared on a monitor, some clumped together, and others were spread apart. Many were divided by what looked like dark clouds of nothingness. Some were oblong resembling an embryo in its mother's womb.

As the cells danced around on the screen, Dr. Burton pointed to the red blood cells which appeared round, separated, and uniform. "These are the healthy cells," he explained. He pointed again, this time to cells that clung together, contained white spots, and / or were distorted in shape, "These are the unhealthy cells."

"Now, see those little squiggly things floating across the monitor?"

"Uh huh."

"Those are parasites."

Circling the screen with his finger he noted, "These are yeast buds, so there is also some candida." He turned to John as though he were his student. "This is called Live Blood Cell Analysis, but it only tells us part of the story; the rest we will see using Dry Blood Cell Analysis."

From the slide holder, Dr. Burton ejected a colorful photo of the blood drops taken from John's finger. The photograph covered the entire snapshot except for the black borders at each of the corners. Large spaces of creamy white masses were scattered throughout the blood pattern, their ends melting softly into the dense areas of red. Heavy black indentations nestled together on the right uppermost corner of the photo, while its center was sprinkled with an orange-reddish brown grainy looking texture overlaying a quarter of the photo. "John, looks like you've got red blood cell damage consistent with prostate cancer," the doctor said, pointing to the problem areas on the photo.

John's eyes shifted between the photo and the doctor. "But how do you know? I didn't put it on the patient history."

"Blood can tell us a lot about the condition of the body."

John looked down, then up again. "They told me, 'you've got prostate cancer too advanced for an operation or chemotherapy. There is nothing more we can do,'" John told Dr. Burton. "This is my tenth doctor visit in less than 6 months. Can you help me?"

"Well, I can't make any guarantees, but I'd like to give it a try." Dr. Burton jotted something down on a note pad.

"I sure hope so."

"Going to get you in treatment here in a minute. Want you to see the girls before you leave. They will give you the list of supplements you'll need to take and a diet I want you to follow. Okay, buddy?"

"Okay."

"Anna!"

Anna poked her head in the door.

"Let's make up a chart on John, would you? Get him ready for his treatment."

"Okay John," Anna said. "Let's get you up here on the table. I'm going to put your feet in water to get your treatment started, okay?"

"Okay."

"When I'm done Marilyn, our office therapist, is going to apply some body manipulations. Alright?"

Anna hooked John up to a machine and adjusted the settings. "There, how does this feel?

"Feels good."

"Great. Don't go anywhere. Going to let this run for about 30 minutes." Anna left the room, returning intermittently to make sure John was comfortable with the machine's settings.

Soon the timer buzzed. "You're all done," she said popping back into the room. "Marilyn is going to come in shortly; when she's done, Dr. Daniel, our office chiropractor, will give you an adjustment."

"Give me an adjustment?"

"Uh huh. It will help to align you. Now when Dr. Daniel is done, Dr. Burton will give you an injection. Do you have any questions?"

"No. I've heard some good things about Dr. Burton. I just hope he can help me."

Dave had not yet arrived. In the waiting room, however, were the Wallaces. Having survived a bout of lung cancer while under Dr. Burton's guidance, Melba was a happy patient. She was a pleasant woman of about sixty whose gaiety permeated the spirits of all in her presence. It had taken some coercing, but her husband Ryan, who suffered from lymphoma, had agreed to give Dr. Burton a try. Her brother Joe, who suffered from lupus, her brother-in-law Miles, a multiple sclerosis sufferer, and Rebecca, a good friend, with her sick infant had also decided to try him. All had shared the long ride from Wisconsin.

Rebecca, a middle-aged brunette with eyes underscored by dark lines, clasped her baby against her bosom, her tresses burying his chest. She lowered herself into the chair next to the doctor.

"Thank God! I'm so glad I finally got to you," Becky exclaimed, wiping the tears from her eyes. "I was so afraid; he's slipping so fast!" Tears spilled into the infant's face. Becky's nose filled with mucous. "I mean, the Wallaces... I've heard so much about you. I sure hope you can help my baby."

"Why don't we get a blood test and take it from there."

Meanwhile, a woman with a big mole accenting the left corner of her mouth sat in a van outside. Her keen features set in a square face were hard, almost callous, accentuated by bobbed black hair. She had an air of pomposity about her, having risen to "Special Agent-in-Charge" status in less than three years, and when she spoke, her twelve-man entourage listened. All of them wore black jackets with 'FBI' inscribed in yellow letters on the left except for Officer Lewis and Special Agent Glenn. Officer Lewis' jacket displayed the word "Police." On Special Agent Glenn's the letters "FDA" were inscribed.

"Okay, our focus is vitamins, computers, records, patient files, drugs and diplomas. We'll scan documents and examine equipment for possible violations, confiscating those we need to prove our case. First, we'll gather the employees in the lobby and later separate them for questioning. Officer Lewis will go first and will give a cue that it's safe to enter."

Officer Lewis moved quickly. His official status went unnoticed by the clinic staff as he made his way inside, losing himself in the throng of patients. He scouted the clinic for any danger of weaponry. All was safe.

"Okay, let's go," the female agent commanded, her feet turning outward as she forged ahead, yielding the lead to Agent Kent.

Thundering knocks preceded the first gunman's entrance. "Don't move. Do as you're told and nobody gets hurt," Kent ordered. Some patients jumped, others gasped. Still others began to tremble.

Sitting in his office, Dr. Burton could hear the pounding, the commotion, and the staccato commands. He sat immobilized as his eyes darted toward Becky, and then the door. It was as though all the air was being sucked from his lungs.

Becky pulled her baby closer. "No! No!" she screamed, "This can't be happening!"

In the patient reception area, the female agent followed close behind the others. She noticed a cherry counter top adorned with various items such as a paper holder, a miniature metal file, two flower arrangements, phone pads, and small wicker baskets with an assortment of cards thrown together in a heap. Behind the counter was a blonde with long hair whose activities had been frozen just as the agent had ordered.

A refrigerator and wooden shelf were straight ahead housing many of the foodstuffs and products recommended by the clinic. Just to the left was a middle-aged man seated at one of the two desks in his office; a woman and her sick infant sat on his left. The female agent charged into the office and flashed her badge. "This is the FBI. Are you Dr. Burton...Dr. Kyle Burton?"

Dr. Burton's eyes darted underneath furrowed eyebrows, "Yes, I'm Dr. Burton," he answered, wondering what this was all about. A lump settled in his throat. Blood rushed to his head.

"I'm Special Agent Marge Newsome." She pointed to the men behind her. "With me are Special Agents Kent and Glenn. We have a warrant to search Natrogenics."

Dr. Burton's furrowed eyebrows gave way to a frown. "What did I do?"

"'That's what we're here to determine. We'll notify you of the charges," Newsome said.

"Notify me of the charges?" the doctor's lips flattened; his cheeks flushed red. "Well, was the sheriff notified?"

"Yes." Newsome answered, her tone matter-of-fact.

But something doesn't add up, Dr. Burton thought. He jumped up from his chair, motioning with sweaty hands.

Armed agents poured through the door; others gathered around. Dr. Burton wanted to speak, but the words would not come. His heart, it seemed, was racing 220 beats per minute. He surrendered, his hands flying over his head as though to shield flying bullets.

"Okay big guy," Newsome ordered, motioning to the doctor, "You'll need to sit here on the couch. Agent Glenn and I will take the desks."

Muttering to himself, Dr. Burton moved slowly to the couch.

"I want to talk to my attorney."

"Now is not the time, big guy," Newsome sneered, cocking her head in the direction of Agent Terrance Glenn. "Agent Glenn and I have some questions for you."

Without his attorney, the doctor vacillated between whether he should or should not answer the questions, but the presence of the armed agents frightened him. What if he didn't answer the questions? What would they do to him? Would they rough him up? Maybe if he answered their questions they would realize that there had been some mistake.

Newsome momentarily joined the agents outside of Dr. Burton's office. She ordered the office staff to be quiet and assemble themselves in the lobby; she gave specific assignments to each agent. While some separated the office staff into different treatment rooms for later questioning, others papered the windows. One agent locked the door and stood guard at the entrance. Still others ordered patients out of the treatment rooms, insisting they sign the registry before leaving the clinic. Some agents would confiscate medical files, records, nutritional supplements, treatment formulations, and other clinic paraphernalia.

Dr. Burton could hear voices and the treatment machinery come to a screeching halt.

Some agents accompanied Newsome back to Dr. Burton's office and began confiscating his microscope, computer, and equipment while Newsome sat at the vacant desk.

"Now just wait a minute here. Just one minute! You said you had an order to search the clinic, not to take away my equipment!"

"Just comes with the territory," scoffed Newsome.

The nerve of these cruel insensitive bullies interrupting my patient's treatments, taking my computer and equipment, even questioning me without my attorney! Surely this isn't legal, Dr. Burton thought.

Becky was confused. "But...I don't understand. I want to get my baby treated."

"Ma'am, I'm sorry, but there isn't going to be any business here today," Newsome said.

"What?" Becky wailed, "But you don't understand. My baby is really sick; he has to be treated."

"Ma'am, there isn't going to be any business conducted here today."

Creases settled across Becky's forehead. Her lips drew back underneath her pug nose. "Listen lady, my baby is dying. I've come all the way from

Wisconsin; there is no way I'm leaving until he is treated!"

"Oh you're leaving lady, but you've got to sign the register first.

"Just watch me!" Becky growled.

"There will be no business conducted here today, Ma'am."

Becky scanned Dr. Burton's expression for direction. He dropped his head. No, he had no words of comfort. He felt as though he had been stripped naked. How will I face my patients again? Becky has come for help only to find herself caught up in a spectacle that should be reserved for criminals. Why I've never even had a brush with the law; these people are treating us like hardened criminals, Dr. Burton thought.

Becky scribbled her name to the registry in the lobby, and forced a long hard stare at the agents. "This won't be the last you hear from me. I can assure you of that!" she said, storming off the premises.

"Okay, let's go! Get the needle out of his arm," one agent ordered one employee, "Go to the lobby." Turning to Ryan, the patient, he said, "Sir, you may leave once you have signed the registry.

Ryan surrendered, stumbling into the lobby where he signed his name and left the clinic.

The painful moans seemed to get louder; Dr. Burton knew the sound. It was John, yet another patient whose treatment had been aborted.

Gone now was the nervousness and apprehension that had characterized Dr. Burton's distress. He could feel the tension growing inside of him, his blood almost coming to a boil, as he witnessed his patients and employees being treated like criminals.

Soon there was a knock. A curious Dr. Burton listened intently, hoping it was someone who could deliver him--someone who could tell them this was all a big mistake--they had the wrong man. Someone who could call the sheriff and his attorney--anyone would do.

One of the agents cracked the door. Standing before him was a lady with a fair complexion and brown eyes. Her hair was in ringlets brushing her round shoulders.

"Ma'am, this place is closed for business today."

"I'm Jane, Dr. Burton's wife. May I speak with him?"

No, it wasn't his attorney, but Dr. Burton was glad Jane had come. Now she could call the sheriff and his attorney, for surely she would read the distress in his eyes, he thought.

Newsome allowed Dr. Burton to meet his wife at the door, their closeness barred by an agent who stood between them. Jane, four inches shorter than Dr. Burton, looked into his eyes at an expression that belied his words; so, too, did his voice. "It's okay, honey. Everything's okay. Go home. Don't worry."

After Jane left the clinic, the door locked behind her. Dr. Burton surrendered once again to the agents' questions.

After interviewing all the employees, the agents huddled together. "There is enough evidence here to suggest some of the products we are seeking are kept at the family's residence," Newsome said to Kent.

Newsome approached Dr. Burton. "May we search your residence?"

"No, you may not search my home!"

"Well, we'll get a search warrant."

"'That is the only way you're going to search my home!"

Dr. Burton checked his watch; it was 4:00PM when the agents dismissed everyone. He phoned Attorney Anthony who met him at the Voyager, the restaurant attached to the clinic. Dr. Burton exclaimed, "Rudy, these jerks have wrecked my office; now they're after my home. Over my dead body! Search warrant or not--I'll be doggone if I'm going to let that happen."

2

Echoes of the agents' voices still rang in Burton's ear. Would they get the search warrant as agent Newsome had threatened? Accompanied by his attorney, Rudy Anthony, Burton barreled his red truck up the winding dirt road leading to his house. As he drew nearer, he saw several FBI agents outside; still others were in their vehicles. Two stood guard at his residence. He gripped his steering wheel tightly and thrust himself forward, squinting in disbelief. They had gotten a search warrant, and so quickly.

Kyle sped into the long dirt pathway and leaped out of his car. This was his residence and he refused to be intimidated by these bullies anymore. Attorney Anthony stayed close behind as Kyle hastened toward the entrance shaking his finger at the FBI agents at the residence entrance, "Get off my property, now." Kyle growled.

"Stop," agent Caldwell demanded, pointing a gun at Kyle's head. "Get your hands up."

Barrels of steel pointed at Burton from all directions. Burton thrust his hands high above his head, choking back words that he didn't dare to speak, not now. His wife was inside.

"Who are you," the agent demanded of Attorney Anthony. "Let me see your ID."

After a quick search, first of Burton then Attorney Anthony, Agent Caldwell shoved his gun back into his holster.

"Okay," he nodded. "You can go in."

The doctor and the attorney trekked upstairs, gaping as agents ransacked the house– snatching out drawers and leaving clothing in heaps upon the bed and floor. The two men were ordered downstairs. "Let's go!" barked another agent, leading the way into the living room where Burton's wife was being held captive.

The phone rang incessantly. An agent stood on guard as Jane answered; he studied her every word.

Burton could feel blood rushing to his head, as he tried to collect his thoughts. It was bad enough that he was involved in this horrific miscarriage of justice at the office—but in front of his wife.

"Jane, did you talk to the sheriff?" he asked.

Jane's speech was slow and calculated.

"We'll talk later honey, okay?" she said trying to force a smile. Jane sat quietly for a moment. "He's out of town," she added.

Kyle's eyelids fluttered. Something is dreadfully wrong with this, he thought. He looked at Jane, his lips puckered, trying to confirm what he had heard. "You mean, the sheriff didn't know?"

Jane looked at him with a raised eyebrow, and just as quickly turned away.

"Unbelievable!" he said, shaking his head from side to side. He looked at Attorney Anthony. "Did you hear that?"

Deep in thought now, he realized that Newsome had lied. The sheriff had not been notified.

Burton fell back onto the couch; his head pounding unmercifully. He wasn't sure what this all meant, but he was convinced he had grounds for a lawsuit.

"I'll look into this," Anthony said. "I want to get my hand on that search warrant."

It would have felt good to just strangle that agent standing guard over him, but there were many others around.

The search finished, the agents gathered outside. "There must be some mistake; this guy is clean as a whistle," Burton heard one agent comment. If the agent was honest and forthright, maybe this ordeal would be dismissed as a big mistake and his equipment and accessories returned. But that was wishful thinking.

In bed, Burton lay thinking about what this meant to his patients. The Wallaces, Becky, and John had sacrificed hours of travel to see him, only to be turned away like cattle driven off a forbidden land. If only he could have seen this coming... Surely there were signs.

After minutes of tossing and turning, Burton's head sank to his pillow; he yearned for a momentary escape. But the rudeness of the agents, Marge Newsome's lying, and the intimidation and fear they had evoked replayed over and over in his mind. Finally his eyes perused the ceiling, staring as though it held answers to his many questions.

Dr. Daniel, the office chiropractor, had also been interrogated, but unlike the others, he had been allowed to pack all of his belongings and leave the clinic. Was there a conspiracy between Dr. Daniel and the FBI? If it wasn't Daniel who had initiated the investigation? And why? Why wasn't the sheriff notified? Why had they taken his equipment? When and how would he get it back? Where did this leave him and his business? More than ninety percent of his patients requested blood tests, a huge draw for the clinic. The equipment he needed to do blood tests and injections was now gone. Without his patient files and office records, his business was as good as dead. He could feel his muscles tightening; it was going to be a long night. What would become of his patients? How many incorrect diagnoses would they receive? How long before many of them would succumb to death in their search for health? He knew the answer. His own experience with illness had taught him well. It had all begun in 1964.

3

Aberdeen, Idaho 1964

In Aberdeen farming was a way of life. It was for the Burtons as well. Beads of sweat streaming down Kyle's face belied the cool crisp spring breeze stirring gently against the wheat brush.

Thick locks of hair matted to Kyle's sweat-stained head as he plunged his tractor headlong into wheat fields stretching far into the distance. There was no time to waste. Big brother Sidney's tractor had forged ahead by nearly fifteen feet. Kyle wanted to catch up, but his eyes were heavy. He felt nauseous and dizzy; an almost paralyzing headache slowed him down.

In the past, headaches and stomach pains had plagued Kyle, but none more vicious than these. As had the others, he assumed that these, too, would pass. The pain, however, persisted. Soon his tractor slowed to a halt. Kyle slumped over the steering column like a wet sack of potatoes, awakening later to the firm grip of Sidney who wrestled him inside of the Burton's dwelling--no small feat for a man who stood three inches taller than did Kyle, but weighed sixty pounds less.

Standing at five-feet-five with a pleasing plumpness, Rita Burton, the boys' mother, spotted the struggling duo. Kyle's head hung loosely against his chest making him appear two inches shorter. He was wringing wet with sweat, his steps slow, and his breathing heavy.

"Oh, Kyle!" Mrs. Burton cried, her chubby hands flying to her mouth. She quickly dampened a towel with cold water and pressed it against Kyle's forehead. "What happened?"

"I don't know. I just happened to look back and saw him slumped over the tractor."

Mrs. Burton helped Sidney maneuver Kyle onto the living room couch. "We have to get him to the hospital."

At the hospital, a nurse helped settle Kyle into a wheelchair; it proved much easier on Mrs. Burton and Sidney's backs. She wheeled Kyle inside the emergency room where a brunette stood ready to get his medical history.

"Yes, blood pressure problems run in my family," Kyle told the nurse. "My Uncle Ben has it." But Uncle Ben wasn't the only one. "His Uncle Billy and Aunt Margaret also have it," Mrs. Burton noted.

Perhaps this is my problem, Kyle thought.

The brunette wheeled Kyle into an examining room where she took his height, weight, temperature, and blood pressure, recorded them on a chart, and disappeared. After scanning the chart for quick reference, a young doctor entered. His youthfulness made him look inexperienced; long legs seemed to swallow up the rest of his body. He extended his right hand for a shake.

"Kyle, I'm Dr. Lesley. How are you today?" he asked studying Kyle's expression.

Kyle shook his head from side to side. "Not so good."

Dr. Lesley studied the chart once again, and then cautiously lowered it onto the examining table. He mounted the stethoscope onto Kyle's bare chest and steered it slowly in a circular motion, listening intently as though the secrets of Kyle's illness were buried somewhere inside, then looked at Kyle. "Have you ever had a heart murmur?"

Kyle's lips puckered and eyebrows furrowed. "No... Don't think so."

Dr. Lesley reached his long slender fingers into a jar containing tongue depressors and pulled one out, thrusting it into Kyle's mouth. "Can you say 'ah' for me?"

Trying to respond as directed Kyle began to gag. Thankfully, this part of the examination ended almost as quickly as it began.

Before long, Kyle's legs were swinging back and forth. "Good reflex action," Dr. Lesley noted. Lesley pressed on the area underneath Kyle's left and right breasts looking for a telltale sign from Kyle. Kyle's frown did not surprise him.

Dr. Lesley looked Kyle in the eyes. "Well, Kyle, a number of things are going on here. Your blood pressure is dangerously high, two hundred ten over one hundred thirty. I'm afraid I'll have to keep you until we can get it down."

"Keep me, for how long?"

"For as long as it takes to get it down. It could take an hour or two—sometimes less than thirty minutes. You also have a slight heart murmur," he said, gesturing with his hands. "It's nothing to be concerned about, just yet, but I'll want to keep an eye on you. You have liver and stomach distress; for confirmation, there are some tests I'd like you to take, including a complete blood workup." He jotted something down on his note pad. "But for now we need to take care of that blood pressure. I'll send in the nurse, and she'll take care of you."

The brunette popped in and took a papered orange-pill sampling from an assortment of pill bottles clustered on a little silver tray. "Mr. Burton, you want to put this under your tongue for me? Just let it dissolve." She checked her watch for the time, and left the room.

Upon her return, she once again checked Kyle's blood pressure, looked at the reading, then at Kyle. "It's much better, Mr. Burton; now it's down to one forty over ninety.

She handed Kyle a small piece of paper with scribbling on it. "The doctor wants you to take one in the morning, at noon, and at night. He wants you back in here next week for an upper/lower GI series. We can't do it today. This procedure has to be done on an empty stomach; it requires hours of fasting. It will tell the doctor what's going on with your stomach."

Upon Kyle's return to the hospital, the brunette took several tubes of his blood. In a darkened room down the corridor, Kyle stood facing a rather huge ominous looking gray piece of equipment. A man in his early twenties ordered, "Don't move." Immediately following was a loud click, a second, then a third. As the technician mounted the flimsy black plastic taken from the machinery, Kyle could see impressions of his skeletal structure; to him it looked fine.

In a similarly darkened room Kyle stood facing yet another monstrous looking machine. A sixteen-ounce cup was filled with a light pink, thick, chalky substance. The technician ordered, "Drink it slowly." A sickeningly sweet aroma penetrated Kyle's nostrils. The awful tasting stuff hung in his throat slithering rather than gliding down and seemed to replenish itself after each swallow; yet the technician urged him to drink it all. It seemed at times that the misery of testing and the treatments was worse than the ailments. But if Dr. Lesley could get to the heart of the problem, the discomforts of testing would be worth it, Kyle reasoned.

Kyle was impressed. The blood pressure medicine Dr. Lesley had prescribed was working wonderfully. With the proper stomach medication, he would be as good as new and able to enjoy an illness-free lifestyle with Jane Henderson, soon to be his bride. At least, that was what Kyle thought…

4

For Kyle, Canada was a long way from home. But it provided a beautiful backdrop for Jane and his wedding. A colorful medley of flowers adorned the acres of freshly cut grass that ascended into small hills and valleys along the open turf. Some formed individual heaps with equal distances between them; others fell into unique patterns of artistry that spelled out the couple's names.

Heaven must have rejoiced on this occasion, for the sun shone beautifully on the horizon as billowy clouds danced across the sea blue sky. The Hendersons had spared no expense in preparing for their daughter's wedding.

Children scurried about in excitement as the wedding party posed for pictures. Sidney, the best man wore a tuxedo, the same hue as the maid of honor's. The groomsmen wore navy blue tuxedos.

Donned with white, beaded corsages above their left breasts, the bridesmaids wore dazzling silk navy fitted dresses; all were cut in v backs, except for the maid of honor's whose was rounded. A silky gray cast gave her dress a distinctive look.

The bride glowed in her long sleeved, white, satin gown. Scattered rhinestones pierced the bodice of the gown while pearls added a regal touch. A long chapel train extended some five feet from the dress' bodice.

Covering Kyle's plump chest was a navy blue tuxedo which extended just below his knees, making him appear twenty pounds lighter. A white shirt provided the perfect contrast. Kyle felt wonderful; any semblance of pain was usurped by this moment of ecstasy. The shy, pretty little brunette was now Mrs. Kyle Burton, and together they would start a new life in Idaho.

Life in Idaho was difficult for the couple that first year. Shortly after Jane discovered that she was pregnant with their first child, a snow storm destroyed five hundred acres of their crops. Fortunately for the couple, Kyle also operated Burton's Repair Shop.

Because of Kyle's older siblings, his parents had already experienced the excitement of being grandparents, but Jane's had not. Jane had not yet told her mother; she looked forward to their upcoming visit so she could see the excitement in her mother's eyes.

Kyle followed as Jane rushed to the door and fell into her mother's embrace. "Mom, guess what? It's happened. I'm expecting!"

"Oh honey, that's wonderful!" Jane's mother exclaimed, her dark brown eyes beaming on Jane's abdomen. "You're carrying it so low. I'll just bet it's a boy."

"Time will tell," Jane answered with a big smile.

In the living room, Kyle's right arm dangled over Jane's shoulder. They had barely settled when the phone rang. A beam still in her eyes, Mrs. Henderson handed Kyle the phone.

"This is Kyle" For a moment he was quiet. A curious Jane looked up at him, her hazel eyes searching his for an answer.

"Okay, I'll take..." There was another pause. "I'll take...yes, when I get back. Okay." He lowered the receiver to the phone cautiously. His sky blue eyes met Jane's. "That was mother," he said.

"What did she want?"

"She says I got a letter from the selective service."

"Oh no!" Jane cried.

Shifting his plump body on the couch, he said, "Ahh, don't think they'll take me. Most of my folks were exempt; they had blood pressure problems."

Jane glanced away from Kyle, then suddenly back again. "Well, what about medication?"

"Nah, I don't think you have to worry. They couldn't pass the… I'll take care of it when we get back."

Jane breathed a sigh of relief. If Kyle was wrong, he would miss three formative years of child rearing. If he was right, however, together they could experience the joys of parenting.

Merle Burton was among the babies born at Pocatello's General Hospital that day, weighing in at six pounds, seven ounces. The proud parents, Jane and Kyle, smiled upon him as he slept. His tiny foot easily fit into Kyle's palm. The timing was perfect. A federal mandate exempted fathers with only one boy from the armed services.

Two weeks later, tiny Merle lay screaming in his crib in the bedroom next to Kyle and Jane's. Panicking, Jane rushed to his side, sweeping the little bundle up into her arms, stroking his little face and rocking him, but little Merle's cries continued. Noticing the little red flat lesions covering Merle's wrists, penis and legs, Jane shouted, "Kyle! Merle is covered with these little... No wonder he's crying." The infant's screams were penetrating and unrelenting.

Kyle rushed to their sides and was overtaken by the sight. "Oooh! Let's get him to the doctor. Wonder what that is?"

Kyle pulled an old shirt from the makeshift chest of drawers and yanked it over his head, his thick blonde hair in disarray. A dizzy spell and gnawing headache overwhelmed him once again. This was no ordinary headache.

"Oh honey, I just remembered the draft," Kyle lied trying to keep Jane from noticing his frown. "I've got to take care of... Why don't you go on? I need to take care of that." He grabbed his forehead squeezing his eyebrows between his fingers and could feel tension building. A bout of dizziness would throw him down if he didn't retreat to his bed and rather quickly. He fell onto it, rolling over, trying to get relief.

He tried to remember if he had taken his second dose of medicine. He knew he hadn't taken his third. Maybe he needed to give the medicine more time to work. But it had been two weeks, already. How much more time did he need before he got results?

At last the headache passed. He was still somewhat light-headed but with time it, too, passed. For added assurance against the draft, Kyle would secure a letter from his physician. From his uncles, he knew the routine well. He would report to basic training as per the order, only to flunk the physical. Then the order would be rescinded. It was true, he wanted to avoid the draft, but he hated that it was at such a price.

A groggy and tired Kyle was getting water from the refrigerator when Jane returned. His thick full lips greeted hers. "So, what'd the doctor say?"

"He says it's the seven year itch," she said, focusing once again upon the baby.

"The seven year what?" Kyle frowned, hoping Jane would elaborate further.

"He says it could last for months, even years," she said somberly. "But he said that this would help." She extended the small tube of cream.

Kyle took a quick look at the tube. "Corticosteroid cream, hum... Must be some pretty good stuff. He's quiet." The quietness lasted for more than a year; the seven year itch appeared to be gone.

But the new year brought Kyle new challenges. He had religiously taken his prescribed medication, but was still plagued with the same old ailments. He could no longer hide it from Jane.

"Oh honey, you look so pale, and your eyes are bloodshot. Maybe you should see a doctor," Jane said.

Kyle grabbed his head, frowning from the pain. "My head! I keep hoping it'll get better but... he groaned, his eyes glancing past hers. "I think maybe if the doctor changes my medicine. I'm just not getting any better. I'll have to go."

The black, glass building that sat atop a hill housed offices of the most respected doctors in Pocatello. Dr. Lesley's was one of them. It was only moments after Kyle had his temperature and blood pressure taken that Lesley appeared with Kyle's chart in his hand. "I understand you've been having some problems with the medication."

"It's just not doing the job. I mean, the headaches and dizziness...I don't know. Just can't get rid of them."

"Are you experiencing any other symptoms?"

"My big toe throbs at times. What do you think may be causing that?"

"It sounds like a touch of arthritis." The doctor looked at Kyle's chart. "Hum...I'd still like to see your blood pressure lowered. But you're right, thirty milligrams of this medication is not working for you. I'm convinced that sixty milligrams would get some results."

Lesley pulled a pen from his white coat jacket and scribbled something onto a small prescription pad. "I'd like to see you increase your daily intake to two pills three times a day. "I've also given you some pain medicine for your big toe. I think you'll feel much better. Keep me posted."

Kyle left the office, with a new prescription and sparkle of hope, once again feeling optimistic. But the following week, the headaches were more frequent. Each successive one took longer to get under control. It became clear to Kyle that it was going to take something other than medication to bring him a relief. He needed the Lord's divine intervention.

At church, Kyle's big arm enveloped Jane's petite neck while Merle sat snuggly against his mother's bosom. Beautiful melodies hung in the air. He pinned his hopes on every word. He needed answers.

Church had been an important part of Kyle's life, but his involvement had been borne of habit. Today, it was borne of need. All of his young life he had been told that Jesus would be his doctor and lawyer in his moment of need. Today he had come asking for what the Lord had already sanctioned--an answer to his prayer.

At the altar, Kyle kneeled, letting his head fall onto his chest. Silently he prayed. "Oh Lord God, I thank You for Your many blessings. Please direct my path. Lead me to a doctor who can help me. Touch me with Your mighty hand, Oh Lord. My family needs me. My wife is going to have our second child. I want to be there for them. I need You, Lord. I need You, Amen."

Jane gave birth to a little baby girl, with golden curls encircling her small wrinkled face. Chelsey was the third reason Kyle could no longer accept failing health. Burton's Repair was yet another. Today a customer had come complaining about work done on his tractor. He needed to oversee the work at the shop; his family's survival depended on it.

More than two months had passed. The headaches were somewhat tempered, but the pain in Kyle's toe was getting worse. With medication, Lesley had gotten his blood pressure stabilized. An aching toe, extreme fatigue, and a sore throat had, however, become his constant companions. Somehow it just didn't seem a bargain. He had to move on. For years, Dr. Dixon had treated his father's family. Perhaps, it was time he returned to him.

Dr. Dixon was an older man who was small in stature. Being of Italian descent, his hair was jet black except for the areas of mingled gray at his temples. Mingled gray sideburns stopped within two inches of his thick silver streaked mustache. His skin had a natural brown tan. He peered over thin wire brimmed glasses that sat on the bridge of his nose. "Howdy, Kyle, what can I do for you?"

"I've been having… I'm so tired. My big toe pains a lot. I can't get rid of this sore throat." Kyle pulled a bottle of pills from his pocket. "I've been taking these."

Dr. Dixon took the bottle from Kyle examining them carefully. "How long have you been taking these?"

Kyle scratched his head. "Let's see, for about a month I took thirty milligrams. I've been taking sixty milligrams for about two weeks now."

Dr. Dixon looked at the chart he had gotten from Dr. Lesley's office. "Let's continue those; these pills seem to be working for you." He handed the pills back to Kyle. "I want to take a look at your throat. Can you open wide for me?"

Kyle obliged.

"Hum, it is a bit red. I'll need a culture to get a proper diagnosis."

"What about the tiredness and my big toe?" Kyle asked.

"I'm sure the big toe is just a touch of arthritis. The tiredness could be caused by a number of things. We'll need to order some tests."

At least it was another avenue, Kyle thought. If it didn't work, he would, hopefully, be no worse off. It's got to get better, he told himself.

Kyle's tiredness had persisted now for weeks, soon to be joined by bouts of depression. He was listless. For days now, Kyle lingered in bed dreading to face the days ahead. He lay thinking, wondering when the nightmare would end. The phone rang. Kyle tumbled over to grab it.

"May I speak with Kyle please?"

"This is Kyle."

"Kyle, this is Dr. Dixon. Your tests showed no abnormality, but your throat culture was positive for mononucleosis. I can give you some antibiotics for that. I'll call you in a prescription with your pharmacist. Alright?"

"Okay," Kyle replied.

Picking up the prescription was yet another chore for Jane, as if she didn't have enough, but the choice was no longer Kyle's.

The antibiotics were helpful in combating the mononucleosis, but what a price to his stomach! For Kyle, bouts of diarrhea now occurred routinely; he knew he could not continue this way. Once again, he fell upon his knees in prayer.

"I come to You again, Oh Lord. Lord, I need You. I want to be a provider for my family. I can't make it without You. I can't..."

It had been three weeks now, but Kyle's nausea, diarrhea, and depression persisted. Still feeble, he sat with his body thrust forward, his index finger pressed against his lips. He had become unbearably weak.

How much more can I take? he wondered. In the past, Dixon always seemed to have the answer. Perhaps if he was just more patient... But time was running out. Since his disability, the shop had suffered a financial setback. He had to get back to work to help recover those loses. There was nowhere else to turn; he would have to give Dixon another try.

Kyle's clothing fitted loosely over his thick frame; gone now was the plumpness that had once filled them. Jane had taken Merle to the doctor's office for a checkup, so Kyle was forced to drive himself to the doctor's office. His palms were sweaty, and his body intense with heat. He could feel the thin liquid settling in his colon. Squirming and fidgeting, he tried to hold it as he launched his truck up to the curve and dashed out.

He rushed to the commode and yanked down his shorts. The thin liquid oozed out of him pouring into the commode with the force of a cannon, filling it with dark brownish green foul smelling feces.

In the waiting room Kyle waited anxiously for the arrival of Dixon. He was to arrive any minute, having made an emergency call at the hospital.

At last a middle-aged nurse with a pleasant smile swung open the door. "Kyle Burton," she called.

Kyle cleared his throat, passed the receptionist, and followed the nurse inside, easing the door shut behind him. Inside the examining room, he hoisted himself onto the big black table. After having taken his weight, the nurse eased a thermometer into his mouth. Minutes passed; she carefully examined it and tossed it in a nearby trash can.

Shortly thereafter, she eased the cuff of the blood pressure machine around Kyle's upper arm and squeezed the attached black rubber bulb. Kyle's arm felt as though it would explode. She marked Kyle's chart. "The doctor will be in shortly," she said, leaving with his chart in hand.

Within ten minutes, Dixon appeared with Kyle's chart. His eyes met Kyle's. "Kyle, I thought we discussed this already."

"My stomach, I just... What can I do about the diarrhea?" Suddenly, Kyle's eyes squinted and his features hardened. "Listen, doggone it! I've lost thirty-five pounds!" He shouted thrusting his hands about in anger.

"Kyle, I've reviewed your tests, including your upper/lower GI series, and your blood work up. All of these tests were normal. Now this illness you claim is all in your head. Perhaps you should see a psychiatrist."

For a moment Kyle froze. The otherwise pale skin turned fiery red, and his lips drew back in anger. He could not believe what he was hearing. A rush of adrenaline propelled him forward. He grabbed Dixon by his collar, almost lifting him off the floor. "What you trying to say, Doc, huh? That I'm crazy? Is that it--huh?"

Dixon was caught off guard. His eyes looked like giant marbles. He was at Kyle's mercy with his brown skin drained of color. His head was thrust backward, his mouth wide-open and his breathing was short. He stood on tiptoes shivering, bound by Kyle's strong grip. "Kyle, I just meant..." He tried to explain, but Kyle interrupted, slamming Dixon up against the wall.

"Oh, I know just what you meant!" He snatched his hand away suddenly and stumped out, slamming the door shut behind him.

The nurse and receptionist standing in the lobby looked at Kyle inquisitively, then quickly back at each other. "Wonder what that was all about?" the nurse said to the receptionist.

"I don't know, but it seems like a personal problem to me," the receptionist replied.

Kyle hastened to his truck and threw himself inside. The truck lunged backwards then suddenly plunged forward, its tires screeching as Kyle sped off. A string of tears streamed down Kyle's face as he headed for home. Moments like these caused him to wonder if God was listening. It was easy for him to have faith when things were going his way. It was not so easy when they weren't. He hoped the altar would help him renew it.

5

Church services had been wonderful; Kyle felt restored. Today was special because Sidney and Liz were coming to dinner. Being newlyweds, they had kept mostly to themselves. Kyle missed Sidney. Growing up, it had been Sidney with whom Kyle spent much of his time when not with his Uncle Ben. And it was Sidney who had rescued Kyle when he fainted in the wheat field.

While Jane juggled between preparing dinner and attending to Merle whose seven-year itch had already persisted for three years, Kyle cuddled baby Chelsey. Her thumb was lost behind her fist and upturned lips. Merle came in with some Legos tucked under his arms. He ran up to his daddy pulling and tugging for some attention. A good age to teach Merle to play ball, were I healthy, Kyle thought. Instead he sat holding Chelsey on one leg, and Merle on the other.

At last little Chelsey fell asleep. Merle insisted on building a house with the Legos, but not without help from dad. Kyle put Chelsey to bed and squatted down beside Merle. It was a strange looking house, but it worked for Merle.

Soon the doorbell rang. Sidney entered first, wearing his tailored suit. Behind him was Liz. A long jacket hugged her curvaceous hips. Her eyes set in a round face danced and gave her a youthful appeal.

"Good to see you," Kyle said, his voice ringing in the air as he ushered the couple to the living room couch. "It's been a long time. Would you like some coffee?"

"None for me, thanks" Liz replied, peeling the lid off a carton of yogurt and shoving a spoonful into her mouth.

"What about you Sidney?"

"I'll take a cup."

"Honey, they're here!"

Jane peeped in, acknowledging their presence.

"What's for dessert?"

"Your favorites: peach cobbler and German chocolate cake."

"Sounds good. Want to bring us some coffee?" Kyle bit into the milk chocolate bar he had grabbed off the coffee table. "Ouch!" His hands flew up to his left jaw and his eyes squinted.

"Oh Honey! Are you alright?" Jane asked.

"It's these darn cavities. Every time I bite down it's… I've got to get this taken care of."

"Yeah, you need to make a dental appointment."

Jane turned to Sidney. "I'll be back with the coffee in a minute," then disappeared into the kitchen.

"Liz, Sidney tells me you're a nurse,"

"That's right. For ten years, now."

"Maybe you could... I've been having some problems. I don't know-- they get one thing fixed, then something else... First there were those God-awful headaches, dizziness, and my blood pressure. Now my stomach aches, my toe throbs and I don't - my doctor and I had it out. He told me I was crazy; said I needed to see a psychiatrist."

Jane appeared with the coffee. She sat next to her husband, trying to get the gist of the conversation.

"Well, Kyle, I've seen a lot since I've been a practicing nurse. I think it's your medication. Have you ever considered nutrition?"

"Nutrition?"

"Uh huh, you know- vitamins, minerals, and herbs. They work better. That's what I do."

Kyle stilled himself for a moment, hoping his disregard for her suggestion wasn't too apparent. He looked Liz in the eyes. "Are you serious?"

"Very. I've seen what medicines can do to people. They can maim and kill. Until people realize that, they're just going to be more people maimed and more killed."

"But you're a nurse, for Pete's sake! How can you practice something you don't believe in?"

Liz laid her yogurt down on the table. "I hadn't seen the devastation of drug therapy before I got into the profession. Now I see it daily. It's not a pretty picture. I recommend nutrition to my patients to counter the negative effects of drug therapy. Some listen. Some don't. For those who listen, the reward is an improved quality of life. For those who don't, well... I think you should give nutrition a try."

"Well, Kyle you can't be any worse off. Give it a try," Sidney added.

Jane nudged him softly. "Well honey, it can't hurt."

Kyle was indifferent to what Sidney and Jane said. Liz's words, however, rang in his ear. "You should try nutrition." He just couldn't understand it. Everybody knew the quality of life drug therapy had brought and continued to bring to many. Why couldn't Liz see that not all drugs were bad? Where would we be without antibiotics and infection fighters, for goodness sake? How could this world stand without the wonder drug, aspirin, and other painkillers?

Kyle cocked his head to the side. "So what do you do when you need to go to a doctor?" He asked beneath raised eyebrows.

"Unless I'm in a bloody accident, I go to naturopaths, homeopaths, and chiropractors-not medical doctors."

"You go to those quacks?" he asked with a slight chuckle.

Liz's face hardened. Gone was the sparkle in her eyes. Her upper torso stiffened and her hands landed on her hips. "Those quacks are doing more for people than those MD's with their drugs and surgeries. There are natural remedies for ailments. But, as long as the public remains closed-minded, doctors will continue to prescribe harmful drugs and do needless surgeries."

Kyle shook his head. He couldn't believe what he was hearing, least of all from a nurse. But everyone had a right to his or her opinion, even if it was ludicrous. Nutrition was all right for Liz if she wanted it. He would stick with regular medicine and real doctors. They had worked for him in the past; they would work again. He just needed the right ones; he was convinced.

Kyle looked away, trying to hide his feeling of disregard. He remembered! His Uncle Ben had high blood pressure. How had he managed all these years? What doctor had he used? What drugs? If the medication was Kyle's problem as Liz had suggested, maybe he needed to have it changed. If not for the medicine, though, he might have suffered a stroke or, God forbid, a heart attack by now. Perhaps Uncle Ben's doctor would have a solution. The thirty-mile trip would be worth it, if he could get answers. But first, he had to get to the dentist so he could enjoy food again without the pain. Since receiving his last fillings more cavities had been found. He dreaded the unpleasant experience, to be sure, but the cavities demanded immediate attention.

Kyle reclined in the dentist chair with his mouth gaped and his stomach growling from hunger pains. He hadn't eaten this morning. Prior dentist visits had taught him better. He dreaded what was coming. Suddenly a sting... The needle plunged into his left lower gums. Relaxed muscles couldn't numb the sensation of the drill grinding through his cavity infested teeth, grating on his nerves, sending chills throughout his body. The constant vibrations made him twinge.

The smells of anesthetic and metal penetrated his nostrils. From the suspended mirror above his head, Kyle could see the silvery substance that the dentist slithered into the holes. It would have to harden for a couple of hours before Kyle could eat. But that was just as well, because by then his swollen lips would have life again. Now he had fourteen silver fillings. He hoped they would be his last.

Days after his visit to the dentist, Kyle's fatigue worsened. Jane had placed a delectable meal before him and he wanted so badly to enjoy it. With hands that trembled, he tried to lift the fork of macaroni and cheese to his mouth only to have it drop, splattering the macaroni and cheese onto the table. A pounding headache returned along with another bout of diarrhea. His medicine proved to be no match. He rushed into the bathroom to relieve himself. Within minutes, he called Jane away from the kitchen, his voice weak and muffled. "Honey!"

Jane stuffed a letter from another dissatisfied repair shop customer into her apron pocket and rushed into the bathroom. She found Kyle sitting on the commode crying, doubled over in pain, his head dangling between his legs.

"Kyle! What's wrong?"

"Get a hold of Dr. Harris, would you? I want to... Uncle Ben wants me to see him."

"Okay," she scurried into the kitchen to use the phone. She lifted the receiver off its hook, fumbled it onto the wall before it fell, and positioned it for dialing. A voice came through.

"Jane, this is Sidney"

"Sidney, can I call you back? I've got to take Kyle to the doctor."

"Listen Jane, that's why I'm calling, can I talk to him?"

"Another time maybe, but... he's, he's in pain."

Sidney interrupted... "I think Kyle should see Dr. Greg Johnson. He doesn't use drugs and all that. He uses chiropractic treatments, massage therapy, reflexology and nutritional supplements."

"Well let me ask him."

His hair sprouting out in all directions, Kyle had maneuvered himself back into the kitchen. His muscles and joints had begun to throb. For a moment, he could no longer walk.

"Honey, it's Sidney. He wants you to see a Dr. Johnson. Liz thinks he might be able to help you."

Kyle, riddled with pain, lifted the receiver to his ear. "I'll think about it, but today I'm going to see Uncle Ben's doctor. Thanks, Sid"

Jane dialed Dr. Harris' office. "Is this Dr. Harris's office?"

"Yes, it is."

"My husband asked me to call. He's in a lot of pain. May I bring him in?"

"Is he a patient?"

"No, but his Uncle Ben referred him; Ben Tyler."

"Sure. Go ahead and bring him, but I may have to work him in."

Jane assisted her struggling husband into the car, strapped Merle and Chelsey in back, and drove off.

Dr. Harris was a tall, man, with white hair and a silver streak at the base of his temples. A neatly trimmed mustache stretched across his lips.

Having gone through the screening process, Kyle entered Dr. Harris' office. Sitting behind his executive desk with his trunk tilted forward, Dr. Harris scribbled something onto his notepad. An impressive assortment of prestigious looking certificates and diplomas lined the wall just above the doctor's head. Kyle eased himself into the chair facing the doctor, grimacing from the pain of every move.

Dr. Harris looked at Kyle's chart, and then addressed Kyle, his eyes focused and intense.

"So, Kyle," Harris paused. "Looks like you've got some pretty severe blood pressure problems."

The words had stunned Kyle. "But...my pressure, I thought it was under control."

"The nurse's readings were quite high," The doctor glanced back at the chart then back at Kyle. "Hum. It says here you've been taking... He began, shaking his head, "but it doesn't seem to be working. Better try another." He thumbed through the big red book he pulled from an adjacent bookcase.

"What about my tiredness, my joint and muscle pain? And the diarrhea?"

Dr. Harris held the pages steady for a moment, and then addressed Kyle. "Well, you're anemic, but I can take care of that."

Kyle waited for a mention of a solution for his pain, but there was none. "And the pain. What about the pain and the diarrhea?" he added.

Harris dropped his head as though ashamed that he had so little to offer. His eyes shifted as he looked up again, trying to gather his composure. "Its arthritis, Kyle. Other than painkillers, I'm afraid there isn't a whole lot that can be done about it. But, at the rate you're going, you could be in a wheelchair by the time you're thirty-six."

Kyle's lips drew tight; he could feel his pulse rising. "You're telling me that...that it's going to get worse?"

"Well, let me rephrase myself. There are painkillers, but there is no cure."

Kyle stilled himself for a moment, his eyelids closing until there was total darkness. A sharp pain grabbed his big left toe and wouldn't let go. "Oooh!" He yelled.

"I think I'm gonna need those pain pills."

"Don't you worry, Kyle. I'm going to take care of your pressure and that pain. The diarrhea could be coming from the blood pressure medicine. We'll try and fix that, too." He thumbed through the book once again. "I want you to take two of these three times a day and the pain pills as needed. I want you back here in two weeks."

"Okay," Kyle agreed easing himself up from the chair. He needed one of those pain pills badly.

One week later, Kyle awakened with a new complaint. Painful redness surrounding a huge mass of puffy lesions covered more than one fourth of his body, including his face and arms. He twisted his trunk looking, trying to examine the awful looking sores. He was much too embarrassed to face anyone. But he had agreed over a month ago, to let Billy, a friend from Seattle, Washington, stop over. He hoped that whatever he had wasn't contagious.

Jane had given birth to their third child, Patrick and was still in the hospital. The two little ones, Merle and Chelsey were under Kyle's care. But, his mother had agreed to help during Jane's absence.

When Billy arrived, Kyle shared the details of his illness with him.

"Man, I think it's the medicine."

It was Kyle's second warning about the side effects of the drugs; the first time was with Liz. And though it had sounded silly at the time, hearing the same thing from two independent people made Kyle think.

"You think?"

"Without a doubt," Billy said, nodding his head. "Without a doubt, based on the things you've told me, I'm sure it's the medicine."

Kyle shifted his focus from Billy a moment, then back again. "Well, there's one way to find out." He flushed the assortment of pills down the toilet and returned.

"My brother's wife told me about a Dr. Johnson. I think I'll make an appointment to see him. Says he uses no drugs to treat his patients."

Dr. Johnson was balding, with wisps of hair in the back and on either side of his head. He listened as Kyle shared his many problems, and then jotted something down on his chart.

"I think I can help. Why don't you stand facing the wall ahead? I'd like to see what kind of motion you have in your neck. Let's have you move your head over to the right as far as it will go. Do you have any discomfort?"

"No," Kyle said, but Johnson noted that Kyle's head stopped within two inches of his shoulders.

"How about when you move it to the left?"

"No," though his range of motion was quite limited.

"Now lie down on your back for a moment." The doctor helped Kyle onto the examining table, maneuvered Kyle's neck gently; with a quick whiplash like jerk, he popped Kyle's neck back into alignment.

Dr. Johnson manipulated Kyle's inner right foot just below the thick muscle beneath the right toe. Amidst Kyle's screaming, Johnson held it steadily until the pain was gone, then released it. He pressed on areas just above Kyle's pelvis, pushing upward. Gurgling sounds abounded as though a sea of bubbles had exploded in Kyle's stomach. It was a strange kind of practice--nothing like Kyle had ever experienced before, but having endured so much suffering, he was ready for whatever--even a chiropractor.

Johnson pressed various bottles of supplements against Kyle's stomach, and with Kyle's arm extended, the doctor pushed down on Kyle's arm, alternating supplements against his stomach until his arm could no longer be pushed down to see if Kyle could tolerate the various supplements He gave Kyle a nutritional supplement chart and a special diet. Though they were expensive, Kyle purchased the products the doctor recommended.

Thanks to Dr. Johnson's program, Kyle's energy level soon returned. The headaches left and he no longer had the indiscriminate bursts of diarrhea.

Even the painful arthritis dissipated after two months of Johnson's treatment. Once again he could eat. All this--and with simple body manipulation and nutrition. Liz had said it; now he, too, had witnessed it. The Lord had answered his prayer. ...And He was right on time.

6

Only two months into Johnson's treatments, healthy color replaced the pale skin that had once advertised Kyle's illness. Thirty additional pounds once again settled over his thick frame. Kyle felt as though he could compete in the World Series.

It was Kyle's first day back at Burton's Repair. Business had slowed to a trickle. He pulled a crumpled complaint from his pants, which Jane had stuffed in her apron pocket the day Sidney had recommended Dr. Johnson. Kyle had come face to face with the shop's financial challenges. Pilferage came to mind, but his accounts revealed the truth.

One disgruntled customer had returned a piece of heavy equipment to the shop for repair. Kyle ripped the equipment apart, its parts covering a wide section of the shop's floor. He maneuvered between parts and examined them with the same curiosity that had consumed him for hours when he was a child. His quick eyes and exceptional skill gave him an instant clue. He moved the suspected malfunctioning part onto a workstation for testing and noted problems with the parts assembly. Before long the problem was solved. The customer picked up the equipment the following day with no further complaint.

As settlement for a botched up job done by one of Kyle's employees, another customer demanded payment in full. Kyle settled with income from his farm. Since the farm was the family's only real source of income now, Kyle hated to continue draining it. He had used Johnson's program for better than six months now; it had become rather expensive. The supplements weren't covered by insurance, as were the drugs, so he had to pay for them out of his pocket, and that was tough. Besides, he was feeling great. There was no need to continue, he reasoned. Yes, he would do it; he would stop taking the supplements. Dan, the latest addition to his family, was the deciding factor.

A couple of months after discontinuing Johnson's program, the awful pounding headaches returned. Yes, Johnson's program is good, but how good if it requires one to continue? Kyle wondered. Except for high blood pressure medicine, you take drugs for a period of time. He had assumed the same would be true for Johnson's program. It was not.

Again on the program, Kyle's symptoms abated. This time, he was determined to find out why. He thought daily meals provided nutritional requirements. Some weekend nutrition classes, however, introduced Kyle to a new realm of knowledge.

Deep in thought, Kyle flipped to a page in his text. Nutritional deficiencies, he learned, were the reasons for many diseases. Contributing to those deficiencies were drug therapy, environmental factors such as toxic fumes, pesticides, fluoridated water, contaminated soils, foodstuffs, and metal compounds. When those deficiencies are addressed by the intake of sufficient amounts of deficient nutrients, the body flourishes. What a simple concept; why hadn't he thought of that before? Kyle asked himself.

Each night, just before retiring for bed, Kyle pored over pages, devouring everything he could on nutrition. Nutrition, he learned, was but one piece of the puzzle. Body manipulation, such as reflexology, was useful in treating and preventing disease. Reflexologists could discern affected organs by merely pressing on various areas on a patient's feet. Kyle remembered his excruciating pain and how it abated after Johnson pressed certain areas of his feet.

But researching these areas was not enough for Kyle. He had mastered the art of fixing malfunctioning machinery; now he hungered for knowledge about the human body--what made it tick. What was different about nutritional therapy? Why did the adjustments and massages make him feel so much better? He was determined to find the answers.

The knowledge Kyle acquired proved helpful for family and friends. Helping people restore their health was a good feeling, but their constant demands caused him to neglect himself, and he was about to pay for it.

The decision to stop taking his supplements a second time, poor dietary habits, and environmental factors found Kyle suffering from an unbearable tiredness that worsened each day. Food had again lost its appeal. Kyle's sense of smell and appetite were gone. Once again, his body was lost in clothes that hung loosely over his thick frame; he had lost some sixty pounds. Although Kyle had once again become faithful to the program offered by Johnson; it was no longer effective.

Jane had watched her husband's deterioration over the years, but until now had allowed him to direct his own treatment. Not today. While Kyle lay totally incapacitated, Jane did a little research. A doctor in New York had been effective at treating various kinds of life threatening ailments. She sat on the edge of the bed next to her husband, stroking his forehead. "Kyle, there's a doctor out east that we're going to try. Like Johnson, he practices with natural remedies," she said.

"Oh, I don't know, Jane," he said, straining to lift his head up from his pillow. "Maybe I should go to an MD for this...I mean, at least for a diagnosis, then go from there." Once again his head fell onto the pillow. "I'm not sure what these natural therapies can. . . I mean, I've been taking my supplements. Let's see what it is first, though," he said, in a whisper.

At the hospital Kyle lay in serious shape, with shooting pains all over his body. A buzzing sound periodically hung in his ear as though a fly had gotten stuck in it, but it was a sound that couldn't be hushed with tweezers. A tremendous headache had returned, and a disabling tiredness crippled him. His blood pressure had become dangerously high again and his stomach was often queasy. The diarrhea returned; this time he was incontinent. Test showed that Kyle had advanced stages of prostate cancer, leukemia, and a bad heart.

"Kyle," his doctor said. "Your prognosis is not good. You have three days at best. I'm afraid there is nothing else we can do." If feeling was an indicator, he had no time to waste.

At home Kyle lay bedridden with piercing chest pains. Jane took a sampling of Kyle's urine and saliva and sent it to Dr. Gary Morris, the naturopath out west. Morris' report confirmed the MD's diagnosis, but he emphasized that Kyle's heart condition was most urgent. "The routine must be followed carefully. Directions will follow, but I want him on bed rest for three days. Give him a PH or alkaline vitamin, enzymes, and food at the times indicated. Most importantly, he must avoid sugar and coffee," Morris urged.

An overpowering exhaustion and headaches were Kyle's companions, the traumatic symptoms associated with drug withdrawals. These symptoms, Morris said, were common during the detoxification period. They persisted for roughly two weeks.

"Open wide," Jane said, as she neared her bed stricken husband. She let drops of homeopathic solution settle under Kyle's tongue to arrest the cancer as he lay listless. Later, a series of colonics cleaned his colon, and chiropractic adjustments aligned his spine. In the weeks following, Kyle's listlessness abated. Six weeks into the program, Morris had literally taken Kyle from death's door, and brought him back to life.

Kyle found himself once again riddled with questions. What was different about Morris's program? Why was it effective and Johnson's not? His search for answers would take him back to school.

7

The smell of fresh eggs, sausage, and toast filled Kyle's nostrils as he yawned and stretched, tumbling out of the bed. It was wonderful having a sense of smell and the appetite to go along with it once again. He was thankful that the Lord had again spared him. He shared the knowledge of nutrition with his family and loved ones and that was a joy, but he yearned for more. His own hairsbreadth encounter with death provided the passion. So when Liz told him about classes in reflexology and massage therapy offered in American Falls, he was elated. It was like an addiction; the more he learned, the more he wanted to learn. Knowing how to maintain ones health, he learned, was precious.

Kyle soon learned that people who wanted massages and reflexology were in plentiful supply, but it was just as well, since applying the techniques learned was one of the course requirements. When he ran into a family member who told him about the degeneration of the spine suffered by Paris Mason, a political heavy in the community, Kyle offered to help.

At Paris's home, Kyle could see through the blinds as Paris walked slowly with one hand bracing her hip. He couldn't help pitying her, as she struggled to let him in. Paris' disheveled hair hung loosely across her face. From looking at her awful limp, Kyle was grieved, just thinking of her pain. He was used to practicing his massages on an adjustment table, not a bed; this put him at a disadvantage. His big hands moved gently from Paris's neck to her shoulder as she lay still on her back. He carefully moved his hands up and down her arms, shoulder, and neck pinpointing the areas that were affected by degeneration. Paris ooohed, ouched, and sighed as Kyle worked his fingers throughout her muscles and joints.

"They want to do surgery next week," she whispered hoarsely.

"Well, let's see what we can do with it," Kyle responded, as he continued to massage her tight muscles.

Paris sighed once again. Though Kyle was as gentle as he could be, Paris was still obviously in much pain, but at least now it felt as though her muscles were being somewhat relaxed. Kyle released his firm hold. "How's that?"

"Some better," she said, slowly taking in a breath, then exhaling.

"Let's get you over on your stomach," Kyle said, trying as gently as he could to roll her over. In spite of his best efforts to be gentle, Paris frowned and yelled. That made Kyle nervous.

"Easy. Easy…" he said as he moved with caution, carefully rolling her over on the bed. He massaged the shoulders and moved downward to the upper torso until he reached the small of Paris's back. Falling tears dampened her pillow.

His touches were gentle, but firm. He kneaded and pressed until her muscles relaxed. But there was more. As Paris sat in a recliner, Kyle began probing her feet starting with her left big toe, and ending with a technique that caused her feet to fan repeatedly from left to right.

The treatment done, cries of relief replaced Paris's falling tears. She settled into calmness, and finally, a deep sleep. This was something she had been unable to do since the horrible pain had begun.

Kyle let himself out, locking the door behind him, relieved that everything had gone so well. He had never known a feeling of exuberance like this one—even on those Christmas mornings when, as a child, he had received his favorite toy. No, this was bigger than that. It was as though something had jolted him into a state of euphoria. That he could give someone back their health was awesome.

The next week Paris phoned Kyle. "You'll never guess...My doctor canceled the surgery!"

"Really? That's wonderful."

"Oh Kyle, I can't thank you enough. If I can ever do anything to help you, just call. Is that a deal?"

"Hey, it's a deal."

Every ounce of Kyle's being rejoiced. This was a calling from God. He was spared so he could give to others what had been given to him. Even though many long hours of study were ahead of him, he knew what he had to do. It was as clear as if etched in stone: "Go ye now my faithful servant and deliver the flock, for the blessings bestowed upon you will be great."

The course work required for a Doctor of Naturopathy degree was demanding. It meant spending a lot of study time away from Jane and the kids. His classes required hands-on training to accompany theories taught. He welcomed the chance to practice his newly acquired techniques.

Paris Mason's one-woman campaign drew lots of people to Kyle. He indulged them with the same devotion. He was crafting his future as a naturopath one person at a time.

Kyle officially opened for business as a massage therapist and reflexologist in his basement, sometimes working late into the night. This arrangement took too much time away from the family. He and Jane decided to move the business to an outside location.

A small trailer was set up within a mile from the back of their dwelling. Kyle loved his work, but sometimes it was overwhelming. A family outing went belly up when a man, who had sprung his ankle, showed up in the office without an appointment before Kyle had gotten away. Seeing the pain in this man's face took Kyle aback. Even an animal shouldn't suffer that way, he thought. He couldn't bring himself to send the man away in that condition. It didn't set too well with Jane, but she respected the man Kyle had become and the decision he had made. Like Kyle, she felt this was Kyle's life mission. She didn't dare stand in the way of that.

Kyle's knowledge once again proved golden when Merle began complaining of extreme shoulder and knee pain three years after contracting the seven year itch. Kyle noticed him shifting unevenly from side to side when he hobbled to the living room. And though Merle was thin, his red, swollen knees and joints were stiff from the weight of his body. Kyle acted quickly, but he hadn't the sophistication to diagnose Merle's condition. Merle would have to be taken to the medical doctor for testing.

"Avascular necrosis," the doctor said. Kyle's research told him that it was a malignant manifestation of the bone possibly caused by steroid use. Kyle suddenly remembered using steroid cream on Merle. A sickening nauseousness penetrated his stomach - to think that both he and Jane may have contributed to Merle's illness. But wallowing in guilt and sympathy was counterproductive. Fortunately, he now had added choices to treat Merle. A doctor of naturopathy and homeopathy degree would give him still more.

8

The grueling course work and residency now behind him, Dr. Kyle Burton could now treat diseases that before were left only to licensed medical doctors. Kyle had been certified as both a homeopathic and naturopathic physician. Through friends and relatives the word spread. With allergies on the rise, a constant stream of patients flocked to the clinic. Since many patients had adverse reactions to allergy and seasonal shots, they sought the kind of relief Dr. Burton offered. Burton's popularity became the nemesis of a local pharmacist whose business normally flourished during allergy season, but dwindled to a trickle as more people learned of Dr. Burton's successes.

While obtaining his degrees, Dr. Burton learned of many diagnostic tools available in Tijuana, Mexico. Until he met Dr. Simmons, a Mormon, however, Dr. Burton had no satisfactory means of diagnosing patients in the United States. He had to rely on the diagnosis of medical doctors.

Dr. Simmons offered an innovative approach to reaching patients hundred of miles away. He only needed a hair sample to diagnose a patient's nutritional deficiencies. Dr. Simmons never met most of the patients he diagnosed, yet for many, his assessment proved effective, especially for those having chronic illnesses. Hair samples, through Simmons, became Dr. Burton's basis for treatment as well.

Renee, a listless, skinny little baby clutched in her father's arms, was Burton's first patient after he was introduced to Simmons's hair analysis. Renee's hair was scant, not enough for a measurable sample, so Burton was forced to use his best judgment. The left side of her body was numbed from paralysis, and Renee drifted in and out of consciousness, episodes that were becoming more and more frequent. Her father, Paul, had come trusting and hoping that Dr. Burton could help his little girl. Since Paul was Burton's brother in Christ, Burton felt a special kinship to him.

Renee's seizures--jerking of the body, foaming at the mouth and convulsions grew more violent with time. Slanted eyes gave Renee a look of Down's Syndrome. Burton could see the stress in Paul's eyes. "What'd they tell you?"

"They say she has . . . he broke down. ". . . A brain tumor. It's malignant. With surgery she could be paralyzed, and with a bone marrow transplant. . . I don't know what to do. If you can help her, Kyle—if you," He dropped his head as though trying to hide the tears. I'll do anything. Just name it."

Since Renee was too small for the standard nutritional regimen, Burton prescribed liquids, small doses of nutrition, and applied body manipulations and a two-week series of daily treatments. Only time would tell.

In April 1982, Mark, a Parkinson's victim, entered the clinic. He trembled badly and moved slowly; his body visibly weak and off balance appeared stiff. Red patches and scars covered his face and neck. Two solid weeks of intense nutrition and body manipulation proved worthless. Mark was the only patient who had not responded to two solid weeks of therapy. "Perhaps Mark needed more time, Dr. Burton reasoned." But the possibility that Mark wasn't properly absorbing the products came to mind.

During Renee's two-month check up, Burton teased, "Is this the little girl who was so sick?" He laughed as he stroked her little hands. Renee lay on the table thrusting her chubby legs about in miniature kicks. Her cheeks had become rosy and plump.

"Keep doing whatever you're doing. The tumor has shrunk considerably," Paul's doctor told him at the time of Renee's medical exam.

"Kyle, I'll never be able to repay you for what you have done," the grateful father exclaimed.

"Seeing this little baby come back to life-that's my pay."

Renee's recovery left Dr. Burton on a natural high. He felt a strong feeling of accomplishment; once again he had given to someone else that which had been given to him, the gift of life.

News of Renee's recovery traveled throughout the congregation. Marie Frances stood ready to receive her miracle. Extreme bloating, fatigue, and memory loss were her complaints. Marie came to Natrogenics for treatment on June 17, 1982. Like Liz, Marie was a nurse and remained true to the profession, but experience had taught her to seek healthcare elsewhere.

Experience told Burton that Marie's symptoms were consistent with parasites and Candida infestation. Once his diagnosis was confirmed by the deficiency assessment from Simmons, he introduced Marie to homeopathic formulations. On a return visit to the clinic, Marie said she felt better than she had in years.

Mark returned. Much to Dr. Burton's dismay, Mark with sporadic scar patches blotting his face, still shook uncontrollably from the Parkinson's. Burton couldn't figure out, for the life of him, what was blocking Mark's progress. Burton recommended other brands of products, but subsequent visits, however, showed no signs of improvement. Mark could not absorb recommended products, so this would present still a greater challenge—what to do when the patient couldn't absorb the product.

Mark's slow improvement, along with that of a growing number of other patients who could not absorb the recommended vitamins or nutrients became a real concern for Burton. He researched the products on the market and found that ascorbic acid, a compound that was implicated in free radical cell formation, was the basis of their vitamin C products. Products claiming to contain "rosehips" had less than five-percent rosehips. Other so-called natural products were heated during manufacturing, destroying the plus and minus charges that distinguished them from their drug counterparts. That destruction, Burton learned, made a natural product "artificial." There was now little wonder why patients like Mark responded so poorly to these products. Better nutrient absorption was the answer, but how, when virgin products were nonexistent?

As a farmer, Kyle had treated his sick cattle by supplying mega doses of vitamin and/or minerals of the deficient nutrient; the animal returned to health. That knowledge, coupled with Kyle's naturopathic training, gave him the impetus he needed to embark on a mission; he needed to create effective products for his patients. Dr. Burton believed that if he could make a product that Mark could absorb, ninety five percent of his patients would be able to absorb it.

When trying to come up with the best diet for his patients, Kyle remembered his cattle. Skim milk and fat free diets tended to make them fat. Obesity would later lead to heart attacks in the animals. This knowledge and his expertise in the field of nutrition and research were the basis for his nutritional recommendations. While the nation's researchers sanctioned a low fat diet for health conscious Americans, Burton told his patients to avoid them: that cholesterol was necessary for the body to thrive and could only be generated by a certain amount of fat intake. He renounced the popular notion that eggs and beef were poor choices of food. In fact, he recommended organic fertile eggs and beef, especially for patients who wished to lower their bad cholesterol. As his patients thrived, Natrogenics clinic continued to grow and was forced to move to a bigger location, hiring its first employee.

Burton's research on aluminum toxicity, fluoride, and the benefits of electromagnetic fields including colored light therapy uncovered invaluable information. Aluminum, Burton discovered, was found in the brains of patients suffering from Alzheimer's and some other central nervous system diseases. Likewise Dr. Burton found that fluoride, once used for rat poison, had been linked with some very serious diseases. It was a known carcinogen; people exposed to fluoride got cancer at a much faster rate than those who weren't. States adding fluoride to their drinking water saw more incidences of cancer than those who did not. Because of this and similar research, Burton urged his patients: "Avoid aluminum cookware, wraps, or deodorants, toothpaste, canned drinks or goods and dinners or snacks wrapped in aluminum, fluoridated toothpaste and water."

Dr. Burton created the first five in his line of products, and waited anxiously to try them on patients such as Mark. Meanwhile, the third Sunday of the month was fast approaching. It was Burton's turn to preach. He needed to prepare for his Sunday sermon.

9

With his family at his side, Kyle slid onto a pew near the front of the church. It was the third Sunday, his turn to preach. This had been the church's arrangement for years.

After a quick trip to the restroom, Kyle slumped back onto the pew letting his arm fall over his wife's shoulder. Clearly the program was in error. Amazingly, there stood his Uncle Ben delivering the message, his baldhead settled into a wrinkle at the nape of his neck.

Kyle looked at the program once again. Perhaps it was not the third Sunday. The program clearly stated that Ben Tyler would be delivering the sermon today, but Kyle had dismissed it as a simple mistake. What had happened? Had he overlooked a meeting?

He looked at Jane and she at him. He could tell from her expression, that, like him, she was confused. Both remained silent, and tried to focus on the message as they allowed the order of service to unfold.

Burton loved preaching and had gone to great lengths to prepare today's sermon. He had so much to say, but apparently not this Sunday. But there was something else in the air—a feeling he couldn't put his finger on. It was strange. He didn't know just what to make of it. It was a lonely feeling, though his family was at his side.

After service Uncle Ben called a special meeting. "It has come to our attention that brother Kyle has been willfully engaging in sinful practices," he said.

Both Kyle and Jane looked at each other alarmed. Kyle sprang to his feet. "What! What sinful practices?"

"Kyle, will you let me finish?"

Kyle braced himself, once again settling onto the pew. He owed it to himself to hear the rest.

"As I said, Brother Kyle has been engaging in sinful practices. Because of that, we, the church body, have voted to ex-communicate him. We have decided that Kyle should be treated as a wicked person. Let it be stated that no one should talk to him, eat with him, or be seen with him. Go now in peace. This meeting is adjourned."

Kyle stood up looking around the church. "Does anybody want to tell me what this is all about?" he asked, as the members spilled from the pews. But for now, the subject was closed. It was clear that the order had already taken effect, for no one would say a word. That his own uncle had put him out of church fellowship was bad enough, but to offer no explanation. How could he ever make amends if he didn't know what he had done? "This is crazy!" he thought.

This explained his discomfort today. Church members had made their decision behind his back. It was a feeling he had never experienced before. All of his life he had attended this church--a place where he could unwind and receive blessings. And now… it was inconceivable that they had done this. He couldn't accept their decision. He just couldn't. They had no right! It was as much his church as it was theirs. So far as he was concerned, he still belonged and had no intention of moving his membership.

With Jane and the children at his side, Kyle left the empty church. Outside, a few families exchanged words among themselves, but disbanded immediately when Kyle approached.

The Burton's piled into their vehicle. Even Mother, Father, and Sidney had left the church without speaking. There were no words to describe Kyle's feeling of emptiness. His excommunication was unprecedented. Its true, the church doctrines was pretty strict; but were his actions not, as always, in accordance with them? He felt so uneasy; he just couldn't rest without knowing what had caused the church to reach its decision.

From these pews Kyle had garnered strength when life seemed so unbearable. He just couldn't imagine life without the church. He didn't want to try. It was as though air was being squeezed from his lungs. Suddenly a thought came to him... And just as suddenly it died. He looked at Jane. "Jane, do you... What are they talking about? I mean, I just don't..."

Jane's eyes shifted nervously as she spoke. "You think maybe, Dr. Simmons... You know, he is Mormon."

"But that's crazy Jane. That's crazy."

"I don't know, Hon, the thought just came to me. That's all." For a moment there was silence.

"But Mom and Dad left, Jane, my own flesh and blood. Even Sidney and Liz have gone," he said, his voice cracking. His red watery eyes were swollen from tears he tried to hold back. He yanked his car into gear, and sped off. Were it not for Jane and his children at his side, he might have never reached home alive. It was a horrible thought, but life without his church would be one thing; life without the family who had loved and nurtured him was quite another. Surely if he talked to Mom she would tell him what was going on. By now it was clear that no one else would. But she wouldn't be home for a while.

At home, Kyle settled into some old khakis and a loose shirt. A cool beer helped him to unwind. There was a game on TV. Try as he might to lose himself in the game, his mind wandered. But it bought him time until Mom got home. Jane settled the children at the table to eat. Kyle phoned his mom.

"Hello."

Kyle tried to be calm. "Mom, you want to tell me what this is all about?"

"Kyle, you were there. You heard the orders."

"Yes, but…I mean… What did I do?"

"I can't talk to you, Kyle. You heard the orders." Suddenly the phone went dead.

"I don't believe she…Doggone it!" he shouted, slamming the receiver back onto the phone base. He dashed into the kitchen. He couldn't keep this to himself. "She hung up on me!"

"Oh honey," Jane said, stopping just shy of serving Chelsey a scoop of ice cream. She stripped off her apron, preparing to follow Kyle into the bedroom.

"But Mom," Chelsey cried.

Jane hurriedly plopped the serving of ice cream into Chelsey's plate and followed her hurt, angry husband into the bedroom. She must have known that words would be of little comfort to Kyle at this moment. She rushed into his embrace. Together, their bodies were energized by the warmth until, for Kyle, the pain had subsided somewhat.

The warmth of Jane's hand soothed his thighs. "You think maybe Sidney will tell you?"

"I don't know. I just… Maybe if I went to mom's... but if she was this rude on the phone, how will she act in person?" He was prepared to do whatever it took to get to the truth, even stopping by unannounced. He knew it was a bold move, but he would just have to take his chances—perhaps one evening after work. How would his father act, especially when he saw Kyle? he wondered. But he had no choice. He had to know.

He felt like a criminal breaking and entering, but it was the only way. After scanning the property for mother's car, Kyle parked, stood out of view, and knocked--an unusual practice in the country.

Soon a pleasant voice rang out. "Coming, coming," she said. Within minutes Mrs. Burton was at the door. Her tightly drawn lips and hardened features told Kyle that she didn't want to see him.

"Mother, please," Kyle begged. "Don't you think...? I'd like to know what this is all about."

Mr. Burton heard the brief exchange between Kyle and his wife and joined in. "Alright, Kyle."

"Well, ca…can I come in?" Kyle asked, gesturing with his hands.

Mr. Burton led the way as the duo followed him into the living room. Mr. and Mrs. Burton seated themselves on the couch, Kyle in a big chair on the opposite side of the room. Mr. Burton's slim body was frail. His thick white eyebrows jutting out from his forehead furrowed as he spoke. "Kyle you know the position of the church."

Kyle cut in. "No, dad, I don't. That's why I'm here."

"Oh come on Kyle--doing business with a Mormon? You know that's not allowed under church doctrine."

"Oh yes, dad, that's right; you went to naturopathic school," Kyle said, sarcastically. "You tell me, how else can I get a nutritional diagnosis? Dr. Simmons's all I've got."

"Kyle, surely you don't believe that. Besides, radonics is not approved by the FDA. ...and associating with a Mormon?"

"Oh dad. What are you saying--that I should just give up my practice?"

Mrs. Burton joined in. "Kyle, no one's asking you to give up your practice, but you need to disassociate yourself from Dr. Simmons. We cannot or will not associate with you unless you do. It's that simple."

It was not what Kyle had wanted to hear. Jane had said it, but he had not wanted to believe her. Without Dr. Simmons, he would be no better off than other naturopaths. He was faced with a strange dichotomy; he had to choose between his family and his patients. Caring for his patients, he felt, was a mandate from God. His family, on the other hand, had made him who he was. They had given him the zest and passion for life through their nurturing. The thought of giving all this up was chilling.

"But mom, I don't... Nutritional diagnosis is the heart of my business. Without it I have no business."

Mrs. Burton's lips turned down, "Then sell it!" she snapped.

"They want me to sell the business," Kyle said, nervously thumping his fingers on his kitchen's table.

Jane looked at him for a minute in silence. "And what about your patients, Kyle?"

"Well, I didn't give them an answer. I told them I would think about it. If they feel I'm seriously considering selling perhaps they will reconsider their decision."

"If you sold the business, do you think it would really matter?" Jane asked.

"Not really. They get something in their heads and... They don't change."

"Well, guess you've got to choose, don't you?"

"No. I have no plans of selling. I mean, I've... My patients come first."

"Well, looks like it's decided," Jane said, tilting her head. "Good. I'm glad. The patients need you."

"I don't know; maybe in time even the church people will reconsider. God, I sure hope so," Kyle said.

The next Sunday offered Burton no relief. Melancholy had replaced the gaiety once fostered by the church. The family arrived late, and planted themselves at the back of the church, departing immediately after services to avoid rejection by the church masses.

Burton had only gotten a glance at the man to his right. An extended stare got Burton no attention; the man was clearly ignoring him. Beside the man was a girl of about seven who sat oblivious to the interchange between Burton and her father. He didn't have to wonder anymore. "My, isn't this interesting?" he thought.

When church adjourned, the man slid off the pew with his little girl as though oblivious to Kyle. "Paul!" Kyle called out to him.

Paul grabbed his daughter by the hand and exited the church, saying nothing.

"Paul," Kyle hollered out once again, but they had disappeared. What a strange twist of fate, Kyle thought. Such an irony; the man who had promised to do anything for him as thanks for saving his daughter Renee's life, was ignoring him.

Kyle's frustration grew. These were churchgoing people claiming to be Christians. Were it not for him, Paul's daughter wouldn't be alive. How could Paul possibly justify his actions? Where was his sense of right and wrong? Where does the boundary of religion end and righteousness begin? In haste, Kyle gathered his family inside the car.

"Jane, do you believe that Paul?"

"Oh honey, try not to take it personally."

"Take it personally? Hey, whose side are you on anyway?"

"Oh Kyle, I didn't mean... He's scared. That's all."

"Scared of what, Jane? What is he scared of? Scared I'm gonna contaminate him? Huh? Huh? Where was that "scare" when his daughter was dying seven years ago? That's baloney Jane...and you know it. Where is the man's sense of loyalty? Then he was about ready to give me the clothes off of his back. Now he ignores me!"

At home Kyle grabbed a beer from the refrigerator and plopped onto the living room couch. The children scattered into various areas of the family dwelling. Jane settled into some comfortable clothing then joined her husband.

Being treated like lepers at the church had gotten to Merle. Chelsey had started to complain about being taunted at school. She had become withdrawn, virtually ignoring Kyle except where necessary, clinging instead to Jane.

"Mom," is daddy a bad person?" Chelsey had asked Jane after coming home from school one day.

"Honey no! Your daddy is a very good person. He helps people. You understand? He helps people." Jane pulled Chelsey into her arms, soothing and rubbing her for a moment, then held her at arms length, looking her in the eyes. "You mustn't... We've got to be strong for daddy, ok?"

"Ok," she agreed, then disappeared into her bedroom.

Later, Jane shared the incident with Kyle.

"I'm telling you, Jane, this thing is just... I mean when it starts to affect the kids...I don't know."

"We'll just have to make them understand, that's all," Jane countered.

"When did this happen?"

"About two weeks ago."

"Why didn't you tell me?"

"I was hoping that things would settle down a bit."

"Merle is irritable. He doesn't want to go to church anymore and its all because of me. He calls them a bunch of hypocrites. You know--what's sad is, I agree with him. They are a bunch of hypocrites."

"But are we going to let those hypocrites run our lives?"

"It kind of feels like that's what they are doing. We still have the farm and repair shop; maybe I should give some thought to selling. I mean, is it really worth having the kids...? But I just--my patients, what would--where would they go? Who would take care of them?"

"Well, that's the thing."

"But I can't just sit idly by and have the children harassed because of me. It's unfair to them. Besides, mother was very clear. If ever they are going to fellowship with me, I must disassociate from Simmons or sell. Quite frankly as I see it, that leaves me only one option. Sell."

10

Who would be a good replacement for the business? Kyle pondered. It must be someone hand-picked, someone who had the patients' best interest at heart. Certain patients would surely die unless they received specialized treatments; these Kyle wanted to treat before selling. Since the sell could take months, this would buy him some time.

Burton placed an ad in the newspaper and some trade publications. His ever increasing 400 patient case load drew the attention of naturopaths looking for attractive ventures. He hoped that both church members and family would see it. Maybe then, they could make peace.

As the church lifted its voices, the family slid onto pews at the back of the church. The sermon had yet to begin. 'Forgiveness' was the message of the day. Hopefully, that word would find its place in the hearts of those present, Kyle thought.

Kyle sat anxiously wondering what the end of service would bring. Would someone from the church have seen the ad? Would they respond in kind?

After services Kyle and his family waited, hoping for an acknowledgement, if not from the church body, from his family. 'Forgiveness' might just as well have been mist in the air that searched endlessly for a place to settle. Just as before, the members spilled from their pews as though oblivious to Kyle's presence. Nurse Marie Frances, who at last, thanks to Kyle, had found some comfort from her Candida, did likewise. But Kyle's encounter with Paul had prepared him for rejection by any of his church members; it had not for what followed.

Outside Kyle ushered his family into their vehicle. Up until now, he had avoided Jane's suggestion, but today it weighed heavily upon him. He stood watching, waiting for big brother Sidney and his wife Liz to exit the church. He felt indebted to Sidney; after all, it was Sidney who had rescued him after his painful episode in the wheat fields and once again from dwindling health. If these were any indication, he knew that Sidney would again come to his aid.

Liz exited first, her short hair in tight curls all over her head and a little black strapped purse slung over her shoulders. Sidney followed close behind. Kyle rushed toward them, his eyes searching theirs for acceptance. "Sid why don't you and Liz join us for dinner? It's been a long time," Kyle said.

Liz lips drew back in anger, her head nodding affirmatively, "Yes, it has been," she agreed.

Sidney's features hardened, "And quite frankly, Kyle, if I never see you again, it won't be too soon!" he added, grabbing Liz by the arm. "Come on, honey, let's go." Together they rushed away.

Sidney's words stung like the blades of a hunting knife. Hadn't they seen the ad in the paper? Kyle wondered. For a moment he stood dumbfounded. A mental fog clouded his focus as his eyes shifted nervously. As Jane had suggested he had played his trump card only to have it fly up in his face.

He watched feeling defeated as the couple vanished into the distance. Nervous and shaking, he snatched his car door open and looked into Jane's eyes. It was the first time since his terrible illness that he had requested this of his wife. "Honey, I'm just...I need you to drive."

She agreed. Kyle sighed, and willfully settled himself into the passenger's seat, plopping his head back on the headrest. He hadn't the words to express his disappointment. Silence was his only refuge.

"Maybe when the business sells... Kyle said, breaking the silence. Jane forced a smile, but remained silent. Though he was grateful for his wife and kids, it was not enough. He missed his paternal family. Constant prayer kept his hope alive.

Absorbing himself in his work proved an outlet for Kyle's pain. He arrived at the clinic early and stayed late as the number of patients continued to climb.

Some local chiropractors called a meeting amongst themselves as their patient load plummeted.

"That Burton's no doctor," the first doctor alleged.

"If he is, how come you never see him at any of the meetings?" another one added.

"I heard his degrees are phony. Are we just going to sit by and let this man ruin our practices?" the third asked.

"No! I think he should be reported," the first chiropractor urged.

With their complaints registered, in March 1984, the State Attorney's office launched an investigation of Burton's Natrogenics clinic. It uncovered Burton's educational authenticity and found that patient satisfaction ran high. To Burton it ordered: "Keep up the good work."

With the investigation behind him, Dr. Burton could now concentrate on patient care, what he did best. Arnold Payton came to the clinic complaining of headaches, a sore throat, and extreme fatigue. Fatigue had robbed him of energy and an inflamed throat kept him coughing. "Epstein Barr Virus," Payton's dad, a medical doctor, had diagnosed, but he had no treatment to offer.

"There's a doctor I want you to see, Arnold. I've heard some good things about his success with the Epstein Barr virus," Dr. Payton, Arnold's father told him. "Nutrition has worked better than anything I have to offer."

But when Arnold returned to Natrogenics clinic with complaints of extreme tiredness, Dr. Burton warned, "Avoid toxic fumes whenever possible. They are hard on the lungs, especially for patients with the Epstein bar virus."

Burton remained troubled about Rick Johnson, a rheumatoid arthritis patient, multiple sclerosis patients who complained of memory loss, slurred speech, and Mark, a Parkinson disease victim. Why their recovery was so slow remained a mystery to Burton. It was not until later that he would discover why.

11

May 1984

A female naturopath assumed new ownership of Natrogenics clinic. Kyle and Jane had barely settled into their living room when Dan, the youngest of the Burtons, burst into the house, panting and gasping, his light brown hair in disarray.

"Mom, Dad!" he yelled. "Come quick! Merle's been in an accident!"

"Accident?" Jane shouted. Both rose to their feet.

At the scene Jane was panicky and badly shaken by the sight of her oldest son; so, too, was Kyle, although outwardly he appeared calm. Merle lay still; his short, injured body was sprawled out on the open turf. His torso was twisted, and his arms were spread out high above his head, bloodied from the motorcycle fall. Merle's head, battered and bruised, lay in a puddle of blood. He moaned and groaned as Jane and Kyle approached, but didn't move a muscle.

Dr. Burton knew from his training that this spelled trouble; he couldn't help wondering if Merle would live to see his twentieth birthday. Burton moved quickly but gently, examining Merle for broken parts, careful not to move him. Blood oozed out of his left leg, as it had been virtually torn from his body. They needed an ambulance, but quick. An ex-employee who had gathered in the growing crowd assured Kyle that he had called one. Merle tried to mumble something, but Jane kneeling at his side, cautioned him in her quiet voice, "Don't try to talk. Okay?"

The ambulance siren grew louder and louder until suddenly the vehicle came to an abrupt halt. Some church members looked on as the paramedics prepped Merle, hoisting his body onto the gurney, but turned away suddenly upon recognizing the injured party. But the Lord never failed in His mercy, sending Kyle Burton just what he needed--an ex-employee who agreed to escort Jane to the hospital. The paramedics lifted Merle's body inside the ambulance. Burton was close behind; the ride seemed like an eternity.

At the hospital Merle lay in a semiconscious state, with Kyle Burton at his side, as three doctors came in. The doctors stood arguing about the best approach to take, given the severity of Merle's injury. Young, stocky, brown haired, Dr. Brody stepped forward poking Merle in various places on his body.

"Ow, that hurts," Merle whispered as he endeavored to push away the doctor's hand.

"Well, you should have thought about that before you got on that motorcycle," Brody rejoined.

Brody's insensitivity irritated Kyle, but he held his tongue. He concentrated on getting a pulse in Merle's leg. It was hanging by the skin, connected by the main artery. Merle's pelvis was broken; it pinched the main artery. Merle was bleeding profusely from his penis. Soon the other two doctors were at his side.

"Why don't we twist the pelvis back to release the pressure on the artery so we can get a pulse in that leg; it's crucial to saving it," Kyle suggested. But the doctors discounted Dr. Burton's suggestions and continued arguing as Merle lay suffering. Burton became annoyed. "We need to save that leg," he insisted.

Dr. Brody turned to Kyle. "Well, you're sure positive."

"Well, why not be?"

Dr. Benn shrugged his shoulders pointing to Merle's pelvis, penis, and severed leg. "Well, what about all those negative things?"

"What negative things?" Dr. Burton asked.

"Well, all those things. He's not going to make it anyway," Dr. Benn snapped.

"Well, you don't know...One thing we know positively, if we don't get a pulse in that leg it isn't going to last," Burton said.

"Wake up man, that leg is gone," Brody said. "All the tea in China isn't going to bring it back."

A deep crease settled between Kyle's eyes as he searched Brody's. "One more negative word and you will land outside that door. I will not open it to put you through it."

A middle aged nurse, a patient of Kyle's, alerted by the screaming doctors, came into the room, her hands on her hips. "Will you all just shut up?" she said, and then pointed to Kyle, "That man is a physician, too! As a doctor, and the boy's dad, he deserves some consideration."

They looked at her, astounded, at each other, then back at Dr. Burton.

Brody turned to Kyle, embarrassed that he had been so presumptuous. "Now what did you say to do?"

Kyle moved quickly resetting Merle's broken pelvis, working until he had gotten a pulse in Merle's leg.

"Well, that worked," Dr. Benn snapped sarcastically, "Now what do you say to do?"

"We've got to get him to surgery to re-attach that leg. I can decide from there," Burton said.

Merle was sent to surgery. Dr. Cousins, one of the most respected orthopedic surgeons in the region, was assigned to Merle's case. He was middle aged, with a medium build. His thick black hair was combed away from his face. Deep waves blended into a neatly lined cut. His tiny lips were set in an oblong face beneath a thick nose.

Kyle joined Jane in the waiting room. Sitting so long with Merle had left Kyle fidgety and nervous. His eyes were heavy, shadowed with dark circles. The stress was unbelievable! At last the surgeon brought news that Merle was out of immediate danger, and his leg was successfully reattached. For the first time in forty-eight hours, Kyle Burton slept in his bed.

The next day, Dr. Burton slipped into some comfortable clothing, grabbed a quick bite to eat, and arrived at the hospital roughly at 9:00. Jane was waiting.

"They gave him some blood this morning," Jane said.

"Who-who gave him... Why did they give him blood?" Burton asked, disturbed by this bit of news.

"Dr. Brody ordered it. He said Merle's count was too low."

"Where is that...?" But before he could speak, Brody had arrived. "You gave my son blood without my consent?"

"His count was too low."

Burton stared at the young doctor for a minute. "A count of 28 is not too low. You had no permission to do it. We will not pay for it!"

"You have no right; he needed that blood."

"Watch me!"

Merle lay with a cast covering him from head to toe. His injured leg, in a sling, extended some twenty-four inches into the air. Only his eyes were visible through the thick cast that covered both his head and face. He looked grotesque, as he was badly swollen.

Once the threat of infection subsided, it was time for another surgery. Kyle, having studied the long-term ill effects of pins and other metals left inside patients during surgery, suggested to Cousins that he use removable pins with Merle. Cousins offered resistance, but honored Kyle's request.

Subject to the reluctant approval of Cousins, Burton used nutrition, daily feedings of yogurt, natural intravenous antibiotics, and green light therapy to speed Merle's recovery. Still Cousins worried that Merle was going to get blood clots.

"Listen Merle," Cousins said, pulling up a chair. "I'm talking to you like a son. This green light is bogus and can in no way improve your condition. We're going to have to thin your blood to avoid life threatening blood clots. To do that I'll need your consent; then I can order you Heparin."

Dr. Kyle Burton, however, did not share Cousins' enthusiasm about Heparin. "Merle's blood is thin enough and in no danger of clotting. Heparin is a dangerous drug with serious side effects. No, I do not approve," Kyle told Cousins.

Cousins had not, however, taken "no" for an answer. Once again, he approached Merle. "You know, Merle, your dad and I disagree on this, but I only need your consent to get you started on the Heparin."

"Why does dad disagree? What are the side effects?"

"Well, there may be some depression; only a small percentage of people have died from using it."

"Then honor my father's request-no Heparin. Let's continue with the green light."

Upon entering Merle's room the next day, Kyle noticed that Merle was hitched to a brand new feeding tube. No one had said anything to Burton about Merle's need for an IV. Had Cousins ordered the Heparin against his better judgment? Kyle wondered. He approached the nurse at the nurse's station, to inquire.

"No," the nurse said, "it is not Heparin; it's Tagamet."

Just the sound of that drug gave Kyle the chills; it had horrible side effects. "Tagamet! I want it stopped immediately!" Kyle ordered, shaking his finger at the nurse.

"I'm sorry, Mr. Burton, but it was the doctor's orders. I can't do that."

"Oooh yes you can, lady--and you will. That stuff causes blood clots!" The nurse looked stunned for a moment. "Now! Lady, now!"

She scurried about nervously, detaching Merle's IV, although hesitantly. Soon Cousins arrived; Burton voiced his concerns.

"You're concerned about blood clots, and you give my son Tagamet?"

"That's right. He has an ulcer. And who do you think you are-coming in here ordering the IV disconnected? What medical school did you go to, huh?"

"I'm his father--that's what qualifies me. Oh, and medical school, it doesn't take medical school. Have you ever heard of the PDR? It's called the Physician's Desk Reference. Do you ever read it?"

"Listen Mr.," Cousins said shaking his finger at Burton. "I'm the doctor in charge on this case. Anymore wild and impulsive acts of yours, and I'm off this case. He's all yours. You got it?"

"That's fine." "A doctor is a lot easier to replace than my son."

Cousins shook his head and walked out of the room. So far as Kyle was concerned, feeding the pompous ego of a doctor ranked between a minus three hundred and five hundred when compared to preserving the quality of his son's life.

It was the thirteenth day of Merle's hospital stay. Upon Burton's arrival, he noticed a helicopter with its motor running. Only the most severe cases were flown to Salt Lake City. What nature of illness had prompted the ordering of this service, and for whom? Burton wondered. His curiosity soon left, however, when he approached Merle's room.

"What's going on? What are you doing?" Kyle asked Dr. Cousins.

"I'm getting Merle ready to go to Salt Lake to see a specialist. He needs that pelvis wired. We don't have that capability here."

Burton looked at him perplexed. "Are you a competent doctor?"

"Well, I think I am."

"Well-why are you sending him there? That pelvis is...he's not going. Now you can go order the helicopter shut off. He's going to stay here."

Cousins offered no resistance. Dr. Burton's suggestions had proved helpful; the proof was in Merle's daily improvement.

"Do you know that man was going to send Merle to Salt Lake?" Kyle asked, settling onto the living room couch besides Jane.

"You're kidding."

"No. I drove up there and saw that helicopter. I thought someone was seriously ill. Come to find out Cousins was prepping Merle for Salt Lake--to see some specialist up there."

"Well, he came to me a few minutes ago and said how he wished he had your knowledge."

Kyle's eyes widened. "What did you tell him?"

"I told him that you'd be glad to teach him."

Merle's improvement, three months later, even shocked Kyle. Now he could treat Merle at home, but needed permission to release him. Cousins resisted, charging that the sinus in Merle's leg was still draining. "If it persists for forty-eight hours, I will scrape it. Don't you touch it," he told Burton.

Dr. Burton offered no comments. He didn't have to. He had to do whatever necessary to keep that leg from draining. Merle belonged at home. Cousins left. From his pocket Kyle pulled out a long Q-tip and covered it with a special ointment. He applied it to Merle's open wound. Now he had a fighting chance of stopping the drainage.

Jane arrived at the hospital bright and early the next day, as did Cousins. "Looks good," Cousins said, satisfied that Merle's leg had drained sufficiently. "Tomorrow he will be released."

"Will you leave a window in the cast so we can continue the light therapy?" Jane asked. Cousins agreed.

Upon her arrival the next day, Jane noticed a windowless cast, just the opposite of what Cousins had promised. She phoned her husband. "Kyle, Cousins didn't leave a window in the cast."

"Okay, I'll be there shortly," Kyle said.

Minute's later Jane confronted Cousins. "There is no window in the cast-You promised."

"That's right. I don't want your husband fooling with it," Cousins said.

Today Dr. Burton didn't bother talking with Dr. Cousins. He came for one thing only. As a physician, Burton was privy to the area where the mold was kept: the one Cousins used to set Merle's cast. He wasted no time. He got the mold, put it in his car, and joined Jane inside.

"You guys ready to go?"

Jane looked surprised at Kyle's apparent calmness. "But what about the window in the cast?"

"Ahh!" Kyle gestured with his hands as though the point was moot. "Don't worry about it. I got it covered. Let's go home."

Though it was awkward at home without the proper tools, Burton used the mold to cut a window in the cast. To speed recovery, he resumed the light therapy and used dressings appropriate for continued doctoring.

The next day Cousins called-wanted to check Merle's leg. Jane agreed and made an appointment. Burton, however, had no intention of letting Merle return to the hospital until it was time to remove the pins; that time was still a while away. Two missed appointments followed.

"Gangrene could set up in that leg without further treatment," Cousins warned.

"Keep your mouth shut about this, but Kyle cut a window in the cast and is treating Merle himself," Jane said.

"Fine! I never want to see Merle again!"

Now Kyle was free of any interference from the hospital. Time was now on his side. With sufficient healing and Merle strong enough to undergo another surgery, Kyle ordered it, this time to remove the pins. A chiropractor made adjustments as needed.

For two months a hospital bed made him comfortable. For ninety days crutches helped him to get around. A cane was his support for three months following. At the end of nine months, Merle had recovered and started a new life.

12

Having sold the business now, Kyle could concentrate on things like reading mail and research materials forwarded to him from the clinic. He hoped he could discover why some of his patients had not responded to his treatment. Research into the British Dental Journal, Canadian Medical Association Journal, Journal of the American Medical Association, Journal of Prosthetic Dentistry, and *others* provided some clues: "Many diseases originate as a result of dental materials. Dental amalgams contain cadmium and mercury. Symptoms associated with cadmium rang from high blood pressure to prostate problems," he noted. He remembered having problems in each of these areas. High blood pressure, prostate problems– what a coincidence!

Mercury, he learned, can cause kidney, heart, and respiratory problems. "Depression, headaches, and digestive problems have also been noted in persons into whose mouth mercury has been placed." How long he had suffered in each of these areas before getting help! "Mercury in small amounts in the sperm can result in birth defects," he read.

How can something in one's mouth launch that kind of assault on the rest of the body? It just doesn't make sense-even with my training in nutrition, Kyle thought. Through relentless research, he learned that when mercury is placed in ones teeth, it sits where the mineral, zinc, should sit and creates a zinc deficiency. Abnormal fatigue, loss of normal sense of taste and smell, poor appetite--he knew the symptoms, oh so well…

Kyle's research revealed that without adequate levels of zinc the "liver, pancreas, kidney, bones, voluntary muscles, eyes, spermatozoa, skin, hair, fingernails, toenails, prostate glands, and white blood cells utilize a bogus mercury mixture, in time flushing away the nerve "B" vitamins. Memory loss, anemia, slow wound healing, sexual difficulties, pancreas disorders, infections, aching joints, and heart disease are just a few problems that can be manifest.

Little wonder, Burton realized, why he had reacted so badly to drug therapy. The drugs and amalgam (silver fillings) combination had proved too much; they had left him deficient in zinc and other minerals, and he had almost paid the ultimate price for it.

Disturbed by this information, Burton had his amalgams removed by a specially trained dentist who used a research based sequence and replaced them with herculite porcelain fillings which, after specialized testing, proved best for Kyle's system. Oral chelation and vitamin mineral-therapy supplemented the removal process. The results were phenomenal. With more energy, he was better able to endure long hours of work without tiring. His thoughts were clearer. Now when Jane made suggestions, he was more prone to listen, not whirl sharp verbal attacks at her, like before. No longer did he suffer from colitis. But perhaps what was most impressive was that high blood pressure and awful headaches were things of the past-even when he missed his supplements.

Further research into the effects of amalgams and root canals in humans revealed anecdotal studies which indicated that these procedures had been implicated in a wide range of other diseases as well, including severe arthritis, anemia, nervous irritability, and convulsive spasms. According to this research, patients institutionalized for years because of debilitating ailments, were able to regain their health after the removal of root canals. A culture taken from a teenager who had suffered from extreme arthritic conditions was later injected into a rabbit. It caused almost complete paralysis in the animal in forty-eight hours.

Mercury amalgams and root canals were not the only dental procedures which could destroy the immune system and contribute, in part to high death rates from many diseases: surgical implants, dentures, caps, crowns, partials, all of which are undercoated with metals, may pose serious health problems for their wearers, Kyle discovered. Like the mercury, these metals can have a severe effect on the mineral composition of the body and health of the individual into whose mouth they are placed. Reactions to these metals were similar to those of mercury: arthritic conditions, central nervous system, blood pressure problems, psychological problems, and blood related illnesses could be precipitated by nickel crowns. Most partials and dentures, he learned, were made of nickel. Even gold, when used as fillings, could, over time, become corrosive and leach into the blood stream creating extreme arthritic conditions for the wearer.

Several studies had linked depression and suicides in teens to the wearing of braces. From this research, Burton concluded that the presence of any of these materials in individuals with predisposition to any condition including acne, allergies, or arthritis could make them worse. What a person who needed dental services was to do was a question yet unanswered. What was clear, however, was that the patients should be tested for any materials being placed in their teeth to avoid future health problems. With this knowledge Burton was certain that he could help bring closure to the patients for whom, in the past, he offered so little help, like Mark.

Former patients wanted Burton to buy back the business. Unhappy with the treatment by the new doctor, they had left in droves. This concerned Burton deeply. Perhaps he should reconsider. He missed it terribly. Besides, there was no sense kidding himself; selling the business had offered no resolution to the rift between his family and him. If only he could convince the physician to sell it back to him!

13

Back in business now, Dr. Burton felt at home. Giving people back their health was as natural to Kyle as breathing.

Prior to the sell of the business, Lori Beverly walked slowly and her vision was poor-- typical symptoms of multiple sclerosis. With an involuntary shake, and a bad limp, she was fast becoming wheelchair bound. She stuttered, slurred her speech badly, and complained of memory loss. Still Lori was frail and peered through eyes that doubled images. No longer ambulatory, she was confined to a wheelchair and incontinent. Her involuntary shakes made it impossible for her to feed herself.

One of the hallmarks of the MS patient, Burton had learned, was deadly parasites whose penetration into the spinal column caused the eventual shut down of the central nervous system. These patients responded quite well to cranial adjustments and a very heavy nutritional program. Paramount for Lori was getting rid of those horrific parasites and building up her body's immune system.

By fall, Lori was no longer wheel chair bound. She walked into the examination room. She was sitting on the examining table stretching her arms high above her head and swinging her legs almost methodically when Burton walked in.

"Hello Dr. Burton. With progress like this, I'll soon be able to run the Boston Marathon."

"Oh you think so, huh?" With the flamboyant use of her hands, Burton didn't have to wonder if Lori could feed herself.

"How's the energy level?"

"I have my days-sometimes good, sometimes not so good."

"Well, we'll see if we can fix that."

A second hair analysis confirmed the presence of candida and something else. Lori's body was saturated with mercury. How could he tell her that the mercury fillings in her teeth had to go? It just sounded preposterous--to say that a substance in one's mouth could trigger havoc in the body. How could he explain this to this patient in a way that she could understand? He wondered.

"Lori you need to have your amalgams removed," He said.

"But why?"

"Your nervous system has deteriorated because of the presences of the mercury in your teeth. It overpowers zinc, a mineral necessary in maintaining the nervous system.

"You're kidding!"

"No. It's like dominos. If you push one of twenty standing dominos, each successive one will fall down. When the body is without zinc, it's like pushing that domino. B vitamins will escape leaving the body susceptible to a whole array of diseases.

Lori agreed. Dr. Burton programmed the order of the amalgam removal. After a dentist provided the service, Dr. Burton gave her oral chelation therapy.

Rick Johnson, now sixteen years old revisited the clinic. Rick had suffered from a crippling rheumatoid arthritic condition since he was eight. Because three mercury amalgam-filled root canals had replaced Rick's three missing teeth from an accident years ago, his prognosis was a bit disturbing. Removal of root-canal-filled teeth and/or cavitations called for more precision. It was expensive. Few dentists were accessible nor were there many trained in this technique. But Rick's suffering was so great that his parents were committed to their son's recovery--even if it meant traveling afar. As he did with Lori, Burton recommended that Rick have the poisonous material removed.

Hair analysis, Burton's basic diagnostic tool, required a considerable amount of hair. For patients with little or no hair, perms, or processed hair, there could be no accurate assessment. Kyle learned that HLB/LBA blood work, another diagnostic tool, could from a single drop of blood, reveal patterns unique to diseases ranging from heart disease to cancer. With it, the sky was the limit. Patients from afar could be assessed and treated, never having set foot in the clinic. Unlike the week's turn-around time for hair analysis from Dr. Simmons's office, the HLB/LBA could be assessed quickly. When used in connection with Muscle Response Testing, and Reflexology, Burton was confident that he could determine the nutritional deficiencies associated with any disease. Thus, he began a course of study.

Two months after her last visit and sequential amalgam removal, Lori phoned Burton. "As time passes, things get better. My energy level is much better." Her speech was clear, no longer was she slurring her words, Burton noticed.

"I still have memory problems, but nothing like before. I'm just amazed. The thought that I could have become another Richard Pryor...is frightening."

"Yeah, no kidding!"

Laughter filled the room as Rick Johnson entered, stumbling over himself with joy. It had been a couple of months since his cavitations extraction. "It's gone! The pain is gone!" he said, demonstrating the ease of moving his arms.

Dr. Burton ruffled Rick's hair. "Well, I guess I don't have to ask how you're doing, huh?" The beam in the child's face, the radiant color and ease of movement... That Rick had suffered from this arthritic condition since he was eight and saw improvement only after the dental material was removed, Burton found significant.

Burton realized that the office was not the right forum for educating the public, yet he knew that patients needed to know about the dangers of some dental materials and procedures that threatened their health. They needed to learn the role that nutrition played in their lives. Only then could they be in charge of their health. Workshops seemed the perfect forum. They would allow him to train practitioners and teach lay persons alike. He could introduce his unique formulations, his primary weapon against disease. Organic ingredients and strict manufacturing conditions kept his products natural. Unlike many products on the market, these products had proved digestible by very sick people, as they contained no preservatives, sugars, or yeast and maintained their plus-and-minus charges to maintain their authenticity.

Shortly afterwards, Burton read a disturbing peace of news about the FDA's July 7, 1985 raid on Zurich's Labs. Per the Report, "The lab was raided because of its interstate shipping of antineoplastic (cancer therapy). The report also indicated that NCI, Aetna Insurance and others pressured FDA into raiding the Zurich's Lab. The FDA reportedly seized 200,000 medical and research documents forcing Zurich to pay to make copies. No charges were filed," the report stated.

Burton's reaction to the report was mixed. There was no denying that the FDA was in a war against nutrition, but if they raided Zurich's lab, the lab must have done something wrong. Burton prided himself on upholding a practice that operated within the parameters of the law. He would not have it any other way. He had a family to support.

The demands of the business required the addition of more waiting rooms, a receptionist, an assistant, a cleaning lady and Marilyn Walter, the office reflexologist. Burton continued to search for therapies that would be beneficial to his patients. He found it in magnetic and nutritional-injection therapy. It could do what no pill could because it went directly to the blood stream: there was no need for the body to break it down. The injection gave patients an immediate burst of energy, unlike any of the supplements.

Burton noticed that since Arnold Payton, another returning patient's amalgam removal, symptoms consistent with Epstein Barr Virus (chronic fatigue) had abated, including aching muscles and joints, deep depression, and headaches. Thanks to shrinkage of the swollen lymph nodes, his sore throat was somewhat better. The disabling fatigue was less prevalent; it was what Burton wanted to hear. With injection therapy Dr. Burton had put Arnold back on the road to recovery. Now he had his third documented case about the effects of some dental materials and/or cavitations.

Now certified in HLB/LBA blood work, Burton was staring into his microscope when his receptionist brought him a piece of correspondence. It was a newsletter, "The FDA Hotline," telling of FDA's harassment on alternative health care providers.

"A raid on Odorless Pets, Inc, a pet goods store is setting a new precedent," it read.

Odorless Pets, Inc offered a product that was designed to prevent pets from giving off foul odors. FDA called it an "unsafe drug" so not only did the FDA appear to be in a scheme to derail interest in alternative medicine for humans, but for their pets. It was the second such raid since the collaborative effort of the FDA and the Pharmaceutical Advertising Council, which began in 1984. Using no cost advertisement to inundate the public, they cautioned against the use of alternative medicine by denouncing it as quack medicine and suggesting that it is dangerous.

With the raid on Odorless Pet, Inc., Burton found himself asking a different question. Was it just possible that this store was a part of that announced nutritional campaign against quack medicine? But this product was for pets, for Pete's sake. Pets don't buy products- ah, but their owners do. It is a booming industry.

The newsletter stated that the FDA had also seized two drums of black currant oil as well as a large quantity of the capsulated product sold by Trott Foods. They claimed that black currant oil, was an "Unsafe food additive."

In a subsequent case the U.S. Court of Appeals ruled against FDA. The Judge said that FDA's definition of "food additive" was too broad - that even water added to food would be considered a food additive.

This was the third raid he had heard about in less than eight months. It had become a real cause for concern. He had to be careful about what he said and to whom. Telling a patient that a certain product could help them medically was, according to the FDA, practicing medicine without a license. Without a medical license, he could make no such claim. So in addition to chosing his words carefully, as a part of the clinic's application process Burton had his patients sign that they were not connected with a governmental agency. Without their signature, the patient could not be treated. It was the only way he could protect himself.

It was May 1989 when Marvis Russell, a middle-aged factory worker, came to see Dr. Burton. Deep lines had settled around his mouth. "I stood watching as several of my buddies died from lymphoma--now I have it. The chemotherapy, radiation, and bone marrow transplant left them weak, tired, and defenseless. I don't know what to do--but I know I'm not prepared to go through that. That's why I came here," Marvis said.

Marvis' blood analysis showed a scant blood pattern, one consistent with the late stages of lymphoma. After getting an individualized nutritional injection a slight blood-pattern emerged. Marvis had lost a tremendous amount of weight, roughly thirty pounds within the last couple of months, as he couldn't hold down his food. Thanks to weeks of nutritional injections, for the first time in weeks Marvis was getting the nutrition he needed. Chiropractic adjustment helped to align him and reflexology helped break up his toxic buildups. A two week daily regimen of nutritional injections would help to boost his immune system.

Burton's next patient, Mrs. Palmer, was elderly with scant hair on her head. The hair remaining was very thin; it more closely resembled strings of thread. She hobbled in with the help of a walker. A double mastectomy, chemotherapy, and radiation treatments had left her frail and energyless. The challenge for Burton was getting her out of pain. The constant pain she suffered made life almost unbearable. Burton was honest with her. "I'll do what I can, but your body's defenses will determine your fate," he said. At the time, Burton didn't know, could not have known, that Mrs. Palmer's fate would be the catalyst that would change his life forever.

14

Lydia looked up from her book squinting, her eyes set in a square face. She brushed her bobbed hair back from her face, losing herself deep in thought about her mother. They were so close; she didn't want to think that her mother's end was near, although all of the signs were there.

Lydia's brother Ronnie had mentioned a naturopathic doctor in Aberdeen. Lydia had her doubts, but no answers. "My buddies swear by this doctor, Sis. At least give him a try. What do we have to lose?"

Lydia had consented. Under Dr. Burton, Mrs. Palmer's improved quality of life made Lydia a believer. Dr. Burton's unique nutritional formulations had given her mom a much greater quality of life. Now, Mrs. Palmer could enjoy Brad, the little bundle Lydia had recently birthed, her only grandson.

Blond curls covered baby Brad's head. For husband Ryan and Lydia, baby Brad was a welcome addition to the family, with his peachy skin and ruby cheeks. Brad's dwindling weight, a loss of several pounds over a four month span, frightened both Ryan and Lydia.

"It's a bad case of chronic bronchitis, pneumonia, and lung disease," the emergency staff told Lydia. "Take Brad to a doctor for follow-up care."

The phone rang late into the night, a sure sign that something was wrong. Baby Brad was safely tucked away in his crib, so clearly the call couldn't be about him.

"Hello Lydia," the voice said. "It's Lilly-- something's happened."

"Daddy! What-what's happened?"

"She fell. We're at the hospital."

"At the...I'll be right there."

At the hospital, Lydia found her daddy pacing the floor of the waiting room. "What happened?"

Mr. Palmer looked down trying to recall the details. "I got up to use the restroom. There was Lillie lying on the floor. I kept calling and shaking her, but she didn't answer, so I just... She was still warm so I tried to get her pulse, and then called the ambulance. God, I hoped she'll be alright. I can't bear to live without Lilly."

"Oh, Daddy!" Lydia exclaimed, embracing her father.

"I'm still waiting for the doctor."

"I don't understand. She was doing so well."

They broke their embrace when a surgeon burst through the double glass doors. "Mr. Palmer, I'm sorry. We did all we could."

"But the fall alone surely couldn't have killed her. What..." Lydia asked.

The doctor broke in. "...She suffered a massive heart attack."

"But there was nothing wrong with her heart," Lydia countered.

"I'm sorry, Ma'am, but apparently there was."

Both Mr. Palmer and Lydia looked at each other. Just the other day she had attended a ball game, Mr. Palmer recalled.

Baby Brad's health continued to decline. In October Lydia took him to another medical doctor in Rexburg, hoping to get answers. "Failure to thrive," the doctor said. Who ever heard of any such diagnosis? But, with Brad's weight loss at one ounce every four days, it was perhaps most indicative, she thought.

Brad's sickly pale skin color and thinning hair told Lydia that Brad was in serious trouble. There was no treatment regimen for "a failure to thrive." She needed something concrete before Brad could get treated. "There is a hospital about 300 miles away that offers hope for sickly children. Perhaps, Brad can get some help from there," the doctor said.

Lydia wasted no time. At Pulmonary Central Hospital, Brad was admitted for a ten-day stay. The battery of tests came back negative. "His electrolytes are incompatible with life. Brad is clearly the sickest child at Pulmonary. The closest diagnosis is cystic fibrosis," the doctor admitted. Finally, a diagnosis; this, Lydia felt, was a step in the right direction.

"The disease is hereditary-genetically based."

"Hereditary?"

"Do you have any other children?"

"I do. Two girls."

"You may want to have them tested, because normally when one child in a family is affected, so are the others."

"But my other children are healthy," Lydia said, her eyebrow furrowed. "Kattie is six and she has had her moments, but nothing like this. As for Amanda, she hasn't been sick a day in her life."

"It is possible that she is affected, though to a lesser degree. Why don't you bring her in for testing?"

Perhaps this wasn't a bad idea because if the other children were affected, they could be treated along with baby Brad before the disease took control. Only Kattie came up positive for cystic fibrosis.

"What are the treatment options?"

"Some enzymes can help the children with their digestion. But other than enzymes, nothing can be done for either of the children until they became more ill. Antibiotics can be used when the need arises. Expect hospital stays at least three or four times a year. Get used to it."

Lydia couldn't believe what she was hearing. "Let me get this straight.

He's got to get more ill before you can treat him?" She shook her head. Utter disappointment overpowered the dash of hope that had kept her sane. The words kept ringing in her ear, "more ill."

"No! No!" she bellowed. Muddled thoughts clouded her focus. She wanted to slap the doctor for suggesting that her son needed to be more ill. Finally gathering her composure she said, "more ill? What kind of reasoning is that?" But he offered no words. She gathered her children and headed for home.

At home, Lydia settled Kattie and Amanda inside and lost herself in a bed of rocks outside. For a moment she stood staring into the distance, as tears streamed down her cheeks. The words were like a dagger driven through her heart. Hospitalized three or four times a year. No! She picked up a fistful of rocks and hurled them across her lawn. With all the strength she could muster, she hurled another into the street. Finally she fell to her knees, cupping her hands about her face, bawling. The scarred knees didn't matter now; how to best deal with this serious diagnosis did. When all else failed, prayer always provided the answer.

Lydia's bedroom provided the forum for a quiet prayer. "Is there no end to this nightmare? I've tried every doctor recommended-finally getting a diagnosis, and for what? Lord, if there's an answer for this, please help me find it. You know what I am going through. Please lift me up, O Lord God. I know that You're the master of all things. "

When Ryan opened the bedroom door, Lydia began. "You won't believe what that doctor told me."

Ryan attempted to speak but Lydia interrupted. She found herself tearing up again as she remembered the doctor's words. "That idiot! He said we could expect Brad to be hospitalized three or four times a year." She wiped more falling tears from her eyes. "What are we going to do? I've exhausted the best of doctors. That hospital specializes in cystic fibrosis."

"Cystic fibrosis; is that the diagnosis?" Ryan asked.

"Yes."

"Well, why don't you try that Burton fella? You know he helped mother."

"Yes, but this is different. Brad's diagnosis is serious."

"Now wait a minute, honey. Listen to what you're saying."

"I know what I'm saying, Ryan. Brad needs a real doctor."

Ryan's voice fell. "Well, Dr. Burton...I guess it depends on your definition of a real doctor, Lydia. But, you know, Brad is my son, too!" Ryan snapped, and then crawled into bed.

"Listen, I don't want to talk about this anymore," Lydia said throwing herself upon the bed, and turning her back to Ryan. Anguishing, she tried silently to justify her position. Alternative medicine was fine for mother, but something as serious as Brad's condition needed special care. Even the specialists were baffled. Give my son alternative medicine and put his life in danger when he should be getting some real help? No, I don't think so.

Three days after his ten day stay at the hospital, Brad was coughing. His skin had become extremely pale, and his vomit contained blood and mucous. He was more listless than Lydia had ever seen him. Seeing her child in this helpless state frightened her. She became terrified. She was losing baby Brad.

Prayer revealed that God had supplied the earth with all of our needs. Was that not the thrust of naturopathy? Ryan was right. Burton had helped mother. If something happened to Brad and she hadn't tried all options, she would never forgive herself. She knew she was taking a chance, but what else could she do?

In November 1990, Dr. Burton's HLB/LBA blood analysis confirmed that Brad's blood pattern was consistent with cystic fibrosis. "His immune system is severely weakened," Burton said. Lydia found it amazing that Burton could come up with a diagnosis solely on the basis of a drop of blood-especially when she thought of all she had gone through to get a diagnosis from medical doctors.

Given nutritional injection therapy, the listless infant now seemed at peace-ready for what ever was to follow. Burton prodded the child in various areas until at last there was a cry. It was strange, Lydia thought, but she was actually glad to hear her baby cry.

Since Brad was a baby, it meant mixing Burton's heavy nutritional concoctions with his food. He frowned, twisted, and turned as Lydia tried to feed him. With each passing day, he seemed a bit livelier.

At the end of two weeks, Brad's pale murky looking skin had changed. In its place was a hint of color. Brad started to show signs of life Lydia hadn't dreamed possible. Smiles had replaced Brad's dismal expression. There was less mucous.

In four weeks, Brad appeared healthy. He had gained about two pounds, no small feat for an infant who had been losing weight so rapidly. He had begun to babble and coo, thrust his feet in the air, and sometimes even cry. Oh what a feeling that was! Brad's once awful thinning hair started to curl, and his cheeks were rosy and supple again.

It was amazing, Lydia thought; this solution was right under her nose. Ryan had tried to tell her. Thank God, she had finally consented. The joy of seeing her baby come back to life was like awakening from a horrible nightmare. Tears streamed from her eyes, but these were of joy. She thanked God Almighty, for it was truly He who deserved all the credit.

In June 1991, Burton's retest revealed what Lydia already knew. Brad had improved drastically. Excitement bubbled up in Lydia as she prepared to take baby Brad to Pulmonary Central for his six month check up. The hospital was noted for treating cystic fibrosis children; the doctors would rejoice in knowing how to better treat their patients. Moms and dads would be happier too. It was a win situation for everyone.

At the hospital, doctors and nurses alike were amazed at Brad's progress. One of the doctors studying the case checked Brad's chart for any medications. When none was listed, he turned to Lydia for answers. "I don't see any prescribed medications. "What have you been giving him?"

Part of Lydia wanted to tell him, but another part of her did not. People believed that herbs were superficial poppycock. She wondered if he would believe her. But she felt she owed him an explanation for the sake of all cystic fibrosis children. To preserve her own integrity, she shrugged "Just some herbs."

"Ahh, herbs. Well...they won't hurt him, but they won't help him either," he said.

Lydia looked down. This was the response she had expected. He didn't believe her, but that was fine with her. The proof, she told herself, was in Brad's health. She certainly didn't need any convincing, not now. The doctor, however, offered a word of caution. "I wouldn't be too optimistic and get your hopes all up if I were you--Brad still has cystic fibrosis."

At home Lydia sat thinking. She had wanted to get through to the doctors so badly. Now her hopes of helping other CF children were dashed. But worse, the doctor's words seem to haunt her, even as Brad had made so much progress. "Don't be too optimistic and get your hopes up--Brad still has cystic fibrosis."

Mother had made progress also; things seemed to be okay. Would Brad's progress be short lived? It was a possibility she had to face. Her thoughts became murky and cloudy as she wavered between decision and indecisiveness. Now, she found herself needing reassurance from the medical community. If anything happened to Brad, and she refused him medical care at Pulmonary, she could be charged with child abuse. Refusing wasn't an option.

Doctors on staff this time were in awe of Brad's progress. Dr. Jacobson, unlike the previous doctor, was interested in Brad's treatment regimen. He had seen Brad only briefly, but recalled the seriousness of his condition. "I remember him in particular, because I wasn't sure if he would live through the spring, let alone thrive like he is doing now. What is Brad taking? It would be helpful to the other CF children."

"I can't remember all the stuff he's taking-it's quite a lot."

"Why don't you give me the name and number of this doctor?"

This was the most exciting thing she had heard since she took Brad to

Pulmonary. Finally someone had listened. What this could mean for the children at Pulmonary only time would tell, but Lydia felt special in knowing that in her small way she would have contributed. She just couldn't wait to tell Dr. Burton.

Burton was just finishing up with his last patient when the phone rang. "Hello."

"Hi," Lydia said with a twinge of excitement in her voice. "You won't believe what happened today."

"Just try me," Burton said jokingly.

"I took Brad to Pulmonary today for his checkup."

"Uh huh."

"The doctor's and nurses were all amazed. They couldn't believe it was the same child."

"Is that right?"

"Dr. Jacobson wanted to know what Brad was taking. I told him there were quite a few things; I couldn't remember all of them. 'Do you realize how much help he could be for our children? What's this doctor's name and number,' he asked. So don't be surprised if you get a call."'

There was a hesitance in Dr. Burton's voice, and then it fell. "Oh, I doubt it; he'll call the FDA."

At Pulmonary Central, Dr. Jacobson discussed his concerns with other doctors. "Do you know what this could mean if patients learn of this Burton fellow."

"Don't tell me you really believe this guy deserves the credit for this," Dr. Depare said.

"The results speak for themselves," Dr. Shipiro admitted.

Dr. Jacobson jumped in. "That child was on deaths door, sicker than any I've ever seen at Pulmonary. As much as I hate to admit it, we've never gotten this kind of result with these children. This Burton fellow has to be doing something that we aren't."

"C'mon, Doc you don't really believe that herb stuff, do you?" Depare asked.

"I don't know what to believe, but one thing is certain; if this doctor has been this successful treating this child, as sick as this child was, he's got something. And you know what, if he is allowed to continue...we're done here at Pulmonary. I don't know about you, but I'm not going to stand for it."

"Well, what do you plan to do about it?" Depare asked.

"I think this is something Mr. Kennard would love to hear about."

Jacobson arranged a meeting with Mr. Ted Kennard, the hospital administrator.

"There are some concerns I think should be addressed," Jacobson told Mr.

Kennard.

Mr. Kennard took a puff off of his pipe. "And what might they be?"

"Well, it seems that there's a Dr. Burton... You remember that Nelson baby, that real sickly infant we were discussing the other day?"

"Uh, huh."

"Guess what. He's not sick any more. His color is normal. His eyes are bright. Why, he's a picture of health."

"You don't say," Mr. Kennard said, pulling the pipe from his lips. "So what do you think?"

"There's this fellow--down in Aberdeen. The mother's been taking the child to see him. Been giving him herbs and such..."

"Oh, come on, Joe! You've not called this meeting for something like this, surely,"

"Well to put it bluntly, Ted, what is it going to mean to us here at Pulmonary if all mothers start taking their baby's down there?"

"You don't think that...."

Joe leaned forward. "Desperate parents will go anywhere to get help for their children. I mean, look at us here at Pulmonary. They travel from all over the world to come here. What's three hundred more miles?"

"Oh, I don't know, Joe. I think you're making more out of this than you should."

"I'm telling you, Ted, if enough mothers get a whiff of this guy, it could force us to close our doors. Drug stocks for cystic fibrosis children would plummet. Think of the embarrassment to Pulmonary. Are you prepared to face that?"

"So what do you suggest?"

"I'm suggesting we make a few phone calls. Something has to be done to stop this guy. If you don't, I will."

Later that year, with Ted Kennard's blessings, Joe Jacobson phoned the FDA and requested an immediate investigation of Burton and his Natrogenics clinic.

15

Two years and two months into his treatments, Marvis Russell still depended upon nutritional injections twice a week. Except for his required injections, Marvis functioned quite normally. And while the injections were demanding, Marvis always boasted of feeling better after having received them. Thanks to continued electrotherapy, Marvis' digestive tract was now less dependent upon injection therapy. For the first time since his first visit, Dr. Burton could prescribe for Marvis a nutritional program.

It had been a long, satisfying day, but patient care brought with it a certain level of stress. It was rare that Burton managed to pull himself away. Today he would. He was going to visit his son Merle and his wife.

At Merle's residence, Kyle and Merle chatted about the church. "I'm not going back, I can't stand being around those hypocrites," Merle said.

"Well, I don't know..."

Merle broke in. "...My wife's father has a church group. I'm going to start going there."

"What kind of church is it?"

"It's the original chapter of the Brethren."

"You check it out and let me know what you think." But even as Kyle was considering leaving his old church, it felt odd; still his family attended. "I don't know...it could be the way to go. Where is it?"

"There's going to be a conference in Calgary, Alberta. Why don't you and mom come?"

"Let me talk to Jane about it, but I'd like to come."

In Calgary, Alberta, at the original Brethren church conference, the spirit was right. Those in attendance were warm, unlike the members at home. It was a treat to be among such friendly church people once again. People freely embraced. This was the kind of spirit Kyle wanted in his church. He didn't have to look any further.

Kyle opened a branch of the original Brethren church in the basement of his home in Aberdeen. It was a small gathering. Merle and his wife, Kyle, Jane, the children-Chelsey, Patrick, and baby Dan made up the membership. Kyle did the officiating. As they had at the old church, they set Wednesdays aside for Bible study.

In August, Steve Chase of the Food and Drug Administration called Terry Forbes of the Federal Bureau of Investigation. "What is being done on the Burton case?"

"No one has been assigned, but we have someone in mind."

"Someone in mind?"

"There's a young chap from the Islands--been hanging around lately. He's agreed to be an informant in exchange for funds to go to chiropractic school."

"When exactly do you guys plan to get going on this?"

"Real soon. Sometime next week," Terry assured Steve.

"Okay, let's get to it."

16

"You'll have to have a blood test," Anna told Wes O'Dea when he asked about the Natrogenics office procedures. Unlike his other patients, Wes was curious about everything. He watched curiously as Burton peered into the microscope. "This blood test thing...what's it used for?"

Burton looked up briefly from the big black microscope. "It helps me determine the patient's blood pattern." Squinting, he stared once again into the microscope. "There appears to be some candida, parasites, and inflammation of the prostate."

"You can tell all that by looking at my blood? Is that why I'm so tired all the time?" Wes asked, his head cocked to one side.

"Un huh."

"Doesn't make a bit of sense to me Doc, but you're the boss. What do I need to do to fix this thing? You're not going to pull that voodoo crap on me now are you Doc?" he said, raising his head with a faint smile, his eyelids flickering.

"Oh, we will get you started on some nutrition and do some body adjustments. You should start to feel better--I'd say in about a week or two."

"I'm all yours!" Wes said, gesturing with his hands--"let's do it." He thrust himself upon the examining table. Burton moved his hands along the prostate reflex. Wes flinched and raised an inch up off of the table--"ouch! What the heck are you doing, Doc?"

"Oh, just releasing the pressure around that prostate."

"Well the last I heard my prostate was somewhere around my penis, not in my foot!"

"Just relax, relax," Burton said continuing the foot reflexology. "Any problems with urination?"

"Yes--somewhat."

"This should help." Burton continued rotating the foot back and forth with one hand and pressing on the prostate reflex with the other.

"I heard one of the girls outside say something about reflex...is this?"

Burton cut in, "...Yes, this is reflexology. It works wonders."

"You don't say. How does it work?"

"It releases the toxins from the problem area, so it can heal."

Burton was used to non-believers becoming believers after having experienced the wonders of these therapies just as he had. He was confident that in time

Wes would, too, even if his cockiness wouldn't allow him to admit it.

His treatment finished, Wes stretched. His air of pompousness had given in to relaxation. "Umm, not bad. I got to give it to you, Doc. That felt good. Maybe someday you can teach me some of those techniques."

It had been two months since Wes O'Dea's first treatment. "Hey good looking," he said, as he approached Anna, the receptionist at the counter. "I'm back!" He wore tight fitting jeans and a black leather jacket that stopped just above his crotch. He plopped his left elbow on the counter and looked Anna in the eye. "So, tell me, sweet thing, what's on the agenda for today?" he asked, wriggling his eyebrows up and down.

"All kinds of good things are in store for you, Wes. Just stick around for the party."

Burton entered soon after Wes was escorted to a treatment room.

"You know, Doc, I got to admit--I'm impressed. I feel so much better. You've got something here. I wish I'd come sooner."

"Well, Wes, I'm glad you're pleased." Burton continued body manipulation on Wes. "That's what we like to hear."

"My wife's been having some real health problems. What do you say if I bring her in on my next visit? You think you could help her?"

"I'd have to look at her blood, but just bring her in."

"Bet," Wes agreed.

In a subsequent visit to the clinic with his wife, Wes was more subdued. His flirtatiousness was buried in professionalism. "Hello, Anna, meet my wife, Angie," Wes said.

"Pleased to meet you. Won't you have a seat in the waiting area?"

While it was her first visit to the clinic, Angie was no stranger to the Burtons. Chelsey and Angie were good friends.

Wes entered Dr. Burton's office. "What do you say Doc?"

"Hello Wes."

Wes seated himself besides Burton, and stretched out his left little finger for a blood re-test.

"So how do you feel?"

"Just great, Doc, just great. I can't believe the improvement already."

"Yep--looks a lot better," Burton said, looking into the microscope. "There's still some candida left, but its some better. No more parasites...and look at that prostate--looks good."

"Yes, between you and me, Doc. I'm fired up and ready to go--if you know what I mean, but my wife hasn't been well."

"Well, it's a good thing, Wes, because candida is contagious--you can pass it back and forth to each other. Let's get that cleared up first."

"You telling me I can't get any cunt until this thing is cleared up?"

"Oh sure, Wes. You can do whatever you want--but you'll end up infecting each other." Wes followed Burton into the examining room where Burton immediately started to work wonders with his fingers.

"You know, Doc, I'm gonna be perfectly honest with you. I'd like to learn your techniques. I want to be a chiropractor some day."

"Oh really. Well, I'm a naturopath, not a chiropractor."

"Still I think learning these techniques will help me as a chiropractor; they are wonderful."

"Well, I'll take that as a compliment. Perhaps one day I can teach you."

Mrs. O'Dea was dainty, only five feet in statue and weighed less than one hundred pounds. Her skin was covered with red circular rashes. Her left cheek was swollen and her mouth twisted to the left due to facial paralysis. She complained of awful headaches, and her eyes mirrored her pain.

Physicians had tried unsuccessfully to diagnose Angie's condition. Unlike many of the other illnesses whose root cause could be traced to dental caries or heavy metal toxicity, its origin was bacteria carried by ticks.

Burton looked up at Angie. "Do you remember being bitten by an insect or anything lately?"

"Well, sure. I mean, you know, I'm a country girl. I'm always getting bit by something or another."

"Looks like a case of Lymes disease here."

"What is Lymes disease?"

"Lymes disease is often misdiagnosed as gout, lupus, or chronic fatigue syndrome. It is caused by a tick bite and can cause lots of damage."

"Yes, but this much damage? I feel like I've been through a washer."

"But I think you've come to the right place."

"Oh, I sure hope so," she said, taking in a deep breath.

Mrs. O'Dea was in the advanced stages of Lymes disease. Her spleen and lymph nodes were enlarged. To make her functional again, Burton offered several adjustment manipulations, electrotherapy, nutritional injection therapy and a heavy nutritional program. For her extreme arthritic condition, Burton prescribed what had become to its users the wonder pill, "black pearls." It had gained its popularity from arthritis sufferers who claimed it provided relief from arthritis when drugs and therapies did not.

Burton's next patient, George Weir an Alzheimer's disease sufferer, showed signs of liver distress, and candida. Burton knew that Alzheimer sufferers often have abnormally high levels of toxic metal and mercury in their brains, so he knew that in addition to recommending the removal of the toxic metals from George's teeth, he would have to work aggressively to help him. For George, electrical stimulation, nutritional injection therapy, and oral chelation therapy would help to detoxify his body, and liver detoxification would rejuvenate his liver.

With the proliferation of horrible diseases, Burton felt a tremendous responsibility to teach the public about the everyday hazards facing them and how nutrition and knowledge could be used to protect them. He would take his show on the road. One such trip was planned for November 1991 to Champaign, Illinois.

It was at this November workshop that Dr. Burton first met the Seymours. Her husband, Cal and a cane supported Danielle as she hobbled forward, having lost her sense of balance. Blond hair hung loosely over her collarbone as she moved slowly toward Burton, her head and body jerking uncontrollably. Weakened muscles had left her incontinent. Her skin was sickeningly pale and she could barely see the figure in front of her. She slurred and stammered her speech badly, and could barely talk above a whisper.

"She is seeing a chiropractor for her back, but she has throbbing pain at the top of her head," husband Cal told Dr. Burton.

"The pains last some three to five seconds," Danielle pitched in. "I'm so weak, I'm numb." She dragged her left leg along, as though paralyzed on the left side.

"She hurt her back and ruptured her disk, and has no sexual desires. Her bowel and bladder are shot--she can't control them. For the last two to three years, she's been bothered with severe bladder and kidney infection," Cal added.

Burton did a blood analysis. "When did these problems start?" he asked.

"In June of 1991 she was diagnosed with multiple sclerosis," Cal said.

Dr. Burton did some body manipulation, followed by an injection, and watched as what appeared to be a miracle unfolded before him. Danielle could now talk in a normal tone, albeit still slurring her speech badly. No longer dragging her leg and shaking uncontrollably, she was overjoyed. "I can walk and without the cane!. I don't believe--I can walk."

Results like these abounded among several patients treated that day. Burton's subsequent visits to Champaign brought increasing numbers of people clamoring for hope--people who had met with ill fate in their search to regain their health. It affirmed that the nation was hungry for this knowledge and kind of medicine.

17

Back in Aberdeen, patients gathered in the waiting room as Burton readied himself for the day's work. Anna called her first patient.

"Hey good looking," Wes said, winking at the long-legged brunette.

"Follow me," she said, as she led him in to the treatment room. In walked Burton.

"My wife is back, Doc," Wes said with resounding laughter.

"I'm real pleased with the progress she has made."

"Listen, I want to learn your craft. When can I come to work here?"

"Don't need any help right now, Wes."

Wes interjected. "Listen Doc, I'm not...if even as a volunteer!"

"Oh, I don't think so, Wes--I always pay my staff. I just don't need any help right now."

"Would you keep me in mind?"

"Okay," Burton said, excusing himself.

Danielle, from Kilbourne, Illinois was on the phone awaiting results of the HLB/LBA blood test she had taken in Champaign.

"Multiple sclerosis, parasites, and a bad case of candidiasis," Burton said. "Just what I thought," he admitted. For Danielle, he prescribed a heavy nutritional supplement program, and a diet.

In an examining room, Lydia Nelson and baby Brad waited. Brad was alert, vibrant, and full of energy. He was cheerful as he crawled about the floor, touching everything in sight. He picked up an object from the floor pulling it toward his mouth.

"No. No!" Lydia cried. Brad jumped, studied her expression then let the object fall to the floor. Born with a hearing impairment, Brad's hearing had in the past created a problem for Lydia. Now he responded readily to any external auditory stimuli.

Angie O'Dea's blood analysis now showed no further signs of parasites or Lymes disease. The once red infectious looking skin had cleared, and paralysis no longer contorted the left side of her face. She moved her neck freely; the stiffness and arthritis had diminished considerably. Her husband, Wes, had said it best, "My wife is back!"

Springfield, Illinois

At birth Ivanna Dion's insides had dangled outside of her body. A concoction and a quick shove back into the body were the only treatment for her condition, then known as "piles." As a teen her weight seesawed. Bouts of constipation were her nemesis. Food sensitivities made eating difficult. She was diagnosed with a duodenal ulcer when she was only seventeen.

As an adult, Ivanna moved with grace. Thick locks of hair cascaded down her thin shoulders. Her bronze oval face was distinctive with high cheekbones, customary of the Indian/Afro American descent. Full heart shaped lips sat in perfect symmetry to her receding forehead. Big brown eyes added a youthful appeal.

After two dental visits in 1987, raging stomach pains humbled her. Her temper was quick. Muscle spasms were all consuming. Yeast infections made life miserable; the extreme bloating and stomach discomforts were unbearable. Inability to remember what she had done that morning, let alone yesterday, was becoming more and more a problem.

In May, Ivanna had discovered Tagamet. Doctors and researchers alike hailed it as a wonder drug. They claimed it would cure ulcers. But, to Ivanna, relief was enough. If only she could get relief from the horrible abdominal pains and discomfort, the chronic muscle spasms, high blood pressure, insomnia, low sex drive, memory loss, and constant yeast infections, nothing else mattered. But the drug had not proved successful in doing any of this.

Depression such as she had never known before overtook her; for that, her OB/GYN prescribed 50 milligrams of Norpramin daily. The side effects of the drug: extreme dry mouth and difficulty urinating forced her to stop using it.

A promotion to a research economist in 1990 meant Ivanna would finally be able to use her skill. Combining her writing with research was, for Ivanna, exciting. Writing was her favorite pastime; technical writing would be a new challenge. But still, digestive problems plagued her. Much was at stake. To be successful on her new job she had to do something. She visited several physicians ranging from internists to gynecologists but persistent stomach problems, high blood pressure, and chronic yeast infections continued.

"Yeast infections" had become the butt of Ivanna and her friend Cheryl's daily conversation.

"Ivanna," Cheryl said, "this herbal product helps to improve energy level, sex drive, vision, PMS and yeast infections. I haven't had a yeast infection since I started taking this stuff. I want you to try it," she said, extending the product with her short stumpy arms.

Ivanna glanced past Cheryl hoping that her inner thoughts weren't apparent.

"Well, I tell you what--I'm under the doctor's care right now. Let me get pass this, and I'll try it. Besides I want to know what is doing what, so I don't want to try them together," Ivanna answered.

Ivanna loved her friend Cheryl; she didn't want to hurt her feelings, but she wondered how she could think such nonsense. Something in a bottle was gonna help somebody--some herbs? Get real! And herbs...everybody knew that they were junk medicine. A doctor in a nearby town had been recently closed for treating children with herbs. It had been shown on television when Ivanna was at her sister in law's house. In fact her sister-in-law had commented approvingly of the closure as they flashed the doctor and her clinic across the screen.

"They closed that doctor down," Yolanda said.

Ivanna had looked at the screen, not sure what she should feel, as they took the lady doctor away.

"Treating children with herbs and things," Yolanda had said, her distaste for this practice evident in her tone.

These things came into focus as Ivanna closed the bathroom door behind her. She had made a promise to her friend. She would keep it. But for now, Tagamet was the order of the day; she needed it for the ulcers she had suffered from since 1967.

Late in 1990, Ivanna decided that it was time to try the herbal blend her friend Cheryl had told her about, and lay the Tagamet aside. Much to her surprise, her energy level improved greatly, she could sleep better, think clearer and her mind was sharper. The depression and bad temper that had plagued her before were lessened. The severe frostbite on her hands was ameliorated with the use of the herbal blend. The blend, which was just under forty dollars a month, was inexpensive compared to the standard doctor office visits.

Embarrassed that she had doubted the potential of the blend, Ivanna was somewhat hesitant to share these results with her friend-even though she had not expressed her doubt, but Ivanna was not one for keeping quiet about such matters. She didn't understand why the blend had succeeded in doing for her what the Tagamet didn't. She started searching for answers among articles that were provided regarding the product; after all she was a researcher.

Some of the ingredients in the herbal blend, Ivanna learned, were vitamins and minerals. One of the minerals was potassium, a mineral necessary for proper bodily functioning, and that without sufficient amounts of it, a person could suffer from various health problems. Potassium and other vitamin mineral deficiencies, she now understood, was one of the reasons she had suffered from such devastation as high blood pressure, poor energy level, and a host of other associated problems. When she took the blend it had supplied her body with some of the required nutrition her body had been lacking. Because her starving body was now getting some of what it had been missing, she got results. For Ivanna, that spelled "relief."

The "to-do" about vitamins and minerals on television Ivanna had dismissed as something uniquely reserved for television personalities. Research on the importance of vitamins/ minerals to the functioning of the body convinced her otherwise. So when her friend asked her to become a distributor of the product, she did. She gladly told others about the wonders of this product, confident that it would do for them what it had done for her.

Overjoyed by the results it had brought her, it never occurred to Ivanna that the benefits to others might not be as great. She had miscalculated. Not everyone was as deficient in the vitamin mineral reserves as she, so the benefit to such individuals was small, if any at all. But she remained undaunted because most individuals did get a benefit; so, for such individuals, the product seemed the answer to their prayers. It seemed so to Ivanna as well, if only for a short while.

There was much tension in Ivanna's family surrounding the use of this blend. Most would not endorse or use it, because to them it reeked of bad medicine--after all this was an herb/ vitamin/ mineral combination frowned upon by the medical community. But what of its benefits? Ivanna thought. But, not everyone suffered from the kind of health ailments she had, nor had they endured an unsatisfactory medical experience. Her family sat and watched, knowing that sooner or later the bottom would drop out, and Ivanna would come to her senses. She would go to a medical doctor and have her problems assessed, as she should.

In 1991 Ivanna enjoyed tremendous success with the product, both financially and personally. But as time passed, she required more and more of the product just to keep a-float. It was no longer just one cup in the morning and afternoon; it became five cups in the morning and afternoon, and still more-too expensive to maintain. Clearly, something was wrong.

Besieged by tremendous headaches, Ivanna's eyes were failing her miserably, and yes, the chronic yeast infections continued. Lethargy overcame her like she had never known before. She had to get answers; she was determined to take control of her health. She contacted her OB/GYN and requested that he order a blood test. Later Ivanna received a call from her doctor's office.

"This is Dr. Osborn's office. Your blood has no clotting factor."

"What do you mean 'has no clotting factor'?"

"Your blood will not clot. We recommend that you see a hematologist."

"Oh, okay," she told the nurse, but Ivanna had no intentions of seeing a hematologist. A hematologist was a medical doctor. She wanted a homeopathic doctor or naturopath, not a medical doctor. She had learned through her research on the herbal blend that holistic doctors got good results with yeast infections. Right now, she would do just about anything to get rid of them. Anything.

She called the doctor's referral service in Springfield. The closest thing to a holistic doctor was an osteopath.

"If I come to your office and there's something wrong with my blood, how would you treat it?" She asked.

"We will send you to a hematologist," the nurse answered.

"Thanks," Ivanna said, knowing that this was not the kind of holistic doctor she was seeking. The kind she was seeking would not send her to a hematologist. Besides, if you go to a hematologist of course he's going to tell you something is wrong with your blood, she reasoned. That's his specialty.

"Would you like to make an appointment?"

"No thanks,"

Things worsened. The headaches grew more severe. She stumbled as she tried to walk. Every ounce of color drained from her body. Yes, she would go to see the hematologist. Perhaps from there she could get more answers. After all, she was a researcher.

Dr. Berry, a middle-aged doctor was very pleasant. As Ivanna stumbled down the corridor, she couldn't help but notice the strange sign as she approached his office. "Cancer patients ahead," it read; the arrow pointed toward the direction in which she was going. Cancer? Why am I going there? I don't have cancer, she thought.

Upon entering the lobby, the receptionist offered her chocolate candy. But Ivanna didn't feel like chocolate- not today. She signed the register then seated herself. To her left was a young girl of about twenty, who sat talking with her mother. The girl slithered out her words clumsily. A closer look told the story. She had been cut from her mouth clear down to her larynx. She willingly displayed the scars, heralding Berry as having saved her life. She had had cancer of the throat. She and her grateful mother cautioned Ivanna to do whatever the doctor told her to. The proof was in their reward; she was still alive.

No, Ivanna thought to herself. I don't want to talk like that or be scarred like that. What am I doing in here anyway? This place is for people with cancer. I don't have cancer. I take this herbal blend. It's a blood cleanser. I know there is nothing wrong with my blood, she thought and shared with her middle-aged doctor as she sat in the examination room answering questions about her medical past.

"So, what do you do for a living?" Berry asked, his receding hairline making him look older than his years.

"I'm a researcher with the State of Illinois," Ivanna answered cheerfully.

He thrust his slim index finger in front of his chin. "So, you decided you weren't going to be one of the statistics. You are going to take control of your health."

"Yes, I don't want to be one of those statistics," she admitted.

Deep creases settled across his forehead as he questioned her further.

"Have you ever had blood transfusions at any time in your life?"

"No."

"Whenever you've had surgery were you required to have transfusions?"

"No."

"Are you taking any prescription medication?"

"No."

"Have you ever presented with any blood infections?"

"No," Ivanna said, wondering what all this meant.

"I don't think you have a problem," he said, excusing himself. Something must have struck a cord in him, because when he returned his message was different.

"Those platelets are abnormal."

Ivanna sat staring in silence, not knowing what to think. "Abnormal? How?"

"You have myelodysplasia."

"Myelodysplasia? What is that?"

"It's sick bone marrow-something that old people have."

"But I'm not old. Why do I have it?" Ivanna asked, rather confused.

Berry studied Ivanna's chart. "Here's what I'd like you to do. Take blood tests over the next four weeks, then we can decide from there what should be done."

At work one day early in March 1992, Ivanna dragged herself up the stairs to her job panting, gasping, from exhaustion. "I don't feel well," she told her boss. "I don't know, I just I don't..."

"It's okay. Why don't you take the rest of the day off, and go to see a doctor."

Ivanna had other ideas; she had called a health food store to supplement the herbal blend she was now taking. "Try this one. It doesn't contain yeast. Yeast is a problem for some people," Andrea the health food store owner said.

Exhaustion overtook Ivanna. She purchased the recommended product. "May I sit on this stool? It was the stool on which Andrea normally sat. Andrea agreed. Ivanna sat resting. "Are you familiar with this herbal blend?"

"Yes, I have some customers who are distributors."

Ivanna continued to sit fatigued, with her purchase in her hand, until at last a dainty blond with long hair walked in with a man two inches taller, who looked quite her senior.

"My, my!" said Andrea. "Just a few months ago you were dragging in here. Now look at you. You look great!"

"Well, thank you. I feel great," the blonde stammered out her words.

Still hailing the herbal blend that she was taking, Ivanna never missed an opportunity to share its wonders whenever she could. Ivanna couldn't help but wonder if the blonde was taking the herbal blend. "Are you familiar with this herbal blend?" Ivanna asked her.

"Yes, we're distributors."

"Oh!" Together they laughed having found common ground.

The girl reached out her hand. "Hi, I'm Danielle Seymour. This here is my husband, Cal. We're from Kilbourne, a little town fifty miles west of Springfield."

"Pleased to meet you. I'm Ivanna Dion. It's so good to meet other distributors of this blend. People here are so hung up on their doctors."

"Yes, well, we're distributors, but this product is not all things to all people," Cal said.

What a strange thing to say, Ivanna thought, especially coming from a distributor. But perhaps some were just not as convinced as others of its wonders.

The blond interrupted. "I've found this doctor, Dr. Burton. He's got all kinds of degrees."

"...Well, I'm tired of doctors with all kinds of degrees. I want a doctor who can help me. These yeast infections--if only I could get help with them."

"I haven't had a yeast infection since I started the program four months ago. This doctor doesn't give any drugs, only natural products."

"Really? Tell me more about this Dr. Burton."

"Well, first you have to take a blood test."

"I've already had a blood test."

"Yes, but this is a different kind of blood test. I'll have to come over and give you one. Do you want to set up an appointment for Saturday?"

"Yes, that'll work," Ivanna agreed.

On Saturday Ivanna vacillated between whether she should bother with this blood test thing. She had a blood test, she told herself. When Danielle called, she'd just tell her that she had changed her mind.

The phone rang at roughly 8:00 a.m. Danielle was making certain that the plans had not changed; after all, this was a fifty-mile trip for her.

"Hello," Ivanna answered.

"Hello?" Danielle said, as though asking a question. "I will be there in about an hour. Give me until about 9:00 o'clock. Now the blood test costs sixty dollars," she said.

"Oh, I don't know..."

Danielle interrupted. "Oh, I tell you--life without yeast infections is wonderful. I haven't had one since I started this program." Danielle's words were like magic.

No more yeast infections, Ivanna thought. She'd crawl to the end of the universe to get rid of them.

"I'm giving you a choice," Danielle said.

"Okay, I'll be waiting."

Before long Danielle was ringing Ivanna's door bell. With her she brought a medical history form, blood slide, a lancet, some disinfecting cloth and cotton. She explained: "the medical history form must be completed and signed. If it is not, Dr. Burton won't analyze the blood--said it has something to do with the FBI and or FDA."

Once the application was completed, Danielle washed her hand with the disinfecting cloth then squeezed Ivanna's left little finger and quickly pricked it. Blood trickled out of Ivanna's little finger in a little stream along the palm of her hand. It didn't bead up like most people's do.

"Oooh! I hope you don't have A.I.D.S. Your blood is running all over," Danielle teased. Together they laughed. It broke the tension.

"Yes, it's kind of weird," Ivanna agreed.

Now Ivanna understood what the nurse had said to her on the phone that day. "Your blood has no clotting factor. You'll need to see a hematologist." At least now she had more answers. The problem was with her blood--no problem. She would go to the health food store and get some alfalfa. It was good for helping the blood to clot--no big deal.

Danielle let the blood sit on Ivanna's little finger for some thirty seconds then pressed the smeared blood from Ivanna's little finger onto the glass slide smearing five smudges of the blood vertically along the slide.

"How long before I hear?"

"You'll receive a nutritional chart in the mail in a week. Then you call Dr. Burton between the hours of one and two o'clock our time. That's when he takes calls on blood work. Then he can tell you what he found."

"Okay," Ivanna said, and then thanked the literal stranger for her efforts.

But following such a program would not be a decision made without discussion with her baby brother. "Gerald. I had my blood taken by a girl from Kilbourne. I want to see what this Naturopath has to say. If he says something strange, I'll know to forget about this whole thing."

"Yes, then you will have two diagnoses; then you can make an informed decision."

18

Something would have to be done-but quick. The awful headaches, buzzing in the ear, and bleeding of her nose told Ivanna that this was serious; needle-and-pin like sensations dancing all over her body left no doubt.

A report was due. Ivanna stared at the blank paper for hours, but no words would emerge. It couldn't be happening at a worse time, just when she had received an opportunity to demonstrate her talents. Life just seemed so unfair. But if she could fix her blood-make it clot, at least then she would have solved part of the problem. She would leave the yeast infection problem for the naturopath.

That afternoon, Ivanna purchased some alfalfa and started taking it right away. The first of her four-week series of scheduled blood tests authorized by her hematologist was Monday. According to Dr. Berry, this CBC showed a marked improvement over the last. But the readings, Ivanna realized, were masked by the herbal blend. That left her but one choice. She would discontinue the herbal blend long enough for the hematologist to get a more accurate reading.

That night she settled into bed, for the first time in months, without having taken the herbal blend. She lay on her back, her head settling onto the down pillow. At that moment it seemed as if all the air was sucked from her body and her insides lifted above her. Empty and hollow, she lay still, gasping for breath. "Jay," she called to her son in agony, "I can't breathe. I can't breathe!" She struggled to lift her head from the pillow.

Jay ran into the room. "Sit up mom, sit up! I'll call the ambulance." He rushed to place the call.

Ivanna eased up in the bed; now she could breathe once again. "Call Uncle Gerald," she told Jay.

"Okay," he agreed.

Ivanna's body shook violently, as though she had advanced stages of Parkinson's disease. Soon it passed-but not for long. Almost as quickly, the shakes started up again.

In the ambulance, the paramedics gave her oxygen as she lay still on the gurney. The technician partially covered her body, leaving her exposed to air. The ride was bumpy. To Ivanna who was riding backward on her back, this three mile ride seemed to take forever. This was Ivanna's first ambulance ride; she hoped it would be her last.

At the hospital, the nurse took several tubes of Ivanna's blood. The myriad tests did not link her intermittent shakes with any major organ, so a hospital stay would not be covered by insurance. For the hospital, Ivanna's pale skin and violent shakes were not deemed good enough reason to keep her, so she was released.

It was late when she returned home. This time she wouldn't take any chances. She took the herbal blend; now she knew she would be able sleep.

It was a day that Burton would never forget. The phone rang.

"There's a call for you on line two," Carrie told Dr. Burton.

"Hello," Burton said.

"Hello Kyle."

Kyle was almost speechless. Mother hadn't spoken with him in years. What had made her swallow her pride and call?

"Mother..."

"Kyle, I have a growth. I can't get it to heal," she said as though nothing had ever happened between them. Perhaps this was what they needed to re-establish their kinship. Maybe the Lord was moving in this way to reestablish what had been lost between them.

"Do you mind if I come in?"

"No. Not at all, why don't you?"

Her blood test showed patterns consistent with a basal cell carcinoma and parasites.

Five days after her blood tests from Natrogenics, Ivanna received a color photo of her blood along with the nutritional chart of recommended products for her improvement. She had stopped taking the alfalfa and noticed that a few days since her hospital visit now, the shakes had became less and less until at last they stopped. The alfalfa was the cause of the violent shakes; now it was clear. It was a product that she now understood she must not take.

After her hematologist's questioning, Ivanna recalled that he told her, "I don't think that there is anything wrong with your blood, as no history of blood problems has ever before surfaced." But this was prior to examining her platelets. This started Ivanna to thinking. If she had no history of blood problems, something had to have caused it. But what?

Dr. Berry's suggestion that she had myelodysplasia made Ivanna curious. She retrieved all her medical records and purchased medical books to try and get answers. Research told her that myelodysplasia is a blood disorder, an ultimately fatal disease facilitated by bone marrow depression. But the question remained. What had caused her bone marrow depression?

Berry's medical report gave her the clue. "I have no documentation in Dr. King's records that he recommended discontinuing the Tagamet."

"Tagamet, in some individuals, creates bone marrow depression where the bone marrow can no longer normally create blood cells. It should not be taken consecutively for more than a nine week period," Ivanna learned. She had been taking Tagamet for 5 years, as much as 800 milligrams per pill in the last year alone under Dr. King's direction. She had her answer.

Meanwhile Berry had gotten the results of Ivanna's last blood tests. "Your blood count is low. There is no evidence of cyclic neutropenia, but we need a bone marrow aspiration for diagnosis."

"Thanks, I'll call if I want anything done."

Ivanna busied herself meanwhile with trying to understand Berry's diagnosis. Myelodysplasia, she noted was pre-leukemia and ultimately fatal. Appleton and Lange's Medical Diagnosis and Treatment book suggested that, "Patients with more than five percent blasts in the bone marrow will almost invariably develop leukemia if they do not die of their cytapenias first. Allogeneic bone marrow transplantation is the only definitive therapy."

Wow! Ivanna thought. This is deep. Berry's analysis had suggested that there was disease in the bone marrow, but to determine the extent of the disease, a bone marrow biopsy was needed. She could hardly wait to talk to Burton to see what his findings were.

"Hello!" a big booming voice responded to Ivanna's greetings.

"Yes, I was calling to get an analysis of my blood," Ivanna said.

"Your blood pattern is consistent with malignancy-stage one, possible leukemia, liver distress, arthritis and a touch of candidiasis."

It was like hearing the voice of a ghost on the other end of the line, this strange man telling you of your condition, yet never having laid eyes on you. Ivanna was speechless... and confused. She had contacted him because of a yeast infection--not malignancy, let alone leukemia. The herbal blend did not camouflage Burton's blood analysis as it had the hematologist's.

"Can I take the herbal blend in lieu of some of your recommended products?"

"You can take it, but it's really no substitute."

"What do you mean?"

"It can't do the job."

Ivanna didn't understand. How dare he make light of this blend. He's only trying to sell his product. No, she would continue with the herbal blend, but this time adding to it Burton's supplements, liquids, and drops. No one would stop her from taking this herbal blend. It had been too good to her, she thought.

Ivanna compared Berry's diagnosis with that of Burton's. Burton diagnosed malignancy stage one-possible leukemia. Two different kinds of doctors in separate parts of the country had independently come up with the same diagnosis, albeit they used different jargon. Now she could make an informed decision; which doctor would she choose?

Choosing Berry's treatment would mean undergoing a bone marrow biopsy, chemotherapy, and bone marrow transplantation which was, according to a study Ivanna uncovered during research, only thirty percent effective. In 1979 alone, the average cost of bone marrow transplant was more than $150,000. This was 1992. Choosing Berry's treatment would mean finding a match for her marrow, after totally eradicating her body's natural defenses. It would mean foregoing treatment for the chronic yeast infections, one of the clinical findings for patients with acute leukemia, not to mention the many other discomforts from which she suffered.

If Burton's program was as effective for her as it had been for Danielle's multiple scleroses, it would address all of Ivanna's problem areas for less than ten percent of the cost of a bone marrow transplant. Her decision was made; she would choose Dr. Burton's program.

In May 1992 more and more patients were flocking to the clinic. Burton received a phone call.

"Hey Doc., you haven't forgot about me have you?"

"No, Wes I haven't."

"Man can't you use a volunteer?"

"No, no volunteers, Wes, but tell you what. Let me give it some thought. We'll see what we can do-okay?"

"Bet."

Monday was another workday for Ivanna. Still fatigued, she struggled to climb stairs, panting, and gasping every step of the way. How could she explain to her boss that she was ill-seriously ill? Yes, the hematologist had seen a problem, but remained uncommitted unless a bone marrow biopsy confirmed his diagnosis. A bone marrow biopsy was something Ivanna didn't want.

What was she going to do? How could she get extended time from work? Who would vouch for the seriousness of her illness? The hospital hadn't linked any vital organs to her illness. No one would accept the word of a naturopath; only a medical doctor had such power.

Ivanna sought the services of a Dr. Brown.

"Depression," he said, and recommended an extended home stay of thirty days, then a physical reevaluation. Brother Gerald took Dr. Brown's findings to Ivanna's boss.

Ivanna hobbled knock-kneed down the descending flight of stairs and fell upon the living room couch; it was the only trip made for the day. Only at bedtime did she ascend the flight--but that was not easy. Arthritis, cramps, and pains made it difficult. Her skin, once bronze in color was now deathly pale. Left untreated, death would surely be her fate; she had no doubt. Taking even two steps left her panting, almost wheezing. Her son Jay got help from some angelic church members. Two members provided a day each of service for Ivanna as she sat idly on the couch, exchanging the couch for the floor, stretching when sitting on the couch became too tiring. The church ladies warmed and heated food for her breakfast, lunch, and dinner.

A week later, when Ivanna's sisters arrived from out of town, so too, did her supplements from the Natrogenics clinic-all 15 bottles. The dosage was massive, some forty-four pills, plus liquid and drops were to be consumed daily. This was no small task for someone as weak and feeble as was Ivanna.

To ensure that all of the products were taken on time and as directed, sister Vernice stepped in. Another sister cooked and stored food, so that in their absence Ivanna would be able to function. Not until their arrival, had they realized the seriousness of Ivanna's condition older sister Debra would later tell her.

The shakes returned, although to a much lesser degree, when she took one of the products. It contained alfalfa. She was concerned and phoned Dr. Burton. "I can't take this product because of the alfalfa; it gives me the shakes."

"Lay off of it about a week or two and start it again."

"That's crazy. I can't take that stuff! Why does he want me to start taking it again?" Ivanna asked herself. Renouncing her own reasoning, she did as Burton suggested and noticed that not only were the shakes gone, she had an immediate boost of energy. From that experience she learned that in the critical stages of her illness she hadn't the nutritional substance needed to tolerate the alfalfa. Once on Burton's program for a week, she had received the base nutritional support needed to tolerate it.

Having now received both diagnoses and realizing the seriousness of her illness, Ivanna decided that she should tell her son that "this was serious; she might not make it."

The word was out that Ivanna was sick, so family who lived in Springfield came over. The varied sizes of white bottles of products dominated the kitchen table. Beside the products was a copy of the nutritional chart containing a Polaroid picture of Ivanna's blood drop amplified one thousand times.

"What's all that stuff?" an older brother, Flynn, wanted to know.

"It's my blood and some products the doctor wants me to take."

Frowning, he looked at the weird looking Polaroid replica of Ivanna's blood, with its mere hint of a pattern of dark red splashes. "How do you know that this is your blood? That's stupid!"

Ivanna was in no position to debate, so the comment was ignored. Ivanna understood that, at least in his mind, she was submitting to what he felt was "bad medicine," something not recognized or sanctioned in the medical community, and that concerned him. She also understood that no amount of explanation would help him to understand. She had made her decision; she had no plans of changing it.

Ivanna was excited about the possibility that she had found something that just might provide relief. Her focus was no longer on just getting rid of the yeast infection--it was on getting rid of the malignancy, and the yeast and other conditions as a secondary measure.

In addition to the many products Burton recommended, he also ordered a change of diet for Ivanna. Following Burton's nutritional program meant scouting out stores that carried organic foods, including fruits and vegetables. Perhaps most difficult for Ivanna, was giving up milk and pastas as she had known them. She loved pastas and breads of all kinds. Instead, she substituted a rice or soy blend for milk, whole grain pastas for white flour based products, and honey and fruit sweetened goods for sugar. Fluoride and aluminum based products including cookware, cans and deodorants were to be avoided. Coffee and coffee flavored foods were discouraged, as they could nullify the homeopathics, the chart stated.

After three days on the products, Ivanna was able to go up and down her steps with ease. She could even warm up the food left for her by her sisters. Things looked bright; it looked as though she was headed for recovery when she was suddenly overwhelmed by a paralyzing tiredness; it was as though her body was being drained. She was concerned, so she called up Danielle and confided. "I'm so tired, I can hardly function."

"Your body is going through a cleansing. That's natural," Danielle said.

Ivanna had heard that before when she was first introduced to the herbal blend, so the concept wasn't foreign to her. Still the tiredness was hard to take; it was even worse than when she was fatigued by the disease. "Yes, but I just feel so bad. I think I need to go to the doctor."

"You're not planning to go to the medical doctor are you?"

"Oh, no-no! I want to see that doctor you told me about in Champaign, that Keiser guy."

"Here, why don't I give you his number, and you can talk to him and see what he thinks, but I'm sure you're going through a body cleanse."

"Okay, I'll call him and see what he says."

Ivanna's call to Dr. Keizer confirmed just what Danielle had said.

"Yes, its natural for you to feel that way in the beginning, but if you don't feel any better after two weeks, give me a call back," Keizer said.

At the end of those two weeks there was no need to call Keizer or take the trusted herbal blend. Ivanna felt great! But feeling better meant Ivanna's mind was free-free to do "idle" thinking. Idle thoughts gave way to self-pity. Some phone calls, but family visits were scarce. Never before had she been so sick. When sick, she got the loving support of her family. Why was it so different this time? She wondered.

Where was Earl who lived only one hundred miles away? And Allen, the brother who was always there to support her when she needed him? During a conversation with Allen, he asked, "If this doesn't work, will you try the other?"

"Possibly but I believe that the body is capable of healing itself given the right stuff." Ivanna knew how strange that must have sounded to Allen. She could almost hear him thinking, yes, that's what you said about the herbal blend. Look at you now!

Others asked no questions about the program, even having endorsed the herbal blend. To them, Ivanna was treading in waters she knew nothing about-and from a stranger? Not to mention, this treatment was illegal. They were hopeful that before long Ivanna would come to her senses.

Some watched from a distance knowing that just as had happened with the herbal blend, the bottom would soon drop out of this treatment too. What, then, would be Ivanna's fate? It was as though she could read their minds. It was like a silent storm raging: a war between them and her, between allopathic medicine and naturopathic medicine, and between the government and the people. Yet, no one dared speak a word.

19

Dr. Burton sat almost chilled as he read a newspaper account of the standoff at Ruby Ridge. Randy, Vicky, and their family had settled into a cabin in the northern panhandle of Idaho. Burton had followed the story from the beginning.

Sought after because of their radical views and ideology, the Weaver family had become targets of the government. Randy's failure to appear in court for a misdemeanor charge, selling sawed off shotguns, had resulted in what would become known as the standoff at Ruby Ridge.

Nearing the end of the standoff, some 250 federal vehicles were summoned to the Weaver's cabin to ward off the attack of a family of five, a friend, and a dog. The standoff resulted in the death of a Federal US Marshall, Vicky Weaver, Sam Weaver, and their dog.

Incredible! Burton thought. Now they are targeting people because of their views. I hope those agents pay for what they've done to that family!

In August 1992, patients came in record numbers to Natrogenics clinic. For Burton, the time was right to add additional staff, so he called Wes O'Dea. "Wes, this is Dr. Burton."

"Yeah, Doc."

"How would you like to come to work for me?"

"I thought you'd never ask. When can I start?"

"How about Monday?"

"I'll do it! See you Monday."

On Monday, Wes reported to Natrogenics for work. He eyed the beautiful Anna who was behind the counter with her long flowing hair dusting her waistline. "You're looking good, girl," he said, his head tilted in a flirtatious slant. "I need to see Doc. Can you get him for me?"

"Sure, he's expecting you. Won't you follow me?" Anna led him to Dr. Burton's office.

"Anna, Wes is going to be joining us here at the clinic."

"Welcome aboard," Anna said, and then disappeared.

"Won't you pull up a chair, Wes? I want to go over what you'll be doing as my assistant. I'd like you to assist Jewel and Marilyn. Marilyn is a reflexologist and Jewel a massage therapist. Both are well trained, so I'd like to have you sit and observe both of them for a while. Follow me," Burton said, taking the lead. "Marilyn, I want you to meet Wes. He'll be coming to work for us."

"Oh, cool, we could use the help."

Burton spotted Jewel coming from a nearby examination room. "Jewel, this here's Wes. He'll be working with us."

"Did you say Jewel?"

"Yes, I'm Jewel."

"He's gonna help us with spinal touch therapy, massage, and reflexology. So, show him what you know. Okay?" Burton ducked back into his office.

Jewel extended her hand. "Wes, so good to have you."

Burton appeared at the door again. "Let's have Wes complete the necessary paper work, then send him back to my office--okay?"

"Okay," Jewel agreed.

"My, my Doc, you're quite a lucky man," Wes said, upon entering Burton's office.

"What do you mean?"

Wes dropped his head peering underneath his brow, with a smile on his face. He slapped his right thigh. "The women man--such fine women!"

"Well, I'm a married man, Wes...and so are you. Let's remember that."

"You know I told you, I'd like my own practice someday. You mind if I take a look at the files from time to time. That'll give me some clues on how to set up my practice and some source of suppliers."

"Sure, just let the girls know."

"Deal."

"So, when do you expect to start school?"

"I tell you, Doc, right now school loans got me strapped, but soon as I find a source of finance."

"Listen, I'll be conducting classes on spinal touch therapy and muscle response testing on some weekends. You'll need to attend. Who knows--you get good enough, I'll have you teaching those classes."

"Bet," Wes said, signaling with thumbs up.

Less than a month after being hired, Wes began scanning files, pulling out files of suppliers.

"Wes, what are you...Can I help you with something?" Marilyn asked, as she noticed Wes stacking a number of files behind the lobby counter.

"No," Wes said sharply. "Just gathering some information on these companies, because some day, mama," he thrust his index finger against his chest. "I'll be doctor in charge."

Marilyn thrust her hands on her hips. "Oh you think so, huh?"

"Just watch me!"

"Hum," Marilyn said, then slipped into the examination room just to the right of the restroom.

Not having finished his lunch, Dr. Burton sat in his office reading a copy of a newspaper that was sent to him by Ivanna Dion. The article was found in the Monday, August 10, 1992, issue of the Springfield, Illinois State Journal Register and was entitled "FDA taking on vitamins--at gunpoint."

> Agency increasing efforts to halt bogus nutritional claims
> (N.Y. Times News Service)
>
> In Texas, state health inspectors raided health food stores across the state in May and, as startled customers and bystanders watched in amazement, removed hundreds of products, including vitamin C, Aloe Vera products, and herbal teas.
>
> In Kent, Wash., armed agents of the Food and Drug Administration burst into the Tahoma Clinic, where practitioners of alternative medicine used injections of vitamins, minerals and amino acids to treat a variety of ailments.
>
> That raid on May 6, captured on videotape by a patient and later broadcast on television news programs, shows FDA agents, dressed in bulletproof vests, bursting into the clinic and commanding clinic employees to freeze. The agency said the clinic was raided because it made illegal drugs, including "vitamin-mineral concoctions," that were being injected into patients.
>
> No charges have been filed in either incident, but officials at the FDA say the raids are part of the agency's increased efforts to stop manufacturers of nutritional supplements from making unproven claims for their products, and to bar their use by doctors unless first it is approved by the agency and to halt their sale as medicines.
>
> The FDA says its actions are grounded in hard science and law. But across the country the agency's tactics have caused anger, frustration and in some areas organized consumer rebellion. The interest groups fighting the FDA represent the makers of health foods and vitamins and the practitioners of so-called alternative medicine--some doctors as well as herbalists and acupuncturists. . .
>
> Last year, the FDA proposed regulations for the labeling law that would classify vitamins and minerals as drugs if dosages exceeded the daily recommended allowances; restrict or prevent the sale of most medicinal herbs like chamomile; prevent unsubstantiated health claims for most dietary supplements; and lower the recommended vitamin-intake levels for various age groups.

> Under the proposal, food labels could not carry health claims about the relationship between the food and specific disease or health conditions, except in the cases of calcium and osteoporosis, sodium and hypertension, fat and cardiovascular disease, and fat and cancer. . .
>
> The FDA, under the proposal, would have the authority to recall or embargo products and impose fines of up to $250,000 on individuals and $1 million on companies for each violation.
>
> Under the proposed recommended intake levels-- which replace the daily-recommended allowances--vitamin C could not be sold over the counter at dosages greater than 60 milligrams, nor could the label say, "Prevents the common cold."
>
> Officials at the FDA say the regulations are needed to protect the public against manufacturers who promote the supposed healing powers of supplements and make phony health claims.

What the…? Where are people's rights in all this? Do what people think matter anymore? This is America for crying out loud! Something has to be done about this. The government seemed determined to thwart any gains garnered by the naturopathic community with their anti-vitamin/mineral campaigns and constant threat to the citizenry at large. The time was right for a meeting with the naturopathic community.

As president of the Idaho Naturopathic Medical Association, Burton sent letters to all member naturopaths, calling for a meeting to take place in October 1992. At the meeting, Burton shared information with his colleagues about the many FBI/FDA raids on clinics between 1987 and 1992. "It's imperative that we remain knowledgeable of what is going on in the naturopathic community. We must continue to push for licensure of naturopaths in the State of Idaho. We must contact our legislators and the governor to find out how they are voting on matters that affect us."

"Yes, but let's face it Kyle, we're up against a huge monster--it's called the AMA. Do you really think that those legislators are going to listen to us? Besides most of the legislators don't understand naturopathy," one naturopath commented.

"We have the support of some of the senators and representatives. In a letter addressed to a Rex L. Furness of the Senate Health and Welfare Committee, several senators concurred that there is a general attitude among the public that in many areas the practice of naturopathy can be and has been an effective form of health care that has served many individuals' needs. They say, and I quote…

"'We are extremely concerned that some law enforcement agencies of the state may prosecute naturopaths for technical violations of the state code. This would amount to unwarranted and excessive enforcement with felony criminal penalties that may violate both the public and naturopathic practitioner's rights under the United States and Idaho constitutions. Because of the lateness of the session, it is the intent and recommendation of this committee that all enforcement agencies that might prosecute naturopaths for mere technical violations should only proceed when there is a clear danger to the public. Harm to individuals must have allegedly occurred.'"

The representatives expressed concern over the fact that law enforcement agencies believe that they can justify prosecution of naturopaths solely on technicalities. As such, they suggest that solving this matter is imperative. The scope of naturopathy should be defined, and the public should be notified whenever non-traditional methods of medical treatment are involved, they said. They believe that if the above criteria are met, licensure may not be necessary.

President Clinton suggested that:

Several consumers had expressed concerns over their rights being eroded by the FDA. He agreed that given the ever rising costs of health care, prevention was a viable approach to health care, especially given that scientific knowledge backs the validity of nutrition as an important factor in disease prevention. He pledged to work closely with Bill Richardson who introduced Bill HR 5746 "The Health Choice Freedom Act of 1992" in resolving this matter.

So some things are being done, but we must keep the pressure on. This means sending letters, making phone calls, and getting the support of patients who will also put the pressure on. It is the only way we can protect ourselves against these unjust attacks. We need to continue to push for naturopathic licensure. I'd like each one present to make a commitment to contact each of our senators and representatives here in Idaho. In the next meeting, we can report and discuss their responses. Then we can decide what needs to be done."

February 1993

At home, Kyle had just settled into bed. The phone rang. "It's your mother," Jane said handing Kyle the phone.

"Hello."

"Kyle..." bitter sobs followed. "Nothing is helping. The sore keeps spreading," she said, after intermittent sniffles. "What am I going to do?"

"Tell you what. Why don't you...you have Medicare don't you?"
"Yes."
"So go ahead and see an MD, since it will be covered. Get a diagnosis, and see what they say. Call me back after the visit. We'll take it from there--okay?"

Drs. Bush and Lange examined the horrible looking sore--now two inches in diameter. Though it was not metastasized, the sore looked dangerous with its purple and black ulceration's, laced with bloodshot lesions and splotches.

"Oh lady, this is...We'll have to do surgery on this immediately," Dr. Bush said.

"Oh my God--when?"

"Lady you're lucky to be alive!" Lange added.

Mrs. Burton's eyeballs swelled to the size of huge marbles. Her thin hands covered her mouth; tears streamed down her cheeks.

"Maybe with chemo and radiation we'll be able to impede its growth, but you'll need skin grafting after the surgery. But you understand there are risks involved. We can't make any guarantee," Dr Bush added.

The doctors looked at each other and chatted quietly among themselves. Suddenly there was silence as they stared and pointed at her chart. Mrs. Burton could almost hear herself breathing. The older Dr. Bush soon broke the silence.

"We can schedule the surgery for tomorrow morning--would that work for you?" But Mrs. Burton was too distraught to discuss it right now. Besides, she needed more than ever now to be able to talk to Kyle.

Kyle was just pulling into his driveway when his mother appeared almost in hysteria. "Kyle--they want to do surgery tomorrow! What am I going to do?" For the first time in years, Kyle would embrace his mother. He threw his sturdy arms around her, drew her up to him, and looked in her eyes. "Don't worry, Mama, we're not at the end of the rope yet--we got a nice long rope to work with. I'll start you on another heavy program, and give you some electrical treatments. We'll go down to Mexico and arrange for the surgery there with Dr. Egore. So don't worry, okay."

Mrs. Burton managed a faint smile.

It was a long journey--the trip to Mexico by automobile. Mrs. Burton was fatigued and very anxious. The hospital provided shelter for his mom and family. Food choices were plentiful, as there were good restaurants to choose from. For the first time, Burton found himself in the position of his distant patients. Now he realized the importance of their need for affordable shelter and good food choices.

For the surgery, Dr. Egan's choice of sedative for his mother was

Valium. Along by Dr. Egan's side, Dr. Burton assisted. The wound, sufficiently cleaned, required stitching. The surgery was done with the precision of a master craftsman. No skin grafting was required. Mrs. Burton was in recovery for one hour. The next morning, they headed home.

20

The trip to Mexico had given Burton an idea. More and more patients traveled from afar to receive his services. If they could find suitable shelter, a restaurant that served whole grain breads and pastas, special breaded and grown tuna-- and other fine food sanctioned under his dietary plan, how much better would be their plight. With that in mind, he purchased a set of townhouses that was physically connected to his clinic for patient shelter.

Dorothy had traveled from California. The HLB/LBA blood screening revealed that her blood pattern was consistent with late stages of lymphatic cancer. Spinal touch therapy would provide some relief. Serving as Jewel's assistant, Wes O'Dea was at her side.

Dorothy slipped into a robe whose opening was at back. She stood underneath a plumb line designed to measure posture deviation.

"Won't you step up on the foot board for a moment?" Jewel requested.

Into the footboard her feet slid. Jewel used a piece of chalk to mark pivotal points on Dorothy's back.

"No Jewel! The mark doesn't go there," Wes asserted.

Wes had been employed at Natrogenics clinic less than a year under Jewel's tutelage; now he had become the expert--and in front of the patient? How unprofessional! Jewel's mouth flew open in disbelief. She didn't want to contribute to that kind of unprofessionalism, especially in front of the patient, so she gave in to Wes' cockiness.

She allowed Wes to mark places of his choosing, instead marking the correct places on the patient with her trained eye. She could override his error when she applied the hand manipulations. When she started to apply the hand manipulation, Wes objected again.

"What's with you Jewel--are you awake? This is where you should be applying pressure," he snapped.

Jewel threw up her hands. "Never mind! I forget you are the expert!" she said then left the room and joined Carrie who was sitting at the desk working behind the counter.

"You know, I can't believe that guy! You know it was all I could do to keep from shoveling my foot up his tail."

"So what now? Was he trying to take over in there, too?"

"I trained him and now he's going to tell me how it's supposed to be done?"

Carrie sighed. "Sounds familiar."

"I need a smoke behind this one. I'll see you after lunch."

Back from lunch, Jewel joined Anna and Carrie at the counter. Both were packaging products. Jewel waited to use the bathroom. Already fifteen minutes had passed.

"Who's in the john?"

Anna's nose turned up as she spoke. "Wes. I don't know whether you have noticed, but that guy's been acting awfully strange lately. He's been in there now for about an hour. This has been going on for the last couple of days. I don't know what's gotten into him."

"No kidding," Jewel added. "I've just about had it with him. I'm going to talk with Dr. Burton about him. I can't take it anymore."

It was Danielle Seymour's first trip to the clinic. A year and four months after her initial treatment, Danielle showed no signs of multiple sclerosis. The speech impediment, extreme fatigue and parasites were still a problem. That overall bad feeling is what brought her to the clinic. Nutritional injection therapy was an instant rejuvenator for her.

Having performed reflexology on Danielle, Marilyn left the room, leaving Wes to do the spinal touch. So advanced now was Wes, that Burton granted him permission to teach classes in Spinal touch therapy on Saturdays.

Wes rolled up his sleeves to perform the spinal touch. "So it's Danielle is it?"

"That's right."

"Hey, I'm Wes. It says on your chart you had multiple sclerosis."

Danielle shook her head, "Not no more."

"It's hard to imagine a fine statuesque woman like yourself with multiple sclerosis."

"Well—it's true."

"Why don't you lie on your stomach for me?"

Danielle obliged, letting her face sink into the opening in the table. As she did, the folds in her dress conformed to her body curves.

"Umm, nice tush," Wes said, as he began his body manipulation. "Are you married?"

Danielle raised her face up out of the opening, and strained to look back at Wes. "Yes. "I'm very much married."

Marilyn poked her head through the door. "Hey charmer, I don't want this to go to your head, but don't forget there's a patient in the other room awaiting your services."

"Hey, I'm good-what can I say. Tell the lady I'll be there shortly."

Danielle didn't want to be in the room alone with this flirt, but Marilyn didn't linger. Saying something to Dr. Burton about his help was unthinkable. What would he think? She would remember this character. Next time she would bring her husband.

"That lady out in the lobby has multiple sclerosis, too. This is her second visit," Wes said, breaking the silence.

Hum, Danielle thought. Here again it was strange hearing a doctor's help discussing another patient's illness.

In the lobby Carrie and Jewel were discussing a new diet product. Carrie had a magazine spread open to the advertisement and pointed with a pencil. "You know, I'm thinking about trying this diet plan. I'd like to shed about fifteen pounds," she said.

"Yes--I wonder if it is any good. I could stand to lose a few myself," Jewel said.

Wes had just returned from treating Danielle in time enough to hear the gist of the conversation. "So, where is it you're trying to lose Jewel--your head? Nobody wants a bone but a dog."

Carrie jumped in. "It's none of your business!"

"You fool!" Jewel shouted, and then left the room in haste only to have Wes follow.

"What did you call me?" Wes snapped.

"You heard me!"

Thus began a shouting match between them. Jane, having just entered Burton's office, was disturbed by this conduct. Burton instructed Jane to handle it while he busied himself with paper work on another patient.

"Wes," Jane cut Wes off from another verbal attack on Jewel. "Kyle wants you to leave--until you can get along with the girls."

The air was stale. Perhaps Wes reconsidered why he was really there. He simply went back to work.

The day had come to a close. Everyone except for Kyle and Jewel was gone. Jewel knew she should approach Kyle with caution about Wes. Kyle rather liked the guy--she didn't want to burst his bubble.

"Kyle, have you noticed how long Wes' been spending in the bathroom?"

"Not really--should I?"

"Well, you know, it's just that he's tying up the bathroom so long that us girls can't get in there. It's been going on now for days."

"Oh I don't know. Have you tried knocking? I'm sure he'd delight in letting you in," Burton chuckled.

"Yes, I just bet he would, but we're not going there," Jewel said. "But seriously, don't you think an hour in the bathroom is a bit much?"

"Yes, no kidding. Even constipation has its...I'll speak to him about it."

Danielle Seymour had followed the demands of the program religiously, i.e. everything but the dental work Burton had recommended. She just couldn't understand the need for it. But for Burton's insistence on amalgam removal, his advice would have fallen on deaf ears.

Danielle had come so far. Burton seized the opportunity to assist a local dentist in removing her amalgams. Each tooth was programmed for removal. Danielle was muscle tested for four kinds of porcelain replacements. Her body could tolerate the herculite.

A rubber dam was used to lessen Danielle's exposure to the poisonous mercury fumes. Injection therapy energized her. Time, however, did not permit Burton to follow the 21-day cycle recommended for sequential amalgam removal. Danielle was going back to Illinois the next day.

In Kilbourne, Danielle lay in bed ill--violently ill. The abrupt mercury exposure had proved too much. It was the first time Danielle found herself questioning the judgment of Burton. She should not have listened to this one, she told herself, as she lay wondering if the illness would ever pass.

After the third week, brighter days were ahead. Oral chelation therapy and a nutritional regimen to accommodate the mineral changes in her body were introduced. The nutrition combination worked wonders. Danielle was amazed. For the first time in months she didn't stammer her words. Energy boosts after injection therapy was common. This boost was totally different; it had its origin in amalgam removal.

Each passing day brought Danielle renewed strength. Her sex drive was back with a vengeance. Her frequent leg cramps all but disappeared. Her nervous system slowly started to rebuild itself. In time, she was no longer incontinent. Constipation was now a thing of the past. Yes, she thought. Burton had once again proved himself.

Dr. Flemming, her gynecologist, was amazed at Danielle's recovery. "You look wonderful. What have you being doing about the multiple sclerosis?"

"I've been using herbs." Danielle said, happily sharing her secret.

"Herbs! That is nothing but a bunch of nonsense! No facts support their effectiveness. That is not why you're getting better," he shouted.

"No, it's true! I've found this naturopathic doctor..."

"Lady, you're nuts. I thought you had better sense," he said, then stormed out of the room.

Danielle left behind him, approaching her husband, Cal, who heard the commotion.

Before entering the hall Flemming turned to face Danielle and Cal. "It's you kind of people that give medicine a bad name. Dealing with quacks and herbs. If that's the kind of practice you seek, don't bother seeking my services!" he snapped.

Cal was incensed by Dr. Fleming's disregard for his wife. "How dare you address my wife like that!" Cal snapped.

"I have some important business to attend. Now, if you'll excuse me," Flemming said.

But Cal wasn't content to let the matter rest. He phoned Dr. Flemming at his residence. "You owe my wife an apology!" Flemming did apologize.

Burton was engaged in a phone conversation when he heard voices and commotion outside of his office. Sheri Whitley, the shipping clerk, was busy in the stock room when Wes suddenly appeared. His right arm was stretched high above his head bracing the railing of the shelves. To exit, Sheri would have to get past him. But Wes was relentless. He had her cornered--he knew it. He moved toward her slowly and held her in an embrace.

"Hey baby, I see the way you look at me. You want me--I can tell."

Sheri tried, though unsuccessfully, to break the embrace. "You wish! What are you doing? Let go of me!" Sheri yelled.

"When the last time you had some real good loving, baby-- Huh? I'm talking real lovemaking. I've got this book--my wife and I do some real lovemaking. You and your husband ought to try it." He pulled her closer to him. "Let me show you how it's done," he said preparing to kiss her.

"Let me go!" Sheri shouted. Burton approached.

"Oh Doc, just having a little friendly play with Sheri here." But Sheri's look said otherwise.

"That's enough, Wes--let her go," Burton said.

"Okay, Doc. Okay," he said thrusting his hands about. "I will."

Wes' innuendos had caused many of the old patients to stop coming. New patients now outnumbered the older ones about two to one, so still there was a need for additional help. In August 1993 Kyle hired Lou Daniel as the office chiropractor. The choice was clear; he was the cousin of Marilyn Walter, a long-standing employee of the clinic. Dan stood at six feet. His broad shoulders and masculine build gave him the look of a sports figure.

Marilyn was the one employee that Wes trusted; she had not taken offense to Wes, so he felt quite comfortable talking to her. She was in the stock room when he approached her. "You know Marilyn, I've been doing some checking around. All those degrees Burton has are phony," he said.

"Fake?" she looked at Wes in disgust. "Oh, Wes, get out of here. You don't know what you're talking about." She started once again stocking the shelves.

"No, I'm serious. Something's going to go down here, so just be careful. Keep your nose clean."

Marilyn looked at Wes stunned, attentive now to what he was saying.

"Someone will come in, someone you least suspect--just be careful," he warned.

Marilyn couldn't help but wonder where Wes was getting his information, but Kyle had been cleared of similar charges back in 1984.

In the lobby just behind the counter, Carrie sat typing out a nutritional prescription when Wes appeared. "Hey Carrie," he said, sneaking up besides her giving her a light friendly pinch on her forearm. "What's going on?"

"Listen Wes; keep your hands off of me!"

"Fine." Wes said, and then snatched open the file cabinet that sat immediately to her right.

"What exactly do you need?" Carrie asked, her lips drawn back in anger.

"The usual business addresses and phone numbers. Oh, but don't worry," he said facetiously, "I have Kyle's approval."

"Yes, well approval or not--next time ask!" Carrie insisted, admonishing Wes with her eyes.

"That's right; you're the big time office manager around here, aren't you?" Wes said facetiously.

Carrie's stern look sent him a message. He slammed the file drawer shut and walked off.

It was Friday, August 31. The week had come to a close. An inoperable toilet at his new church building had caused Kyle to stop by. With a flick of the switch, a streak of light flashed then died. A slight tinkering sound sealed its fate; the bulb had blown. But there are some bulbs at the clinic, he remembered.

It was dark. It felt so lonely as Kyle pulled up to his Natrogenics clinic. It looked so barren with his being the only car on the parking lot. The tightly secured door sprang open, with one turn of the key. Off to the right, Burton saw a flicker of light coming from the inner office area. He hastened his pace. Bending over on hands and knees there was Wes with a flashlight in one hand peering over one of the files. A tall stack of files was on his right.

"What are you doing?" Burton asked.

Wes was jumpy and jittery. "I'm mmm... just running things off so that I can set me up a practice. I'm just learning how to do it because you are so successful. I want to get information," Wes stammered.

Boy that's strange, Burton thought. Why the secrecy? Why is he so nervous- something Wes had never been? Why wasn't his vehicle parked on the lot—and all the lights off? Something funny is happening here, Kyle thought. He wasn't quite sure what was going on, but it forced him to make a decision.

"Wes, I'm gonna give you your next month's check. I want you out of here. We're all done."

A nervous Wes started to gather up the files.

"Don't bother," Kyle said. "Ill take care of them."

Wes crept out of the clinic looking like a wounded puppy. Burton didn't know what Wes was up to, but he wasn't taking any more chances. He changed the locks on the door and called it a night.

September 1, 1993

Thundering knocks pounded at the door. It was 12:00 midnight. Who could it be, this time of night, Sheri wondered? She approached with caution and peeped through the peephole. It was Wes. Under normal circumstances she would have merely ignored him, but the sound of the knocks told her he was frantic. Besides, her husband was in the bath. She felt that in his state of mind, he wasn't a threat to her. What could he possibly want this time of night? she wondered. He was about to pound the door again when Sheri snatched it open.

"Wes--what's going on?" Sheri asked.

"Kyle--changed the locks to the clinic," Wes said.

"What are you talking about, Wes?" Sheri studied his expression.

"Kyle changed the locks," he jabbed his finger toward the direction of the clinic. "It's like the guy doesn't trust me or something."

"Wait a minute, Wes. Just settle down. Kyle couldn't have changed the locks--my key worked just fine there yesterday morning."

"Sheri. I was just by the clinic; I'm telling you, he changed the locks," Wes took a deep breath and quickly exhaled shaking his head. "That lousy scumbag!"

"Hum," Sheri shrugged, not knowing what to make out of this one. Sheri couldn't believe it, but she actually felt sorry for Wes at this moment. She attempted to calm him.

"If Kyle changed the locks, I'm sure he had a good reason, but what makes you think you're the reason? It could be any number of reasons."

"I should have known better than to come here. He's got you... Never mind!" he shouted, and then stormed off.

Sheri had to take a few minutes to get her breath. Wow, she thought. Now she was wondering. Why would Kyle change the locks? Still more importantly, why would Wes be down at the clinic this late at night? Something was going on...

On Monday the girls arrived early at the clinic, Burton having given each of them the new key, over the weekend. They were in a huddle in the lobby. Wes was in the center.

"You girls are working for peanuts! Kyle's taking advantage of you. The man owns a Lincoln town car, a snowmobile...."

In walked Burton, confident and assured. Wes looked shocked. "That's right Wes. I do own those things. Perhaps when you're fifty, you will too. I didn't have them when I was your age. Now--if you will excuse us, the staff and I have work to do."

"You'll be sorry. You're gonna get raided. I guarantee you that!"

"You feel that's necessary? That's fine, because I'm not doing anything illegal. Everything I'm doing is according to code. So, if you feel that's what you have to do, you have to do what you have to do."

Wes looked at Kyle, this time pointing his finger at him. "I hate you! I can't stand the sight of you. I don't ever want to have anything to do with you again."

"Well, I'm sorry you feel that way, Wes, after all I've done for you, but I want to wish you the best in whatever career you pursue in life."

Wes hastened to the door and slammed it shut behind him.

Jewel shook her head; her hands on her hips. "I just can't believe the nerve of that guy--to issue a threat like that."

"Ahh, its just hot air. He'll get over it."

21

In October 1993, the Idaho Attorney General's office began its formal investigation into allegations made by former employee of the Natrogenics clinic, Wes O'Dea, based upon information supplied by the Criminal Investigation Unit, Idaho Attorney General's office.

November 1994

Another of Burton's yearly visits to Champaign, Illinois was but days away. Ivanna couldn't wait. For the first time she would lay eyes upon him-the man that had saved her life. She looked forward to matching the deep phone voice with the face. She had heard good things about his visits and lectures.

Burton's deep blue eyes held a mystery. His silvery gray hair glistened beneath the rays of sunlight shining through the open window. When Ivanna first met him she was cautious, but anxious; she wanted to say something, but was not sure what.

He sat staring into the distance, indifferent to Ivanna's presence. How she yearned for an acknowledgment, as she studied his blank expression. He was non-responsive; his blue eyes were fixed somewhere between eternity and never land. She wanted to thank him, but the words hung in her throat. Didn't he know it was he who had breathed life back into her diseased body? She felt slighted, disappointed, as though rescued only to be later rejected. Is it my color that offends him? Ivanna wondered.

Soon Burton was discussing the horrors of dental amalgams and other dental materials with another patient. Well-maybe those amalgams were bad for people. But, the real question was--were those things in her mouth considered amalgams?

She had seen something on 60 Minutes, A CBS Weekly News Magazine's December 1990 airing entitled "Is There Poison in Your Mouth?" a few weeks ago after the airing, but it made no sense to her. She couldn't identify with those people on 60 Minutes. She didn't have multiple sclerosis, arthritis, depression, allergies, or any major illness. Roughly two weeks following that 60 Minutes airing, she received more amalgams. Apparently upset at its airing, an article was placed at the office's sign-in desk in defense of dental amalgams. Unsure about the debate, Ivanna never questioned the dentist when he did her amalgam fillings that day. But Burton had gained her trust; if he said something was wrong with those things, there must be.

Springing up from her chair she approached Dr. Burton. Her short bodice rested on a long pair of legs blanketed by a full skirt that swept the floor as she kneeled down to show him. "I want you to tell me if these things in my mouth are causing me problems." Her mouth opened wide.

He shook his head and chuckled. "Every time you chew, that stuff is…."

Enough said. When her mouth had became the butt of a chuckle by a man she had come to respect and trust, no more words need be spoken.

"It interferes with digestion," he added.

"Things just keep getting better and better," friend Danielle had said after her amalgam removal. Two people she had come to trust had said it. Burton had become Ivanna's EF Hutton; when he spoke, she listened.

The time could not come soon enough. The dentist was booked solid until May the next year. Meanwhile Ivanna suffered from tremendous digestive problems, including gallbladder attacks, illeocecal valve problems, TMJ and colitis. She stammered her speech, was plagued with a bad temper, bad memory, thinning troubled hair, and fluctuating high blood pressure. No longer able to endure the colitis, she called Dr. Burton "I'm not able to hold the product. "It runs right through me," she told Burton

"Have you had your mouth done?"

"I've made an appointment, but I haven't got in yet."

"Carob powder may provide some temporary relief," he said. But the relief she got from the powder was just that, temporary. She couldn't wait to start the removal process.

Although Burton had gained Ivanna's trust, his insistence on the removal of her amalgams just made no sense. As a researcher, she wanted to understand his reasoning. Through research she learned that mercury amalgams contribute to a zinc deficiency, indicated by white fingernail marks: marks she had since she was a child. In recent years the abnormal fatigue, loss of normal sense of taste and smell, poor appetite, low sex drive, disorders of the nervous system, poor circulation, and fainting tendencies she suffered were, she believed, caused by this deficiency.

Because of Dr. Burton's teachings, Ivanna had learned about reflexology, so she understood the connection between reflex areas in the feet and corresponding glands and organs on the body. Further research into the theories of Weston A. Price, DDS, Hal Huggins DDS, MS, George E. Meining DDS, FACD, FICD and others taught her that there is *also* a connection between the teeth and the body's organs. Now she understood why amalgam removal was so important. She also understood why she needed to have a *biological* dentist remove her amalgams; *they* understood the clear connection between the teeth and body health and the proper sequencing for amalgam removal. Not only could *biological* dentists test a patient's health status by examining their teeth, *they* always tested the compatibility of dental materials before placing them in patient's mouths. With this knowledge at hand Ivanna could hardly wait to start the removal process.

Behind the counter, Carrie busied herself typing a nutritional chart for a patient. Just as Anna entered from an adjacent room, a redheaded man appeared. A navy sports jacket stopped within two inches of his crouch; his hands were buried in his pockets.

"May I help you?"

"Yes, I have a 3:00 o'clock appointment," Ben Byrd said.

"I'll need you to complete this application. Please read, sign, and return it. The doctor will not treat you without your signature, okay?"

Ben obliged, and then seated himself in the waiting area.

Soon Jewel appeared. "Why don't you follow me," she said, leading him to a treatment room, and took the chair behind Burton's desk.. "How are you feeling?"

"I've been real tired lately. I wanted to get to the bottom of this."

"Can I have your little left finger?" From his little finger, she smeared five drops onto a glass slide.

Burton entered. Jewel moved to a desk on the right hand side of the room.

"Hello. So, what brings you here?" Burton asked, seating himself at his desk. He mounted the slides of Ben's blood into the monitor. Live cells of various shapes and sizes danced around.

Burton looked at Ben's blank application, then up at Ben. "Is there anything in particular you'd like us to check for?"

"I need to get to the bottom of this situation here--why I'm so tired all the time."

"What did your doctor tell you?"

"A doctor there in Boise wanted to do a battery of tests; I don't have time for that. I took a few, but never bothered going back to the guy."

Burton pointed first to a normal white cell, then to an abnormal one. "These are abnormal. It shows a weakened immune system. That could account for the tiredness." Burton peered once again through the black microscope. "Have you ever had hepatitis B or HIV?"

"What, you mean AIDS?"

"Not necessarily. Having HIV doesn't mean you have AIDS."

"I just don't... I'm not sure what tests that jerk ran."

With the flick of a button a Polaroid replica of Ben's blood, magnified 1000 times was ejected. Burton placed the photo in front of Ben.

Jewel stood up pointing and showing from the wall depiction, what normal versus abnormal blood looked like.

Ben looked at the Polaroid. "Mine resembles that," he said, noting that his resembled the section of blood that Burton and Jewel had noted was abnormal.

"Yes, it's rather large," Jewel admitted.

"That in the center, that white stuff--what's that?"

"It shows some spinal deterioration there, inflammation of the colon, prostate gland irritation and digestive problems," Burton said.

"Humm," Ben said. "Can it be cured?"

"I've had lots of success with this."

Burton looked at the Polaroid of Ben's blood. "Any history of heart condition, heart pain?"

"Yes, well it was a pain when my old lady dumped me. But to be honest with you, that drained my purse more than it did me emotionally. No, not really. I just--my energy is gone. Can't buck and bang beaver the way I once did, you know. Now you, Doc, look like you've got a lot of juice left."

"Well, Dr. Burton has a personal stake in caring for himself--his wife," Jewel said.

"That's right," Burton agreed amidst laughter.

"Standard treatment for your condition is covered in the office visit. Injection therapy is quicker. It lessens the healing process," Burton said.

"Thanks, but no thanks. Needles are not for me."

"Ok. We'll just do the standard. I'd like you to come back in a couple of days. It won't cost you. I can tell if we're on the right track."

"Sounds good--because I don't like throwing away my money."

"Oh, it's not--we'll take care of you. Why don't you follow Jewel? She'll work on you."

Byrd lay on a table in a treatment room as Jewel began reflexology. "Oooh, that's sore," he said, frowning as Jewel massaged the area just below the ankle.

"That's the prostrate area"--Jewel said continuing to work. "Remember how your blood showed that you had an infected prostrate gland? Well, this is helping to relieve some of the tension off of that prostrate."

Anna greeted Byrd back in the reception area.

"Can I bill my visit to Blue Shield?" he asked. Anna turned to Carrie Doyle, the office manager.

"Yes, the visit, but not the supplements."

Subsequent visits found Ben trying to bill his insurance for supplements and services rendered by staff; each time he was denied.

At the close of the business day the latest FDA Hotline newsletter appeared on Burton's desk.

"Warning! The FDA Octopus is Spreading," was a main heading. It claimed that:

One company, whose sin was to tout the benefits of calcium, now finds itself tied up in litigation at least until July, 1995."

FDA's Raiders Keep on Coming, a subheading in the "FDA Hotline" newsletter told of documented cases of suspected abuse.

> "There is an aggressive pattern by the FDA when they pull these raids. In addition to the contraband, they end up seizing computers and manufacturing equipment, virtually forcing a company to shut down." Bionetics was raided by an army of eleven armed FDA agents and Postal Service officials who took all of his products, his processing equipment, computers, and his customer and distributor lists. Bionetics is fighting the FDA and struggling to stay alive."

"Charges are being billed to the insurance company by the Natrogenics clinic," Undercover Agent Ben Byrd told Special Agent Newsome.

"We'll be working in conjunction with the Food and Drug Administration and the State's Attorney General's office to investigate payments received by the clinic as a result of these billed charges," Newsome said.

After reading the article, Burton remembered he needed stamps. He checked his watch-not long before the post office closed. He dashed in and out of the post office only ten minutes before its closing. Pulling up to the curb was a red Ford mustang, a familiar car.

The short cocky Wes O'Dea dashed out of his car throwing his brief case inside, and hurrying inside the post office. Just the sight of Wes and a whole flurry of thoughts came rushing back to Burton. Like the "FDA Hotline" newsletter's statement that, "Bionetics is fighting the FDA and struggling to stay alive." The words Wes had spoken upon leaving the clinic. "You'll be sorry. You'll be raided." Was it just an idle threat? Now he had to wonder…

22

At the Idaho State Attorney General's office in Pocatello, Wes O'Dea met with two investigators, Ron, from the FDA, and Russell of the AG's office:

"I was a paid employee at Natrogenics Clinic. My primary function was in Spinal Touch therapy, stocking shelves, and teaching classes in Spinal Touch therapy."

"We've got to get Daniel out of that office. It's not him we are after," Ron said, thumping his pencil on the desk.

"Listen, there's a local chiropractor here in Pocatello, we'll have him pay Daniel a visit--convince Daniel that Burton's practices are illegal. Maybe that'll light some fire under his butt," Russell said laughing.

Russell's body leaned forward. "Better yet, I'll take this matter before the chiropractic board. Keep us posted, Wes."

In Aberdeen, a nervous Dr. Burton became more cautious than ever. He became paranoid, not knowing whom he could trust, who would be his Judas. With Wes' threat, he wondered just how much he should tell his patients. The constant threat of the FDA, the fear that the long arm of government would destroy what he had worked so hard to build: a health clinic that truly addressed the needs of the people, was too much to bear.

That unrelenting pressure made Burton appear distant, even curt, to his patients at times. Questions raised by the patient were often short circuited with jargon that left the patient distrustful, for they did not know the tremendous pressure facing this man. If he told the patient he could cure them, he was said to be practicing medicine without a license. If he did not tell the patient he could help them, the patient became distrustful, nervous, and frightened. It was after all, for many, their last hope. They wanted some kind of reassurance-and natural medicine was for most a strange and different kind of practice.

The raid conducted on February 1, 1994, on Missouri Research Foundation, a Miami facility, only heightened Burton's fears. The owner wanted to know:

- Why would the FDA, an agency that is sworn to uphold the constitution of the United States and protect the American people, suddenly raid our company and threaten criminal charges.
- How can a government agency be so totally devoid of compassion

for the very citizens they are obligated to serve? Equally, why did the FDA sabotage medical research efforts on GH-3 and Entelev (the forerunner to Cantron and Cancell)?

The editor notes that, "our legislators continue to justify the FDA."

Ivanna's success with Dr. Burton's program had been amazing. Even prior doubters had started to look on her with a kind of admiration. Gone now was the belief that she was totally "wacko." Some started to ask genuine questions about the program; Ivanna delighted in sharing it. Just as Danielle had shared it with her, she felt it her duty to share it with others; it was Danielle's only request.

As a researcher for the State of Illinois, Ivanna had access to statistics on the rising disease rates in the U.S., and particularly in Illinois. She found comparable statistics on disease rates of whites' verses non-whites disturbing. Illinoisans should be made privy to knowledge of this program, she thought, as Illinois was one of the states with a disturbing growth rate of cancer. Illinois' soil depletion of the vital mineral, selenium, fluoride in their drinking water, combined with the dental materials placed in Illinoisans' teeth and the All-American poor diet, placed citizens of Illinois at tremendous risk for getting cancer, Ivanna believed.

In January 1994, warfare was raging over the U.S. health care crisis. First Lady Hillary Rodem Clinton was appointed to solve this dilemma, but designated the newly elected Illinois State Senator, Carol Mosley Braun, to scout the country for ideas.

When the Honorable Carol Mosley Braun visited Springfield, Illinois, in January 1994, Ivanna was on hand to deliver the valuable package, a letter which, she felt, would possibly open up the program to citizens in the state. She wrote:

Honorable Senator Braun:

In March 1992, I was diagnosed with myelodysplasia, the early stages of malignancy, and an ultimately fatal disease. The 1992 "Medical Diagnosis and Treatment" book by Appleton and Lange states that: 'Patients with the disease often develop leukemia if they do not die of their cytapenias first." It states further that, "Allogeneic bone marrow transplantation is the only definitive therapy."

According to the Illinois Health Care Cost Containment Council's Technical Report Series: 91-05 "Organ Transplants at Illinois Hospitals in 1989," the average charges for bone marrow procedures in 1989 were $127,753. My layoff, coupled with the expenses of bone-marrow transplantation, made bone marrow transplantation impractical as a treatment option for me. Fortunately, I was introduced to an alternative treatment that restored my health for less than ten percent of the average charge per discharge for bone marrow transplantation. This treatment is known as Naturopathy. I feel blessed that this option was available to me, especially in light of the fact that I lost my mother, brother and a brother-in-law to the dreaded disease cancer. Each was treated under traditional allopathic medicine. I only wish that all 'Illinoisans' knew of this option.

The Illinois Medical Practice Act of 1987," however, makes it impossible for naturopathic, homeopathic and other health care providers to administer health care in the State of Illinois, since they do not hold medical licenses. This is unfortunate since naturopathic and homeopathic physicians do not treat their patients with traditional allopathic medicine; instead they use natural products, products that work in conjunction with the body's own defenses to heal itself.

The Illinois Medical Practice act of 1987 (60/3) states that: 'No person shall practice medicine, or any of its branches, or treat human ailments without the use of drugs and without operative surgery, without a valid, existing license to do so etc.

The Illinois Medical Practice Act of 1987 (60/49) further states that *Persons without license holding themselves out to the public as being engaged in diagnosis or treatment of ailments of human beings-Penalty,* Section 49 applies. If any person does any of the following and does not possess a valid license issued under this Act, that person shall be sentenced as provided in Section 59.

This impeding Act is keeping many good physicians out of Illinois and many otherwise intelligent beings from making alternative choices concerning the nature of their treatment because they know not that such alternative physicians exist.

This pervasive lack of exposure prompts insurance company executive officers to:

- Disqualify alternative treatment methods, claiming they are experimental and forcing people to pay for them out of their own pockets.
- Pay exorbitant sums of money for illnesses that could under naturopathy be treated far less expensively.

While homeopathy and other alternative treatments are far less expensive than traditional medicines, these treatments often run up into thousands of dollars. This makes it impossible for persons who have no means of paying for the treatments to obtain them, unless their insurance companies (assuming the person has insurance) will pay for the treatment.

The gesture of providing health to all citizens in the (United States) indeed is a noble one. Failure to incorporate the utilization of all kinds of health care providers into the universal package is to deny the kind of competition that would ultimately drive down medical costs.

While managed care offers some palliative relief for the current medical crisis through its encouragement of competition among 'medical doctors,' it fails to incorporate within its mix competition among all kinds of physicians be they allopathic, naturopathic, homeopathic or otherwise.

Some petitions are being circulated by concerned citizens such as myself, -- citizens who want to be able to make choices about the nature of their treatments. Please find enclosed a petition on which some signatures appear. What we as citizens would like is as follows:

- To be able to make choices concerning the kind of physicians administering our care.
- Insurance coverage regardless of our choices of physicians.
- Naturopathic physicians and alternative health care providers added to the proposed health care plan.
- A law or bill introduced to make it possible for alternative health care providers to practice within the State of Illinois for this would represent the truest form of competition in the health care industry.

Please consider the above proposal. It hurts to see so many people lost to illnesses because they are unaware of options available to them. People in Illinois deserve to know.

It was March of 1994 when Ivanna's friend, Cheryl, brought her some disturbing news. After a month's stay at Bayles Hospital, the doctors had found Ms. Helen's problem.

"I'm sorry Ms. Helen, you have pancreatic cancer. You can go home and eat anything you want," the doctor had said.

"Mom was disturbed by this strange paradox. She had been on a special diet and taking insulin injections, three a day, as a diabetic for some fifteen years. How could she all of a sudden eat what she wanted? Something's not adding up. She turned to me for advice. Ivanna, my mom has been diagnosed with pancreatic cancer. Do you think the program you're on could help her?"

"Well, you know, I'm sure she'd get some help, although I don't know how much. Look at how much it helped me."

"But you know you're young; sure it helped you. My mom is old."

"If she hasn't had chemotherapy, radiation therapy, or surgery, actually she stands a good chance at getting tremendous benefit. You know, you can tell her about it. Let her decide."

Ms. Helen's cancer was so advanced the doctors hadn't even offered chemotherapy, radiation, or surgery. They did offer to biopsy the tumor on her neck, which had grown to the size of an egg. Ms. Helen refused.

"What do I have to lose?" Ms. Helen reasoned when she agreed to try the program. Incontinence and tremendous pain were signs that she was clearly in the latest stages of cancer. The pain in her leg was so great that she required frequent massages. Fluid retention had sealed one eye shut. She just hurt all over.

The first days on the program, Ms. Helen felt horrible, as her body was going through a cleansing. After three weeks on the program, she started getting impressive results. Food started to taste like food again. Within a month the unbearable pain had diminished, and in time she was no longer incontinent. Now there was hope.

But Ms. Helen had Medicaid. To keep her card active she had to make occasional visits to her doctor. The doctor proclaimed that her blood sugar level was normal, no more need for insulin shots. Three months on the program, and the tumor had gone away. Almost as miraculously, her eye opened. Cheryl and Ivanna rejoiced together. How ironic, Ivanna thought-what a strange twist of fate. The friend, who had led her to a wonderful and new kind of medical adventure, was now reaping the benefit of the very seed she had planted.

Both Ivanna's beloved mother and brother had gone through standard allopathic traditional medicine for their cancers and had suffered greatly before their deaths. At the time, she sincerely felt that her efforts, if she was ever financially able, would be made providing monies for cancer research. Experience with Burton's program would cause her to redirect her efforts. It was a different kind of fight, to be sure, but she was prepared, now, to see it to the end. Ms. Helen had been given another chance at life.

On June 24, 1994, Marge Newsome phoned Wes O'Dea.

"So, what's the scoop on the Burton case? Has Daniel left Natrogenics?"

"I've been asking some questions. Two people say he is planning to leave, claims his salary sucks."

"Good work, Wes. Keep us posted."

On June 28, 1994, Wes's wife, Angie, was shopping at the "Voyager," the store in the back of the clinic, when she ran into Chelsey Burton. While conversing, Dr. Daniel crossed their paths. Angie's eyes widened and her mouth sprang open. Her head turned gradually, her eyes following Daniel until he disappeared. Is that Dr. Daniel?"

"Yes—why?"

"He still works here? I thought he was gone. Does he still work for your dad?"

Chelsey couldn't understand the look. Why did Angie appear so surprised? What is the big deal if Lou still works for my dad?

"Sure -- why?"

"I heard he was moving."

"Oh no. No, he's still with us. Says he passed the boards in Montana; will move there once his wife has the baby."

Ivanna had gotten her amalgams removed. She couldn't believe the changes! The extreme muscle spasms in her left arm, her mouth cramps disappeared immediately after the first amalgam's were removed. She noted changes in her sleep patterns. She required less sleep to function. The colitis stopped almost as quickly. She no longer stammered her words. Her blood pressure was normal. With the passage of time, she became calmer. No longer was she given to neurotic thoughts, depression, and a bad temper. Amalgam removal meant better vitamin/ mineral absorption that paved the way for the healing that had begun to take place. For Ivanna, the tooth-body connection that she had read about in Dr. Hal Huggin's, DDS *Its All in Your Head*; George E. Meinings's, DDS "*Root Canal Cover Up*", and others was now confirmed.

But amalgam removal, from her once mercury toxic body, also meant extreme sensitivity to foods containing mercury, and to products wrapped, packaged, stored, or containing aluminum or other metals. Consuming any such products would bring unbearable headaches, stomach cramps, hiatal hernia attacks, illeocecal valve problems, and other digestive problems. Hair and household products, facial products, makeup, medications, lotions containing aluminum or other metals had to be avoided as well.

In the lobby of Neutrogenia clinic, behind the counter, Marilyn sat. Just as a female patient approached, the phone rang. Marilyn clasped the receiver against her ear, and signaled to the patient that she would be with her in a moment.

"Hello. Yes, this is Natrogenics."

For a moment there was a pause. Marilyn anchored the phone with her shoulder as she prepared to take down information.

"Natrogenics clinic, this is Marilyn."

"Did you say Marilyn?" A man asked.

"That's right."

"Marilyn I'm--I need some information. I was hoping you could help me. What payment arrangements do you have for your services?"

"You'll need to talk with our manager about that, but she's out until Wednesday. Perhaps if you'll call then she can help you."

"Can-can you, who should I ask for?"

"You know what--I bet Anna can answer your question. Hold on, okay. I'll transfer you."

"Is this Anna?"

"It is; what can I do for you?"

"Anna listen. I- I- I- I'm --I want to get some doctoring done."

"Yes?"

"...But I, I'll need some kind of a payment arrangement. You think that maybe we can work something like that out?"

"Well, we mostly expect payment when we render services, but on occasion we can hold a check."

"I'm not sure what you mean--hold a check?"

"Well it's --I mean, if you want us to wait for a week or two before we cash your check--sometimes we will do that."

"Oh, I see. Well, I'm, I don't have a lot of money, but I am covered by Medicare."

"Uh huh, Medicare doesn't cover Dr. Burton's services. They will cover an adjustment if the patient has an X-ray of their back."

"Which companies will honor your services?"

"That decision is made by the individual company."

"Who submits the claim? Do I have to?"

"You do."

"You telling me, I have to mail it in? I mean, can't you guys do that for me?"

"Blue Cross and Blue Shield are the only insurance we will submit claims to."

"Oh good because that's what I've got-Blue Shield. So you say you'll do the billing. I won't have to, right?"

"That's right. But unless Medicare approves, Blue Shield won't either."

"I don't get it, what is that...?"

"Okay. Let's try it again. Medicare will honor the claim only if you've had a recent back X-ray."

"So far as I know, there is nothing wrong with my back, but..."

"Uh huh well..." Anna said.

"That's... Why would I have to get an X-ray when I don't have back problems?"

"Yes. That's kind of how we feel, but Medicare requires that. Let me talk with our office manager about a payment plan for you. She'll be in Wednesday."

"When can I come in?"

"Sometime next week."

"Will I be able to see Dr--I believe it's Burton?"

"Sure."

"So-Anna, that's your name right?"

"That's right."

"Okay, you've been a big help."

"Glad I could help."

August 1994

Inside Dr. Burton's office, Marvis Russell rejoiced.

"You're looking real good. That digestive track is coming along nicely. Think we'll be able to reduce those injections now to once a month," Burton said.

After identifying herself and informing Winston Earl Whiteside, a licensed Chiropractor in Boise, Idaho, of the reason for her visit, FBI Special Agent Marge B. Newsome began her questioning on allowable practices for Chiropractors in the State of Idaho.

Whiteside told Newsome that blood work was considered one of the acceptable practices of a chiropractor in Idaho. "So too are urinalyses, galvanism, or electrical stimulation, and ear washes."

On August 25, 1994, Carrie Doyle returned from her vacation.

Anna warned, "This one is a rare duck. He is very long winded, and boy is he dumb. He wants to discuss a payment arrangement with you, says he has Medicare and Blue Shield. He says he'll be calling sometime this week, but he didn't leave his name. But I'm sure you'll hear from him--soon."

At approximately 9:50 am, Carrie did hear from him. He made an appointment with Sheri for an August 31 visit to the clinic.

"The name is Porter Lance," the man told Sheri.

23

On August 31, 1994, a disheveled man in his fifties entered Natrogenics clinic. A thick unkempt beard outlined his pear shaped face. Dusting his buttocks was a flannel shirt that flared over his protruding belly. Anna looked up from the counter as he approached. "Hi. What can I do for you?"

"I'm here to see Dr. Burton,"

"Your name?"

"Porter Lance."

"Okay, you'll need to read, complete, and sign the back of this patient evaluation form for me." She pointed in the direction of the waiting room. Why don't you go in there...?"

"You mean in there?"

"Yes, return it when you're done-okay?"

Porter stared at the form for a moment. "Well, can you answer one thing...?"

"What's that?"

"Can I make payment on this visit? I don't have a lot of money, but I do have Blue Shield."

"Blue Shield doesn't cover Dr. Burton's visit. They'll only cover Dr. Daniel's work, since he is licensed under their plan."

"But I've got to see him...Dr. Burton. Can't you help me out here?"

"Well, you can postdate a check, if you wish."

"Don't have any checks and have very little money. How much are we talking here?"

"That depends on whether or not you will be taking the blood test."

"Blood test--what are you talking about?" Porter asked looking confused.

"Are you going to have the blood test?"

"Here?" Porter asked his eyebrows furrowed.

"Yes."

"How would I know what they're gonna do? This is my first time here."

"Tell you what. I'll get you in to the doctor. He'll decide."

"Yes, well, what about my Blue Shield card?"

"But I told you, Blue Shield won't cover Dr. Burton's charges."

"That's right."

"Here, let me make up a file on you. Can you sign the sign-in sheet please?"

"Sure. Listen, I need to use the... You got a bathroom?"

"Just around the corner here," Anna motioned with her hands. Porter excused himself.

Anna was addressing the doctor in his office when Porter came up. "Dr. Burton, Porter would like to talk with you a moment."

"I was wondering if I could pay on this treatment at the end of the week."

"Sure. That will be fine. I'll let the girls know."

Jewel seemed to appear from nowhere. "Hi, I'm Jewel."

"Hi, Jewel, I'm Porter."

"Soon as the office is free, I'll get you in." She led Porter into Burton's office.

"So, how'd you hear about us?" Burton asked.

"A buddy in Twin Falls," Porter said, intermittently coughing and clearing his throat.

"My, you've got a nasty cough. We need to take a look at that-- sounds pretty bad, like chronic fatigue syndrome."

"What's chronic fatigue syndrome?"

"Well it's. . . don't be alarmed. I'm just looking at your symptoms. I'll need to draw a little blood to tell. It'll show up here on the screen. You'll get to see what's going on with that terrible cough. If it's mono, it can lead to chronic fatigue syndrome. With the cough, there is often a recurring sore throat."

"Well, can you help me?"

In walked Burton's wife, Jane. "Let's get his blood, will you?" Burton said, passing Jane the lancet.

"Oh no--not a needle," Porter said, squirming at the sight of the lancet.

"It'll be just a little stick. Got to stick your little finger. "We both can look at it on the screen. It'll tell me what treatment you need. How old are you?"

"Fifty-five--getting old."

"Not older, just wiser," Burton teased.

Jane added her own special brand of humor. "Just mellowing out a bit, huh?"

"Are you gonna prick my finger?"

"I'm the one."

"I see. Sure hope this doesn't hurt."

"Nah! Little finger please."

"Little--yes, okay," Porter repeated.

"We go after the little guys."

Porter thrust out his little finger and turned his head. "Okay, just hold steady," Jane said, squeezing his little finger in preparation for the quick prick. "There we're done. Just let it sit for a minute. Going to smear it onto a slide."

"O-o-o-h--blood!" Porter said, looking at the beaded blood on his finger.

"There better be."

"Oh, I must be in bad shape."

Jane pressed Porter's finger, gently placing four smudges of the blood onto two slides, and handed Porter a cotton ball. Porter pressed it against his little finger, intermittently checking to see if the bleeding had stopped.

"Why did you make four little spots?"

"It'll show various stages."

Porter coughed once again, and lifted the cotton ball from his little finger. "What should I do with this?"

Jane looked at his little finger. "It's still bleeding?"

"Well, yes."

"Told you I go after the little guys--boy did I get it that time," Jane teased.

"Yes, you got me. But it didn't hurt."

"Nah, it kind of looks scary, but most patients are amazed at how painless it is."

"Hey, I'm a tough guy."

Burton placed one of Porter's slides inside the slide holder. "Okay, let's take a look." He pointed to the monitor.

Porter leaned forward looking at the funny looking shapes as they danced around on the screen. "Why is my blood dancing around like that?"

"It's called live blood. It'll tell us the condition of your blood cells."

"Oh!"

"The other slide has to dry. We'll look at it later."

Burton pointed to the red cells, distinguishing them from the white.

"How do you know them apart. ...Oh--the red cells are darker."

"That's right. For every seven hundred red blood cells, you should have one of these. Also, you have your blood fats. This is a live white-blood cell," Burton said, pointing.

Porter's hands motioned toward his ears. "Didn't hear you Doc--want to repeat that. I'm awful hard of hearing."

"This one is live and... Well, we know that this one is dead. This is common with EBV. See that there?"

Porter looked on...EBV? What's that?"

"It's chronic fatigue syndrome, just what I thought."

"Aw I don't get it Doc; what you looking at?"

"That there. We can't see the virus, only its effects.

"This one's large, too."

"Way too big. You see that one dancing across the screen. It's alive. You can see it moving."

"Yes, it's moving," Porter said coughing.

"What do you do for a living?"

"I'm a truck driver."

"The fumes could cause the toxic buildup."

Burton pointed to a black squiggle on the screen that was moving quite rapidly. "See that thing there?"

Porter moved closer to the screen, his eyes squinting. "It's a little hard for me to tell. Where is it again?"

"Right there..."

"Oh yes, you said something about parasites?"

"Yes--worms."

"How common is that?"

"It's quite common. Burton placed the other slide into the microscope. This is a crystallization test. It'll develop in a minute. A normal one is shown on the wall in the left hand corner." Burton pulled the undeveloped Polaroid from the slide holder and laid it aside.

"Is this a picture of my blood?"

"Uh huh."

Burton picked up a small wooden slab, smeared a drop of Porter's blood on it and examined it. "No problem with your blood sugar--it's good. Now, let's take a look at the photo. If you look here, these red cells have been destroyed-possibly by a parasite. He pointed to another grouping on the photo. None of these are good."

"Wow, Doc-Wow! Now you've got me confused."

Burton pointed to the grouping once again. "These here."

Porter frowned and pointed to a blotch on the picture. "This blotch is white blood cells"

"They're in pretty bad shape--probably destroyed by the virus."

"What virus?

"This is that EBV virus I mentioned before -- you know the Chronic Fatigue Syndrome. There's a clear problem here."

"Now I'm worried. What problem?"

"This area shows an inflamed prostrate gland; it's infected."

"You are saying my prostate..."

"Uh huh--but it's not cancer."

"Whew, you had me..."

"I see a bit of heart stress here; it could be coming from that nasty cough. That shows stress on the adrenal glands."

"Oh, okay."

Burton pulled out a chart and began writing on it. "We'll have the girls type this so they know what to do nutritionally."

"All right. So, we'll have to kill both the parasites and the virus. Also need to clear up that prostrate gland."

"But how?"

"It'll be done nutritionally."

"You mentioned inflammation of my prostate, that's frightening. Does that mean that it's...?"

"It's common for middle aged men."

"Really?"

"Quite. I mean, it would have shocked me if I hadn't found it."

"But does that mean it's almost...? I mean I'm--I always hear so much about prostrate cancer."

"Well, inflammation comes before cancer."

"Are you saying my condition is pre-cancerous?"

"We can take care of it."

"Can you cure me?"

"The only thing I can cure is ham. Have any trouble urinating or waking up to...?"

"Sometimes, but not all the time. But when you say cancer I just...I panic."

A sharp and cautious Jane interjected. "He never said cancer; you did!"

"But isn't pre...?"

"No!" Jane countered with forced laughter.

"Well, pre-cancerous, isn't that..."

"That's all it is; not cancer. If people catch it early they wouldn't have a problem. So what brought you in?"

"Low energy mostly and these coughs. I hope you can get me back on track."

"Well, we'll try and kill the virus with our sound frequency machine. Hopefully it will destroy the virus. Then Jewel will do some reflexology on you. Ever been adjusted by a chiropractor?"

"No, I haven't."

Jewel poked her head inside Burton's office. "Why don't you go with Jewel--she'll take good care of you," Jane said.

"Have a chair. Take off your boots and socks for me," Jewel instructed.

"So what's this you are going to do?"

"First I'm going to have you soak your feet in water, and I'm going to attach it to this machine. You'll feel a little electrical stimulation."

"So, how's that going to help me?"

"It'll destroy the parasites and break up any body inflammation lessening the effects of any disease."

"Should I go ahead and stick my feet in?"

"Go ahead now... Let's put one foot in this pan, and the other in this one okay. "I'll take it easy, okay. Let me know when you feel it."

"What's it supposed to feel like?"

"First, a little tingle."

"Yes, I feel it. It's a slight tingling."

"Should I turn it down?"

"Nah, it's okay. The higher you go, the worse it gets or what?"

"No, when it's turned up, it just increases the intensity of the frequency, but it won't execute you, I promise. It treats your body, not your feet."

"What do you call this machine?"

"It's an FG three machine. Ever had a reflexology treatment?"

"You mean what you're doing now?"

"No. We use our hands to massage your feet."

"Will I be getting that too?"

"Yeah you sure will, when you're done with the FG machine. My hands can work wonders. Usually I can tell what problems you have because of your reaction when I work on certain areas. Your feet have nerves for each of your organs."

"I didn't know that."

"It's true. Our feet can tell us a lot."

"The tingle has almost stopped."

"Would you like me to turn up the volume a bit more?"

"Yes."

A polished Dr. Daniel, the office chiropractor, walked into the room, his masculinity encased in a six foot three inch frame. "Are you ready for him? Take it easy on him; he's afraid of being electrocuted. I've got another patient to attend," Jewel said leaving the room.

"I'm kind of nervous about being shocked. The tingling is okay, but…,"

"Okay. So I'll slowly turn that knob to the right. Tell me when you feel it."

"Are you sure I won't be shocked or something?"

"Definitely not. Just sit and relax."

"This doesn't feel too bad; actually it feels pretty good."

"It's very relaxing. A researcher named Rife learned that different frequencies of electricity can kill a virus."

"How can you tell if the treatment helped me? Do you take another blood test?"

"Exactly. Normally we recommend retest in two months. But, you can call for a retest if you're having problems."

"Well, yes, I want to know if my prostate improved. He mentioned that it was inflamed, and I'm scared especially being my age."

"Why don't we increase that frequency?"

"Yes, now it's tingling."

"Oh good. Burton's going to have one of the girls type up your nutritional program," said Daniel.

"Oh okay. How come I don't feel the tingle anymore?"

"Your body is now in the accommodation mode. So I'll turn it up again."

Jewel popped back in. "Pardon me, but here's your nutritional program. The numbers on the bottle tell what formula it is. The doctor wants you to take these just like it's written here."

"Where can I get these?"

"We have them. Stay away from all the things that are underlined. Any items that are circled, you can use in moderation. Those not underlined or circled, you can eat as much as you like, okay," Jewel explained.

"Am I going to…I mean what if I'm short of cash to buy all these? Can I order the others through the mail?"

"You'll need to talk with our office manager about that"

"But I also have insurance with Blue Cross/Blue Shield."

"Okay, they won't pay for anything Dr. Burton does. His program is for research only, so the insurance companies won't cover it. They will pay for my treatments since I'm a licensed chiropractor and Blue Cross/Blue Shield provider."

"Are you saying that this treatment is considered chiropractic?"

"Since I'm doing the work, I can bill Blue Cross/Blue Shield."

"Oh, I see."

"The doctor will probably have me give you an adjustment. That, too, can be billed," Daniel added.

"An adjustment for what? There's nothing wrong with my back."

Daniel pointed to a wall replica of the spine. "All your nerves are in this area, that's why we have to adjust you."

Porter had a strange look on his face. "What is that?"

"That's the spine."

"You mean a human spine?"

"Sure is," Daniel said pointing to the area on the spine depicting the third, fourth, and fifth lumbar.

"Okay, now look at this area. If the space here is decreased, a bone is misplaced and will create inflammation, putting pressure on the nervous system; that impacts all the other bodily functions."

"So as a chiropractor, you can adjust me, right?"

"Exactly. After adjusting the area, the prostrate gland can heal a lot faster."

"Is the FG machine something chiropractors usually use or…?"

"Some of them do, but not that many; others use the Tens unit."

"What kind of machine is this?"

"It's a Rife machine."

"Who made it?"

"Doctor Lynch, a naturopath over in Twin Falls."

"Really? Is he still over there?"

"No. He was a little bit too successful. The FDA and FBI came in and shut him down."

"You're kidding!"

"I wish."

"Why did they close him down?"

"He made claims of curing his patients with this machine. That's forbidden--something the FDA won't allow."

"The FDA?"

"The Food and Drug Administration."

"I see."

"Oh they're very powerful, more so than any law enforcement agency in this country."

"Is that right?"

"They're pretty powerful."

"Well, what is he doing now?"

"Well, they fined him and forbade him to practice, so he does research. He's on probation, not even allowed to leave the country without permission from his parole officer."

"You don't say."

"It's frightening and very disgusting because all he did was help people. Yet, he is being treated like a criminal. Lots of his old patients are ours. They still talk about him. Dr. Lynch was quite a guy."

"Was he a young guy or older guy?"

"I would say he was about Dr. Burton's age--middle aged. Won't you come with me?" Daniel motioned with his hands as he led Porter to another room. "Why don't you lie on your back for me?"

"You mean on the table?"

"Yes."

"I feel something vibrating midway my back, first it goes up then down again."

"It's the rollers."

"I couldn't put my finger on it, but yes 'rollers' that's what they feel like."

"They help calm your nerves."

"So what kind of treatment is this?"

"It's just a massage, just done by a machine, just relax. Jewel will be in soon to do your feet."

"Alright, I appreciate your help, Doctor."

"Take care," Daniel disappeared.

Minutes later Jewel returned. "Okay Porter, let's do some reflexology on you. This will make you sleep real good tonight."

"Good. I could use some sleep."

"If I'm too harsh let me know."

"Oh, no this is good. You're on my toes."

"Yes-- your sinus area."

"What are you talking about, my sinuses? Oh! You mean my sinuses? Okay."

"Uh huh," she moved her fingers up to the ball of his toes, this is your head."

"Oh, okay--my head."

"These are your ears," Jewel said, as she pressed on the area at the base of his middle toes.

Jewel slid her hand over the 'eyes of his foot.'

"And where are you now?"
"These are your eyes."
"Okay," Porter said, closing his eyes. Yes, I can feel that. It's a little tender."
"That's because of your glasses."
"Toxic buildup because of my glasses?--oh, okay."
"Right," Jewel said.
"You mean my eyes have nerves that run down to my feet?"
"Actually, they're pressure points."
"Are you going to do both feet?"
"Uh huh."
"What's that you on now?"
"I'm on your colon now."
"That's in my foot?"
"Mm-hm."
"Well, I'll be. I notice you're on my heel...," Porter said.
"This is your sciatic nerve; it runs from your buttocks and then down the back of your leg."
"Is that what you're working on now?"
"Mm-hm."
"Is everything the same on the right foot?"
"Much of it is, but your heart and spleen are on your left foot; your digestive track is on your right foot."
"Okay."
Jewel began rubbing the back of the ankle leading into the heel of the foot. "Okay now I'm in your prostate area, so this might be a bit tender."
"Yes, that's really tender. I'm not sure why."
"Did the doctor say you have a problem in that area?"
"He said something about it... said it was enlarged, that's it."
"That's why it's so tender. Yes, that's your prostate. It's common in men."
"I heard that men my age have problems."
"Even some young guys do."
"Young guys--with prostate problems?"
"Sure do. Lots of them are on blood pressure drugs—they can screw up the prostate."
"That's scary, you know? You're back on it again."
"Getting the congestion out. Your feet are tattle tales. They tell it all. I can feel the toxic buildup."
"You say this is reflex action?"
"Reflexology."
Jewel moved her thumb back over the eye reflex on Porter's foot.
"These are the eyes; it's really tender," Porter said.
"Uh huh."

"Cause I wear glasses."

"Well, see when your eyesight starts to fail, toxins build up in that area, so there will be pressure in your eyes.

Jewel began working on the prostrate gland pressure points in the other foot.

"Oh boy does that hurt!"

"Do you have any trouble urinating?"

"I sure do."

"When the prostate is enlarged, it cuts off the urinary track. That's why you have trouble urinating. Jewel pressed on other surrounding areas.

"Ow! That really..."

"He'll give you something for it, because he saw a problem there."

You're on the top of my foot, right?"

"This is your chest and lungs."

"That's my chest and lungs--on top of my right foot?"

"Mm-hm."

"Feels good."

Jewel began slapping Porter's foot to loosen up the toxins. "You have to go to school for weeks before you can become a certified reflexologist."

"No kidding?"

"Mm-hm. So, have you been adjusted or...?" Jewel asked.

Porter broke in... "What do you mean, adjusted?"

"Did Dr. Daniel adjust you?"

"No, not unless, is this... Am I getting an adjustment now or...?"

"Right now, you're only lying down."

"Do I just lay here, or what?"

"Mm-hm. Just lie back and relax. Going to let Dr. Daniel check to see if you're all lined up."

"Okay--I appreciate your help." Jewel left just as Daniel entered the room. "Are you going to adjust me now, Doctor?"

"Yes, I am. I'll adjust the lower back so that energy can be released to the prostate allowing it to heal itself."

"I see. So that's why I need this adjustment?"

"You've got it. Now can you slip off your glasses and lie on your stomach for me?"

"You mean right here on this table?"

"Right here."

Porter turned, preparing to lie on his stomach.

"Put your head in the hole here. Let your arms rest on the arm rests."

Daniel adjusted Porter's 3rd, 4th, and 5th lumbar. "Before the adjustment your right leg was longer than your left. Now both legs are the same length."

"My legs were different lengths?"

"Yes, your left leg was shorter."

"Wow!"

"I'll need you to hold out your leg for me; don't let me push it down," Daniel attempted to push Porter's leg down. "It's strong as an ox. Okay, now let's do the other. Hold it." Porter's leg didn't budge. "Very good. You're all done. That wasn't so bad was it?"

"No, it wasn't."

"Now your blood can flow freely throughout your body, especially your nervous system and lower back area."

"Should I go to the reception area now, Doctor?"

"Sure."

"Well I'm… what's I'm supposed to do with this?" he asked Anna who was at the reception counter.

"Well, these are the things Dr. Burton suggests you take to get better."

"You mean these here?"

"Uh huh, all of these. Would you like me to tell you what they cost?"

"Well, what do I have to pay for now? I want to get all these, but I'm short on cash. If I can just get the main ones now, can you ship me the rest if I mailed you a money order?"

"Uh huh, that'll probably be best, because we can't charge it."

"Okay. Now I've got Medicare and a Blue Shield card."

"I'll need a copy of it. The only thing I can send to Blue Shield is your adjustment and the electrical treatment. Alright. Now Blue Shield will only pay for Daniel's work—the chiropractic adjustment, and your electrical stimulation treatment. The blood test was sixty dollars, so I can't turn that in since Dr. Burton did that. He cannot turn in anything under his name."

"What about the other?"

"They won't cover any of your supplements."

"So what is all this going to cost me?"

"Your treatment alone was eighty-five dollars. That includes the sixty dollars for the blood test and twenty-five for the office call."

"Alright, can you folks bill me for eighty-five dollars, so I can get some of these pills? I can pay for some of 'em."

"Okay, let me talk with Jane about this. She's the boss, so…"

"Well, I'm going to give you some money, and I've got my Blue Shield card. But I want to use the money to get some of these pills, if you can… Help me out here… Can you tell me the ones that I need to get started on the most?"

"Mm-hm." Anna summoned Jane's help. "Jane, can you…"

"…I want to get to feeling better."

"Jane, Porter wants us to bill him for the services so he can get some of the pills."

"I've got this insurance, and she said it would…"

Anna interrupted. "It'll cover only twenty-five dollars."

"But it won't cover...," Porter added.
"No, they will not cover the sixty dollars for the blood work," Jane said.
"Well, can you send me a bill?"
"We can take a check."
"Don't have any. I just got this money on me."
"Well, just pay for the pills with your money."
"But see, I really want to get better. I want to buy what pills I can today, and order more when I get home. I can send you a money order for the balance."
"We can only ship the pills to you C.O.D.," Jane said.
"I need to know the most important pills to get started on, if you can tell me that."
"Alright let's see," Jane said, looking at Porter's chart.
"Go ahead and charge him for the services, and he can pay cash for the pills he gets," Jane told Anna.
"But I need to know which are the most important pills for me to start taking. Cause he said I had prostate problems."
"Well, let's see... he want's you to take the parasite formula--it'll kill the worms, and the number thirty-two, that helps with the prostate. You'll want to get started on the number 40... that'll kill the EBV," Jane said.
"What is EBV?"
"Epstein Barr or whatever."
Porter looked confused, "Epstein Barr?"
"The virus, okay?" Jane said, annoyance evident in her tone.
Porter began thumbing through the papers. "That's not what he told me, and it's not on these papers ...."
Jane joined Porter in thumbing through the papers. "Okay, it's not listed here. This is our natural antibiotic."
"Well, will you put that on here?" Jane paused for a moment, disgusted.
Anna interjected. "I can do that for you."
"Suppose you can write it down here," Porter said, pointing to the paper.
"That's yeast infection," Jane said.
"Yeast, okay."
"He wants you to take Cal Mag # 2, okay?" Anna said.
"What's this # 4?"
"That's Vitamin E. Number eleven is an energy drink. Seventeen are enzymes, and # 28 is like barley green. It purifies the blood. This # 32 is a male hormone. You'll definitely want to take that one. The # 41 is for parasites—parasites are what set things off," Jane asserted.
"Okay."
"You'll only need one bottle of it—it lasts thirty days.
"Will you put that down here? How to take it."
"That's right on here," Jane pointed to the directions on the bottle.

Anna joined in. "Everything's right here—how to take it. The # 42 is catalase, # 48 is for energy, and # 49 is for infection."

"This is a lot of stuff. Which ones should I start on right away?"

Jane's fingers scanned the page. "Well, let's see…"

"Okay, I'll put a check by the ones you want to start on."

"Alright, if I gave you fifty dollars cash, what could I get?"

"Not much."

"What about # 32?"

"That's sixteen." She looked at some of the other pills she felt were necessary for Porter and totaled them. "Okay, we're looking at a hundred dollars already."

"Can you let me have them on credit? What about me paying the office call? My insurance…."

"If you've met your deductible," Anna said.

"Yes. I've met my deductible."

"So what you're saying is that you have only fifty dollars?" Jane asked.

"Well, I have more, but I'm trying to hold on to some cash. I don't want to break myself."

"Let's see, so if you got the thirty three…."

"Don't you folks extend credit—I mean I'm going to give you a fifty dollar bill."

Jane interrupted. "… Okay, this is something we had to stop doing. It's gotten us into financial problems in the past, so we just—we just had to stop it."

"Well, what can—what do you recommend?"

"I mean, if we extended you credit, then we'd have to do it for everyone else. I feel really bad that I've got to say 'no' when you really need the pills and all, but…."

"What if… How about sixty dollars. Would that work?"

"Okay," Jane said.

"What could I get for sixty dollars?"

"Okay, those with the check—I'll give you those."

"Well, what all am I going to get?"

"Well, let's see."

"You're going to get five of them."

"How much is that going to be? Can you tell me that? … and tell me what the balance is so I can pay it when I get home."

Jane placed her hands on the gathered bottles of products and turned to address Anna. "Go ahead, let him have these."

"Okay, now I'm going to give you sixty dollars."

"Why don't I give you a price list?" Anna said.

"… And a receipt showing what I got and owe for, and everything I have to get."

"Okay, I'm going to give you ten percent off, but normally we give it only on cash purchases. It should help a bit...," Jane added.

"Okay."

"Let me tell you what it'll cost you to get the others," Anna said.

"I want to know what I paid and what I got to get. Then, what's it going to cost for the other."

"Okay, so if you give me sixty dollars, you'll still owe 118.79," Jane said.

"Alright"

"Now that's only for the pills," Anna added.

"Well, will you put that down here, because now I'm really confused?"

"It's all here: Your vitamins, services, the total of which comes to $118.79," Jane said.

"The charge to Blue shield is separate. Twenty-five dollars will be billed to Blue Shield," Anna said.

"Okay, so that's what I need to know. Then my bill is $118.79 minus $25.00 dollars since I've met my deductible. Will you guys send it to my insurance?"

"Yes. Carrie, our office manager, will send it to Blue Shield."

"So can I order the pills next week?"

"Sure," Anna said.

"Can I have them sent to me C.O.D.?"

"You want it sent to your P.O. Box?"

"No, I won't be in...I may be in California."

"Just give us an address. I'm underscoring the vitamins you are taking, okay. I'll make a copy. Then when you call, I'll have a record of what was sent so I'll know what to send."

"When you call ask for Anna," Jane said.

"Okay, so Anna will you put your name on here for me because I may forget. So should I ask for A-N-N-I; is that how I say it?"

"No, it's Anna."

Porter jotted her name down.

"Are you all set now?"

"Just one question: Blue Shield will pay $25 dollars of that $118.79 right?"

"Only if you have satisfied your deductible."

"Okay, that's all I want to know."

"So if I place my order..."

"...You will get them automatically," Jane said.

"What if I'm not any better—what then?"

"He'll want to see you."

"No problem. I camp out anyway."

"Good."

"Okay, so I'm done, right?"

"You're all done."

"Thanks, Anna. See you."

In late September, Special Agent Marge Newsome collaborated with Porter Lance, listening as he phoned Natrogenic's clinic.

"Yes, the August 31 service claim was sent to the insurance mid September," Jewel said.

"Is Dr. Burton in?"

"Sure. Let me get him for you."

"Ah—Dr Burton--this is Porter Lance-doubt that you remember me, but...."

"You bet I remember you. Why wouldn't I?"

"You have so many patients and all...."

"Yes, but it's the good ones that I remember most."

Porter laughed. "You said I have a couple of things that I needed to work on, but these pills you gave me I've been taking, they ain't did nothing for me."

"Do you have Epstein Bar virus--chronic fatigue syndrome?"

"I think that's what you said. You also said something about my heart, parasites, and an enlarged..."

"...Prostate," Burton filled in the blank.

"Prostate, that's right. Okay, well I followed all the directions and everything. These pills ain't doing the job."

"Yes, that's a real tough virus. I get best results using injection therapy."

"But I thought these pills were supposed to..."

"Uh huh, well...We'll need to do injection therapy."

"I see."

"I've had a lot of success treating this virus. You may need to slow down a bit, to give your body a little time to heal—maybe just hang out here about five days or so."

"Alright, so when can I come?"

"Well, I'll be able to work around your schedule."

"Okay, thanks Dr. Burton."

"You bet."

In October, the FBI received a statement from Natrogenics clinic showing a $90.79 balance outstanding on charges incurred for Porter Lance's August 31, 1994 visit. It also received, a statement from the Blue Shield of Idaho showing reimbursement of $25.00 of the $35.00 charges Porter Lance had incurred during his visit. Both were entered as evidence into the files of the FBI for the prosecution.

Special Agent Marge Newsome phoned Wes O'Dea, the cooperating witness. "Have you gotten any more info on Daniel's plan to leave the clinic?"

"I talked with Daniel's wife yesterday. She claims they are going to be leaving for Montana in a couple of weeks since the baby has been born."

"Does Burton use Laetrile in his practice?"
"I swear to it. I handled it myself."
"Where is it kept?"
"Some is kept in his office, but most of it is kept at his home."
"Who's the supplier?"
"I believe it comes from the Radcliff Institute in Mexico."
"...What about the FG3 machine, the one that supplies electrical frequencies to the body--where did it come from?"
"From a Ben Lynch."
The next day, 1994 Porter Lance set up a 4-day series of appointments, his first for November 7th.

24

On November 7, 1994, Porter Lance returned to Natrogenics clinic for the first in his series of appointments.

Anna looked up. "How are you doing?"

Jewel joined in. "How have you been since the visit?"

"Well, I ain't no better.... Dr. Burton told me to come in. I remember your face, but not your name."

"Anna."

"Doctor will see you in a minute," Jewel said.

"Okay, so Jewel, what are you going to do to me today?"

"Well I'm not the doctor... Chronic fatigue is a very stubborn virus. You got to stay on it to beat it."

"That's why I'm here. I want to beat this thing. I'm scheduled for today, tomorrow, Wednesday, and Thursday."

"Come on back." Jewel said motioning with her hands.

Porter followed Jewel into Burton's office.

"Hi Porter, how are you doing?"

"Well, not so good."

"Been working hard, or hardly working?" Burton teased.

"I'd say a little of both."

"Working is good—it keeps you out of trouble. Just sit down and relax. Now tell me what's been going on?"

"Well, I just don't feel good."

Burton looked briefly at Porter's chart. "Looks like you've got chronic fatigue syndrome. Still tired like before?"

"Yes, I'm still tired."

"Have any trouble staying awake when driving?"

"... Then I'll be all right for a minute but still tired."

"How's your throat?"

"About the same; I still have the cough."

"Sounds like the virus is still there. Okay, let's get another blood test; see what we've got here. That virus is a tough nut to crack. Why don't we get some IV's together. I want to give Porter an IV and some oxygen." Burton told Jewel.

"Wait a minute, you're going to do what?"

"Well, it's what I call injection therapy."

"You plan on needling me, Doc?"

"Well, only if you want to ...It's our best attack against the virus. But it's entirely up to you..."

"What about some other kind of pills? I'd rather do..."

"Well, I've got this new machine. I can't make any promises, but we can try that... . I'm told it can kill the virus."

"Should I come everyday for treatment or...?"

"Yes."

"Well, I'm coming tomorrow, Wednesday, Thursday, but Friday afternoon I'm leaving for Reno."

"Okay, so we'll work on you up to Friday."

Jewel pricked Porter's little finger for some blood, smeared it onto a slide, and placed it on a nearby stand. Burton placed the slide into the microscope.

Porter's blood projection appeared on the screen.

Burton was deeply engrossed with the live blood analysis. "That one is alive," he said.

"Let's use that new machine on you--see if it'll get rid of that virus."

"Okay."

"We're going to do it everyday, so..."

"You say my blood sugar is okay? So is that my blood I see moving right there?" Porter asked over a brisk coughing spell.

Burton was still focused on the live cells on the screen, however. "How is your digestion, as far as gas and that?"

"I have gas sometimes."

"These are your white cells, those are your red ones," Burton said, focusing once again on the monitor.

"Say that again—oh I see, the large one is the white cell right?" Porter said over a brisk coughing spell.

"That's right. It's barely alive; this is common with the Epstein Bar virus victims."

"What is Epstein Bar--a virus?"

Dr. Burton interjected, "Its chronic fatigue syndrome."

"Oh, okay."

"...Caused by the Epstein Bar virus," Burton continued. He pointed to other problematic areas of the blood. Those little dancing shapes there--they are blood fats." He pointed to yet another area. "This tells me you have digestion problems."

"You telling me my digestion is screwed up?"

"Okay, now look at this one. Did you see that move, that in the middle?"

"Yes, so..."

"Looks like bacteria." Burton pointed again. "When you see these dead white cells, that means those cells have been attacked by the virus. Okay, here's a good one," Burton said.

"How do you know it's a good one?"

"Well it—if you notice, it'll light up. That means it's still alive. But look at how dark the other one is; those cells are your immune system."

"I don't get it, doctor. You said something about my white cells…."

"They are your defense against disease. When your defense doesn't work properly you can't fight the virus. The virus is killing them, and you feel the effects of it. It's called chronic fatigue."

"Is that the reason I'm so drained?"

"Yes, that's why. Your white cells also help the Central Nervous System."

"They do all that?"

"Yep."

"I stay so tired. Am I going to get A.I.D.S?"

"Well, left untreated it can lead to HIV."

"You mean A.I.D.S.?"

"Well, someone can have the HIV virus and not have A.I.D.S."

"What am I going to do, doctor? I don't want HIV."

"Lots of my EBV patients are other doctors. They come because tranquilizers and antibiotics are all they have to offer. That'll settle you a bit, but not for long."

"Can you help me?"

"I've been very successful at treating this."

"But how? What are you going to do?"

"First, we'll try the new machine on you, but if that doesn't do it, we'll need to use injection therapy."

"These pills you gave me, I've been taking them."

"Well, this virus is tough, not easy to get rid of it. I've had good success with the IV's. Going to put you on that new machine. Make sure to drink lots of water; otherwise, you'll get a headache. This machine can break up the virus without damaging the cells. You'll feel just a slight twinge."

"Oh, it's that electrical sound frequency machine, I remember. Jewel used it last time."

"No, this one is different. This machine can break up crystals using various frequencies. It is similar to the FG3. Why don't you go with Jewel so she can get you started."

"Thanks, doctor."

Jewel led Porter to an examination room with lots of naturopathic paraphernalia.

"You've got a lot of stuff in this room."

"Just stretch out here on the table for me, and let's get rid of those boots, okay?"

"You want me on my back?"

"Uh huh."

Porter lay on his back and got a terrible cough.

"After his treatment, Porter joined some other patients at the counter.

"I'm supposed to see you here--is it Anna?"

"No, Sheri," she said, and then gestured toward Carrie who was standing next to her.

Porter's confusion was evident in his expression, so Carrie explained. "No, I'm Carrie."

"So it's Carrie and Anna, right?"

"No, it's Sheri."

"Oh I see, you're Sheri." Sheri stood laughing at the confusion that she had caused Porter.

Carrie tried to explain, "You saw Anna before you got treated. That's the lady you paid."

"And your name again?"

"I'm Carrie."

"Oh boy, I'm really confused," Porter said.

Carrie, like Sheri, stood laughing capitalizing on Porter's confusion.

She thumbed through the pile of folders that had stacked up on the counter. "Okay, here is your blood work."

"Okay, now I have my Blue Shield card."

"I'll take care of it," Carrie said, handing Porter a copy of his nutritional chart. "This is what Dr. Burton wants you to take."

"I'll be here until Thursday. Should I wait to get the pills then, too? See, last time she sent me the bill."

"Oh, well...."

"I think Anna-- and I think it was Jane--agreed to just bill me for the charges. Since my cash was low, I bought only some of the pills and they sent the charges to Blue Shield. They billed me for the rest. I paid the balance today," Porter said.

"Yes, that's right here."

"If we could do that again, that would be great. I think I can pay you some more before I leave on Thursday, but I got to keep some cash on me to eat with. But I want to get some more pills."

"Okay, I'll allow you to charge the week of service, but I'll need at least half. But you can't charge the vitamins."

"So I can't have the pills on credit?"

"We don't do that anymore."

"Can't you just bill Blue Shield for some of the pills then let me pay the rest?"

"It tells you on the contract that your payment is due when services are rendered."

"Yes, I know it does. I'm going to see if I can; it's Carrie right?"

"Uh huh, I'm Carrie. Are you scheduled to come in the rest of the week?"

"Yes, but I need to know times for the other days."

"Okay, now, these are all of your appointments."

Porter looked over it and noted the times. "Okay, looks like I'm all set. These match with what I had written down when I called earlier."

"Okay, we'll see you tomorrow morning at ten."

"Thanks."

Special Agent, Marge Newsome conducted her own investigation. Knowing the products that Burton sold was necessary to help the government build its case against him; she phoned Wes.

"Hi Wes, Marge Newsome here. Are you familiar with a product called, 'black pearl?'"

"Yes, it's an herb from China; it resembles a little black marble."

"How is it labeled?"

"It carries the label H-21, but the herb does not appear to be a Natrogenics formula."

"Are you aware of any drugs or narcotics used in the product--anything that might be considered illegal in the United States?"

"No."

"Who are the suppliers?"

"There's a Gem Manufacturing. Luther Bain is the contact person."

"Does Burton use any injections in his practice?"

"I'm aware of two. One is a vitamin mixture; the other is used for cancer patients."

"Okay thanks, Wes--appreciate it."

"Yes!" Marge thought, clutching her hand into a fist. According to naturopaths who were interviewed, injection therapy was not an acceptable practice for naturopaths in the State of Idaho, so a case could be built around Burton's use of the injections. If they could prove that Burton used drugs in his product that alone would be the catalyst they needed to shut him down, but how? Even Wes had said that he wasn't aware of any narcotics used in the products.

Anna was in a phone conversation when Porter Lance arrived at Natrogenics for the second in his series of appointments. It was 10:00. Just as she looked up, Porter was standing before her.

"Hi Anna."

"Porter--how's it going?"

"Uh, I believe my appointment is at 10:00?"

"Let me check for you," she said, and then disappeared returning with Lou Daniel.

"Uh—hi doctor."

"How are you? Why don't you come on back?" Daniel beckoned.

Suddenly a young man appeared before them in the examination room.

"Derrick, come on in. Porter, this is Derrick. He's preparing to go to chiropractic school, and would like to do some observation. Do you mind if he sticks around?"

"Should I leave?" Porter asked.

"No, you're fine. He just wants to observe, if you don't mind," Daniel said.

"Oh, okay."

"You won't find this FG3 machine in most chiropractors' offices," Daniel told Derrick.

"Uh huh."

"Since I'm in a naturopathic environment, I have access to this machine. I've been real pleased with the results so far."

"Uh huh…"

"When we have the patient's feet in two separate buckets of water, sound frequency is produced throughout the body. It is based on the theories of Dr. Royal Rife."

"You said something about the currency running through my body…"

"Yes, it vibrates according to the frequency applied."

"Can you break that down for me?"

"Chronic fatigue is a virus."

"Okay." Porter jotted it down.

"Viruses tend to have protein clusters around them, so are difficult to treat. This machine destroys those abnormal protein structures that are not vibrating at the proper frequencies; this leaves the virus exposed for attack."

"Should I put my feet in, now?"

"Sure go on. I'm letting the machine--warm up."

"That's really fascinating," Derrick added.

"What's your area?" Porter asked.

"Biology. I've done some independent studies in genetics research too. It's really kind of neat. I got hooked."

"And after graduation what are you going to do?"

"I'll be applying to some chiropractic schools. I've always wanted to be a chiropractor."

"I recommend Parkway highly. It's where I went. It's down in Florida," Daniel said.

While Porter lay on the table getting treatment on the Rife machine, Derrick and Daniel struggled to disassemble an older table to make room for a newly purchased one.

While the two men stepped out to get the table, Porter took note of his surroundings.

"Looks like I came at the nick of time," Derrick said, helping Daniel mount the table in the room.

"Why is that table moving?"

"It's an adjusting table," Daniel said, adjusting the machine to a higher setting. "We're going to let it go for two minutes then turn it back to D and start the process again."

"Okay."

"People are tired of taking drugs and having surgery, so chiropractic is becoming very popular," Daniel told Derrick.

"Is that why you're here in Idaho?" Porter asked.

"Like anything else, there are some areas that are saturated.".

"Yes, but Burton is a naturopath."

"Right," Daniel agreed.

"So…combining the two… Does the demand seem to be there? Is that what people are seeking?" Porter asked.

"Well Dr. Burton and I work well together. Our patient load is good, although it's met with disfavor by the chiropractic board."

"Why wouldn't they like it?"

"Well they don't want me over here. They want me out of here."

"Why?"

"They don't like me associating with a physician in another discipline of medicine, especially when that discipline has no licensing board. They can't control Dr. Burton, and that bothers them."

"Yes," Derrick agreed.

"So they want me to disassociate from Dr. Burton. They've been trying to convince me to leave."

"How?"

"They've threatened to revoke my license… take me before the council. Things like that…"

"And you mean you're still here?"

"I'm told they plan to do some investigation…."

"You're not afraid for your job?"

"Well, I figure I'm doing only what I was trained to do."

"Well, I don't see how they can stop you."

"Because of my association with Dr. Burton."

"Well, no one ever complained to me about him."

"Well, he frightens them."

"Everyone's always told me how good he was."

"They're threatened by him."

"But why?"

"Because he gets the patients they used to have, all by word of mouth. He doesn't advertise. Patients from Pocatello, Idaho Falls, and Blackfoot are coming in droves. Twin Falls and the…."

"That's right, because I'm from Twin Falls."

"Uh huh. See that's what bothers them; he's taking their patients. Some local chiropractors reported me."

"Gee."

"Some right around here. Pocatello doctors are reeling because lots of their patients come to us. We treat them, because we feel it's their right to choose where they get treatment."

"So what's wrong with that?"

"Well, Dr. Burton has to be cautious. He can't really diagnose, but he can recommend helpful supplements."

"What other medicines does Burton use--I mean, other than vitamins."

"Homeopathy. It means, 'like equals like.' Minute quantities of remedies that, when massive doses are used, produce effects similar to the disease being treated. That tends to have a positive effect upon diseased conditions."

"Yesterday he mentioned giving me an IV. What's in it?" Porter asked.

"Well that's determined by your disease. We still have an adjustment to do. Why don't you lie back on the table for me? Let me have those glasses..." Daniel put Porter's glasses aside and told Porter to grab the bar which extended underneath the head of the table and did the adjustment.

"Now that we are finished with the adjustment, we're going into the other room."

"Okay, so what is this room used for?"

"See the coffin," Daniel said rather calmly.

Porter's eyes bucked, as he eyed the yellowish bumpy coffin looking box.

"A what? A coffin!"

"Yes."

"No, you can't be serious!"

"When we treat certain diseases we have the patient lie in there...."

"Kidding aside, what is this?"

"It's a sun tan bed."

"Oh, okay. What's next?"

"I'm going to plug in that other machine, but first let's slip those boots off," Daniel said, then left the room.

As he lay, his ankles covered with electrical currents, Porter could feel rollers going up and down, between his upper and lower back. It seemed that out of nowhere Sheri appeared. "Hi Sheri."

"Hi Porter."

"So I heard you say earlier that you're from all around. Where is your husband from?"

"From Southern California."

"You guys new here in town or...?"

"Well, for about twelve years we lived in California, but had to leave because all the jobs were going to the Hispanics. They worked for pennies. That left us out in the cold. That's when we decided we had to move."

"Is that right?"

"Yes, we couldn't even pay our rent. It just sort of wiped us out, but it's like that in Vegas too."

"So how long have you folks been here?"

"A little more than two years."

"You've got kids?"

"Yes, four of them."

Shortly thereafter Daniel returned. "Dr. Burton went to this national convention in Las Vegas a few weeks back and learned about this electrical machine. It comes with a money back guarantee for curing the Epstein Bar virus, chronic fatigue syndrome, and A.I.D.S…"

"You mean the machine I was on?"

"Right. He said if used twenty minutes each day for a month, it can get rid of those viruses."

Porter was at the reception desk when Anna approached. "Anna, do you need my Blue Shield card?"

"No. They will send in all of the charges, all but the sixty dollars for the blood work."

"But the blood tests are so expensive, why can't it be included?"

"Because Blue Cross works only with Dr. Daniel, not with Dr. Burton."

"Well, why didn't Dr. Daniel do the blood work?"

"Because he's not … that's not what he does."

"Oh, okay, well…well, I want to get all the treatment I can this year cause I've met my deductible. I don't want to have to start all over."

"We'll send it in for you."

"Alright, I'll see you tomorrow at two o'clock."

The information Porter had received on the staff was immeasurable. Driver's licenses, addresses, criminal records, etc. could now be at Porter's fingertip. Derrick Glenn had provided the kind of diversion Porter needed to pull additional information out of Daniel. His attempt to bate Anna to try and implicate Dr. Burton by using Daniel to solicit unwarranted insurance payments from Blue Cross/Blue Shield for blood work, was unsuccessful. But that was today; tomorrow was another day.

On November 9th, Porter entered the clinic once again, just in time for his 2:00 o'clock appointment.

The room behind the counter was in clear view now; it resembled a little laboratory. Little bottles lined a wall full of shelves. Background conversations were audible--but Porter couldn't make out the words.

Children's voices hung in the air. A little girl brushed past Porter.

"Oh, let me move," he said.

An attentive and sensitive female cautioned the child. "Tell him you're sorry."

Jewel and Daniel were slowly approaching.

"Porter, how are you?" Daniel asked.

"Good."

"I'm going to go ahead and get you back in a room. Dr. Burton will be in to see you," Jewel said.

"Which room do you want me in?" Porter asked, clearing his throat.

"Just follow me," Daniel said as Jewell lead the way.

"You want to make sure you're drinking lots of water to flush out those toxins," Jewel said as Porter entered.

"I've had a couple of beers."

"Beer doesn't take the place of water. Got to get some water in you."

"Do you have anything that can help me sleep?"

"Um hmm. Little black pills."

"Can I get any today?"

"We have them."

Suddenly Burton appeared. "Porter--what's new?"

"Do you have a minute?"

"What you need?"

"Well, my buddy's got prostate cancer and I've been telling him about my treatment. I believe it's helping. Can you help him? He doesn't want surgery, because he's in his late fifties. He's retired."

"There are other patients that I have treated with that same problem. I've had some come about four days before their surgeries. After our treatments, the surgery was cancelled. They got a clean bill of health from their doctor."

"Well, he's scared to have surgery."

"I treated a seventy-five-year-old man for prostate cancer ten years ago. He's still very much alive."

"I'll tell him to come see you. If I'm not better by tomorrow, I'm going to get an injection."

"I'd recommend the IV's."

"Okay. I've also been having a hard time sleeping."

"Maybe you're drinking too much coffee before bed. That'll do it."

"Not into coffee so... I drink beer. I've been going to bed early, but I still have problems sleeping. I need something to help me..."

"Well, we can give you a Chinese herb; it's a concentrated valerian root. It'll help, but if you're stopped and they give you a blood test, it'll show up as Valium in your urine. I can get you some samples to see if it helps you," Burton said, reaching up in the cabinet and pulling out a few.

Burton's statement was the magic bullet for Porter. If Valium was in the pills, Burton could be charged with practicing medicine without a license. Valium, a controlled substance, could only be legally dispensed by a medical doctor; Burton was no medical doctor. Those pills just may be the nail needed to drive Burton's clinic into the coffin, he thought.

But Burton had learned during research that valerian has the same outward structure as Valium, but is an herb, not a drug. "Let's have you try these," he said handing Porter the pills.

"Can I get some of them if it works?"

"Yes. Tomorrow we'll know."

Porter examined the pills closely. "Alright, now what do we have here?"

"Some Chinese herbs. They should help you sleep. They're also good for pain. Have you been in any pain?"

"Not really."

"Alright then you'll only need about two of them. These little pills are really good for arthritis."

"You telling me these will help with that too?"

"They can help relieve the inflammation a bit. Alright let's get you on the other machine. Lou, where do you want Porter to go?"

Daniel pointed to an adjustment room," the one right there."

"Are you going to use that FG machine on me again?"

"Yes. Why don't you go ahead and sit in the chair for me." Daniel turned on the current. "Let me know when you want me to turn it up or…?"

"Okay--I'm starting to feel it… So, how long have you been here Doc?"

"One year now."

"Your future here looks promising?"

"I'm planning to move soon. I want to open up a shop of my own."

"You mean in Idaho?"

"No, I'm looking at Utah, near Provo. I won't rule Idaho out. I have an uncle in Provo who is a chiropractor."

"I think that's near Salt Lake."

"It is. I don't know if you remember Marilyn, but it's her dad."

"What's his name?"

"James Kelly."

"Oh, are you thinking of going into practice with him?"

"Yes, but he hasn't gotten started. He's getting ready now. He's trying to get another practice opened. He's done well with his past three practices. Each grossed $400,000 a year."

"No kidding."

"Just think if that were split in half. Compare that to the $36,000 I'm making here."

"How'd you happen to hook up with Dr. Burton?"

"My cousin, Marilyn, works here. She's the one with the silvery-gray long hair."

"I Don't believe I've…."

"She's always here. She's behind the counter today."

"Well I can't see her, but that's your cousin, huh?"

"That's how I found out about Dr. Burton--through Marilyn."

"And your uncle is her dad?"

"Right."

"Okay, Marilyn is your cousin. Her dad, your uncle James Kelly is planning to open a practice, right?"

"Exactly. Plus I figure, he knows how to start a practice. I could learn a lot from him, like how to do the books..."

"I'm a little confused about something though. You said that you're not into naturopathy... See, I understand something about chiropractic care now, but what is a naturopath?"

"Well, Dr. Burton is a naturopath."

"And Dr. Kelly?"

"Since the requirements were different when he graduated, my uncle was not licensed to practice as a chiropractor. So when he moved to Utah, he studied naturopathy."

"Oh--I see."

"The law forced him to close. But he had been practicing more than a decade."

"But why do you want to leave here?"

"Well, I'm really not all that anxious to leave--I mean Dr. Burton and I work well together--he's a pleasure to work with. I've never had a better job, but I've just.... It's time to move out on my on. The chiropractic board is breathing down my neck, so...."

"But why?"

"They don't like me associating with Dr. Burton. See in Idaho, there's no licensing board governing Naturopaths; therefore, the chiropractic board can't control him. That's why they don't like him. ...And for me to associate with him...."

"Yes, but who says they don't? How you know?"

"Well, I got a call from a member on the board. He told me. 'We don't like your being there with Burton.'"

"Well, if you stayed, what problems could it cause for you?"

"Well they could revoke my license if they suspect I'm involved in illegal or unethical practices. They'd investigate, but meanwhile I'm out of business... Of course legally I can decide Ill just practice as a naturopath, and tell them to stuff that license. There's nothing they could do about it."

"Un huh."

"Heck, I've got proof of my education. They couldn't stop me, but I couldn't advertise. I would have to change my cards from chiropractic to a naturopathic physician."

"So how long do you think you'll stay?"

"I got my home on the market. It's been on the market for a month and a half now, but no offers. When it sells..."

"So where would that leave Dr. Burton--I mean he needs a chiropractor doesn't he?"

"I feel bad about leaving but, that's ... I let him know so he could be looking for someone to replace me. How's your back and neck today, Porter?"

"Well okay. I'm not hurting."
"Alright then--you're done."
Marilyn walked in with her silvery gray hair brushing her waist.
"I don't believe I've met you. What's your name?" Porter asked.
"I'm Marilyn."
"Oh--okay so you're Marilyn. I hear you do reflexology too."
"Oh, definitely."
"Well, do you work here at the clinic, too?"
"Uh huh. Monday, Wednesday, and Thursday."
"Seems to be a nice little town."
"Yes it's got its good points."
"Okay now it makes sense. You're the one Dr. Daniel was trying to point out to me. He said you were cousins."
"Uh huh. So you see, I've been around."
"Yes. Are you married?"
"Um hm. Got three kids: fourteen, ten, and three."
"You've got a handful then."
Marilyn laughed. "Uh huh." She proceeded down to the base of Porter's toes with her fingers until done. "Come back to see us."

On November 10th Porter came to Natrogenics clinic for the last in his series of the four-day treatments

Porter looked around the clinic. "My, this place is packed, and it's only ten o'clock," he noticed as he conversed with the lady next to him. She was a bubbly, jolly lady who had only praises for Burton.

"So, what brought you to the clinic?" Porter asked.

"Let me see, where do I start? Well I guess you could say pancreatic cancer--but I had a bad case of sugar diabetes."

"Really? I got this buddy over in Twin Falls with prostate cancer. I've considered telling him about the clinic. He doesn't want surgery, but I was trying to see if this treatment helped me."

"What are you here for?"

"Chronic fatigue," Porter said.

"Well, the lady that recommended me had chronic fatigue. She's doing so much better since she's been coming. She still has bouts of tiredness on occasion, but nothing like before."

"Is that right?"

"She's only been coming now for about four months."

"Maybe I should go ahead and tell my buddy to come over."

"Listen, when I first came to the clinic my legs pained me so badly that I couldn't walk, the circulation in them was so bad. My doctor told me that they were going to have to amputate them. But that was... Can you imagine? I live alone and have no family. With no legs... The Lord heard my prayer, sent me an angel. I'm retired, got a good pension, so... I feel really blessed."

"You could barely walk before? You don't even have a cane!" Porter exclaimed.

"Right," the lady said laughing.

"Porter!" Sheri called out.

Porter neared the counter looking around at the gathering crowd of people in the waiting area. "Is it gonna be like this all day?"

"Probably so. This isn't unusual. We're booked solid today," Marilyn said approaching. "I don't know what it is about Thursday's, but probably because Dr. Burton is in on Thursdays," Sheri added.

"Isn't he in most days?"

"He's not in on Tuesdays."

"Oh I see," Porter said.

Daniel, lead Porter to an examination room where Marilyn was preparing for his treatment.

"Well, I slept like a baby last night," Porter told Marilyn.

"That's good to hear. Why don't you slip off your boots and socks for me?"

"Oh okay. I've got a question. Those pictures of my blood said something about research."

"Well, that just means that it is not a program the FDA approves. Since they don't approve of it, Dr. Burton has to state legally that it's a research program." Daniel said.

Marilyn joined in. "Is this your last day?"

"Yes, this is it, but I want to ask Dr. Burton if I should get treated again in about a month."

"Okay."

"The FDA tends to want control over treating illnesses. Dr. Burton can't claim that his blood tests are scientifically proven, so they insist that he say that they are for research purposes although clinical studies support its value," Daniel explained.

"It's to protect us," Marilyn added.

"Exactly. Without it, they'd put him in the slammer," Daniel said.

"How can they do that?"

"They're very powerful," Daniel said.

"They're wealthy--very wealthy," Marilyn added.

"Right. For one, they're associated with another giant, the AMA. The AMA is loaded," Daniel explained.

"Yes, but what's that got to do with you folks? Are they spying on you or something?"

"Well, if word got out... See they've done tons of research on these diseases and have gotten good results."

"Yes, but the AMA would never approve of this treatment," Marilyn said.

"Oh all right, because I was wondering."

"Listen I've got to step out a minute," Daniel said.

"But if it helps people. He couldn't stay in business if he weren't helping people," Porter said.

"See they know they would lose money. But now medical doctors are starting to realize that nutrition plays a part in maintaining health. Course most won't even.... They're into drugs."

"Well, if I didn't believe I was being helped, I wouldn't come," Porter said.

"Most of our patients come to us as a last resort, after they've tried everything else."

"Well I've got this buddy with prostate cancer."

"Has he had surgery?"

"I really don't think he has, though."

"Chemotherapy and radiation damage the body so badly."

"That could be what he's been doing."

"Well yes--that destroys both the good and bad cells."

"Right," Porter murmured.

"But those we've treated that died, their quality of life improved so much... Some of them were active until the very end. I mean, I know this lady that went to the ball games up until the end. When she first came to us she could hardly walk."

"Are they getting the same basic treatment as me for the cancer?"

"They get injections. It goes directly into the blood stream; the body doesn't have to break it down."

"Oh, okay. Where can I get more of those black pills?"

"If you call us we'll be happy to send you some. These are the pills that the FDA wants."

"These black pearls, -- why?" Porter asked frowning.

"Because they're very good for arthritis. They want the stuff that works."

"Well, what makes you think they want these pills? How do you know?"

"Well, they've raided other doctor offices for these pills."

"No kidding? Was that here in Idaho?"

"Uh huh."

"Where?"

"One of the naturopaths up in Blackfoot. They closed him down and put him in jail."

"What makes you think it was the FDA?"

"That's who they identified themselves to be."

"Hmm."

"I can't believe they get away with this stuff. Those guys can make your life miserable."

"Well I hadn't heard of them. Well I had, but I didn't know what they did.

When Daniel said something about the FDA I didn't know who they were."

"What's really sad is people don't know they have an alternative because the medical doctors will not tell them. But this is an alternative, and I think people have a right to know about it. I mean--I'm not against medicine but I believe there's a time for it, and then a time for alternative therapies. To me, cancer is the time for alternative treatments."

"So you're not against medical doctors."

"Oh, definitely not. There's a place for them."

"Okay."

"I'd like to see them put their brains together--but they don't."

"Ummm."

"If the wrong people find out about what we do at the clinic they'd squeal on us not because we're doing anything wrong or illegal, but because we're good at what we do. We have many satisfied patients, and to be honest, they want these treatments. That's wrong? We should be free to choose our doctors," Marilyn said.

"Well he's got a good reputation, so…"

"But don't think they aren't watching us."

"Um hm."

"Our treatments are effective because we treat the cause, not the symptoms."

"I think I must really be in bad shape."

"You think?"

"Well I'm always tired. I've got this cough, and wasn't sleeping. But last night I did, so I feel better."

"Sleeping is very important."

"The problem is I'm always on the road."

"It's tough without the proper amount of sleep."

"So he gave me these little black pills to try. That did it. How much longer do you think it will take before I…?"

"Let your body be your judge."

Suddenly Jewel was standing at Porter's side.

"So Jewel--How are you?" Porter asked.

"I'm good. How about you?"

Dr. Daniel entered and proceeded to adjust Porter. "Lie on your stomach for me," Daniel said.

"Ohh--I felt that," Porter said.

In walked Sheri. "Daniel here likes giving orders."

"Why not," Daniel teased.

"Seems to be enjoying, it doesn't he Sheri? Bet you don't take that, right?" Porter asked, winking at Sheri.

"She doesn't," Daniel said. .

"No because I'm a liberated woman," Sheri asserted.

Burton came into the treatment room."

"Hi. Dr. Burton."

"How are you, Porter?"

"Well I had two--they worked. But she said I should've taken three."

"Well, for patients who have to take more than two for pain, they have to take their bottle of valerian root with them. Then they can see what they've been taking just in case Valium shows up in their system. See Valium comes from valerian root," Burton explained.

"So these pills got Valium in them?"

"No, they've got valerian root, the whole plant. It's not addictive because the plus and minus charges are still in there the way nature intended. That's why it has no side effects. It's natural."

"Okay."

"When they see the bottle with valerian root, they'll understand that it's okay."

"I'd like a bottle of the valerian root also. When I need more can I just order them?"

"Just let the girls know. There are sixty in the bottle so…"

"Okay thanks, Dr. Burton."

"You bet," Burton said, leaving the room.

"One of my friends has a business in Provo. I think Utah is the place for me," Daniel told Porter.

"Still not sure about when or where you're moving to?"

"Well maybe one day I'll move, but…"

"Sounds like a good opportunity there for you."

"I'd like to get some years under my belt first, and then set up there. But the longer you wait, the harder it gets, plus you run the risk of someone else settling in there. My uncle's been asking me to join him." Daniel left the room.

Porter stopped at the counter where Sheri was standing. "You're such a hard worker, Sheri," Porter said teasingly.

Sheri laughed. "Boy do I have you fooled."

"I'm supposed to pick up some pills."

Anna interceded. "This is the valerian root. Keep it with you when you're on the road."

"Okay, I understand, but I need to talk with Carrie."

Carrie explained, "You're going to pay twenty percent of the services."

"But you understand, you're responsible for the sixty dollars for the blood test because that was what Dr. Burton did," Anna said.

"But I don't understand…"

"I explained that to you before," Anna said, disgusted.

"I don't remember, but whatever."

"You owe us twenty percent of charges which is $23.00 plus $60.00 for the blood work. That is $83.00, okay? Carrie will take care of the insurance."

"I'm not going to be able to buy any pills today, so I want to have you ship some of them to me."

"That's fine."

"But I want to buy the valerian root and black pills to take with me."

"Alright, that's $29.24." Porter handed her that amount.

"Here is your receipt."

"Thanks for your help. I'm off to Reno now. Take care."

Just outside, Porter ran into a lady who recognized him from a previous visit. "Aren't you the fella with the friend, who has prostate cancer."

"Yes."

"You should have him come over. Listen, I have breast cancer. I've been on the program here for three months now, and I tell you, I just feel so much better. Those injections are wonderful. I don't think your buddy would be sorry," Ms. Goodman said.

"Thanks, I'll be sure to tell him." He entered the pills as evidence at the FBI headquarters in Boise.

25

December 5, 1994

Dr. Daniel had moved slower than Special Agent Newsome wanted. In spite of threats by the chiropractic board, he was still at the clinic. While Daniel was not initially the subject of the FBI investigation, he was fast becoming a target with his stubborn resistance to leaving. This left Special Agent Newsome but one choice.

She phoned Joel Barnett, Staff Attorney at the Blue Shield of Idaho office requesting Daniel's provider number, a number which entitled him to receive payments for services rendered; it could provide a paper trail to Daniel.

Burton, she learned, had a provider number with Blue Shield of Idaho, but unlike Daniel's, his number was deemed nonpayable since his services had no federal billing codes.

Wes O'Dea was ever vigilant in his watch over the clinic through the eyes and ears of Dr. Lou Daniel. Wes phoned Special Agent Newsome to discuss his visit with Daniel at a Christmas party earlier in the month.

"Hi Marge. This is Wes."

"Wes, what you got for me today?"

"Well I got lucky. I visited with Lou at a Christmas party."

"What can you tell me about Burton? What's his schedule like, say over the next month or so?"

"Burton plans to spend a month and a half in Europe next month."

"Is that so? Hmm... Yep. I sure as heck can't afford a trip like that and I've got news for you, my friend, in a couple of months nor will he. I intend to see to that personally. What kind of income does the clinic bring in?"

"According to Lou, between $55,000 and $75,000 monthly."

"So that explains how he can afford to hang out in Europe for a month and a half."

"According to Lou, he recycles part of the profit into his farming business, and is making big plans to remodel the clinic. Also plans to get a new computer system."

"Is Daniel making any plans to leave?"

"No, not yet. He claims a deal to open up a chiropractic practice in Utah fell through, so plans to leave the clinic are off for now."

"Did he mention the chiropractic board?"

"He didn't seem very concerned, but he said the Board questioned him about whether or not he was using his insurance provider number to cover treatments performed by Burton."

"He leaves us no choice. Looks like we're going to have to conduct that raid with him there. How does Burton file his insurance claims, electronically or through regular mail?"

"They are mailed."

"Okay. Good. Hey, keep it coming, buddy."

December 22, 1994

It was three days before Christmas when Lance phoned the clinic. Agent Newsome listened intently.

"Natrogenics, Anna speaking."

"Ah Anna, this is Porter Lance. Listen, I want to wish you a Merry Christmas, but I got to ask you something."

"Uh huh."

"What's my balance?"

"I don't believe, any, but let me check."

"Okay, I ..."

"Blue Shield paid the balance."

"They paid it all?"

"Uh huh. You're all clear."

"Good. I'm glad to hear that. Thanks, but I got another question for you."

"Okay."

"You know those little black pills I got from you?"

"Yes."

"I need to get some more. If you can send 'em C.O.D..."

"Uh huh. That's how we shipped to you last time."

"All right, why don't we do that?"

"Okay."

"Well, I still have some left, so just send one package. That'll last until I come back over."

"Is this going to Boise?"

"Yes, I'll be here until Christmas."

"Alright, I'll get them out to you today."

"Okay, alright, Merry Christmas to you. Be sure and tell all the others: Jewel, Marilyn, Dr. Burton, and Dr. Daniel, Porter Lance wants to wish them a happy holiday season."

"I sure will."

"I hope to see you next year. Thanks for everything."

Confirmation of black pearls and injection therapy given to patients at the clinic had been a common thread shared by interviewees of the Burton investigation. Newsome believed she had enough information to justify a search. But when? She phoned Wes.

"Burton's going to be unavailable from January 14, through January 20. He is scheduled to attend a seminar in Las Vegas, Nevada."

"Where does Burton keep his patient records?"

"There's a storage room at the clinic, that's where he keeps his current records. Some of the older ones are stored at Burton's apartments on the porch in boxes. Other older ones are kept upstairs in his office at his home."

From the Natrogenics clinic a package of small plastic zipped bags with sixty black round pills and a bill for $24.00 C.O.D made out for Porter Lance, was received; it was entered into evidence at the FBI headquarters.

A new year was dawning. It had been now more than a year since Wes was fired, and the clinic had already grown considerably. Patients who had once stopped coming to the clinic because of Wes, started coming back. Word quickly spread. Soon his clinic case load increased to about ninety eight percent of Burton's prior case load.

Ninety percent of Burton's patients were from outside Aberdeen. They came from across the country and abroad seeking what they had found in no other, a return of their health.

26

In an interview with Special Agent Newsome, Idaho State Bureau of Occupational Licenses, Attorney Pat Melcher, verified Walt Lou Daniel's license to practice chiropractic in Idaho.

"Have there been any admonishments to Walt Lou Daniel or Kyle J. Burton?" Newsome asked.

"According to our records, the chiropractic board has never applied any discipline to Walt Lou Daniel or Kyle J. Burton."

According to Lisa Harris, Benefits Administration Specialist at Blue Cross of Idaho, code 87177 is a direct smear for ova and parasites and could not be used for blood analysis, such as used by Kyle J. Burton. Code 97014 delineates the use of electrical stimulation equipment, equipment Blue Shield assumes to be approved for use by the physicians submitting the claim. According to Ms. Anderson, Blue Shield does not monitor equipment approval.

It was not until January 12, 1995, that the FBI got what it believed was a real break in the Burton investigation. Linda Reichart phoned Special Agent Marge Newsome from her residence in Stratford, Wisconsin, having been referred by the Attorney General's office.

"I have important information for you on one of Dr. Burton's patients," Reichart told Newsome. "I was suspicious of his treatments."

"Who was the patient?" Newsome asked.

"Leslie Child." Reichart said.

"What kind of things makes you suspicious of Burton's treatments?"

"Well, for one, I think Dr. Burton brainwashed Leslie."

"Brainwashed, how?"

"Some pills Leslie received--little black ones, I was suspicious of, and so I had them analyzed. Diazepam was in them."

"What was Child's response to that?"

"'So! He's a doctor,' she said. I said, 'He is not a medical doctor. So he shouldn't be prescribing pills with drugs in them.'"

"Why do you think she got on Burton's program?"

"He scared her to death, that's why. He told her that if she didn't get treated, she could end up with cancer."

"Did she buy that?"

"She's in Idaho as we speak--for a couple of weeks or so."

"Listen, I would like to have you talk personally with one of the agents from our Milwaukee Division about Burton's treatments of Leslie Child." Linda agreed.

On January 13, 1995, in the presence of Special Agent Marge Newsome, Porter Lance recorded a telephone call he made to Natrogenics.

"I want to bring over my friend, the one I told you about that has cancer, but I want to make sure that you're going to be there," Porter said to Burton.

"I'll be out of the office from February 14th through late March or early April. I'm scheduled to go to Europe and then to Dallas," Burton responded.

Now the constraints were before them. They must plan the search before Burton went to Europe or wait until April. Daniel would have to be forced out.

Under direction of Special Agent Newsome, on January 23, 1995, Investigative Assistant Terrance Seargant secured a copy of the Natrogenics clinic's 1994 Annual Report.

Prior to visiting the clinic, Special Agent Porter Belt (Lance), had been examined by Dr. Jordan, a graduate of the University of Alabama, and given a clean bill of health. In a subsequent interview with Newsome, regarding Burton's diagnosis of Lance, Jordan stated:

- Neither chronic fatigue syndrome, parasites, an inflamed prostate, heart stress, digestive problems, weak immune system, nor blood sugar levels are discernible by a single drop of blood.
- Chronic fatigue syndrome can only be diagnosed over a lengthy period. Mononucleosis is common and is caused by a combination of infection and the EBV virus. Only when the cells are stained and a high powered microscope is used with the ability to magnify the cellular activity 800 - 1000 times can a diagnosis of chronic fatigue syndrome be solidified.
- Parasites and or worms are diagnosed through a stool sample. If blood is the basis of the analysis, staining of the blood would be necessary in addition to running other specific tests before such a diagnosis could be obtained.
- An enlarged prostate is diagnosed using a digital rectal exam. Heart problems are diagnosed using an Electrocardiogram or EKG, stress test or ECHO cardiogram.

"I am not aware of crystallized blood tests requiring the drying of blood, such as that used by Burton. When blood tests show signs of bacteria, the patient is a severely ill patient, not merely the victim of parasites or worms."

Jordan renounced the notion that EBV could lead to HIV. "HIV is diagnosed through a series of steps, one of which requires examination of the serum in the blood. To assess the patient's immune system, their blood count is analyzed, specifically their white blood cells. Staining of the cells and magnification with a high powered microscope would have to be done to complete the process."

In an interview with Special Agent Newsome, Joel Barnett, Staff Attorney Blue Shield of Idaho, verified that the codes 724.2 and 839.0 used for Porter Belt (Porter Lance's) services rendered by Walt Daniel on January 25, 1995 were for a painful lumbar area and extreme exhaustion.

Dr. Gary Pickston, Chairman of the State of Idaho Chiropractic Board told Newsome that prescription writing is not within the scope of practice for chiropractors in the State of Idaho, nor are chiropractors granted permission to give injections of any kind. "They are, however, permitted to draw blood."

On January 30, 1995, Porter Lance placed a final call to the Natrogenics clinic.

"Natrogenics clinic, Anna speaking."

"Yeah, Anna. Porter Lance here. Dr. Burton in?"

"Ah yeah."

"I need to speak with him… don't you remem… I was in last month."

"I know who you are."

"I just need a few minutes."

A tired, almost breathless, Burton came to the phone.

"Porter, how are you?"

"You sound tired."

"Oh man--busy."

"Hmm. That friend I've been telling you about wants to come in to see you. I'm going to be over that way this Thursday. Will you be in?"

"Yeah--all day."

"Would like to get in there as soon as possible, so how early can we come?"

"Eight-thirty is fine."

"Now should I arrange this with Anna or…?"

"No. I'll let them know."

"Thanks, doctor."

On January 31, 1995, Special Agent Marge Newsome petitioned the U.S. Magistrate, Judge Lewis Winston for a search warrant on the Natrogenics clinic, in Aberdeen, Idaho. Judge Winston consented, requiring that the search take place on or before February 9, 1995. The search warrant was to include the property to be searched and list of evidence to be seized.

Marshfield, Wisconsin Special Agent Norris E. Broyhill walked into the

Tan and Slim Clinic in an undercover operation. Several exercise tables were stationed throughout the clinic, three of which were occupied by customers.

A white female whose jet-black hair was piled atop her head stood manning the floor. She had a certain glow about her. Her demure stature belied her prominence, but it was apparent when she introduced herself.

"I'm looking for a Patty Florence, the owner," Broyhill said.

"Yes, I'm Patty Florence. May I help you?"

"Just curious, how did you get into this business?" Broyhill asked.

"Well, I was lucky enough to have survived a bout with lymphatic cancer thanks to a wonderful doctor."

"Really?"

"Yeah," she said, pointing to the products that were shelved under a counter near the entrance of the clinic.

She handed him some pamphlets. "See all those products there…, Dr. Burton formulated them."

"What are the tables for?"

"They're a form of exercise for rarely used muscles. When used with nutrition they can provide relief for the user."

"How much does it cost to use the tables?"

"The first visit is free. Thereafter they are $8.00, for one-and-a-half hours of therapy."

On February 1, 1995, Natrogenics was buzzing with patients. Sheri and Anna waited on the incoming patients while Carrie busied herself with phone orders.

The phone rang. The statement was short and blunt. "You're dead tomorrow!" the caller warned. Just as emphatically the caller slammed the phone in Carrie's ear.

The voice was a familiar one. It was definitely a male, Carrie thought. But the threat… She asked Sheri and Anna to cover the phones. She had to share this with Kyle.

"Kyle. Someone just made a strange call. I'm not sure what…" She said, motioning with her hands.

"What did they say -- was it a male or female?" Kyle asked.

"It was a male's voice. He said, 'You're dead tomorrow!' I don't… What do you think they mean?"

"It was a male, right?"

"Yeah."

"Probably Wes," Burton said, with his lips flattening. "Probably that doggone Wes O'Dea," he said slamming his ink pen down onto the desk. And for a moment there was silence as they looked at each other.

Soon Anna was at Burton's office. "Marvis Russell is in," she said.

"Send him in," Burton said. Carrie left just as Marvis, the lymphoma patient, entered for his injection. Marvis didn't know that this would be the last of his desperately needed injections.

27

On February 2, 1995, several patients and employees filed into the clinic shortly after Burton's arrival.

In the waiting room were the Wallaces. Melba had survived a bout of lung cancer under Burton's care. It took some coaxing, but husband Ryan, diagnosed with lymphoma, had agreed to give Burton a try.

Along with the Wallaces was Becky, a middle-aged woman with dark hair and hazel eyes, and her deathly ill infant. All had shared the long ride from Wisconsin.

A thin frail man with pale skin walked into the clinic. His red eyes had sunk deep into their sockets. Walking slowly, using his cane and daughter for support, he eased into a chair in the lobby. His clavicle protruded underneath his open collar. Faith healers, hypnotists, magic potions, and massive doses of chemotherapy and radiation had brought no relief. He wanted to believe that his suffering was nearing an end. He wanted to be there for his grandkids.

Burton was staring into his microscope when Anna walked in.

"Dr. Burton - John's here."

"Won't you send him in?"

Anna wrapped her arms around John's waist lending support until at last he was seated in the chair next to Burton. John's body odor reeked of slowly decaying meat.

Dr. Burton extended a hand to John. "Hi John, I'm Dr. Burton. What brings you here?"

"I'm in constant pain. I have a terrible time urinating-keep having to go over and over."

A quick poke with a lancet and a drop of blood settled into a small bubble on the tip of John's little finger. "Your blood is consistent with stage four of prostate cancer, parasites, and a touch of Candida." Dr. Burton told John.

After months of medical testing, John had finally been given a diagnosis by traditional doctors. How could Burton have possibly known…and from one drop of blood?

Anna made up a chart on John and settled him onto a table in the treatment room.

Becky clasped her baby to her bosom; her waiting was over. Tears of joy streamed down her face as she seated herself next to Dr. Burton.

"He's been slipping so fast! I just…" As her tears spilled into the infant's face, she wiped them away gently. "I've heard some wonderful things about you. I hope you can help my baby."

"Let's see what we can do."

A man sneaked in from outside the clinic. There was nothing conspicuous looking about his garb, Anna noted as he pushed his way into the room behind the counter where liquid vials of herbal medicines were contained.

"I thought he was an employee's relative since he was back in this area, until I saw the word 'police' written on the back of his jacket," she later said in an interview.

Immediately following, the clinic's front door was thrust open.

A gunman dressed in black burst in. "Don't move!" Do as you're told and nobody gets hurt." Thoughts of a possible robbery had entered Kyle's mind but quickly faded when a woman similarly attired charged into Dr. Burton's office. "Are you Dr. Burton...Dr. Kyle Burton?"

"Yes, I'm Dr. Burton," he said, his brows furrowed.

She flashed her badge before him. "This is the FBI. I'm Agent Marge Newsome. This is Carlton Kent," she said, pointing to the gunman who was now at her side. Another agent approached. "This is Agent Terrance Glenn, from the Food and Drug Administration. We have a warrant to search Natrogenics."

Kyle's usual baritone voice changed into a husky squeal. "What did I do?" he asked, motioning with his hands, thinking that surely there must be some mistake.

"We're closing you down. We're taking all your stuff, including records and equipment," Marge said.

"What did I do?"

"You'll be notified of the charges."

"Has the sheriff been notified?"

"Yes."

Burton jumped up from his chair. "I want to talk with my attorney."

An entourage of armed agents poured through the door. Kyle could suddenly feel a lump in his throat when he noticed that Porter Lance was among them. "You know me as Porter Lance; I am Agent Belt."

Burton stumbled back into his chair, his hands flying over his head as if to shield flying bullets. His lips flattened and the once tan cheeks were red with anger.

"Employees are to come into the waiting room, now!" Newsome demanded. The employees rushed out of the patient's rooms, some accompanied by an official. Jewel, who was ushered into the waiting area had been prepping Ryan Wallace for an injection.

A man whose jacket was marked, "Police," hustled Anna Lange, Lou Daniel and Carrie Jean Doyle into the waiting room. Sheri Whitley was directed by one of the agents to join the other employees in the waiting area. One of the agents papered the clinic window and secured the entrance. "No employee is allowed to leave the premise," he said.

"I want you all to stand facing each other. Do not talk. Don't touch anything, and don't move," Agent Newsome said arrogantly.

The employees looked at each other in disbelief. One attempted to speak.

"There will be no talking among you," Agent Samuel Briggs reminded them.

Briggs allowed the employees to sit as the agents huddled together planning the course of the day. Carrie sat quietly, staring into the distance with her hands in her lap. Sheri sat trembling, looking periodically at her watch as though to accelerate the time. Her facial expression revealed her personal distaste for what was going on.

Anna sat with her head back against the wall, her eyes shut. Jewel was leaning against the wall, her head tilted and her tresses hung to one side.

Some agents summoned the employees into separate treatment rooms for questioning. Other agents gathered equipment and items for seizure.

Patients in the examination rooms were left shaken, crying under the watchful eye of the policeman who stood where he could see into their rooms.

Kyle sat in his office with his shoulders hunched forward, his elbow on his desk, supporting his chin. He felt so helpless, so anxious, with fear.

"Oh no." "Oh God, no! This can't be happening…", Becky cried. The force of her bellows was overpowering. She sat squeezing the small infant against her bosom as tears streamed down her face.

"Please, please. I'm from Wisconsin. My baby is…" She said, stammering for the right words. "My baby is very very sick. Can he just-I mean….."

"Ma'am there isn't going to be any business conducted here today," Newsome said.

"But…"

"You heard the lady, Ma'am," another agent retorted.

Arriving patients were turned away.

"This place is closed for business, today. Everyone sign the register, then you are free to go," one of the agents told the patients. Soon patients began drifting out of the treatment rooms.

John moaned and groaned as he was ushered off the treatment table and out of the clinic.

"Okay, let's go lady. Let us have your John Hancock and address, then you can leave," Newsome told Becky whose pitiful look begged for mercy.

"I'm not leaving until my baby is treated."

"Oh you're leaving lady, but you've got to sign the register first."

"Just watch me!" Becky growled.

Becky pulled her listless baby up to her, frowning. "You can't do this. No. No!" she shouted at Marge. "It's not right," she groaned.

Marge gave Becky a look of condescension and repeated, "There will be no business conducted here today."

Becky angrily scribbled down her name and address onto the register. "You won't get by with this!" she said, slamming the pen on the board. She thrust back her head and continued to hurl threats at Agent Newsome as she left the clinic.

It was like being in some strange movie, Burton thought. He was one of the actors, but didn't like his part.

"Okay big guy, you'll need to sit here on the couch. Agent Glenn and I will need these desks. We've got some questions for you," Agent Newsome told Burton.

Burton's lips flattened as he moved slowly toward the couch. "Listen, I want to talk with my attorney."

"There'll be plenty of time for that, big guy. Now is not the time."

Kyle plopped onto the couch as they proceeded with the questioning. Both agents, Glenn and Newsome, pulled a pen and tablet from a briefcase she brought into the clinic and prepared to take notes.

"So what's the procedure for receiving treatment here?" Marge asked.

"First the patient is asked to complete an application, which he must read and sign before he is treated. If the patient agrees, we'll draw some blood."

"How is the blood drawn?"

"The little left finger is pricked, for a smidgen of blood."

"Once you've got the blood, what do you do with it?" Agent Glenn asked.

"I'll perform two tests: the HLB and the LBA or whole blood test."

"Do you add anything to the blood when doing the test?" Glenn asked.

"No." With the LBA blood tests, a microscope having four lenses is used. Its range of magnification is 40 to 12,000."

"How do you perform the HLB blood test?"

"I take two Polaroid pictures of the blood; one is given to the patient, the other is for my file. The LBA tests are projected onto the monitor so that the patient can see it."

"Which test is conducted first?" Agent Glenn asked.

"The LBA test is done first to allow the blood for the HLB blood test to dry."

"What happens to it then?" Marge asked.

"I explain the nature of the blood-- white and red blood cell activity."

"Are the patients aware that this blood test is for research?"

"Patients are asked to read and sign an application which states that these tests are for research."

"What certification do you have?" Glenn asked Burton.

"I'm a naturopathic doctor."

Agents Glenn and Newsome continued questioning Burton while Agent Chester, in a separate treatment room, questioned Carrie Jean Doyle, the clinic's office manager.

"I'm Office Manager here at the clinic," Carrie told Agent Chester.

"What are your duties as Office Manager?"

"I take care of the accounts receivables and payables, the mail, and clinic orders."

"Who orders the black pearls?"

"Dr. Burton does. They arrive at the clinic in bulk. He takes them home, returning with some in zip lock bags each day."

"Were you ever given any instructions regarding the black pearls?"

"Employees were told that the pills were made up of 21 Chinese herbs including valerian root, and because of the valerian root a person taking it could show positive for Valium, if tested."

"Where are the black pearls kept?"

"In Dr. Burton's office in the cupboard above the sink."

"Do you have records reflecting who was given the black pearls?"

"It's listed as H-21 on the patient's file."

"What are they used to treat?"

"They are used to treat arthritis, people with sleeping problems, or those in a lot of pain."

"Do you know who supplies the clinic with the black pearls?"

"Yes, Adrian Frontier," I've got the book containing the company's name and address.

"How were the pills paid for?"

"With a business check."

"How could one identify whether or not the black pills were prescribed?"

"The H-21 would be typed. The code identifying the black pills is 99070. This is indicated on the patient's ledger card."

"Have you ever taken any of the black pearls?"

"Yes, I have for a painful headache."

"Are you aware of any research being conducted at the clinic?"

"Yes, the blood test is referred to as a research project."

"What do you think the purpose was in calling the blood test research?"

"It was to let the patient know that the treatment was not guaranteed."

"Do you have any knowledge of injections conducted at the clinic?"

"Yes, patients are given liquid vitamins."

"Where are they kept?"

"In a brown briefcase in Dr. Burton's office, which he carries home each night."

"Did Dr. Burton take the briefcase home last night?"

"Yes, and he returned with it this morning."

"Where are the patient records?"

"They are in the ordering book I turned over to you earlier."

"What code distinguishes a patient who has received injection therapy?"

"Code 90015."

"Have any patients experienced any problems as a result of receiving the injections here at NGC?"

"No."

"Who hooks up the patients for the electrical stimulation procedure?"

"Jewel or Marilyn would administer the electrical stimulation."

The agent showed Carrie various codes. "Code 97260 is for manipulation and is used only by Dr. Daniel."

"Who does the blood tests?"

"Jewel or Marilyn sticks the patient's finger, but Dr. Burton is the only one who analyzes the blood."

"Have you ever seen any patient cured?"

"I have seen many patients receive tremendous relief. I can't say whether or not they were cured."

"Are you aware of any deaths that occurred as a result of treatment administered by Dr. Burton?"

"No."

"Do you have any code that suggests that a patient's deceased?"

"The patient's file will be marked with a red pen and put in an inactive file."

"Where are these inactive files kept?"

"They are kept in the office."

Carrie's questioning continued as other employees were similarly interviewed-employees like Walt Lou Daniel. At six foot three Daniel towered over the agents. He was summoned into a treatment room.

"This is Criminal Investigator Roy Evans of the Attorney General's office," Belt motioned with his hands. "I am, of course, Special Agent Porter Belt of the FBI, known to you as Porter Lance," he said to Dr. Walt Lou Daniel as he flashed his badge and Daniel's personal information before him.

"Your cooperation is essential. We have gathered enough information on you to make you a subject of our investigation. It's all here, your date and place of birth, social security number, your wife Sheila and your three children. You get what I'm telling you? You're a graduate of Parkway Chiropractic School and no criminal record. I'm sure you want to keep it that way, right?"

Daniel had heard Wes's threat that a raid was coming, but had never really taken it seriously. Nor had he really understood before why the chiropractors had tried to get him out of the clinic. He did now.

"Of course. What do you need?" Daniel asked.

"I need a statement from you after we finish our interview. You are to leave this clinic at once and have no further contact with Burton for a year. Is that clear?"

"Okay." Daniel agreed.

Daniel hopped up on the treatment table. The officers pulled in chairs from the clinic waiting area.

"So, what brought you to the clinic?"

"My cousin, Marilyn Walter, told me about the opening for a chiropractor."

"What are your plans when you leave the clinic?"

"I'm making plans to move to Provo, Utah, but my debt from Parkway is out of hand."

"What are your duties here at the clinic?"

"I do chiropractic treatments, use the FG-3, and Sweep 4 machines."

"Explain the treatments administered by the FG-3 and Sweep 4 machines."

"The FG-3 helps with inflammation, such as sprained wrists, and destroys certain types of parasites. The sweep 4 relieves pain by stimulating the nerves."

"Is there any research being conducted at NGC?"

"Dr. Burton conducts blood research."

"What all do you treat patients for here at the clinic?"

"Our treatments include cancers, brain tumors, arthritis (various types), nervous conditions, migraines, and impotency, multiple sclerosis, cystic fibrosis, and a host of other debilitating diseases."

"How are the diagnoses of diseases noted on the patient files?"

"When Dr. Burton does a blood analysis, he notes his findings on the patient's file."

"If you're not involved in blood work, how do you know?"

"My mother was treated here at the clinic in June, 1994. Dr. Burton noted on her chart "metastasis tendencies."

"We'll need to take a look at that file."

Daniel retrieved his mother's file from the room just behind the receptionist's counter and returned.

"What treatments performed here at the clinic can be billed to Blue Cross/ Blue Shield?"

"The only treatments billable to Blue Cross/ Blue Shield are those done by me, since Dr. Burton's services are not approved for payment."

"Has blood work ever been submitted to Blue Cross/ Blue Shield under your authority?"

"Carrie asked me when I started working here which code could be used to send blood tests to either Blue Cross or Blue Shield. I told her the code for malaise."

"Since your line of work doesn't involve blood work, how did you know that?"

"It was something I learned at Parkway."

"Did you give Carrie permission to submit such blood work to insurance companies under your name?"

"No."

"Well, we know for a fact that in the past blood tests have been submitted to Blue Cross/Blue Shield under your name. Let me remind you. You are expected to answer these questions truthfully. It would be a pity to lose the license you've worked so hard for.... So how do you explain this, huh?"

"If it was occurring, it was because Dr. Burton authorized Carrie to do it."

"If you didn't authorize Carrie to send the bills for blood tests to the insurance company under your name, why would she do it?"

"No, I told Carrie not to use my number to send in to Blue Cross/ Blue Shield."

"Were you aware that in the beginning Carrie was using your number to submit claims for blood tests to Blue Cross/Blue Shield?"

"Yes. In the beginning I was aware."

"Did you at any time receive any verbal or written reprimand for billing blood tests under your number?"

"A Dr. Naples, one of the Idaho Chiropractic Board members, asked me to meet with him. He wanted to know why I had agreed to take a job with Dr. Burton. I told him my cousin, Marilyn had told me about the opening. He warned that if I am found to be involved in any illegal activity it could be to my detriment. He instructed both Carrie and me to stop this practice of billing blood tests under my number. I did."

"Were you the only male employee at the clinic?"

"Wes O'Dea and I were here for a short time together. Wes was later fired."

"Do you ever give any injections?"

"No."

"Do the black pearls contain any drugs?"

"To my knowledge they are all natural; they have been tested and showed negative for drugs."

"Why aren't these pills displayed along with the others on the shelf?"

"Because Dr. Burton said that the FDA was after them."

"Are these pills kept any place, here at the clinic, other than Dr. Burton's office?"

"Yes," Daniel got up and pointed outside to the treatment room containing these pills. "They're in a cabinet for our personal use and/or given out to patients as samples."

"Yeah, I remember when I was here back in November undercover, Burton got some of the pills from a cabinet in that room."

"Alright we need you to write a statement concerning everything you know about the black pearls, injection therapy, billing practices and anything else that would be helpful to us in our investigation here at NGC."

Daniel wrote a statement, signed it and left the clinic just as previously ordered. The statement was witnessed and signed by both Special Agent Porter Belt of the FBI, and Criminal Investigator Roy Evans, and entered as a signed confession of Daniel's allegations against Burton and his own personal involvement in an insurance fraud scheme.

It was roughly 10:00am when Jane arrived at the clinic. She noticed the big van sitting outside in the barren parking lot. The employees' cars were there but there were no patient cars, quite unusual for a Thursday, she thought.

As she got out of her car, she noticed that the window was papered. Just what in Sam Hill is going on in there? She wondered. She slowly put her hand on the doorknob and tried to turn it, but the door wouldn't budge; it had been bolted shut. Her curiosity wouldn't allow her to leave until she knew what was going on inside.

She knocked. A man dressed in a black outfit slowly cracked opened the door. "Ma'am I'm sorry, but this place is closed for business," the agent guarding the door said.

"May I speak with my husband?"

"Who are you Ma'am?"

"I'm Jane Burton."

With Newsome's approval, the agent opened the door, allowing Jane to step inside. "Okay, but only for a minute."

Kyle could see his wife's confusion and bewilderment, as he moved within three feet of her. He moved still closer; so, too, did the agent. "Not too close," the agent warned.

"Hi Jane," Kyle said. Kyle's expression was borne of secrecy-something was going on. Jane could sense it.

"What's going on?"

"Well, you know, it's nothing, really. These guys… just wanting to check some things out. But it's okay. Make sure Patrick catches his flight this afternoon. I'll be okay."

"Are you sure?"

"Yeah."

Jane knew differently. She rushed home and phoned Sheriff House. "Sheriff, Hi. This is Jane Burton."

"No, this is… The sheriff is out of town," the official said.

"Well, when will he be back?"

"Sometime later this afternoon. Can I help you with anything?"

"Well, I don't know what to make of it, but there's something strange going on at the clinic."

"Does it look like a robbery?"

"Well, I don't know what's going on, but the windows were papered, the door was bolted. And I… A man was standing guard at the door when I tried to get in. He stood between Kyle and me as we talked?"

"Well, I haven't heard anything about a raid ordered on the clinic. Listen, you call your attorney and let me do some checking on this. I'll make sure to let Sheriff House know when he gets in."

Kyle sat watching helplessly as the agents gathered several items for seizure, including his high-powered microscope, patient files and his briefcase containing the injection solution. It was as if his children were being taken. He could feel tension mounting as he sat trying to control himself. Can these people legally get away with this? He could hardly wait to talk with his attorney.

From his office, Kyle could see Special Agents Newsome, Belt, and Kennedy all gathered in a huddle near the door entrance. He heard whispering, but the words were muddled.

"Do we have your permission to search your home? Agent Newsome asked Burton.

"No!"

"Fine, we'll get a search warrant!" Agent Newsome snapped, then disappeared back into the lobby joining the other agents.

It was roughly 10:30 when Investigative Assistant Carlton Kent left the premises to obtain a search warrant on the Burton residence. Although some agents remained, Burton was released— stepping into his freedom for the first time in hours. He understood now what it must feel like to be locked up. There were so many unanswered questions. Attorney Anthony met Burton at the Voyager Café in front of the clinic; they headed for Burton's residence.

The Burton's residence and detached garage looked almost haunted from a distance as it sat overcast in a shadow created by the greenery surrounding it. A wide country dirt road fanned out in front of a grassy field and back left until it disappeared into the distance then to the right of the detached garage where it dusted the edges of a two-thousand acre wheat farm.

The two car garage sported a basketball goal just beneath the pointed roof. Five tractor trailers and other farming equipment could be seen among towering trees that hid the mechanics shop where Burton's sons were working.

The two-story dwelling was covered with beige siding. A brick tapered chimney on the house's right front stretched from its basement in between the first and second story window all the way up to the roof of the house; to the left of the chimney was a second story balcony. Immediately below was an arched canopy that shielded the door just beneath it. Two rails extended outwardly roughly four feet in front of the house where they supported three steps between them. On either side of these railings, Agents Briggs and Caldwell stood guard as Kyle and Attorney Rudy Anthony approached. Other agents were sprinkled throughout the landscape. Kyle hastened to the entrance, leaving Attorney Anthony a couple of feet behind. "If you don't get off my …," Kyle growled at the agents.

"Stop," agent Caldwell demanded, pointing a gun at Kyle's head. "Get your hands up."

Barrels of steel pointed at Burton from all directions. Burton thrust his hands high above his head choking back words that he didn't dare to speak— not now. His wife was inside. Agent Caldwell shoved his gun back into his holster and did a quick search of Burton's person. Patrick and Dan, Burton's sons, ventured outside of the mechanics shop and were headed for the house when they noticed the men standing at the entrance.

The Investigative Assistant, Terrance Seargant, arrived at the Burton's residence with the search warrant.

"Nobody's going in there. Got a warrant to search this place," Agent Caldwell said. Patrick and Dan looked at each other, their dad, and Attorney Anthony who was fast approaching.

"What's going on, dad?" Patrick asked as he moved toward the twosome, Dan at his side.

"These guys have a warrant to search the place."

Dan looked puzzled. "But why?"

"I'm not sure."

"Can they do that…I mean what are they looking for?"

"They're the Feds, Dan; they can do whatever they want. Our best bet with these guys is to just cooperate," Attorney Anthony said. Patrick looked at Attorney Anthony, and then thrust his head back.

After a quick search of their persons, the agents gave their okay for Kyle, Attorney Anthony, and Burton's sons to go inside... As Kyle and Attorney Anthony entered, they could hear men talking in the basement, but decided to follow the trail of voices upstairs. The boys joined Mom who was in the living room, guarded by an agent.

Kyle and Rudy watched as Agent Burns rummaged through Kyle's bedroom, yanking open his dresser drawers, scattering their underwear and other clothing onto the bed. Agent Burns made himself comfortable on the Burton's bed reading his personal letters.

Agent Burns scooped up the drawer contents and threw them back into the drawer, slamming the drawer shut, and then joined Agent Caldwell in the other room. "Looks like we're about done here," Burns said to Caldwell.

"We got to do the bedroom," Agent Caldwell said.

"You've already done the bedroom," Kyle said.

"Yeah, well we're going to do it again," said Agent Caldwell. "And you go downstairs, and don't hang around the corner, either."

Kyle and Attorney Anthony looked at each other, and then settled themselves in the living room with Jane and the boys.

As the agents prepared to leave the house, Kyle could hear one of them remark, "You know, I think we're in the wrong place. This guy is clean. There's nothing here."

In the basement, the agents had left evidence of their presence. Kyle and Attorney Anthony scanned the half dozen or so gifts that had been wrapped for an upcoming wedding that were now ripped apart and scattered all over. A plant whose contents had once been neatly displayed in its planter now lay in a dirt heap on the carpet.

"My wife's gonna ... When she sees this mess!" Kyle said.

"Yeah, you know, I'm just curious. I'd like to see that search warrant. Just what did they hope to find rummaging through your drawers and reading your mail?"

The phone rang. It was Kyle's sister Katty who had learned about the raid on their Baltimore, Maryland news. "Kyle, I'm so sorry, she said sobbing into the phone. "What is your attorney saying about all this?"

"Well you know it's...He's trying to sort this all out. And, you know, they even raided my house."

"What! Oh Kyle, that's awful," Katty exclaimed.

"They took Jane's prescription medication, my bank books, gold coins, and letters and left the house a mess."

"Well, did they tell you what this was all about?'

"You know that's the tough part--they didn't even tell me what I had done."

"I'm going to be praying for you."

"Okay thanks, Sis. Thanks for calling."

The phone rang once again. He hoped it was the sheriff, but how could it be? The sheriff was out of town, Jane had said.

"Kyle, this is Sheriff House. So what's this I'm hearing on the news about a raid?"

"You mean you didn't know?"

"Heck no. Course I've been out of town... This is the first I've heard of it-- when I turned on the news."

"They even raided my house; forced me and Rudy to stay downstairs while they rummaged through it."

"Kyle, listen. I should have been notified. Any outside officials coming into this town for something like that are supposed to go through me first."

"That doggone Marge Newsome said you had been notified."

"I want you to call your attorney. Tell him everything you've told me. I don't think they can get away with this. They're on my turf."

"He's here. I already talked with him about it."

"Well, what did he say?"

"Well, he said that it may be legally okay but not very courteous. He said it could cause a lot of hard feelings, and to talk with you about it."

"Let me speak with him."

"Rudy. What do you make of this?"

"Well, Sheriff, I mean you know who we're dealing with. These guys make up rules as they go. You know that."

"Well this is my turf, and I'll be darned if I'm going to just sit back and let them take over. They're going to hear from me."

"There may be some legal technicality we can muster; I'll check it out. I'll get back with you on this."

Later that evening Burton took Attorney Anthony to the clinic. As they approached, they could hear voices. "Looks like they're still here. I can hear them," Kyle said.

"So can I."

Attorney Anthony looked around in Kyle's office, hoping to find clues of things he might be able to use in Kyle's defense. Kyle followed the trail of voices into the little small medicine room.

"Get out of here!" Agent Chester ordered.

"Quit watching us," another said.

Kyle just stood looking.

Soon Agent Chester got up and headed toward Kyle. Kyle retreated back into his office, joining his attorney.

"Listen. Have your patients inundate them with phone calls and letters, the more the better. You'll need to start a petition drive rallying support for your cause. In the meantime, I'll be checking around to find out what you can and cannot do legally."

It had been a long day. Jane had settled into bed when Kyle crawled in just after midnight. Still perplexed by many questions, Kyle found himself tossing and turning with his eyes wide open. How could this have happened? Suddenly he recalled, "You're dead tomorrow!" It was the threat that caller had made yesterday, the one his office manager, Carrie Doyle, had told him about. How could he have been so blind? It had to be Wes. Now this explains why Wes was on his hands and knees searching documents in the dark at the office that day. He was spying for the FBI. But how could the Feds come after him based on just one person's allegations? What were the grounds for the search?

The feeling of shame and degradation hung over Kyle like a wet blanket. He had been treated like a criminal in front of his employees, his community, and possibly the nation. How could he clear his name when he didn't even know what the charges were? Now Dr. Burton understood what Dr. Lynch, whom they had crucified, Dr. Daton, and all the other health care practitioners who had been raided, felt like. The deception by (Agent Belt) AKA Porter Lance, who was going to bring his friend, Dave, over for treatment, now it all made sense.

What would he tell his employees? Which employees would he keep and which ones would he let go? He pondered a myriad of questions that night, but the one that weighed most heavily upon him was would he resolve this matter in time to save his patients?

28

The FBI had given Kyle little justification for reporting to work. "You can resume your practice," Newsome told Burton.

"But how, without my equipment?"

"That's your problem."

The girls would have to be told who would stay and who would go. With so little to work with, Burton was certain that only one person was needed to administer patient therapy. Marilyn was a natural, so she would be his choice; today would be Jewel's last. For bookkeeping and other duties, he would keep Carrie Doyle. Now he needed only one shipping clerk. He would keep Sheri Whitley. Her past performance had told him that the orders would be shipped both timely and accurately. He called a meeting to inform the staff.

To garner support for his legal cause he directed the employees to send petitions to the patients whose files remained at the clinic. The petition, the work of Dr. Merle Fry, was short, but to the point.

> We, the undersigned, petition the return of all records and equipment taken from the office of Dr. Burton on or about February 2, 1995. Our personal experience with Dr. Burton is one of exceptional expertise, knowledge, and caring. It is incomprehensible to us that Dr. Burton would do anything derogatory to his profession or to any patient under his care. We hereby demand that all records and equipment be returned, and all charges against him dropped.

As news of the raid spread, many patients called. Each patient was asked to get as many of the petitions signed as he could and return them to the clinic. Accompanying the petitions, was a letter asking patients, friends, and/or relatives to call Idaho senators and representatives whose names, addresses, and phone numbers were enclosed.

Patients were informed that the clinic would not be open for business until February 13, 1995, as many legal issues needed to be worked out. Legal questions abounded. Could he still sell his vitamins? What treatment, if any, could he legally administer? How long before he would get his equipment back?

After letting go of some employees, would he be able to finance his business debt? Would he be able to meet the farming, mechanics shop, and clinic payrolls? What kind of income could he reasonably expect to generate without the ability to perform blood work or give injections; that was, after all, the draw of his business.

FBI Special Agent Marge Newsome received a call from cooperating witness, Wes O'Dea. "I understand that yesterday you pulled it off."

"We did--what do you have for us?" Newsome asked.

"I got a buddy who thinks I should talk with a Dr. Merke over in Blackfoot. He says he has some important information on Burton and his practices."

"Go for it."

"What about school? I'd like to start as soon as possible," Wes said.

"I'll be getting the paper work together on that real soon. It'll take a while for the processing."

"How long are we talking?"

"A couple of weeks."

"Okay."

"Okay Wes. Let us know what you find out."

"Count on it."

On February 6, 1995, Special Agent Newsome received a call from a number of Burton's patients. Daisy Ducksworth suggested that her confidential files had been taken from Burton's clinic, and she demanded to know why.

"According to our files Ma'am, you took GH3," Agent Newsome told her.

"That's right, lady I did take GH3. Those are my confidential files. How dare you take them away from Dr. Burton without my permission? I would like them returned at once. This is a violation of my rights!"

Shortly thereafter, Kate Russell phoned Newsome. "I feel that what you are doing is wrong, and it's a waste of our taxpayer dollars. Dr. Burton is an honorable Christian man. Ma'am, Dr. Burton saved my husband's life, and he did it using all natural products. I want this case dropped now! Let the man get back to saving lives. He can't do that since you took all of his files and equipment."

"How do you know that all the files were taken? Who asked you to call me?"

"That's not important. I want his files and equipment returned!" she demanded, slamming the phone in Agent Newsome's ear.

But Agent Newsome was wiser when she questioned Mr. Luther Bain. Having gotten dust blown in her face from questioning prior interviewees on how they knew the files were taken, Newsome would be more cautious. "How did you learn about the raid?" Newsome asked.

"I called the clinic this morning to order some supplements and learned that my file had been taken. I would like it returned to Dr. Burton."

"A copy of your file will be returned to you," Newsome said.

"I need the files returned to Dr. Burton, he's my doctor. I don't know what to do with it."

Along with Special Agent Newsome, Investigator Roy Evans of the Idaho Attorney General's office was also interviewing Burton's patients. He phoned Arlene Webb at her Wisconsin home. "I am conducting a criminal investigation of Dr. Burton and his Natrogenics clinic."

"I am appalled that you FBI and FDA people seized my personal medical files from my doctor. I want my files sent back to Dr. Burton now! You people are always snooping around where you don't belong. Every time I turn around you are raiding some naturopath or alternative doctor," Webb yelled.

"Were you ever treated by Dr. Burton?" Investigator Evans asked.

"Yes. I bought some natural supplements from him because that's all I take. I went to those medical quacks for years. No more."

"This is a criminal investigation, Ma'am."

"I don't believe for one minute that Dr. Burton is a criminal. He is a good man, and I want my file returned to him," Webb demanded.

"We are working with the originals, but would you like us to send you a copy of your files?"

"I would like my records sent back to Dr. Burton. I'm not able to send those records back."

"Would you be willing to submit to a personal interview with the FBI?"

"I have nothing more to add to what I've already said," Webb snapped.

But like Special Agent Newsome, Investigator Evans, too, had gotten smarter after his interview with Webb. When he returned a call to Mary Black, he introduced himself only as an investigator with the Idaho Attorney General's office who wanted to offer help rather than play detective.

"I would like you to help me get my medical records back if possible," Black said.

"Would you like them sent to you?"

"Yes, if you would, please."

"Okay Ma'am. Let me check on that file for you. I'll keep you posted."

Investigator Evans responded to a request that Cynthia Zina had previously made to the US Attorney's office in Boise regarding her file. "I can't believe the nerve of you low lifes.... You did the same thing to Dr. Wayne in Washington State."

"Have you ever been treated by Dr. Burton?" Evans asked.

"Yes, I have for arthritis. He's done a wonderful job--thank you very much! I'd like to know just what is it you're looking for?"

"I can't give out any information on this case, since it's still under investigation."

"So for as I'm concerned, Dr. Burton should be allowed to practice his way. Nobody is being hurt. You have no right to stop him from practicing his craft," she told Investigator Evans.

On February 7, 1995, Agent Newsome phoned Tamara Borders for questioning.

"Both my mother's and my files have been taken from Dr. Burton's office, and I would like them returned."

"So you've received treatment from Dr. Burton."

"If it weren't for Dr. Burton my mother, Lorna Horn, would be dead. My mom had a brain tumor which had been treated by a doctor in Idaho Falls, but it didn't do any good. Dr. Burton has been treating her for some years now, and she's improved tremendously since he's been working with her.

"Well, we can't release the originals; this case is under investigation. We can mail you a copy of your file."

Special Agent Newsome telephoned Ernest Sojourn, a resident in Spokane, Washington, and explained the nature of the interview.

"What you're doing to Dr. Burton! It's a shame! What in the heck do you think you're doing? You have no right!"

"Have you ever been treated by Dr. Burton?" Agent Newsome asked.

"I'm being treated for the Epstein Barr Virus."

"Did you receive your treatments at the clinic?"

"What I'd like the FBI to do is this; either return a copy of my file to Dr. Burton, or me, because Dr. Burton has never hurt anyone. In fact, he's helped a lot of people. I want you to return Dr. Burton's things to him."

"Was Dr. Burton's treatments helpful for you?"

"Ma'am, the Epstein Barr Virus would have killed me but for Dr. Burton."

Peter Kirsten told Agent Newsome, "Ma'am with all due respect, I am with Dr. Burton one hundred percent--one hundred percent."

Lonnie Knox told Newsome, "My son Bill is fifty. He just freaks out if he doesn't get this supplement from Dr. Burton. You took it when you raided the clinic. Please drop all charges against Dr. Burton. We rely on him heavily."

When Newsome learned that Dr. Burton had worked on Liz Regan's back she asked. "Are you aware that he is not a chiropractor, Ma'am?"

"Lady, you don't need to be a chiropractor to massage a person. I think you FBI people are just on a fishing mission. And I want you to know that I contacted Congressman Crapo and Senator Larry Craig about this!"

"How long have you been a patient of Dr. Burton's?" Newsome asked Gertha Jamison in a phone interview.

"For about 18 years. Now the FBI has taken the machine he uses to treat me."

"Can you describe that machine to me?"

"He would put my feet in water in a bucket with metal plates and cords attached to my ankle."

"Why don't you go back to whomever you were going to before you started going to Dr. Burton?"

"Because you guys shut him down! Both Dr. Lynch and Dr. Nelson were shut down."

"Why not just go to a medical doctor?"

"Medical doctors screwed me up. I'll never go back there. I want my file returned to Dr. Burton at once!" Jamison snapped.

"We can't return the originals to Dr. Burton, but you can receive a copy of your file."

"I'm not interested in a copy of my file. I'll tell you something, lady. If my leg has to be amputated because you won't allow Dr. Burton to practice, somebody is going to get sued. We're not living in a free country when you can't even choose your doctor because you FBI people shut him down. You go after innocent people like you did with poor Randy Weaver and those innocent people."

The calls, requests, and personal visits to prosecutor Leonard McClain's office on Burton's behalf were numerous. It prompted McClain to confront Dr. Burton's legal counsel, Attorney Anthony, to limit the requests to only those patients whose files had been taken. But Anthony rebutted:

"Burton needs the patient files to keep his business open. Many patients have come in, and it is hard to service these people without having the records. It is impossible to predict who will call or come in. Therefore, we ask that all the patient records be returned."

Outbursts from angry patients flooded the courts and FBI offices.

Becky, the lady who had brought her small dying infant into the clinic the day of the raid for treatment but was denied it, railed: "You vile, miserable piece of trash, my baby died and it's all your fault! You can bet I will be on that witness stand testifying on Dr. Burton's behalf."

"The 13 agent FBI/FDA raid on Natrogenics clinic in Idaho on February 2, 1995, was a little bit like Ruby Ridge in Northern Idaho. Please don't allow the Attorney General's office to be used like the past Governor, State Police and other agencies were used in the Ruby Ridge, Randy Weaver case," one patient pleaded.

"The more these things come into the light of day, the more they stink to high heaven," another said.

"What this country needs are more people like Dr. Burton to keep us alive and well. The medical profession could learn a lot from health practitioners. Or don't they want to?" another patient exclaimed.

Hundreds of letters showed continued support for Burton during this tumultuous time. Now he needed legislators to pass a bill grandfathering in naturopaths who had earned their place in society before their states' licensure requirements were in place. He needed someone to rally behind his cause so he could get his equipment and files back. He placed his hopes in Helen Chenoweth, a trusted Member of Congress who wrote,

> When the Founding Fathers wrote and ratified the Constitution of the United States, they had in mind a government of limited powers that would leave the people to live their own lives, free from governmental interference. They knew that protection of the rights of individuals to liberty and free use of their property was the key to both individual and national prosperity. With that end in mind, they wrote a constitution that listed the powers of government and made it abundantly clear that government had no other powers. The protection of private property rights was one of their greatest concerns.
>
> The Founders also knew, however, that left to itself, government would not be content to stay within its proper bounds. This led them to include a bill of rights to establish a strong court system that was intended to be a shield between government and the people. The federal government has grown at an incredible rate and has intruded into the daily lives of Americans to an extent that would amaze even the Founders... Your property and rights are no longer your own if these regulations and government actions are not challenged.
>
> I have been a member of the Stewards of the Range, a national constitutional and property rights advocacy organization, headquartered in Boise, Idaho, since its establishment in 1991. Stewards have become one of the leading forces fighting governmental intrusions into the rights of Americans.
>
> But Stewards, and organizations like it, cannot be everywhere and do everything. We must all do our part to protect our rights when government attempts to invade them. You need knowledge of the law. You need to know how governmental agencies, legislatures, and advocates of regulation work. Only in this way can we 'fight smart.'

Supporters also sought the backing of Governor Phil Batt, for he held in his grip the decision that would ultimately determine Burton's fate.

29

February 13, 1995

"I have been sick for years. I went from one doctor to another, and they couldn't find anything wrong, but I felt awful. I kept asking myself, if there's nothing wrong how come I feel so horrible. Finally a friend of mine told me about Dr. Burton," Carlton Fisher told Agent Newsome in an interview.

"How do you know that some of what you're taking doesn't have illegal drugs in them?" Newsome asked.

"Because I can't even take supplements on the market, let alone drugs. I shared this with Dr. Burton. It's something about my stomach… I just can't take them."

Burton reopened for business. Erma Summer came in for her bi-weekly injection; three weeks now since her last, digestive discomfort was creeping back. Complaints of pain that had only recently begun to fade away had resurfaced. Burton watched her grab her stomach, doubling over in pain.

"I wish I could help you but they've taken my equipment and files. I'm sorry." But just watching her it reminded him of the suffering he'd endured. …And it was so unnecessary.

Meanwhile Agent Newsome phoned Pattie Florence, owner of the Slim and Firm. "Are you a patient of Dr. Burton?"

"Yes. "

"Dr. Burton is not a medical doctor. Why didn't you go to a medical doctor?"

"Lady, I've been to several medical doctors at Marshall Clinic. I kept telling them how bad I felt. They said it was all in my head. Finally, I learned that I had Lymes disease, and Dr. Burton treated me with natural supplements. I wouldn't be here today if it weren't for Dr. Burton."

Genieva Bee of Utah told Newsome, "My daughter, who was five years old, had been treated for leukemia with a bone marrow transplant and massive doses of radiation. They didn't work."

"So how did you hear about Dr. Burton?"

"A friend of mine. When I took my daughter to Dr. Burton she was barely alive. With Dr. Burton's treatments she lived about a year longer."

It was only two weeks ago that Marvis Russell had last received his injection. Upon entering, the clinic he noticed that it looked bare. The girls weren't stirring about the counter, ringing up the register. Nor were there many patients in the usually packed clinic.

Burton ventured out of his office and noticed Marvis in the waiting room. "Why don't you come back? I'm a little short on staff now, I guess you've heard," Burton commented, leading Marvis into his office.

"Heard what? I came in for my injection."

Burton slid into his big chair behind the desk. "Didn't Carrie tell you what happened?"

"No. No one was at the counter when I came in. I thought it was kind of strange, but I didn't know what to make of it."

"Thirteen FBI agents came in and raided us a couple of weeks ago."

"So that's what it is. I noticed the place looked awfully bare."

"Yeah they took all my equipment, and many of my patients' records."

"Are you kidding?"

"No. They took my injection solution."

"Awh man! But there must be something you can do."

"They even took my microscope."

"Oh man! What am I going to do?"

"I wish I knew."

"What do you think brought this on?"

"An angry ex-employee. Trying to get even I guess."

"But why?"

"Well, I had to let him go. He was stealing from me. He sexually abused my patients, he just... Hiring that guy was one of the biggest mistakes of my life. But he kept bugging me about working here. Said he wanted to be a chiropractor and learning from me would help him. I fell for it. Now it's costing me. So, I don't know what to tell you. My hands are tied. I'm hoping it won't be long before this thing is resolved."

"There must be something I can do."

"Listen, call and write the legislators, the prosecutor, and the judge." Burton pulled a list of names and numbers from his drawer and gave it to Marvis. "Let them know how you feel. Yours was one of the 400 files taken, so call the FBI and the Attorney General's office and ask that my equipment and your file be returned."

"Man! This is unreal. I'll get right on this."

It was Kate Russell's second time speaking with Special Agent Newsome. "I want my original files returned to Dr. Burton now! He is my doctor."

"Mrs. Russell, this case is still under investigation," Agent Newsome said.

"I don't give a care about your investigation. Dr. Burton is my doctor and I want my files sent back to him."

"Sounds like you're afraid we'll find something Ma'am."

"I've got nothing to hide, but these are my family's personal medical files, files that are supposed to be private. They do not belong to the FBI."

"The files are being held in the strictest of confidence."

"They ain't doing a bit of good being stored away in no darn boxes. Dr. Burton needs them to treat my family."

"Ma'am we cannot release the originals at this time."

"My files shouldn't be in you goofy FBI agent's office where all they'll do is sit and mold," Russell quipped.

"We will send you a copy of your family's file. But no originals will be released to Dr. Burton at this time," Newsome said.

"What brought you to Dr. Burton?" Newsome asked Erma Summer," another one of Dr. Burton's patients.

"I've had different types of cancers. They went into remission and returned. Now I have lung cancer."

"How do you know you have it? Did you go to a medical doctor?"

"Yes. I've received treatment by Drs. Sears, Monte and Zelda in Idaho. But now the cancer is back."

"So are you a patient of Dr. Burton's now?"

"Yes I am."

"What are his methods of treatment?"

"He gives me injections. Please don't close him down. I'll die if you stop him from practicing."

"Where were these treatments administered?" Newsome asked.

"At the Natrogenics clinic," Summer said.

Burton followers were loyal and creative in getting needed assistance for Burton. Eleanor Manson wrote to Dr. Nathan Daton whose clinic had managed to flourish in spite of the FBI/FDA raid previously launched on him in 1992. She asked Dr. Daton if he could offer any suggestions to Burton in resolving his case. He offered the following:

"I am sure you have done this already… But if not… Contact the staff of Senator Hatch (Utah) in Washington DC, and point out that the FDA did not give you 10 days notice as called for in the Hatch/Richardson Act just passed, and the agency violated this new law!"

Another supporter suggested that Burton contact Lorraine Prince of the Channel 3 news, since she was interested in having Idaho restore its image, especially in wake of the Oklahoma, and Ruby Ridge fiascoes.

Gale Parsons, a satisfied patient and avid supporter of Burton mounted perhaps one of the most aggressive campaigns. She spearheaded a national campaign to convince concerned patients to write news shows, senators, prosecutors, judge, probation officers, television personalities, etc. in support of Burton. Several of Gale's articles were featured in local newspapers. The response to Gale's articles was phenomenal.

Undaunted by the barrage of letters flowing into her office, Special Agent Marge Newsome continued investigating. Was Daniel in compliance with their order regarding contact with Burton? On board at the clinic was Marilyn, Daniel's cousin. Through Marilyn, Daniel could still be in touch with the happenings at the clinic. Through Daniel, so could Wes... He contacted Agent Newsome to answer more questions about Burton.

"Has Lou been in contact with Burton?"

"Burton tried to find Lou a few days after the raid."

"Why would Burton want to talk with Dr. Daniel?"

"He wanted to find out what happened."

"How is Burton functioning since the raid?

"He called his employees together at the office and asked them what questions they were asked by the investigators."

"Is he being cautious now, or is he practicing as per usual?"

"He's being cautious; he thinks the telephone is bugged. He advised the employees not to accept any more packages from United Parcel Service or the U.S. Mail because he wanted to know what was considered acceptable practice before he got in any new shipment of products.

"Does Burton know why he's being investigated?"

"He thinks he's being investigated for practicing medicine without a license."

"Who does he think turned him into the authorities?"

"He is convinced that I turned him in, since I was fired."

30

March 3, 1995

Burton stood looking out of the window that had been papered by the agent during the raid. Still Burton's equipment wasn't returned, and no charges had been filed against him. His temper grew short. If what Dr. Daton said was true, the FBI was in clear violation of the Hatch/Richardson Act. That should account for something, he thought.

He remembered the chronic patients he had had to turn away, and was moved to tears. Each passing moment was so crucial to these patients. He just had to figure out a way to get his microscope, injection solution, and equipment back.

"Agent Newsome, this is Burton. I would like to clear my name. Can you tell me what charges are being brought against me?"

"Mr. Burton, as you know, this case is still in investigation. We cannot comment on it at this time."

"But what about my equipment when can I…?"

"You'll need to talk with Leonard McClain," Agent Newsome cut in.

"I've tried contacting him a hundred times. I can't even get the guy to return my phone calls."

"Have your attorney call him."

"Okay," Burton said.

But Newsome told Burton's patient, Kirston Hopson, "There possibly won't be any charges."

"That's strange, she told you that; she won't even talk with me about it," Burton said.

Otis Lewis confirmed Hopson's statement, but added that Newsome was friendly and assured him that Burton could still practice.

It was from a letter written by Senator Dirk Kempthorne that Burton first learned of the FBI charges: mail fraud, using misbranded drugs, and administering unapproved medications. Some concerns had also arisen about Burton's having a proper license.

Burton sat at his desk, eagerly waiting, hoping the ringing phone would bring good news. "This is Kyle," he said, pressing the receiver against his ear.

"Kyle this is Bart Richie."

"Yeah, Bart."

"I talked with the US Attorney's office."

"Uh huh, did they tell you anything?"

"They said that no charges have been filed, and there was a good chance that there won't be any."

"Did they say anything about when I can get my equipment back?"

"They wouldn't give out any information regarding the case, but said that you have a good reputation, and they don't want to ruin it."

Seven days later Ryan Walsh phoned. "Kyle I visited with this lady FBI agent that I know in Pocatello and discussed your case."

"What did she say?"

"She said that if no charges are filled within forty eight hours, your equipment is supposed to be returned. But guess what! She also said that they have orders to get rid of all naturopaths from Boise to Pocatello."

"You mean she admitted it? Right from the horses mouth, huh?"

"Yeah, this thing is crazy. I'm going keep you posted on what I find out."

"I appreciate it. Thanks," Kyle said.

Neither Ivanna's busy school, nor work schedule, could keep her from campaigning for justice on behalf of the doctor who had given her a second chance at life. She reasoned: if he is in trouble, I am in trouble, and addressed correspondence to US Prosecutor Leonard McClain, probation officer, Stacey Cannon, USA Judge Winston, national news shows and local newspapers to try and get Burton's equipment back. All efforts proved futile.

Dr. Coals phoned Burton. "One of your patients was in my office today. Says they talked with Marge Newsome. Newsome claims all charges have been dropped."

"Thanks, but you know… I keep getting these stories, but they won't return my equipment. Heck, I'm dead without my equipment."

Ryan Walsh stopped by the clinic to visit. "I just went by to see Agent Shirley, one of the FBI investigators."

"That son of a gun took my gold coin collection. Just hearing his name makes me want to puke."

"He said it's going to be a while before you get your equipment back, but they don't plan to close you."

"You're telling me they're still not talking charges, but they're going to keep my equipment? Crap! What's it going to take? What do they want from me?" Kyle asked furiously. They looked at each other, both filled with disgust.

"I wish I knew, Kyle," Ryan said.

Later, Dr. Ronald Feagan, the president of the IMNA phoned Burton. "If a person practices for seven or more years without any complaint from the state, the practice is considered to be in good standing. They can't close you down."

"Ronald I tell you, I don't know what to think anymore."

"Well that's law--I can prove it. Maybe you can talk with Rudy about it. It may be something you can use in the grand jury hearing."

"Yeah well, we'll see."

"President Clinton advised Kessler to lay off the health food industry," Paris Mason told Burton.

"Yeah, let's just hope he does."

"Also, you may want to call Tyrone Morrison. He can help. Just let him know you're a friend of mine." Paris was attempting to return the favor as she had promised when he rescued her from back surgery years ago.

Dr. Burton walked through the clinic lobby into the Voyager, a clothing store that was attached to the front of the clinic. Just on the other side was his restaurant; inside was Erma Summer's daughter, Mandy.

"After the raid I took Erma to see a regular doctor. I mean, what else could I do?"

"Yeah, this thing is just…." Burton said, his lips flattening.

"I had to take her to a nursing home. Her health is poor. I feel this is wrong. She should be able to go wherever she wants, especially because of her poor health. We've tried all that medical stuff. I went to her attorney the other day. He's going to be writing the FBI."

The FBI continued to gather whatever evidence they could on Daniel; it could prove useful later. Agent Newsome spoke with Blue Shield of Idaho's staff attorney, Joel Barnett. "I'm trying to locate a chiropractor by the name of Walt Lou Daniel."

"If you'll hold on I'll check on that for you. … Okay, looks like he has a shop in Provo, Utah."

"What company name is he using?"

"Not long ago we received some claims submitted from Daniel under the name of Provo Chiropractic," Barnett said.

"Thanks." Newsome said.

A letter from the Law-offices of Justin & Joseph, attorneys for Erma Summer, caught Agent Newsome's attention.

Dear Agent Newsome:

It is on behalf of Erma Summer, a patient of Kyle Burton's that we are writing you. During a search at the Natrogenics on February 2, 1995, you removed patient files, one of which was my client's, Ms. Summer.

She has tried repeatedly to have you return those files to her, to no avail. This file is her property and the information in them personal. A personal relationship with Mr. Burton is her right to be enjoyed by the "doctor-patient relationship."

Ms. Summer is terminally ill; without treatment she will surely expire. She has chosen Dr. Burton as her practitioner. Mr. Burton cannot provide her adequate treatment, however, without her files. As such, we are asking that you return the original file to Erma, the one removed from Mr. Burton's office on February 2, 1995.

Thank you in advance for your cooperation.

"You know I talked with Sheriff House. He said he learned about the raid on the news that evening. He was quite upset." Gertha Jamison told Dr. Burton.

"Yeah, I mean they oughta... I don't know, maybe that'll be what we need to have this case dismissed," Kyle said.

"I also talked with the governor. He said they are looking into the matter. He was very supportive."

Jeanette Hogue reported, "I've been talking with someone I know at the FBI's office. I hear they can't find anything to charge you with, and feel that the raid was a waste of time."

"Then maybe they'll dismiss the case," Kyle said.

"You know, I talked with the reporter who was assigned to this case. He claims that the judge served the warrant believing that you were practicing unorthodox medicine," Donna Hunter told Kyle.

"Yeah, well, I heard that they are trying to get rid of all naturopaths from Boise to Pocatello."

"Sure looks that way. I mean, Dr. Lynch and I can't think of the other fella's name over in Twin Falls, but they shut him down, you know."

"Yeah, it doesn't look good," Burton said.

It was April 3, 1995, when Ryan and Merle Sattles visited Burton.

"We talked to that defensive witch a while ago," Merle said.

"Very nasty," Ryan added. "She had the gall to say: 'You know he's not even a doctor.' I told her' I don't give a crap if he's an ape. He helped my family and me. No doctor ever could!'" Ryan said.

Burton couldn't help laughing. It was a testament of the Lord's mercy upon him. He had sent His angels to fight this battle with him. For that, he was grateful.

According to Merle Fry, both the US Attorney and the governor were very kind and supportive. They promised they would do what they could so that Burton could continue to practice.

Conflicting calls continued to flood Burton's office. One came from Luther Bain.

"I talked with Agent Newsome. She said that the equipment is being kept for awhile, but they have no intentions of closing you down."

"The heck they aren't, Luther! They have as good as closed me down. I don't have any equipment, or my patients' files. What exactly is that, if it's not closing me down?"

"Well those are my thoughts, too, especially since she admitted that they don't have anything to charge you with. So I told her that if some of these patients die, this would be grounds for a class action law suit by the families."

"What good is my microscope to them? They don't know what to do with it. They don't know what I do!"

All the conflicting second hand information was getting to Burton. He wanted the truth. He called US Assistant Prosecuting Attorney, Leonard McClain.

"I can't talk with you because you have an attorney," McClain said. But Burton wasn't about to release him so easily.

"I just need to know if I can lease another microscope from the research center while I wait for mine."

"You'll need to talk with your attorney," Leonard snapped.

Kyle slammed down the phone. "Crap!" Why can't I get answers when no charges have been filed against me? How long is this going to continue? Perhaps his attorney could make sense out of some of this. But the call to Attorney Anthony yielded no new information.

On April 9, 1995, Kyle received a call from Erma Summer's daughter, Mandy. "Erma died April 8, 1995. I will be suing the FBI," she said.

31

In April, Special Agent Brett Kerske conducted an interview with Doug Smith, a Regulation/Compliance Investigator with the State of Wisconsin. Smith stated that there were currently no laws or regulations governing the practices of naturopaths or homeopaths in the State of Wisconsin. On visits to Wisconsin, it was in Merle Fry's office that Burton treated patients. Dr. Fry explained to Agent Burns how Burton's treatments were differentiated in the files.

In her followup personal interview, Linda Reichart told Agent Burns, that "according to Leslie Child, her husband, Andrew, who dismissed Burtons' patients as 'medical outcasts,' agreed that she could try the program for a couple of months, Pattie Florence, who was supposedly successfully treated by Burton, convinced Leslie Child to get on Burton's program.

Florence had her husband remove H-21 (black pearls) from her Slim and Tone store and take them to her home when she found out about the raid on Burton. Florence also had Laetrile, something used to treat cancer, even though it's illegal here in the United States."

The Russells enthusiastically shared their FBI interview with Burton. "We got a visit from an FBI agent. He was very nice. I told him we started going to see you when a psychiatrist, indirectly referred by our medical doctor, prescribed a drug that made Donald's tongue swell up, and have been seeing you ever since," Kate said.

"Did he tell you anything?"

"He said he didn't know why they were investigating you, because you've had many calls and letters supporting you."

"Did he say anything about whether or not there will be charges?"

"He didn't mention the charges. We told him how much you had helped us. He said he was wondering how in the world you could make such a good diagnosis from the blood. I told him, 'well, you know, it's a research project, and Dr. Burton tells his patients that."

Burton supporters kept the pressure on. They continued to clog the judicial systems begging for mercy for their doctor. One patient wondered how the FBI/FDA could come in and seize her medical files when her husband couldn't get it when she was sick, without her signature or a letter of request. To Senator Luther Craig, she wrote, "I am trying to determine:

- What law/statute gives them legal jurisdiction

- What conditions give them the right to raid and confiscate patients' records and/or other items?
- Is there a stature that provides for the length of time they can hold them?
- Are there guidelines to be followed for seizing properties?

Eula Lucas wrote in protest, "I have been treated by Burton for years because I haven't gotten results from approved medical personnel. I pay far too much for medical insurance not to be able to choose my own form of care."

Conflicting stories continued. Helen Hope called Burton about her encounter. "I talked with Marge Newsome."

"Now what is she saying?"

"They said that they can't find anything to charge you with.... Said they won't be closing you down."

"Thanks Helen."

Pattie Florence told Burton, "You know I had an FBI agent stop in my office a minute ago. He wanted to know what kind of treatments I had received while at the clinic. He asked if I had gotten injections or used the electrical machine. I told him yes, I had gotten spinal touch therapy and some adjustments."

"Did he ask about the H-21?"

"Yeah, he saw it on my report. I told him that we used to have a homeopathic remedy called H-21."

"That's true, we did."

"He asked me about the round black pills. He wanted to know where I got them. I told him I got some from you and some from Marshall Clinic."

"Uh huh."

'"Well, you know they have Valium in them,"' he said. I said, '"That's a lie because they were tested at the clinic in Marshall. They said there was nothing in them that would hurt you."'

Dr. Ryan Radcliff, Burton's partner in the HLB/LBA research, extended an opportunity.

"Kyle, this is Ryan. Listen, Ronald Feagan and I just got back from Washington, DC. They're talking about reopening the Hewitt College in conjunction with another college that enrolls 18,000 students."

"What kind of degree are they offering?"

"They're going to offer a four year program for naturopaths and a one year program for MD's to get their NMD's. "

"With all these raids going on what does the demand look like out there?"

"Well, there aren't many NMD degrees out there. It's a highly respected degree, and the response was good. They want to have charters in different locations, but they need someone to teach the blood work. Will you be willing to teach it? It's going to be a requirement in order to get the degree."

It sounded like a good opportunity. Would the judge give his consent? Kyle couldn't help wondering. "Well, you know I'll have to see what these guys here say. Don't know if they'll agree to it or not. Let me get back with you on this one."

Maureen Scales told Burton that Agent Newsome refused to discuss the case. "She claims it's her job to protect the public from unscrupulous practices."

Shortly after an interview with the FBI, Dr. Merle Fry phoned. "Kyle this is Merle. You won't believe who was just in my office."

"Who?"

"Agent Norris Broyhill from the FBI field office."

"Why doesn't that surprise me? I bet he asked you about the H-21 didn't he?"

"He asked several questions, but yeah one was about the H-21. I told him that I only used the natural H-21."

"That's the only kind we use, can't seem to get that across to them. You can get drugs from medical doctors. We don't need drugs to do what we do. Don't they get it?"

"He seemed amazed at the blood work. I showed him pictures of my initial and current blood work and he was amazed. He asked how I could see the improvement. I told him that you were the expert, but that I was doing a lecture on it soon. He asked if he could attend. I told him that would be fine."

"Yeah, well, let's just see if he shows up."

"I told him that you'll be lecturing in September on the blood work… and I gave him some pamphlets."

"…I don't think I'm going to make it. These people are… They won't let me travel."

"If it's any consolation, he told me that everything is going to be okay."

"Yeah, well, I've heard that before, but I still don't have my equipment back."

"There's only one thing that concerns me."

"What's that?"

"He asked if I had been involved in your petition drive. I told him that I made it and you approved it to be sent out."

Disturbed by the FBI's maneuvers, Ronald Feagan called Burton. "Ramsey Holland (the attorney for the ANMA) said that he heard that the FBI was visiting your patients, and that they cannot take files and then visit the patient. He suggests that something needs to be done."

"Yeah… Like what, Ronald? What are we going to do about it?"

It was early May when Stacy Wren phoned Burton.

"I talked with Marge Newsome, and she told me that they do not have anything to charge you with, and they are not going to close you down."

Letters from supporters continued to pour into Burton's office. But progress was slow and he became more and more frustrated. He urged Attorney Anthony to speed up the process.

Attorney Anthony wrote Assistant U.S. District Attorney Leonard McClain.

> *Some time has passed since we last spoke. I have attempted to reach you by phone, but you are unavailable. My client would like to have this matter behind him. We have not received anything back from the numerous items that were taken during the search. We would like to know the status of the investigation, and would like to have equipment returned.*
>
> *At the time of the search, it was indicated that the microscope would be returned shortly after the search and after it had been examined. To date, we haven't received all of the files, which were to be copied and returned, nor have we received any of the other items that were seized. I would appreciate your response in this matter as soon as possible.*

When Lydia Nelson learned of the raid she felt bad for Dr. Burton, but it was Brad's health that most concerned her. Burton had given her baby life with his natural approach to health. Because of that, she had come to rely heavily on him for all of her family's health care needs.

The paranoia typical of a frightened mother returned. What if Brad fell ill again? What about Kattie? Where in the world did this leave her? Her family? She shuddered to think of what could be.... In a letter to the FBI she wrote, "My husband and I are taxpayers, we are outraged that our tax dollars are being spent harassing Dr. Burton."

Jeanette Snyder phoned Burton. "I talked to that Marge Newsome today."

"I appreciate all the support you've been giving me."

"I asked her why she did what she did to you."

"We're doing an investigation."

"Well did you find anything to charge him with?"

"No.'

"Then why don't you return his equipment?"

"Because we are still investigating him."

"'I wish you all the bad luck in the world,' I told her and then slammed down the phone."

In Early May, Dr. Ronald Feagan phoned Kyle with what he believed was promising news. "I understand that your equipment is going to be returned in 19 days," he said.

"Well, that sounds good, but…"

"The attorney suggests that we have a 'show cause' hearing and a motion to enjoin them from consulting with the patients. If Rudy gets too much flack from it, Ramsey Holland will help."

May 15th had brought Burton no closer to a resolution. In a letter to Leonard McClain, Anthony discussed Burton's concerns.

Dear Leonard:

In speaking with my client, he has a number of questions that he would like you to respond to. First, could you please delineate what he can or cannot do in his practice so that he can continue practicing without fear of interruption or prosecution? Secondly, he is concerned that part of his practice is being limited because he does not have his microscope. Do you contend that his use of a microscope is illegal? If you do not contend it is illegal, Mr. Burton plans on purchasing another microscope to use if his is not returned to him.

Next, at the time of the search warrant, the agents took oxygen tanks. These were not listed on items to be seized. He would like the oxygen returned. If you contend that his use of oxygen in his practice is against some law, please let us know what that is. Third, there was an ozone machine taken, which was also not on the list of items to be seized. Dr. Burton states that he hasn't used the ozone machine that much, but wants to know whether you contend the use of that machine is prohibited by State or Federal Law.

There are also certificates taken. Under the search warrant some certificates could be taken, which were Dr. Burton's certificates. However, the agent seized all of Jane Burton's certificates. Those were not provided for under the search warrant, and she would like those returned to her. Also, Dr. Burton had his Washington D.C. license for naturopathic practice taken. He would like to have that returned to him as well.

If you could answer these questions it would be greatly appreciated by Dr. Burton. Further, Dr. Burton remains willing to sit down and discuss with you, under a use immunity agreement, any questions you might have. There have been multiple statements by the FBI and the U.S. Attorney's Office that your office did not wish to put Dr. Burton out of business. With that in mind, he wants to make sure that he can continue to service his patients, and that he does not run afoul with your contentions of improper acts.

McClain responded.

A use-immunity agreement is unnecessary if Dr. Burton believes that his medical practices are lawful. Should you find our terms unacceptable, we will continue our inquiry and render our judgment. You may, however, find a meeting more expedient. Until there is a resolve in this issue, Burton's equipment will remain under our jurisdiction.

"Kyle this is Rudy. I talked with Leonard. They have agreed to meet with you; however, they will not meet under use immunity."

"Use immunity. What's use immunity?"

"That means that whatever comes out in the meeting cannot be used against you."

"Heck Rudy. You know those guys… I've got nothing to hide, but these guys don't…."

"…I think we should go ahead and meet with them, Kyle. Without it, they will just drag things out, and that could have devastating results on the business, not to mention your patients. Perhaps we can come up with some resolve. Let's give it a try.

"Let me think about this, Rudy. I'll get back with you," Kyle said.

"By the way, McClain totally ignored my question about whether or not you can purchase another microscope, so I would lay low on that until we get clearance."

"Okay," Burton agreed.

The desire to know what was legally acceptable for him to do, in and outside of his practice, weighed out over Kyle's insistence of the use immunity agreement. Grand opportunities awaited him, like the new naturopathic college for which they were seeking faculty, speaking engagements, seminars, and conferences. Clearing his name was important so that he could get back to what he loved best--helping his patients. But how could he make any plans when things were still up in the air?

He phoned attorney Anthony. "Rudy lets do it. You'll be there with me in the meeting so… Let's go ahead with it."

Continued efforts to reach McClain by phone failed, so on May 24, Anthony drafted yet another letter.

Dear Leonard:

I have had an opportunity to speak with my client and he is willing to meet with you and discuss your questions concerning his practice. My client would like to resolve this matter, get his equipment back, and continue on. We look forward to a fruitful meeting with you to discuss the matter in detail and find out what you claim he is doing that is improper and if there is something improper, to appropriately adjust his practice.

Mr. Burton has always wanted to comply with the law and do things that would be in his patients' best interest. Please let me know a time that you will be available for such a meeting here at my office.

Sheila Holland did get through to McClain and shared her conversation with Burton.

'"We don't have any charges against Dr. Burton, we're just looking into how he conducts his business.'"

"'That's ridiculous. This man has helped people that no one else could. He needs his equipment to continue,' I told him. Leonard said, he was sorry and would get it back as soon as possible."

"Soon as possible…. What the heck is soon as possible? Did they give you a date?" Burton asked.

"Unfortunately not. No date."

32

In late May, in the presence of Special Agent Terrence Glenn of the FDA, Assistant US Attorney Leonard McClain and Special Agent Marge Newsome interviewed Adrian Moore, a naturopathic physician at his Boise, Idaho office.

Moore told the investigative team that, "When patients require a blood test, the patient's blood is drawn by a member of our staff and sent to a lab for examining. The standard blood tests CBCs, and chem strip are later analyzed by the National Health Labs." He furthermore asserted that: "Neither parasites nor cancers can be diagnosed by simply analyzing a drop of blood using a microscope." His would be the standard against which Burton's practice methods would be measured.

Kelly Hadley offered the investigative team materials she felt would help to clear Burton's name.

"The materials you've gathered, Ms. Hadley, are not in the best interest of the government," Newsome and McClain agreed.

"What I'm doing is in my best interest, because I need those injections to stay alive. I want to help clear Dr. Burton's name."

"Is Dr. Burton currently giving injections?"

"No. That's why I want to clear his name, so he can. I can't work because of my health. I'm dying from cancer."

In early June, Special Agent Marge Newsome interviewed Hank Naples, the Pocatello chiropractor who urged Daniel to discontinue his practice with Burton. "How long have you been practicing?" Newsome asked.

"Since 1970."

"Are you licensed here in Idaho under the Idaho State Chiropractic Board?"

"Not only am I licensed under that Board, I am currently serving on that board."

"Who appointed you to that Board?"

"The governor."

Newsome looked down at her notes. "I see here that there's a Harold Naples who is also a chiropractor here in Pocatello. Any relation?"

"Yes, Harold is my cousin."

"How did you learn that Burton had a chiropractor aboard?"

"Well, one day Harold and I were talking. He told me that Burton had a chiropractor named Walt Lou Daniel practicing with him."

"Did anyone from the board talk with Daniel concerning this?"

"Yes. I called him in May of last year and told him that he could get in trouble practicing with Dr. Burton since he does not have a license. I asked him to come in and chat with me about it."

"Did Daniel ever come in to see you?"

"Yes, a few days later. Again I told him that any prudent person would not practice with an individual who did not have a license, even though it was not considered unlawful. I told him that it is unlawful to allow Burton to charge his services under his license; I warned, 'It could spell trouble.'"

"Do you know whether or not Daniel was doing this?"

"No. I don't."

"Is there any other information that you'd like to add? Anything you think would be helpful to us?"

"Someone mentioned that Burton is diagnosing patient's cancers using hair analysis and curing them with injection therapy."

The National Forensic Chemistry Center for Analysis analyzed products purchased by undercover agents Porter Belt and Ben Byrd, while supplements seized during the Natrogenics clinic's search were sent to a FDA office in Seattle, Washington.

Equipment inspection, on the other hand, was handled by FDA's Winchester Engineering Center in Massachusetts. It was not until June 6, that the FDA released a report of its findings to the FBI. They questioned Burton's assertion that he is a Doctor of Naturopathy and made the following charges:

- Neither Burton's services, nor medical devices have been FDA approved.
- Burton uses unapproved drugs to treat his patients.
- Burton is in violation of Title 21 U.S.C.

"In certain states licensed naturopaths can prescribe drugs and give injections. They can do neither in Idaho since naturopaths are not licensed in Idaho. The Idaho Association of Naturopathic Physicians (IANP) has been trying to get legislation passed regulating naturopaths," Moore told Agent Newsome.

Special Agent Newsome interviewed H. David Lloyd, a Pocatello chiropractor. Per her request, Lloyd gave Newsome sixty black pearls, that he had gotten from Burton, for analysis. He made one request:

"Could you let me know the results of the tests?"

Newsome remained non-committal.

Tennessee convened its investigative team, Special Agents Joseph Bosley and Carlton Spacey, who interviewed Harold T. Snow. Snow was a white middle aged male whose long thin gray and black mane encased his face. The long gray and black beard and round, wire rimmed glasses gave him the appearance of an Amish.

Though demure in stature, the self-employed farmer was not intimidated by the agents. He refused to reveal what he was treated for at the clinic, but boasted that under Burton's care his health had improved tremendously.

"Is there anything you want to add?" Agent Bosley asked.

"My personal feeling is that the FDA wants to put Dr. Burton out of business. No one I have ever known suffered from Dr. Burton's treatments. In fact, they've been helped."

Marilyn, the only employee absent on the day of the raid, shared her FBI interview with Burton.

"Marge Newsome interviewed me for about two hours," she told him.

"Did she have a lot of questions?"

"She asked a lot of questions about our practice and business. She said that they aren't going to close you down, but there might be a need for some adjustments."

Newsome recalled Carrie Doyle's statement that a red notation in Burton's files signified that a patient had died while under Burton's guidance. She noted one such notation, and interviewed Ryan Aldridge of Pocatello in connection with that death. Aldridge admitted that although his wife had passed away while under Burton's care for pancreatic cancer, he had no regrets. "With Dr. Burton's treatment she had a good quality of life up until she passed away."

Sheriff Dan House, still incensed that the raid was conducted without his knowledge, paid Burton a visit. "Kyle I've been checking into this thing. You know I just can't believe they'd... I still can't get over it. I'm sheriff of Bingham County, and I find out about a raid on a business in my town on the news. That stinks!"

"What's worse, they searched my home and left it a mess."

"You know, the killing thing about it is, I've got a stack of letters in my office about a foot high in your support. That should tell them something."

"Those people are despicable."

"That's an understatement. They have shown no respect for my position here in Bingham County, whatsoever. You can bet I'll be working to help resolve this matter so you can get your equipment back. Listen, I want to bring my deputy in here to visit with you. Let's see what we can get going on this."

"Six of my patients whose health was deteriorating under traditional therapies were restored under Dr. Burton's guidance. Your interference with freedom of choice and the results from non-allopathic method of treatment have to tell us all something. This something is that standard medical care is not for everyone. Those who choose to seek other forms of health care should be given this choice," one health practitioner asserted.

"For agencies to leap WAY beyond their authority to deprive us of our constitutional rights of Life, Liberty, and the Pursuit of Happiness is gross fraud against the people of our free, sovereign republic," one supporter said.

"'Guilty until proven innocent' is not the American way for citizens.... or is it?" yet another cried.

"I am most happy with the care I received from Dr. Burton--to the extent that I pay for it out of my pocket in lieu of treatment approved by the AMA which would be paid by my insurance." one patient bragged.

It was mid-June when Bart Richie again phoned Burton. "Kyle, I talked with Leonard at the Governor's office. He says they plan to have your equipment back to you in a couple of months."

"You know, Bart, I've ... I have no faith in what they say anymore. They won't stop until they've closed us all."

"Governor Batt claims there is nothing against naturopathic practices in Idaho."

"Right, and Christmas doesn't come in December."

"Leonard says that you seem okay, but they're still looking at the business aspect of your practice, such as insurance and the use of your machines."

Later that day, Sheriff House stopped by with his Chief Deputy, Luther Connors, who scanned the search warrant carefully. "This warrant is very broad. If they didn't go through the sheriff's office, it's illegal," Deputy Connors said.

"We may be looking at a lawsuit here. This thing was cleared up back in 1984 with the AG's office, right?" House asked.

"Right."

House looked at Burton inquisitively. "Has the practice changed at all since 1984?"

"No. We're doing the same thing we were doing in 1984."

"I'm going to do some research on this. I'll see what I can do with it. We're with you buddy," Connors said firmly clasping Burton's shoulder.

"Thanks. I appreciate it," Burton said.

While Burton continued his search for answers, the FBI questioned the Arizona Naturopathic Medical Board records about the validity of the Hewitt Memorial Institute of Health Science, the institution from which Burton had graduated.

J. Washington, Director of Advanced Wholistic Health Institute, phoned Burton to report his conversation with Leonard McClain. "Leonard said that there has been enough information gathered now for a Grand Jury, but he would visit with you to see if they could get some things settled."

"Yes, a grand jury-- that's what I'm afraid of…"

"I felt that everything was going to be okay after I spoke with him."

Four days had passed when Sheriff House and his deputy stopped by Dr. Burton's office.

"Your job is to get those FEDS out of this county. Make them tow the line like they expect us to do," ex-County Commissioner Victor O'Connor told the sheriff.

"Well, I've been talking with an FBI agent. They finally told me that they have two charges against Burton: one is selling drugs, the other is insurance fraud. Say they don't have to answer any more questions concerning any other charges. I'm going to write a letter to the FBI tomorrow and request the return of all of your equipment. It'll go out tomorrow," House said.

FBI's George Curran interviewed J. Washington in Washington, D.C. regarding Burton's education. Washington told Curran that Burton had passed the federal exam and was honored because of his excellence.

"He asked if you had been feigning a federal license. I asked him, 'What are you charging him with?'"

"He said, 'selling drugs,' but assured me that those charges had been dropped. He said the only charge left was that they thought you were using a MD number to get the injection solutions."

Ronald Feagan never missed a chance to give Burton information he thought useful for his defense. "If they try and make those drug charges stick, John has agreed to testify to the statement Curran made saying that the drug charges had been dropped."

But Burton had grown almost numb from the continuous fight. All he wanted was resolve.

"Why don't you have Rudy talk with Leonard and assure him that if the FBI would return your equipment and drop all drug charges, the sheriff will not file a lawsuit. Nor will we," Feagan added. Burton called Rudy.

"Rudy, I talked with Ronald. He suggested that you should talk with Leonard. Let him know that the lawsuits will be dropped if they'll return our equipment and drop the charges."

"Kyle, let me tell you something. Do you honestly think the FEDS are afraid of a lawsuit? I can assure you they're not. They want you to sue them. Then they've got you where they want you."

"Well, I mean…Jerry Sparks has won several cases against big government."

"Jerry Spark's retainer is a quarter of a million dollars. Kyle, I'm telling you, file a lawsuit and they'll bankrupt you for sure. Think about it."

"I don't know. Please, just… get this thing settled. Do whatever you can to stop the Grand Jury hearing. I've had several patients to die last month, all because I couldn't give them the proper treatment."

Dr. Damon Carter, a dentist in Suring, Wisconsin, and a satisfied patient of Burton's, was unaware of the latest in the investigation. He wrote Agent Newsome and Senator Larry Craig. "I want to know why my files have not been returned to Dr. Burton along with his equipment."

Senator Craig replied, "If your file was confiscated by the FBI, you can contact the agency and request a copy. However, because this is an ongoing case, it would be improper for me to intervene any further until the investigation is completed."

As promised, Sheriff House wrote the FBI, voicing his concerns and telling of the 500 names he had gotten on petitions in support of Burton.

> *"The raid came as a total surprise, and I had absolutely no knowledge of what was taking place. Working in Law Enforcement, I feel it should be common courtesy to notify the Sheriff of a County that another Department will be serving a search warrant.*
>
> *You took equipment that is needed for his patients who are still under his care. I would appreciate some information that I will be able to pass on to Dr. Burton in this regard, i.e. reason for the search and the taking of his equipment."*

33

Sharla Reed of Telephone, Texas, told Special Agent Page that both she and her brother, who was a quadriplegic, used the black pearls."

In Van Alystine, Texas, Nina Dammons admitted that she was familiar with black pearls.

"I've been taking them for more than a decade now. A truck hit me. The pain was so severe; I was trying to get relief. The black pearls helped so much that I stopped using the expensive prescription medications I had been taking."

"Were you aware that the black pearls have drugs in them?"

"No, they do not contain drugs, because I sent a sample to a laboratory in Texas for analysis. They didn't find any drugs. A friend of mine also had them tested by Dow Chemical in Houston, Texas. No drugs showed up."

"These pills are illegal here in the U.S. Knowing this, would you consider purchasing these pills again?"

"Yes, if I could find someone who carried them."

"The FDA is stopping businesses from selling products that are helping people. One of the television shows exposed the FDA's attack on black pearls back a few years ago," Liz Washington of Houston, Texas, told Special Agent Murray.

The agreement between Wes and the FBI had been settled and his student status solidified at Eastern State Chiropractic. Wes felt he had earned his place in this school; he dared not let anyone take it from him. On June 20, he called Special Agent Newsome, frightened.

"Ms. Newsome someone's trying to destroy me."

"What are you talking about, Wes--we've honored our agreement."

"Yeah, but someone's called the school. Somebody told the director that I ruined their back when I adjusted it. You're not going to let that stand are you?"

"Wait a minute, Wes. Back up. Why would anybody say you did that unless there's some truth to it?" Newsome asked.

"Someone wants go get me kicked out of school."

"Alright, Alright, Wes. Was it a male or female?"

"Well, I'm not sure, but Dr. Roundtree the director, can tell you more about it. It was left on his answering machine."

"No ideas on who this might be?"

"I think it's one of Burton's patients."

The Grand Jury was little more than thirteen days away, yet Burton still wondered about the allegations being made against him. On June 27, Lillie Houston phoned.

"One of those darn FBI agents visited me today--wanted to know about the H-21."

"They're still looking for drugs, I guess.... Thought they had resolved that."

"The agent asked if I knew what was in them. I told him, 'No--I trust my doctor.'"

"He said, 'Well he's not an MD so he shouldn't be prescribing H-21, because it has Valium in it,' and gave me a list of the side effects of Valium."

"Well these are clean. They've been tested, so if drugs are what they're looking for, they're wasting their time. Besides, I heard that they cleared me of the drug charge--what are they trying to prove?"

"Well, I told them that I never experienced any of those side effects. ' I feel fine. Furthermore, I don't believe the pills have any Valium in them, and I don't appreciate what you're trying to do to Dr. Burton.'"

Six days before the Grand Jury hearing, Alice Fredo phoned Burton.

"Kyle, I talked with Marge Newsome. She said that it's okay for you to do the injections. She said no one's reported any problems with them."

"Well that's interesting, because they haven't returned my injection solution. I'm going to contact Rudy for clarification on this."

The FBI continued its search into the standard guidelines for naturopaths. In Olympia, Washington, Kenya Jones, Program Manager of Naturopathy Licensing in Olympia, Washington told Special Agent Byron Hardy and Special Agent Josephine Wren, of the Defense Criminal Investigative Service, that naturopaths cannot prescribe any controlled substances, such as drugs.

Shon Hogue, ND, Associate Director of Admissions, Bastyr University in Seattle, Washington, said he was not familiar with the HLB/LBA blood research program, but was familiar with the Dark Field Microscope, the kind Burton used in his practice.

On hand in Woodland Hills, California, was Special Agent Cathy Seigel, who interviewed Wayne Charleston, Acting Dean of Bellafontaine University. Charleston verified the authenticity of the copies of the Bellafontaine University Diplomas issued to Burton. He told Seigel that Burton had graduated cum laude from the school.

Clarence Keaton of Washington, DC, who licensed and registered businesses operating within the District of Columbia, told Agent George Curran that naturopathic certification could be gotten through a course of study at a university in naturopathy or training directly under practicing physicians who are certified in naturopathic study.

J. Washington verified the validity of Burton's certification by the American Naturopathic Medical Certification and Accreditation Board. "The American College of Homeopathic Physicians is a component of the now defunct Hewitt Medical Society of America. Burton was given an honorary doctorate and is highly regarded by the American College of Homeopathic Physicians," Washington said.

The FBI felt it had gathered enough information to convince a jury that there was just cause for indictments to be served on Kyle J. Burton, so on July 11, 1995, a Grand Jury of the United States District of Idaho, in Boise, Idaho convened in the presence of 21 jurors. Leonard W. McClain, Assistant United States Attorney, represented the United States Attorney. Employees of the Natrogenics clinic were interrogated first. Next Ryan Radcliff was called to testify.

Radcliff told McClain that Burton, in conjunction with the AM Biogenics Hospital in Mexico, had been involved in research to determine the effects of free radicals on the body and to design protocols to address the problem should one exist. The research, Radcliff explained, was analogous to a footprint.

> *If a deer walks through this room and nobody is here but we recognize the footprint, we don't have to see the deer. We know the deer went by. Like the deer, free radicals leave footprints behind and, as such, affect coagulation systems. Every disease involves free radical mechanisms.*
>
> *The microscope is used to observe pathology. Dr. Burton and I have been working in that effort since 1990. The goal of the research is to try to develop diagnostic procedures, as well as therapeutic property goals primarily for degenerative disease processes.*
>
> *Naturopaths who use injections are practicing under a Supreme Court ruling which said 'that the medical society shall not interfere with the practice of naturopathy,' so that is the way they were practicing.*

Radcliff told the jury that, contrary to Moore's interview, "things such as Candida Albican, parasites, and other fungus can be seen in the blood, and that has been cited in the Journal of Otolaryngology."

34

While the Grand Jury continued its hearings, investigation into the Burton case continued from coast to coast. Still at issue were what naturopaths could and could not do and what certifications Burton had.

Derrick Cellini, ND, Chairman of the Washington State Naturopathy Advisory Committee of the State Department of Health in Seattle, Washington, told Special Agent Byron Hardy that he believed the American Naturopathic Medical Certification and Accreditation Board, an organization in which Burton claimed an affiliation, was a subset of the American Naturopathic Medical Association (ANMA).

"Only a few states regulate naturopathic activities, although the American Association of Naturopathic Physician's (AANP) has introduced some legislation. In Washington naturopaths can diagnose and treat using standard diagnostic tools, and even deliver babies. They can also bill insurance," Cellini said. He verified the validity of Burton's certificate from Bellafontaine University of San Diego, California.

"For admission into the National College of Naturopathic Medicine in Oregon, an individual must have a minimum of three years of study from an accredited college or university, including science courses basic to premed. In Oregon, naturopaths can prescribe medicines, do injections, submit claims to insurance companies, practice pretty much like an MD, except they are restricted to minor surgery," Dr. Steve Norton told Special Agent Sidney. "But since Idaho is an 'unlicensed state' naturopaths can practice in accordance with provisions set forth by the State Attorney General's office or a regulatory body of alternative professionals," he added.

Meanwhile, at his Seattle, Washington office, Special Agent Hardy conducted an interview with Penny Hull, ND, former President of Washington Association of Naturopathic Physicians (WANP). According to Hull, Washington naturopaths can give vitamin injections and anesthetics when minor surgeries are necessary.

A day after the Grand Jury convened, Sheri Whitley entered the Radio Shack just down the street from Natrogenics clinic. A pale looking man moved toward her, barely able to put one foot in front of the other. He looked familiar, but she didn't want to stare. She couldn't help but notice his red eyes and his frown.

"Hey Sheri, did Burton get his stuff back?"

"Oh Marvis!" she said. "I'm sorry, no… No he didn't. As a matter of fact, there was a Grand Jury hearing yesterday, so it's still up in the air."

"I'm not gonna make it. I'm not gonna…."

"Well, maybe things will break soon," Sheri said trying to calm his fears.

He had come such a long way…But now things just didn't look good. It was such a pity. It seemed he would be following the same dread path as his buddies, unless he could get more injections.

"I sure hope so," he said, then turned and left the store.

Amidst the madness, Kyle sat in his office reading H.R. 1951, The Food and Dietary Consumer Information Act of 1995, glad that at least some representatives were fighting for the public. Introduced by Rep. Dennis Hastert (R-IL) and Rep. Frank Pallone (D-N.J.) 6/29/95, H.R. 1951 sought to: 'Reduce Health Care Costs through A Better Informed Citizenry By':

- Allowing food and dietary supplement companies to make truthful, non-misleading statements for their products while not altering the FDA's current statutory authority to prosecute and remove misleading or mislabeled products from the market.
- Preventing the FDA from classifying foods and dietary supplements as drugs.
- Providing for uniform definitions of foods and dietary supplements and their labels across the 50 states.
- Abolishing a recently created Presidential Commission on Dietary Supplement Labels that would have delayed the public for 4 additional years from having truthful, non-misleading information on how nutrition can help prevent the onset of chronic disease.

In support of the bill The Coors Decision: Pallone states: "In Rubin v. Coors Brewing Co., the correct legal precedent was set by Justice Stevens regarding the communication of truthful information in a commercial setting. He wrote:

> *Any 'interest' in restricting the flow of accurate information because of the perceived danger of that knowledge is anathema to the First Amendment; more speech and a better informed citizenry are among the central goals of the Free Speech Clause. Accordingly, the Constitution is most skeptical of supposed state interests that seek to keep people in the dark for what the government believes to be their own good.*
>
> *Incredible as it may seem, at the present time, it is a serious federal crime for a company to tell the truth about the disease prevention benefits of a Food or Food Supplement until the U.S. Food and Drug Administration (FDA) has precleared the claim.*
>
> *It has only approved two health claims in 88 years: one for folic acid*

preventing neural tube birth defects; and one for calcium preventing osteoporosis. Until it is changed by H.R. 1951, the law will permit FDA to continue to ban true health claims for Food or Food Supplements as 'unproven' drug claims, Claude P. Milton, Health Freedom Legislative Advocate for Improved Health, noted.

Sheri's entrance into Burton's office caused Kyle to look up.

"Kyle, you know Marvis Russell was in Radio Shack this morning. I didn't recognize him, he looked so bad."

"Yeah, he was in here shortly after the raid practically begging for treatment... I had to tell him that I didn't have the equipment. I could tell he was slipping."

"You know this is the kind of thing that just boils me over... And that Grand Jury hearing was a big joke," Sheri said.

"Well, it's just a waste of the taxpayers' money. I'll bet the jurors were all medical people. They don't know jack squat about naturopathy or alternative medicine. They don't know what I do, and if I told them they wouldn't understand it. How can they judge me?"

"It's no doubt they were all medical. Their minds were already made up, no matter what you said. It was all a big show. Each time I spoke, they looked at each other and shook their heads as though I was crazy."

"That's what I thought. That's why the idea of a grand jury just turned me off."

"I just hated it. McClain rehashed the same questions he had during the raid, except this time it was in front of a jury. He was trying to make you look like a liar."

Carrie Doyle, Jewel, and Marilyn joined Sheri in Burton's office.

"It was just a waste of time, trying to get across to those people. You wouldn't believe what one of the jurors asked me," Marilyn said.

"Try me," Kyle said.

"Well, I told them that I sometimes mixed the serum for the injections based on what you told me to mix. One juror asked: 'Well, if he told you to put cyanide in it would you do that?' I wanted to tell her to go suck an egg."

Burton leaned back in his chair. "That's--It's this kind of thing that just.... grand juries are so one sided. I hear they were all medical people."

"I have no doubt. They were just snickering and laughing, but I told them that this stuff does sound strange to you if you've never been exposed to it. McClain asked if we ever refer people to medical doctors. I told them, 'yes, there are some occasions when we have.' They had a lot of questions about the electrical machines, and I told them they work because I had used them myself. They thought that was hilarious," Marilyn said.

"What kind of questions did they ask about the equipment?"

"Well, he wanted to know what the Tens unit felt like. I told him it just felt -- like I said, it relaxed your muscles, and it feels like it grabs them once in a while to help them relax," Jewel said.

"Did they ask anything about Daniel?"

"They asked when he started working at the clinic. And when I guessed about the date, they tried to belittle me. There was just no winning with those characters. I knew it was going to be bad if they were making such a big deal out of when Lou started."

"It'll be interesting to see what they come up with."

Marilyn pitched in. "Oh yeah, they wanted to know something about how we got along. I told them always real good, but I left to be home with the kids and start selling Mary Kay. 'Did he tell you what to say when you got here?' McClain asked. I said. 'No. I talked to him when I got a search warrant, and he said, 'All the other girls have been served with one, too.'"

"I told Leonard McClain that I was scared by the raid because, I didn't know if it was my butt, the doctor's butt, or what. Hell, there were thirteen armed agents. They were stern and matter of fact. 'You don't talk or move.' Yes, I was scared!" Jewel added.

At the Grand Jury Hearing, Anna Lange testified that she shipped on average 15 packages of product a day, which sometimes included black pearls. Sheri Whitley admitted that she had mailed information to patients about the raid, asking them to contact their congressman.

"I tried several medical doctors before I tried Dr. Burton. None of them helped. If it weren't for Dr. Burton I'd be dead," Larry Taylor of Phoenix, Arizona told Agent Harrison.

When Special Agent Paris Bender interviewed Candy Beard at her place of employment in Kansas City, Missouri, Beard told her: "My medical doctor diagnosed arthritis. I didn't tell Burton what was wrong with me. I wanted to see if he could find the problem. He did, and prescribed some natural products. I didn't want to take all those drugs that my doctor was prescribing."

Special Agent Newsome, in the presence of FDA's Terrance Glenn, interviewed Tamara Borders at her Idaho Falls residence.

"Are you a patient of Burton's?" Newsome asked.

"No. My mom was. She had a cancerous brain tumor."

"Had she sought medical attention for her illness?"

"She did with a neurosurgeon here in town, but the cancer returned. He suggested another surgery and radiation treatments. Mother didn't want either of these so she decided to see Dr. Burton."

"What was Dr. Burton's treatment for this?"

"He recommended some herbs and a new nutritional program."

"What is the status of that illness today?"

"My mother is much better."

"How do you know the cancer is gone?"

"I sought the services of Dr. Morgan for re-testing, and he said, 'What ever you're doing keep doing it--she is much improved;' he didn't bother re-testing her. An eye doctor had found her tumor through an eye exam. After receiving Burton's treatments, he could find no signs of the tumor."

"Do you remember a guy named Wes O'Dea?"

"Yes, he adjusted my back. I remember he taught some acupressure classes at the clinic. Both my husband and I took them."

"Who did you pay for these classes?"

"I remember this as if it were yesterday. We were told to write the checks to Wes, not the clinic."

Agent Newsome interviewed Ola Hughs in the presence of her husband, Nick Hughs, and Special Agent Terrence Glenn.

"What brought you to the clinic?" Newsome asked.

"I had a virus. My medical doctor said it would go away on its own. I didn't see how--I was so sick… I decided it was time for a change. Dr. Burton treated me with some natural supplements."

"Were there any ill effects from taking these products?"

"None. Dr. Burton saved my life. He saved my life."

"Did you ever feel that Burton was faking it--playing doctor?"

"Lady, Dr. Burton has more knowledge in one little finger than those medical quacks will in a lifetime. He's proven himself."

"Do you remember purchasing Liquitrile from Natrogenics clinic?"

"I don't know, and what bothers me is, how the heck you know!"

Agent Newsome showed Ola the invoice.

"Well, quite frankly I don't remember taking it, but I took whatever Dr. Burton recommended. I'm told the FBI has my medical file, and I would like it returned to Dr. Burton."

"A photocopy will be sent to you, but the FBI will be keeping the original to pursue further investigation, unless, of course, you will agree to discuss the nature of your treatment and the illnesses you were treated for while at the clinic." Hughes declined.

Newsome telephoned Troy Sanders at his Grace, Idaho residence. "I understand that your wife, Rose, sought treatment from Dr. Burton at Natrogenics clinic in Aberdeen, Idaho," Newsome said.

"Yes, she was treated for cancer."

"Had your wife sought medical attention for her condition?"

"Before she went to the clinic she had been given radiation in Pocatello for a cancerous brain tumor."

"What treatments did Dr. Burton offer your wife?"

"He offered natural products and nutrition as a treatment for Rose."

"But she's deceased now, so what does that tell you about that treatment?"

"Well, the tumor disappeared after Dr. Burton's treatment, because it was confirmed by Dr. Hinckley."

"Do you remember your wife's ordering Liquitrile?"

"Yes."

"How was it packaged— in pills, liquids?"

"It came in a liquid. My wife used to put it in her drinks."

"You said, yourself, that your wife is deceased. Still think that these treatments were effective?"

"Quality is something the radiation treatments had stripped my wife's body of. Dr. Burton extended her life, but more than that, he added quality to her extra year of life. Unfortunately, she lost the battle; the cancer returned."

"Mr. Sanders, why do you think we're conducting this investigation--it's because of things like this....?"

"I believe you're investigating Dr. Burton because of one of Dr. Burton's ex-employees who got fired. Dr. Burton mentioned that the ex-employee was caught stealing."

On July 25, 1995, Idaho's Attorney General's office investigator, Roy Evans, interviewed Melba Wallace's husband Ryan at his Rexburg, Idaho address.

"Were any other members of your family patients of Dr. Burton's?" Evans asked.

"My granddaughter had Leukemia. Dr. Burton helped her with that, now she's fine. Then, my wife Melba was treated."

"Were these services billed to insurance?"

"No, I paid cash for my treatments."

"I see you ordered H-21 on some occasions. Have you ever heard of it referred to as black pearls, or been told that they were illegal in the United States?"

"No."

"Have you ever used Liquitrile?"

"What, are you trying to say— that's illegal too? Sir, if it had not been for Dr. Burton, four members of my family would be dead, including me. Quite frankly, I don't care what this investigation uncovers--I support him. My brother and his wife, my wife and I were in the clinic the day you people came in, ordering everybody around, just as I was getting an injection. You wouldn't even let the girl finish with me. It was a disgrace! Illegal, my foot! I have nothing more to say to you!" Wallace bellowed.

It was at last time for Burton to sit down with the investigative team. It happened on July 26, 1995. Special Agent Newsome conducted the interview. Also present were Burton's attorney, Rudy Anthony, and Peter Walter, an investigator hired by Anthony, Assistant United States Attorney Leonard McClain, Special Agent Terrance Glenn of the Food & Drug Administration and Investigator Roy Evans, State of Idaho Attorney General's office.

Questions abounded about the specifics of Burton's education, course curriculum, length of courses, and the validity of Burton certifications.

"Where did you first begin your medical training?"

"At the Utah College of Chiropractic."

"Tell us about that college."

"It was a correspondence school but it also included hours in the classroom."

"How many classroom hours did you attend at this Utah College?"

"Hey-that was a long time ago. I don't know."

"How long did the course work take?"

"It was a four year program."

"How many times did you go to Utah to further your degree?"

"I don't know, but some lecture classes were required. Most of the classes, however, were correspondence."

"What degree did you obtain from the Utah College of Chiropractic?"

"A Doctor of Chiropractic, but I was never licensed to practice in any state."

"Where were these classes offered?"

"Some were in Dallas, Texas; Las Vegas, Nevada; and Reno, Nevada."

"How long did these courses last?"

"They would vary."

"In what other medical areas did you undertake course work?"

"I got other degrees from Bellafontaine University."

"Were these courses in a classroom setting or through mail order?"

"All the courses were correspondence type courses."

"Were you given tests in these courses?"

"Yes, I was tested."

"You were tested through the mail," Newsome said arrogantly.

"Yes."

"What were these tests like?"

"The tests were rather extensive."

"What degrees did you receive from Bellafontaine University?"

"One in homeopathy, the other in cancer theories."

"If these tests were done through mail, how did you know whether or not your answer was right?"

"The tests would be returned to me showing what I got wrong and what I should have marked," Burton explained.

"Did you take followup courses?"

"I've taken other courses in Canada and British Columbia in anatomy and reflexology."

"How long was this course?"

"It was an accelerated intensive study that included hands on and lecture type classes. They were short but very intensive. We were given homework."

"Was there a test?"

"Certainly."

"What other courses did you take?"

"I studied spinal touch therapy, muscle response testing, and nutritional studies from the Natrogenics Foundation which is in Salt Lake City, Utah."

"How many times did you go to Salt Lake City for training or course work?"

"It was quite a bit. Each of the courses was accelerated."

"You mentioned having taken courses abroad. Have you ever worked abroad?"

"Yes, I have at the AM Biogenics Hospital in Tijuana, Mexico."

"Tell us about that hospital."

"It's a hospital in Tijuana, Mexico, approved by the Mexican government."

"What kind of training did you get to prepare you for treating patients at that hospital?"

"I did roughly one thousand hours of study at the hospital."

"How many times did you go to Mexico for training?"

"I can't remember the number of times, but each trip, I stayed months at a time."

"Are you still continuing your studies in Mexico?"

"Yes, I've continued those studies whenever possible."

"What kind of training did you receive in Mexico?"

"I received special training in administering injections and mixing the solution used in the injections."

"Were tests given for this special training you received in Mexico?"

"Tests were hands on. Not written."

"Did you receive any degrees or certificates for the HLB/LBA blood work?"

"I did receive a certificate from US Logistic Hospital and also privileges at the Tijuana Mexico Hospital."

"When did you begin class work on blood analysis?"

"It was sometime in the eighties."

"How much of this was in a classroom type of setting?"

"I don't recall."

"I can see you have a certificate from Radcliff Research Institute. What does this certificate allow you to do?"

"It allows one to do research using the HLB/LBA method."

"So what are some of the facts you have uncovered as a result of this research?"

"Well, one is the fact that candida can now be tested using the HLB/LBA blood analysis."

"Did you submit the results of your finding to the Center for Disease Control?"

"That was something that the Radcliff Institute did. But it's my understanding that the CDC has that report."

"How long have you been conducting this research?"

"Since 1983, once I received my certificate and equipment."

"How many of your patients participate in this research?"

"About twenty percent."

"Do you inform your patients that you are doing research on them?"

"My patients must read and sign a consent form which tells them that this is for research purposes before I test them."

"What percent of your patients have blood work done?"

Disenchanted with the questioning, Burton looked at Anthony, and Anthony at Burton. Burton pulled himself up and stumped out of the room.

"If you'll excuse me," Anthony said, following Burton. Welsh followed, only to return later and inform the panel that neither Burton nor Anthony would be returning.

35

Outside now, Kyle shook his finger at his attorney. "You know, that is what I was afraid of, Rudy! Those people aren't interested in any thing I have to... They just want to crucify me," he said throwing up his hands. "They just... What exactly are they trying to prove, anyway--that I didn't attend an Ivy League school? Is that a crime? They trying to say I'm incompetent? Why don't they want to talk about the numbers, huh? The numbers... How many cancer patients are those big Ivy Leagers curing, huh? Heck, I get to clean up their messes. How many of the multiple sclerosis patients are they giving better lives--quality lives? And what about the CF children--what about those? What about the growing number of chronic diseases in this country, huh? What about the patients, Rudy? Do they account for anything? There is no way I'm going back in there."

"Well I had hoped for better... But I agree. We we're getting nowhere in there," Anthony agreed.

Anthony sent Assistant U.S. District Attorney McClain a letter.

> *I hope you understand that our decision to discontinue the interview was my decision. I would hope that you will not use that against my client; I did not believe we were getting anywhere with the interview, other than arguing over trivial details with no one on the same page.*
>
> *My client would still like to resolve this matter, but it appears clear to me that we are not headed toward resolution at this time; The case is still well into its investigative stage with more investigation being anticipated. With that in mind, we remain willing to talk, but we will not discuss the matter for investigation purposes. The only way we would discuss the matter again would be with the idea of the matter being resolved, and with Mr. Burton being granted immunity.*
>
> *If you have any questions, please don't hesitate to call.*

Gale Parsons, a patient of Dr. Burton's, was growing more irritable as time passed. Burton's equipment had not been returned. To date the Grand Jury had issued no indictment against him, so on August 1, Parsons intensified her campaign. She sent letters to US Senators, Representatives of the US Congress, the Sheriff of Bingham County in Aberdeen, President Clinton, Allan Lance, Attorney General, and various syndicated television personalities, and urged her followers across the country to do the same. She urged news publications to print her press release.

> WACO, RUBY RIDGE, and now ABERDEEN
>
> No one died when 13 armed FBI/FDA agents raided Natrogenic's Clinic in Aberdeen, Idaho on February 2, but hundreds and thousands of individuals are suffering and may die as a result of a naturopathic doctor being limited in his ability to practice alternative medicine.
>
> On Feb. 2, 1995 the FBI and FDA, with a search warrant in hand, raided Dr. Burton's clinic taking herbs, vitamins, and equipment valued at $100,000 and patient records. Now, five months later and after a grand jury hearing, no evidence of wrong doing or any charges filed! So why hasn't the personal property of Dr. Burton been returned?
>
> Dr. Burton's infuriated patients have demanded their personal patient files from the FBI office and have only received copies of their confidential information! Thousands of letters, phone calls, and petitions have been sent to Marge Newsome and Leonard McClain. There is no indication that these public servants consider what the public demands! Many patients called Ms. Newsome and said she would not hear them out, was rude to them, and even hung up on them. Are federal employees not to listen to the taxpayers?
>
> There is a rumor that an individual in the Idaho State Attorney General's office is taking bribes to close down all naturopaths in Idaho, possible payoffs from the American Medical Association or drug companies. Does money speak louder than honesty and ethics? Who do we trust any more? Is our government getting so corrupt that it will not allow us to have freedom of choice in health care?
>
> Marge Newsome, Leonard McClain, and their staffs are wasting our taxpayers' money on a frivolous 'witch hunt.' Dr. Burton wonders 'why tax dollars are being spent to harass people' when he is trying to live an honest life, devoted to helping people.

"We should have freedom of access to health care. It's tragic that the FBI and ATF have the right to raid, whether it's Dr. Burton or Waco. Our government shouldn't dictate how everyone lives and what they should do according to Clinton and Reno. It's time for government to get out of our lives!" Dr. Ronald Feagan argued.

But "getting out of their lives" was something the Feds had no intentions of doing. Special Agent Keizer Wayne Page interviewed Jon Wheaton at his residence in Powdery, Texas. Wheaton told Page that he suffered no side effects from the black pearls; in fact, because of them, he had been able to cut his Prednisone usage in half. "I would continue to purchase the black pearls knowing they are illegal, because it helped both me and my wife," he said.

Senior Editor Columnist Bob Chester, from "The American Republic", printed Gale Parson's "Waco, Ruby Ridge, and Now Aberdeen' press release.

"You would be amazed at the response that column produced from around the country. The FEDS are evidently abusing their authority from coast to coast," Chester said.

Like Gale Parsons, Ivanna Dion was disgusted that no resolution was in sight. She made her final plea to Leonard McClain.

> *"I can no longer afford to sit quietly as a patient whose life is threatened by this injustice; if Dr. Burton's patients' records and HLB/LBA blood research equipment is not returned immediately, I am prepared to expose this ugly injustice to the public."*

In spite of the many cries from the public, the FBI investigation continued. It sought to build its case against Burton for insurance fraud, drug charges, injection therapy, and mail fraud. In Shrewsbury, New Jersey, Special Agent Andy Boston interviewed Mrs. Jewel Star at her business.

"Did Dr. Burton ever tell you where he got the pills?" Boston asked.

"No--but I can't say I asked either, just like I wouldn't ask my medical doctor where his drugs came from."

On August 18, 1995, Ryan and Melba Wallace phoned Burton. "I talked to governor Batts office and was told that he is in favor of naturopathic care and was doing what he could," Melba said.

"Well, we've got a bill that's coming up next year. Let's see if he puts his money where his mouth is," Burton said.

"I also got a call from Leonard McClain, and he was very friendly. He implied that they do not have any charges against you, and will not be closing you down. He says he has not returned the equipment because they anticipate needing it for evidence. 'Well if you're not closing him down, get his equipment back to him so he can operate,' I told him."

"And what did he say to that?"

"Nothing. What could he say?" Melba asked.

"Listen, I talked with an FBI agent that I know and was told that, if they have not charged you, they don't have anything on you--that they should be returning your equipment soon," Ryan added.

Ivanna hadn't any word yet that anything had changed for Dr. Burton. She sent letters to some local newspapers as well as nationally syndicated television talk shows. But once again, the request to the newscasters that they print or report it fell on deaf ears.

Professor Arnet of Switzerland joined the bandwagon of supporters for Burton. He wrote a letter to Assistant U.S. Attorney Leonard McClain, renouncing the search on Burton. "I am encouraging you to move on, and let him carry on this work with all the means that he is entitled to use. Or else your insistence to examine his practice in every detail to the point of stalling him completely may turn up as a case study, some new book or newspaper item which would bring you a lot of bad publicity."

"So far as I'm concerned, I feel the investigation is wrong and is a good example of you jerks wasting our tax dollars. We never asked for this investigation," Lana Pierce told Agent Newsome.

"I contacted Kirk Kemthorne and he said you have no right looking at my medical file. I will be getting in touch with the US Attorney about this… I want this investigation stopped," was a message Pierce later left on Newsome's voice mail.

Barry Mathews, the vice-president of the Boise branch of the Idaho Association of Naturopathic Physicians (IANP), told Agent Newsome that Burton was a member of the Idaho Naturopathic Medical Association (INMA), which is an offspring of the IANP.

The split up had come because the two organizations couldn't agree on what should be the requirements and scope of naturopaths. At the heart of the dispute were Dr. Ben Lynch's methods of treatment. Those who approved of his practices joined the INMA. Those who did not stayed with the IANP.

Agent Newsome questioned Patty Hornberger about whether or not services she received while at the clinic were billed to her insurance company.

"I hope this investigation won't take long because I need Dr. Burton," she answered.

Investigator Roy Evans telephoned Gladys Hains at her Boise, Idaho home about injection therapy. Hains admitted to having had injection therapy while at the clinic. "I'm telling you I don't know what I would have done without that…I feel much better. Dr. Burton has helped me to regain my health. He's worked wonders with me. I know I would be in bad shape, if alive at all, if it were not for him," Hains said.

Subpoenas were served on various people to appear before the next United States District Court of Idaho Federal Grand Jury.

36

The investigation into the Natrogenics did nothing to discourage those who knew of Burton's fine work. Tony Henderson invited Burton to teach classes to medical doctors in capillary blood analysis and video microscopy at the New Age Center on Aging Medicine in Playa Dorado on the north coast of the Dominican Republic.

The investigative team continued to confront the suppliers of black pearls. Prior interviews convinced Special Agent Baker that Jason Bartrell was a supplier. But a call by Agent Marge Newsome to Linda Mallory at Bartrell's Advanced Construction could not tie Bartrell to the black pearls.

An article entitled "Naturopathic Clinic Raided" by Eleanor Manson of Hotline Printing Publishing, gave the status of the investigation.

> The FEDs are alleging that non-FDA approved drugs H-21, and GH3 were dispensed. However, they did not report any injury or complaint by a customer consuming the company's products.
>
> As of September 8th, Dr. Burton still hasn't gotten any of his illegally detained property back, no charges have been filed, the Federal Grand Jury that convened on July 11 failed to return an indictment, and the probable cause affidavit remains sealed. When reached for comment, FBI Agent Porter Belt of the Boise office declared that it was a case of insurance fraud and that he couldn't discuss it because the investigation was 'ongoing'. When asked why they stole the doctor's coin collection, Belt had nothing to say. A Texas report shows that Burton's black pearls were not adulterated.
>
> In an airing of Nightline, Dr. Lucian Leap stated that 180,000 annual deaths can be attributed to hospital and doctor mistakes, and estimated that 1.3 million suffer injury related to treatment. Dr. Sidney Wolfe said most people are not aware of the preventable death and injury that are caused by the health care system. Dr. Burton's patients left mainstream medicine behind in search of something better. They found it in Dr. Burton's care, and were justifiably enraged at how their doctor was being persecuted.

The article urged people to call Marge Newsome and express their views.

- Demand that the stolen property be returned to Burton at once.
- Help pass H.R.1951 The food and Dietary Consumer Information Act of 1995. This will stop the FDA from turning dietary supplements into drugs, and will allow us to make truthful health claims about dietary supplements.
- Also, help pass H.R. 2019/S.2140 - The Access to Medical Treatment Act, which will stop the FDA and other Federal Authorities from harassing alternative practitioners such as Dr. Burton, who represents an economic threat to mainstream doctors and to the pharmaceutical industry.

"If we don't get behind Dr. Burton and his peers with protective legislation, we may not have them around when we need them," the article concluded.

Ronald Feagan of the ANMA, Burton's member affiliate, had made it known that the agency was going to investigate the clinic to see if Burton's practices were in keeping with their guidelines. Special Agent Ryan Sanders of the FBI questioned Ronald Feagan, the ANMA's president.

"What is your current occupation?"

"I'm a psychiatrist and a naturopath."

"Where did you attend school?"

"I received my Dr. of Naturopathy from Clayton University in St. Louis, Missouri."

"Are you a member of the American Naturopathic Medical Association?"

"I used to be the president of it back some years ago."

"And is this ANMA a recognized association?"

"It's nationally recognized."

"What are the requirements to become a member of the ANMA?"

"The person must be a certified practicing naturopath."

"Do members of this organization include any profession other than naturopaths?"

"Sure, other professions included are dentist, chiropractors, veterinarians, and osteopaths."

"Who gave naturopaths the legal right to practice homeopathy and naturopathy in Idaho?"

"The Supreme Court, through a state amendment which allows naturopaths to use class I and II equipment."

"What are some of these devices that you are permitted to use?"

"Some examples are syringes, and stimulating machines."

"What is the difference between a naturopathic doctor, doctor of naturopathy, or naturopathic medical doctor?"

"They all mean the same thing; it's just that different states call them different names."

"What sets a naturopath apart from a medical doctor?" Sanders asked.

"A naturopathic doctor doesn't use prescription medicines or do surgeries."

"What kind of educational requirements is there for a person who wishes to become an N.D?"

"A person, who has been trained, such as an MD, can become an N.D. through correspondence."

"When did colleges for doctors of naturopathy become accredited?"

"It was in the later part of the 80's when the push was on to make these colleges accredited."

"What university did Burton attend?"

"Hewitt's University, which was located in Arizona; a branch was in Florida."

"Is it accredited?"

"When it was founded accreditation standards were not in place. It was a well-respected institution, and was highly regarded in the community when it existed. When the owner passed away in 1983, it was dissolved."

"How long was this course of study at Hewitt?"

"That depended upon the course of study chosen."

"What about Burton?"

"Burton completed the course of study in four years and continued taking courses in things such as medical microscopy, cancer therapies, and homeopathic studies. He's well respected in our community."

"What can you tell us about Dr. Burton's practices at Natrogenics clinic?"

"We haven't completed our investigation into the matter, but we don't support illegal activity," Feagan said.

As the investigation into Burton continued, the United States District Court for the District of Idaho conducted a second Grand Jury hearing in mid September. Assistant United States Attorney, Leonard McClain's first witness was Agent Terrance Lloyd Glenn of the FDA

> *"My function," Terrance said, "is to investigate allegations of criminal misconduct and violations of United States Food & Drug & Cosmetic Act. This includes individuals trafficking in unapproved drugs, making health claims for unapproved treatments where there has been no scientific evidence to show that they are safe and effective for their marketed intent, and also in counterfeit prescription drugs, steroids, and various types of food products that may be counterfeited.*

Terrance told the jury that his investigation involved not only the use of unapproved drugs and injectable type drugs, but also medical devices determining whether or not these devices are effective for the conditions for which they are claimed to be, whether they are safe and whether or not they are approved by the FDA.

"I doubt its reliability, since no research reports that diagnosis using this microscope is repeatable. The microscope, while used as a standard medical device, is not typically used as a diagnostic tool. When it is, written permission should be acquired from the Review Board for its use in that capacity. I have not seen any such paperwork from Burton."

"As a result of the search warrant, were there substances seized from Dr. Burton's office which were later analyzed to determine whether or not there were controlled substances in them?"

"Yes. During analysis we found that all except for one of the packages of black pearls tested positive for diazepam; exhibition No. 6, said to be 'for employee's use only,' tested negative for diazepam, but contained other prescription drugs. It was found in an office at the clinic behind the receptionist's desk in a cabinet. Exhibit #7 was obtained from H. David Lloyd by FBI Agent Marge Newsome; it also contained diazepam.

Because diazepam (Valium) is a controlled substance, there are regulations that the product has to be labeled for use only by a physician or prescribed by a physician. Valium must be labeled letting the patient know that 'it could be habit forming. Terrance indicated, however, that he had never seen such a label applied to any of the black pearls in talking with Marge Newsome or any of the patients that were given the black pearls from Burton's office. Terrance stated that the amount of diazepam found in the black pearls varied from .7 to 1.5 milligrams per pill."

"Are black pearls prescribed by medical doctors?"

"It's more of a black market type thing. A lot of these products are smuggled into the country from the Far East. The pills also contained other prescription drugs that were potentially harmful, Indomethacin, Mefenamic Acid, and Hydrochlorothiazide," Terrance said.

When questioned, Dr. Moore, ND, told Leonard McClain that Idaho has no regulatory board which oversees the practice of naturopathic medicine. Your practice in Idaho is limited to natural remedies; even clipping a patient's toenail would be in violation of the law because of the possibility of breaking the skin.

Moore admitted that he was not familiar with two of the electrical machines that were used in Dr. Burton's practice, but was familiar with the dark field microscope that Burton used.

37

The investigative team's challenge was to show mail fraud and fraudulent insurance practices by Burton.

"Billing insurance charges was common at the clinic; it was the only way some of Burton's patients could afford treatment," Carrie Jean Doyle told Agent Newsome in a September interview.

Newsome became suspicious when she noticed that insurance claim forms at Natrogenics clinic were not signed by the attending physician. She questioned Lisa Harris of Blue Cross of Idaho. "Did you require the attending physicians to sign claim forms submitted to you?"

"Attending physicians are not required to sign claim forms as long as they provide their provider number."

Newsome interviewed Walt Lou Daniel. In attendance were Daniel's attorney, Winston Gilmore, an assistant to Gilmore, Jasmine De Angelos, and Assistant United States Attorney, Leonard McClain. At Newsome's request, Daniel told them that he was currently practicing in Provo under the name Provo Chiropractic, and that he held licenses to practice in Idaho and Utah.

Daniel admitted he knew the FDA had not approved Burton's blood test, but felt it was legal since it was used for research purposes.

"Who told you to bill insurance companies for work that Dr. Burton performed?" Newsome asked.

"Dr. Burton said that as long as I treated the patient it was alright to use my number to bill the blood work."

"And you mean you never even questioned this practice?"

"Well I did initially, but after Dr. Burton explained it, I was okay with it."

"Was Dr. Burton billing insurances for his services before you were hired? If so, under whose number?"

"I think he did it under his own name."

"...And you didn't think this a bit strange, when all of a sudden you come aboard, and he suddenly needs to bill insurance under your number?"

"Well, most insurance companies won't reimburse for naturopathic services."

"The electrical treatments performed by Jewel Haley or Marilyn Walter, did you think that their services should be billed using your provider number?"

"As long as I was within reach while it was being done, I figured it was okay. I was told that if I used electrical machines to treat a patient, the charge was billable to the insurance."

"Are these electrical machines approved for use by the FDA?"

"Guess I never really thought about it one way or the other."

"So you didn't bother checking this guy out before you went to work for him...?"

"I spoke with Dr. Burton's attorney in a meeting when I came to work here. He assured me everything was above board."

"What were the black pearls (H-21's) made of?"

"It was made up of twenty two herbals and, according to Dr. Burton, contained a heavy concentration of Valerian Root."

"If these pills were so innocent, why did Dr. Burton feel the need to hide them?"

"There were some bad ones on the market, some that had drugs in them. These had been tested at the University of Houston, and were said to be drug free."

"Did anyone ever come to you and discuss your being employed at Natrogenics clinic?"

"There was a Bart Naples who had asked me what my plans were in working with Dr. Burton. I told him it was a building block toward my future."

"Did Dr. Naples discuss any concerns he had about your being employed there?"

"He mentioned that he had gotten a complaint from another chiropractor who said Dr. Burton wasn't licensed. Naples warned that it was in my best interest to stop engaging in any suspect activity, that he wanted it stopped."

"Is that when you stopped having blood work billed to insurance under your provider number?"

"That following Monday I asked Carrie not to bill anymore blood work under my provider number."

"On October 5, 1995, Special Agent Terrance Glenn of the Food and Drug Administration issued its findings on the black pearls. It stated that all of the bags of black pearls plus the bag of 60 pills mailed to Porter Lance contained indomethacin, diclofenac, mefenamic acid and hydrochlorothaozide.

Some bags of Gerovital H3 or GH-3 taken during the search was said to contain Ibuprofen and Procaine Hydrocloride; however, a small bag housing six bottles of (Gerovital) GH #3 found in Dr. Burton's office at the clinic was said to contain no drugs.

The final Grand Jury hearing began Thursday, October 19, 1995. Ben M. Byrd, Jr., the first undercover agent at the clinic, was called to witness.

Byrd testified that he visited the Natrogenics clinic feigning tiredness; for that he had been given undercover money. He carried a remote microphone that was built into his mobile phone.

He refuted Burton's notion that he suffered from a weakened immune system, inflammation of the prostate, pre-cancerous condition, and degeneration of the spine, since, prior to his visit, he had been tested by a medical doctor and given a clean bill of health.

> *"I gave them the address of an undercover post office box which had been previously supplied to me by FDA personnel. Blue Cross-Blue Shield had also issued me a special undercover Blue Cross-Blue Shield card," he testified.*

During Porter Belt's undercover capacity at the clinic, he admitted to wearing a body tape recorder to record the visits.

> *Prior to visiting the clinic, Agent Newsome told me to get a very, very thorough physical with all possible blood tests that they could give me, because she was aware of Burton's blood test. I had four vials of blood taken and everything. I was given a clean bill of health. According to Burton I had EBV (Epstein Barr), which he claimed could eventually develop into HIV, so I felt like he was telling me that possibly I was – eventually, I was going to get HIV.*
>
> *Burton diagnosed heart stress, and an inflammation of the prostate, which he said, 'was typical for a person my age.' He said my condition precedes cancer, but offered that he had cured patients with similar problems.*
>
> *I was trying to find out how they billed charges when I first called the clinic. Daniel explained that as long as he worked on me, they could bill the insurance for services rendered. I contacted the clinic once again to determine if the insurance company had paid the bill for the charges submitted on prior visits.*
>
> *Terrance advised me to tell Burton I couldn't sleep, since the black pearls were used for sleeping. I did. Dr. Burton goes to a cabinet in a room, and he brings back a sample of these black pearls. He instructed me to take two, and claimed they would help me relax and sleep. He explained that Valium is made from valerian root and gave me a bottle of valerian root to show police in case I was stopped for drug testing. I telephoned the clinic from Boise and ordered some black pearls COD, which were subsequently mailed, to my undercover box."*

Adrian Frontier, an alleged supplier of the black pearls, testified, "I have seen lab reports on the black pearls show up negative for drugs. Airline pilots and many people go through security programs for drugs and nothing shows up. Valerian root is a natural form of diazepam," he added.

H. David Lloyd told McClain, "I went in front of the lab technician at the lab. I ran a drug test on myself and paid for it. It came up negative for drugs. I went back the next week. In front of the lab technician, I opened up a package and I took two of the black pearls. I ran another drug test on myself. It, too, came up negative."

"You gave Agent Newsome the pills that are in this bag. Are you saying that you had more pills? McClain asked.

"Yes. Yes, I had other pills."

"You had other pills that you kept. You didn't give Agent Newsome all the pills that you had?"

"No I didn't. I have never seen anything like this, that's helped people. I have always kept some on hand. I feel like we have too many organizations and too many people, and sometimes I feel like they are the bad guys. I'm sorry, but that's what my philosophy is, sometimes," Lloyd said.

"You indicated you had some feelings about big government. Do you feel like there is a vendetta against alternative health care, and this is what's happening in this case?" a juror asked.

"I personally wonder why they came in on him. I question ten armed agents. To me, it's like killing an ant with a tank. If somebody was doing something wrong, I wish they had gone in and said, 'show us your insurance records,' or something, 'we have had a complaint against you.' Instead they take all your equipment, they take your records, and you can't do anything about it. And then they just sit on it; and there are people-they sit four, five, six, eight years, and they never get their stuff back, and they don't charge them, because they haven't found anything. I just don't think that's due process, and I think it's against the Constitution, I personally do. If he's doing something illegal, he should have to stand up for that."

"He should be shut down," a juror said.

Agent Newsome would be the next person to give testimony. Since Lloyd had testified that he had kept some of Burton's black pearls and had them analyzed, and found them to be negative for any drugs, this was information McClain must impart to Agent Newsome prior to her testimony about the black pearls.

Newsome's testimony would begin at 11:40 a.m. "I was going to change into a new topic, so now would be a good time for me, if we want to take a break," McClain said.

It was 12:00 noon. McClain and Newsome met in the foyer.

When the jury convened at 1:40 p.m. Newsome resumed her testimony and told McClain that all packages of pills tested for drugs came back positive for diazepam except the one in a cabinet in a room where patient files were kept. "At the clinic there was a small used package of black pearls that was said to be for the clinic employees' use; it was later marked exhibit #6. There was no diazepam found in that one package of pills," Newsome said.

Newsome's misleading testimony would go undetected by the Grand Jury; now it appeared that Burton was poisoning all the black pearls except the ones being used by the staff. Her testimony seemed to justify H. David Lloyd's earlier testimony "my testing of the black pearls revealed no drugs," But Lloyd was not referencing to GH#3 but rather to the black pearls,which Terrance Glenn had previously testified were ***all*** positive for indomethacin, diclofenac, mefenamic acid, and hydrochlorothiozine. Only (Gerovital) GH#3 found in Dr. Burton's office at the clinic were said to contain no drugs.

When asked by a juror how much diazepam in the black pearls would be illegal, Newsome replied:

"Any amount of diazepam was illegal. Leonard and I were talking amongst ourselves, because a previous witness testified that he had taken these black pearls, and had a drug test done on himself after eight to 12 hours, and that the— drug test on himself came back negative. No patients had reported any detrimental effects on them from the black pearls, although some said they didn't affect them one way or the other.

The FBI got involved because of Dr. Burton's possible mail fraud and fraudulently billing insurance companies. (The alleged fraud to insurance companies, Newsome learned, over the periods of 1993 and 1994 amounted to $1,200.)

I questioned Special Agent Terrance Glenn about the FDA's stand if a doctor uses unapproved devices. 'If the doctor is using an unapproved device in their practice, there's nothing the FDA would do except send him a letter saying, 'you should apply for an investigational device exemption. The FDA would not do anything to the doctor,'" Newsome noted.

On October 20, 1995, the United States District Court for the District of Idaho's Grand Jury for the case of "UNITED STATES OF AMERICA vs. Kyle J. Burton, DEFENDANT" issued its indictment. (Vio. 18 U.S.C. & 1341 and 21 U.S.C. & 841, 331(a), 352(f) and 333(a) (2). It cited 44 counts of violations.

38

Ten days after the Grand Jury hearing, Attorney Anthony's head was buried in the Idaho State Journal, which had just today released the indictments of Kyle J. Burton handed down by the federal grand jury in Boise on Oct. 20.

United States Attorney Patty H. Richardson announced Friday the indictment of Kyle J. Burton of Aberdeen for mail fraud, distribution of controlled substances, and mislabeling controlled substances that had been distributed.

He is accused in counts one through 33 with mail fraud for improperly billing insurance companies for a diagnostic procedure that is in the research stage, which carries a 30 year imprisonment and/or $1,000,000 fine. In counts 34 through 39, he is charged with the illegal distribution of a substance containing diazepam, commonly known as Valium, which carries life imprisonment and/or $4,000,000 fine.

In counts 40 through 45 he is charged with improperly labeling the substance containing diazepam which carries a 3 year imprisonment and/or a $10,000 fine.

Counts 1 through 33 of the indictment relate to a scheme devised by Burton, a naturopathic physician, who operates the Natrogenics clinic in Aberdeen. It is alleged that as part of his practice, Burton conducts a blood test for patients which is not approved or accepted in the U.S. as a diagnostic test.

Medical Services Bureau, Blue Shield of Idaho and Blue Cross of Idaho were mailed bills for these tests under the name of Dr. Lou Daniel, a licensed chiropractor who was working for Burton. Neither BSI nor BCI provide benefits for services provided by naturopaths.

Counts 34 through 38 allege that on four occasions between Nov. 9, 1994, and Feb. 1, 1995, Burton illegally distributed a substance containing diazepam, a controlled substance commonly referred to as Valium.

In count 39 Burton is accused of possessing the same substance on Feb. 2, 1995, with the intent to distribute.

In counts 40 through 44, Burton is accused of delivering the substance containing diazepam into interstate commerce, and that they were misbranded in that the labeling failed to bear adequate directions for use and warnings against use under conditions where their use may be dangerous to the health of the users.

The indictment was cruel and biting, but now the months of waiting, wondering and guessing were over. Now Anthony knew the huge monster facing him. But there was little he could do until he could get the Grand Jury Testimony and Jury exhibits that lead to the indictments. He would petition the courts.

For Burton, the indictment meant one thing. There was yet more work to be done. He needed the aid of his supporters, perhaps now more than ever. The word jail itself for Kyle was frightening enough; even one day in that place was unthinkable. Incarceration conjured up some awful images.

Rudy had mentioned the possibility of entering a plea bargain. The outrageous fine -- why he was as good as dead unless he could… He needed to talk to Rudy.

"Rudy this is Kyle. When is the… Have they told you when the sentencing is going to be?"

"Listen, I spoke with Leonard. He said the court appearance on the indictment has been set for November 9, 1995, at 2:00 p.m. Now, we talked for some time about what he wanted. He didn't feel that you were serious about coming to a resolution."

"I'm not serious? I'm the one who can't practice my profession and I'm not serious. Well if-- …No! I don't want to be destroyed. But if he can come to a reasonable solution…I'm all for that."

"I told him that 'that was a preposterous statement' that you've been trying to resolve this since February, by being cooperative."

"We've given those blood suckers everything they've asked for… What more do they want?"

"He said our leaving the meeting in July shows that we are not serious about the matter."

"Sitting there being humiliated. Doggone right! It was a joke."

"I let him know that I was not happy with those people whose only purpose was to pick you apart either. Nor was I happy with his decision to prosecute the case. I talked about a possible plea agreement with him. He said that the only way they would consider a plea agreement is if you will agree to one count of mail fraud, one count of distribution, and one count of mislabeling."

"Those crooks took those pills and poisoned them… and they want me to plead guilty to that! No, I don't… No! Okay the mail fraud charges--okay."

"The mail fraud charges amount to $1200.00."

"Twelve hundred dollars? Fine. They want $1,200.00 lousy dollars, I'll give them $1200.00, but what's with this imprisonment crap? What's he going to do about that?"

"Well there are a lot of things that determine federal sentencing, things such as: the amount of drugs and or money along with the nature of the alleged plan to plot the scheme. Oh, I believe he wants to come to some kind of resolution now. It's the details of the resolution that I'm uncertain about. But he's going to get something over to me in writing after he reviews sentencing guidelines."

"Yeah, well, the sooner the better."

"I'll keep you posted."

Given the expense of continued legal counsel and the time frame of a trial, the plea agreement seemed to Burton the best way to go. He received a fax from a supporter of his who disagreed.

"I would never presume to give legal advice, but if it were me, I would not plead at the hearing. The judge should ask if there are any preliminary motions, and you or your attorney must challenge jurisdiction prior to pleading. The hearing will be postponed, giving you time to research the jurisdictional issues while waiting for the plaintiff's response. We do not have to argue the jurisdictional question for the plaintiff," Ricky Burns told Kyle.

But on November 9, 1995, Kyle J. Burton appeared before the United States District Court for the District of Idaho. The Procedural Order from that appearance cited that a thirty-day "Jury Trial Date was set for December 13, 1995, at 9:00 a.m. in Pocatello." In accordance with that Order, an Order Setting Conditions of Release specified that the defendant, Kyle J. Burton, could be released on Unsecured Bond if he promised to appear at all proceedings as required and surrender for service of any sentence imposed. The United States Marshal ordered that the defendant be released after processing.

Anthony had yet to receive any discovery regarding this case. In a letter to Leonard W. McClain he wrote:

> *I would like to have this material as soon as possible, so that I can prepare for trial as it is scheduled. Numerous people who wish to testify on Mr. Burton's behalf have contacted me. Also, there may be outside defense counsel that will come in to assist at the time of trial. The matter addressed in this discovery letter needs to be responded to immediately so that proper preparation can take place.*

On November 18, 1995 a U.S. Congressional member of the House of Representatives in whom Kyle had placed his hope, asked for specific details of the case.

> *We have found that the FBI has been lying in the charges. No one has ever been harmed in our office or had any severe side effects. An FBI agent posed as a truck driver and received treatment for himself. He*

wanted it turned in to the insurance company by our licensed chiropractor. We told him at the front desk that we do not do this. He repeatedly asked us to do this. We said, "no." We feel like that is entrapment. He signed our papers that stated that he was not an undercover agent or government entity, Kyle responded.

It was not until November 20th, 1995, that the Honorable A. Lewis Winston ordered the return of Burton's equipment. He ordered that transcripts of Grand Jury testimony, Grand Jury exhibits and other Grand Jury items seized during the February 2, 1995, search be released to defendant's counsel, Rudy Anthony.

But Leonard McClain provided only a partial list of the items Anthony had requested for discovery. He withheld all Grand Jury testimony, citing that it would be submitted "upon orders by the Court as provided in Federal Rule of Criminal Procedure 6(e) (3) (C) (I)."

Burton's supporters' calls and letters continued to clog the judicial system, the FBI offices, and the judge. Dr. H. David Lloyd D.C., the chiropractor who had the black pearls tested, expressed his disappointment with the indictment.

Dear Mr. McClain:

I was quite impressed with the sincerity of those serving on the Grand Jury, even though disappointed with an indictment of Dr. Burton. There are several issues I would like to relay to you.

I was at a chiropractic convention in Utah through the past weekend and was impressed to see Xactrun, a company using the same microscope as Dr. Burton, doing live blood analysis and then giving vitamins and enzymes and noting the change particularly of the separation of the red blood cells. That helps the efficiency of the blood system and how it carries oxygen throughout the body. It will be a valuable demonstration before a jury to understand the process.

Also, the FDA agent in Boise stated at the hearing that Valium and three anti-inflammatory agents were in the black pearls. I question their finding because valerian root is in the black pearls, and does this show the same spike on their tests as Valium? If I can do a drug test and Valium does not show up, I question their results. I double checked and I no longer have any pearls from Mai Soo; and the ones I gave to Marge Newsome were from Dr. Burton. I also ran another test on November 14, 1995, taking three black pearls on November 13, 1995, and once again the results were negative.

Three years ago a company out of Salt Lake was going around to doctor's offices doing live blood analysis for patient evaluations and using billing codes. Enclosed are code numbers that Dr. Burton used. He stopped using the codes when their validity came into question. I was told several years ago that the blood analysis could be billed to insurance companies.

I marvel that the insurance companies, did not complain, and yet you made such a big deal out of it. I heard $1,200.00. When an insurance company questions my billings or says something is not covered, they simply send a bill for me to refund what is in question or not covered.

This attack on Dr. Burton is unwarranted, unjustified, and even unconstitutional. It follows the same abuse and overuse of power that was demonstrated with Weaver and in Waco. I believe someone in power wants Dr. Burton out of the way.

When I was the unit command of a Calvary unit in Nebraska, I remember our training as a result of Kent State. Using a bullet against unarmed citizens was not justified; you have tried using a tank to kill a fly.

Considering the deaths of people by prescription and illegal drugs, I would think that the FBI and the FDA have a lot more important business than slandering Dr. Burton and attempting to ruin his reputation, I would hope so anyway.

I think you know you have made a mistake and are afraid to admit it, or to let it go. I would hope that you would be honest enough within yourself to close the case and immediately return his equipment. If not, I look forward to testifying on Dr. Burton's behalf on every charge brought against him.

A jury here in Pocatello will acquit him and wonder why the government has spent hundreds of thousands of dollars on $1200.00 in insurance claims, a microscope, and an herbal combination (black pearls), that does not show up on drug tests. The money could and should be used to stop the abundance of illegal drugs being trafficked here in our state.

Mr. McClain I think you are honest, and I hope you listen to your heart in doing what is right, and not what Marge Newsome needs to justify 10 months of work and to further her career. There have been many LIES and cover-ups that will be brought out, and if justice is to be met, maybe some government employees losing their jobs with charges brought against them would be in order. Maybe justice would then be served.

On November 30, 1995, the Government furnished Anthony a Second Supplemental Response to Request for Discovery. It included Grand Jury Testimony, audiotapes of the accounts of Special Agent Porter Belt's visits, and conversations to employees of the Natrogenics clinic.

As he read through the transcripts, Anthony couldn't help marveling at some of the testimonies. That special agents Ben Byrd and Porter Belt's only purpose at the clinic was 'entrapment' was evident when both Byrd and Belt told Leonard McClain under oath that they had told Dr. Burton that they had been feeling tired, when they visited the clinic.

Byrd stated how he had convinced the girl at the clinic to put the charge on his Blue Cross card, even as she felt that the charge was not a covered expense. He told Burton he was 'very concerned about his medical condition,' and admitted to giving 'the clinic' the address of an undercover post office box.

Belt admitted that surveillance was conducted during his visits to the clinic. It was the kind of stuff that, if taken to trial, could be damaging to the prosecution.

Anthony phoned Kyle. "I've been looking over these transcripts and... Well, those guys really set themselves up. It's clearly a case of 'entrapment'--one lie after the other. The question, though is: Do you really want to take this to trial?"

"Well, I mean, if we can beat' em -- It'll clear my name."

"Kyle, let's get real, here. They'll drag this trial out until you're bankrupt. You can't win--not really. Sure I can--we can fight this thing if you want, but I want you to think about what it could mean to you financially."

There was silence on the other end of the phone. "But these drug charges, Rudy. I mean what I am supposed to do, let them pin that on me. If I don't take this thing to trial--what will that mean to my reputation? I mean, how are people going to react if they think I'm selling drugs at the clinic?"

"What it comes down to, Kyle, is this. You're going to have to choose the lesser of the two evils. You can plea bargain, in which you'll have to admit to the drug charge and one count of mail fraud, or end up bankrupt. And that's what they want."

"Admit to these drug charges. What would my patients think?"

"Can't answer that, but it's a chance you have to take. These people don't play fair. The most astounding testimony came from Marge Newsome. Now, get this, she testified that," The black pearls that were labeled 'for use by employees' contained no diazepam." This was after Dr. P. David Lloyd testified that 'no drugs were found when he had his black pearls tested by a lab.' If you'll remember though, the drug analysis showed that drugs were found in all of the black pearls. Do you smell a rat? I do."

With the Third Supplemental Response to Request for Discovery, McClain supplied Anthony with the findings on the black pearls by Peter Metzger of the Department of Health and Human Services. Metzger had received a separate shipment of the black pearls for analysis; all were said to show drug infiltration. Diazepam, Mefenamic Acid, Diclofenac, Indomethacin, and Hydrochlorothiazide, the same drugs found in the black pearls analyzed by the FBI/FDA, were found in Metzger's analysis. The Liquitrile product was said to contain Amygdalin.

McClain held the taped account of the raid on February 2, 1995, the video tape of the raid on the Burton residence, and the tape of Special Agent Ben Byrd's second visit to the clinic. The Grand Jury transcripts of Carrie Jean Doyle and the cooperating witness Wes O'Dea, both of whom testified on July 11, 1995, were held as well.

Kyle Burton's plea was given in an article in the "The Aberdeen Times":

> Aberdeen naturopath Burton pleaded guilty in U.S. District Court last week to one count of mail fraud and one count of mislabeling a prescription drug, Valium.
>
> The guilty pleas came as part of an agreement Burton and his attorney, Rudy Anthony, made before Judge Lewis Winston on Monday, December 18.
>
> Burton will be sentenced by Winston on March 18. Winston said Burton may call character witnesses and present more information prior to sentencing, but the plea bargain reached by Burton and the Idaho Attorney General's office is not binding on the judge's sentencing.
>
> In return for the guilty pleas, the Attorney General's office dismissed the prior indictment, which listed 44 counts against Burton, including mail fraud, distributing controlled substances and mislabeling controlled substances.
>
> In the agreement, Burton will have to pay between $237.60 and $840 to Blue Cross of Idaho and between $234 and $850 to Blue Shield of Idaho, as reimbursement for money he received for some of his services.
>
> He also agrees not to practice as a naturopath, but he will still be permitted to operate his health food store and sell health food products. If Idaho should adopt licensing or certification procedures for naturopaths, Burton could practice again after becoming licensed under the Idaho law.
>
> The attorney general's office also agreed to recommend a jail sentence of no more than six months for Burton. That sentence could be served as home detention, with Burton wearing electronic monitoring with work release privileges.
>
> The government also agreed to recommend that fines not exceed $50,000 since Burton had incurred a net loss in income over the past years under investigation.

Burton's net profit for the year 1993 had fallen by 80 percent below that of 1992 due to thievery, sexual harassment of patients, and contemptuousness by the cooperating witness, Wes O'Dea. After Wes's firing, the business profits in 1994 had once again started to climb, but fell by 54% in 1995 due to the investigation.

The pressure was now on to rally support for the passage of Senate Bill 1428, The Complementary Health Care Act. This bill would grandfather in old naturopaths whose acceptance had been won because of their contributions to society.

Ivanna Dion shared her story with Judge Winston, and begged for mercy in the sentencing of Dr. Burton.

Dear Judge Winston:

In March 1992 I was introduced to alternative treatment under the care of Dr. Burton for myelodysplasia, an ultimately fatal disease. This program proved both economical and convenient. Dr. Burton's treatments were made possible thanks to the HLB/LBA blood research test which Dr. Burton used to determine which of his products could be used to address my individual needs.

My friend's mother, Ms. Helen, a 64 year-old insulin taking diabetes patient, who was hospitalized at Bayles Hospital was subjected to a battery of tests for a month, only to learn that she had inoperable pancreatic cancer. Her cancer was so advanced that her doctor felt it useless to recommend chemotherapy or radiation. Instead he said, "Ms. Helen, I'm sorry but you have cancer. You can go home and eat anything you want." Having received this death sentence, she, too, would seek help under the guidance of Dr. Burton. I am happy to report that recent hospital X-rays have confirmed that Ms. Helen no longer has cancer, and is no longer taking insulin shots, thanks to the ingeniousness of Dr. Burton.

Having witnessed the success of both myself and Ms. Helen, other persons across the country from Chicago to Memphis who have not met with success under traditional allopathic medicine, have followed me in seeking health care under Dr. Burton's guidance. If you, Judge Winston, were confronted with a life threatening illness, would you not want the right to choose your health care? That is the position in which we, as patients, find ourselves.

The fundamental right to choose the administrator of our health care needs has been taken away from us due to the FBI and FDA's seizure of Dr. Burton's HLB/LBA medical records and equipment. It is indeed, my honored sir, as I'm sure you will agree, a travesty of justice if we as United States citizens cannot have the fundamental right to choose our method of health care. When levying any charges against Dr. Burton, please consider not only the health of his patients, but the nation as well. Our very existence depends on it.

It appeared as though his nightmare would never end, but there was always a ray of light that helped Burton remain optimistic. He received Federal Codes for his HLB/LBA blood work. Now he could legally bill his blood work to insurance companies. Good news, but it meant nothing if Burton could no longer do the blood work. He hung his hope on passage of SB 1428.

Even as the letters continued to pour in to Judge Winston, Burton's practice was limited to selling his supplements and doing massages. Ninety percent of Burton's business, doing blood tests was now only a memory of a privilege that could only be restored by the governor's magic pen--the signing of SB 1428.

On January 29, 1996, Ronald C. Feagan, N.M.D. now former President of the American Naturopathic Medical Association wrote Judge Winston:

> *I am writing regarding Dr. Burton. As a practitioner, and the President of the ANMA for the past twelve years, I have familiarized myself with state and federal laws. Having completed investigation of Dr. Burton and his practices, I am convinced of his innocence.*
>
> *Dr. Burton has successfully met the requirements of a naturopath, is Board Certified, and is a member in good standing with the ANMA. No complaints have ever been registered against him. He's well respected among peers and patients across the country. As such, I believe he could win if this is taken to trial.*
>
> *Under pressure, Burton has yielded to the "plea," pleading guilty because of his financial inability to pursue good legal counsel. Knowing the laws as I do, I could successfully defend him, myself. His willingness to plea suggests that he feels overwhelmed by this system of injustice.*
>
> *...I discount the allegations against Burton as false, and feel that he should have remained steadfast in his stance of innocence.*
>
> *I extend my support for Dr. Burton. Please exercise leniency when rendering a sentence.*

Anthony received the Presentence Report and faxed over a copy to Burton. Perhaps of most concern was the government's level of sentencing. If a level 6 was assessed, the fine would range from $500 to $5000. For level 8, the fine would be $1,000 to $10,000.

In his "Objection to the Presentence Report," Anthony asked that the court consider the defendant's ability to pay the fine, the restitution, and the impact of the plea agreement in limiting defendant's ability to earn equivalent income in the future.

It seemed that Burton's efforts with Senate Bill 1428 had paid off. The Bill passed both houses: the Senate floor on which it was tabled and the House of Representatives Health and Welfare Committee. And though he urged his supporters to keep pressure on the governing bodies, he had little doubt that Governor Phil Batt would sign SB 1428; he had long expressed his support for it.

March 14, 1996, at Governor Phil Batt's office tension ran high. It seemed that everyone wanted a stake in Senate Bill 1428. Lobbyists were hustling about nervously hoping for a last minute conference with the governor, hoping to influence his hand.

The Bill had arrived for the governor's signature on March 11, 1996, some three days ago. Supporters held that SB 1428 would stamp out fraudulent providers. Some thought its passage meant that the bill would broaden their choices of health care coverage. Those in opposition argued that the governor's signature would infer that provider standards were mandated.

Ruth House, the governor's secretary had her own opinion about SB 1428; she had been a satisfied patient of Burton's. Even a few moments ago the governor had pledged his support, so Ruth was certain he would sign it.

Ruth couldn't help but wonder who the stately looking fellow was that was approaching her desk with his neatly tailored navy suit. In one hand was a maroon briefcase. It was clear from his demeanor that he was a lobbyist--but for whom?

The man extended his hand for a shake. "Hello, I'm Steve Brent. I'm here to see the Governor," he said.

"May I ask what company you're representing?"

"I'm with the American Medical Association."

"Won't you take a seat? I'll let him know you're here," Ruth said, then disappeared into the governor's office. She was at her desk again when, moments later, her phone rang. She motioned to her guest. "The governor would like to see you now," she said.

"Thank you very much," he said.

It was not until she was asked to type the letter to the Honorable Byron Olson, president of the Senate, that she learned Governor Phillip E. Batt had vetoed SB 1428. According to the governor, "its registration policy for alternative health care providers was far too lax. Given the controversies of the bill, and in the absence of a clear line of demarcation concerning regulating and registering of 'complimentary health care providers,' I am vetoing SB 1428," he wrote.

For Burton, the governor's veto of SB 1428 was crushing. But the 'cat and mouse game' had just begun. It would be another year now before the matter could be tabled again, let alone passed.

Still ahead was the sentencing for the charges brought against Burton.

On March 18, 1996, Burton received the "Condition of Probation and Supervised Release."

> Under the terms of your sentence, you have been placed on probation by the Honorable Lewis Winston, United States District Judge for the District of Idaho. The

defendant's term of supervision is for a period of four (4) years, commencing March 18, 1996.

The defendant shall report in person to the probation office in the district to which the defendant is released within 72 hours of release from the custody of the Bureau of Prisons.

The defendant shall not possess a firearm as defined in 18 U.S.C. & 921.

For offenses committed on or after September 13, 1994:

The defendant shall refrain from any unlawful use of controlled substance. The defendant shall submit to one drug test within 15 days of release from imprisonment or placement on probation and at least two periodic drug tests thereafter, as directed by the probation officer. It is the order of the Court that you shall comply with the following standard conditions:

The defendant shall not leave the judicial district without the permission of the court or probation officer. The defendant shall support his or her dependents and meet other family responsibilities.

The defendant shall work regularly at a lawful occupation unless excused by the probation officer for schooling, training or other acceptable reasons.

The defendant shall notify the probation officer ten days prior to any change in residence or employment.

The defendant shall not associate with any persons engaged in criminal activity, and shall not associate with any person convicted of a felony unless granted permission to do so by the probation officer.

The defendant shall permit a probation officer to visit him or her at any time at home or elsewhere, and shall permit confiscation of any contraband observed in plain view by the probation officer.

The defendant shall notify the probation officer within seventy-two-hours of being arrested or questioned by a law enforcement officer.

Special conditions ordered by the Court followed:

- The defendant shall not incur new credit charges or open additional lines of credit without the approval of the probation officer unless the defendant is in compliance with the installment payment schedule.

- The defendant shall be placed on home detention for a period of six (6) months, to commence April 17, 1996. During this time, the defendant shall remain at place of residence, except for employment and other activities approved in advance by the probation officer. The defendant shall wear an electronic device and shall observe the rules specified by the Probation Department. Cost of electronic monitoring shall be paid by defendant.

- The defendant shall not be employed in any capacity related to practicing as a naturopathic/homeopathic physician, nor shall defendant perform any unpaid or volunteer activities in this area during the term of probation without the permission of the probation officer. The defendant may operate a health food store and recommend/sell health care products.

- The defendant shall publish a statement in the major newspaper-type publications in Pocatello, Idaho; American Falls, Idaho; and Aberdeen, Idaho, acknowledging he fraudulently submitted billing statements to Blue Cross and Blue Shield and knowingly dispensed Valium without being labeled as such. Further the statement will indicate that as a consequence of his actions, he is precluded from practicing as a naturopathic/homeopathic physician until such time as he is licensed to do so.

- Upon a finding of a violation of probation or supervised release, I understand that the Court may (1) revoke supervision or (2) extend the term of supervision and/or modify the conditions of supervision.

- The defendant shall make restitution to Blue Cross and Blue Shield respectively in the amount of $588.00 each for a total of $1,176.00.

The "Judgment in a Criminal Case" which was issued on March 19, 1996, stated that, "The defendant shall pay the following total criminal monetary penalties in accordance with the schedule of payments set fourth on Sheet 5, Part B."

	Assessment	Fine	Restitution
Totals:	$ 75.00	$ 10,000.00	$ 1,176.00

Burton believed, with the plea bargain, he had made the right choice until he received, from the court on April 2, 1996, additional probationary terms.

- Defendant shall submit to search of his home, vehicle, and/or person upon demand of probation officer, or person authorized by probation, without necessity of a warrant, and shall submit to seizure of any contraband found therein.

- Defendant shall provide the probation officer with access to any requested financial information.

- Defendant shall post a sign at his business establishment stating that he is precluded from practicing as a naturopathic/homeopathic physician.

Though Burton's sentence was reduced, Judge Winston was adamantly against Burton treating patients. According to Cal Garrison, U.S. Probation Officer, in response to Burton's request to recommend a $25.00 nutritional program valuation/ treatment for his patients, "Judge Winston indicated he does not want you involved in either homeopathic or naturopathic practice. Your letter implies that reflexology/deep muscle massage is a form of homeopathic treatment. He said you can give massages without a license, but there can be no hint/ recommendation of any treatment involved. In summary, you can sell your products, but cannot give any treatment advice."

Judge Winston was likewise concerned about the article that Burton had published in the newspapers pursuant to the sentencing in his case. "He does not believe you accomplished what the court ordered via the very small personal ad seen in the Idaho State Journal. Neither the court nor probation officer has seen the other articles, but assume they are the same. It was the court's intentions that you publish articles that are clearly visible for the public to read (without having to go through numerous small personal ads). For example, the judge expected an article more in line with the announcement of a new employee at a local business or a new small business being opened ...at least something that will be clearly visible when people are perusing the newspaper."

Epilogue

- Many of Burton's patients died between the time of the raid and the time Burton's probation was lifted in March 2000, including Ryan Wallace who was receiving an injection when the agents entered, his brother-in-law, and his sister. Some patients' health declined considerably.

- Similar FBI/FDA raids have been conducted against numerous health care practitioners throughout the United States.

- The business of Dr. Merle Fry, the Wisconsin chiropractor who offered support for Burton and wrote the petition to be signed by Burton's supporters on his behalf, was closed by the IRS. According to the IRS, Fry was delinquent in his taxes.

- Medical research confirmed the Association of Fibrinogen in finding heart problems before recognizable symptoms appear. Burton's work contributed significantly to those findings.

- Kyle Burton was offered a Peripheral Blood Assessment Teaching Position at Capital University. His acceptance would depend on whether or not the probation officer would grant his permission to take it. He did.

- Today Burton offers his services as an instructor in his HLB/LBA techniques to health care practitioners across this country.

- Dr. H. David Lloyd, the chiropractor whose drug test discredited the FBI/FDA case against Burton, reportedly failed to complete some areas of Medicare documents submitted for payments. He was fined $91,000 and ordered to repay $91,000 for a total cost of $182,000.

- Burton paid $11,261.80 which included the $10,000 fine, $1176.00 restitution, and the $75.00 assessment. Burton has been given full rights to practice as he had prior to the search. He resumed his practice in April 2009 and is still in practice today.

www.ingramcontent.com/pod-product-compliance
Lightning Source LLC
Chambersburg PA
CBHW030425310726
48979CB00009B/1625/J
* 9 7 8 0 9 8 9 1 6 5 2 0 4 *